SLAVE TO DESIRE

Jolene's thoughts were so muddled, both from
having bumped her head and from having imbibed
so much bourbon, that she was having trouble
sorting out her thoughts. Kurt, finding himself in her
unresisting arms, lost his self-restraint. His lips
descended to hers. Their initial touch was gentle, but
as a flame took hold within him, his kiss deepened
fiercely.

Responding, Jolene's flimsy grasp on reality was
completely swept away as she became lost in a world
where only she and her dream lover existed.
Forgotten was the slave jail, the man who had
attacked her, and that she herself was a runaway
slave. She had no life outside this room. Destiny had
brought her to the arms of the one she loved! Here,
in his warm embrace, she would stay . . . forever!

Kurt, his lips still on hers, murmured hoarsely,
"Sleeping Beauty, what we're about to do is wrong.
But I can no more turn away from you than I can
stop breathing. You're forbidden fruit, my love, but
too tempting for a man to refuse."

And, gathering her in his arms, Kurt kissed away
the nightmare of Jolene's day. . . .

MIDNIGHT SLAVE

ROCHELLE WAYNE

ZEBRA BOOKS
KENSINGTON PUBLISHING CORP.

ZEBRA BOOKS

are published by

Kensington Publishing Corp.
475 Park Avenue South
New York, NY 10016

First printing: November, 1988

Printed in the United States of America

For Dick, with love from Wayne's sister

Prologue

Part One

1840

Charlotte Warrington's face was etched with worry and her eyes were glazed with anxiety as she watched the young slave who, racked with pain, tossed and turned on the bed.

"Millie," Charlotte pleaded. "Try to relax. Stop fighting the contractions."

Millie wanted to make Charlotte understand that she wasn't fighting. Something was wrong—terribly wrong! Although Millie had never given birth, she instinctively knew that her labor wasn't progressing normally. She was going to die! She could sense death lurking in the shadows, waiting patiently to claim its next victim. Would it also take her baby? The likeliness of the possibility shot through her with an emotional pain more excruciating than her physical one. Then, suddenly, her grief was replaced with serenity: her baby would be better off dead. She had never wanted to bring a child into the world; she had always sworn she never would! But she hadn't taken into account that she'd have no choice in the matter, that her master would insist that she accommodate him.

She tried to speak to Charlotte, but a severe contraction impaled her with so much pain that she screamed in agony.

Alarmed, Charlotte whirled about, calling frantically, "Della! Della! Do something!"

Responding, the large black woman turned her gaze from the open window and looked at her mistress. She had been paying scant attention to what went on inside the bedroom, for birthings were commonplace with Della. She held several positions on the plantation, her most important as cook, but along with her other responsibilities, she was also midwife to the slaves. Another wench giving birth made little impression on her.

"What you want me to do, Miz Charlotte, ma'am?" she asked respectfully.

"I ... I don't know," the woman stammered. "But surely there's *something* you can do to ease her discomfort."

Della, moving with incredible grace for such a big woman, crossed her mistress's bedchamber and paused beside Millie, who occupied a small bed in the corner of the room.

Eying Millie unsympathetically, Della folded her arms beneath her heavy breasts and muttered, "You gotta stop fightin'. Let nature take its course."

Weakly, desperately, Millie cried, "I'm not fighting! Please believe me, something's wrong!"

"You's too pampered, that's all that's ailin' you," Della said with a harrumph.

"Della!" Charlotte reprimanded sharply. "I insist that you show poor Millie compassion!"

"Yes'm, Miz Charlotte," the woman mumbled, feigning contriteness. However, Della, accustomed to speaking her mind, continued as though she hadn't been chastised. "Miz Charlotte, ma'am, them wenches in the fields have babies without all this screamin' and cryin'. They lay down, open their legs, the little sucker pops out, and the next day they's back to work. Millie here's just too pampered! You'd think she was a white lady, the way she's carryin' on."

"Della, that will be enough!" Charlotte spat sternly. Her glaring eyes met Della's until the servant lowered her gaze and pretended submissiveness.

"I's sorry, Miz Charlotte," she murmured, though she didn't mean it.

When Sam Warrington had first brought his young bride home, Della had welcomed her warmly. However, she had taken an instant dislike to her new mistress's personal maid, Millie. She was a mulatto, which in itself was enough to arouse Della's distaste, for she had no use for light-colored Negroes. In her opinion, which stemmed from personal experience, Negroes with white blood were always uppity and acted as though their white origin made them superior to their black kinsmen.

When Della, incredulous and somewhat envious, saw that her new mistress treated Millie almost as an

9

equal, her animosity toward the servant grew.

Deviously, Della kept her feelings for Millie well concealed. She didn't want to do anything to arouse her mistress's disapproval. Della was the most important slave on the Cedarbrook plantation and wasn't about to gamble losing a prominent position that had taken her years to achieve. She knew which side her bread was buttered on. Sam Warrington buttered it, and his young wife was now the most influential person in his life. Della, out of self-preservation, hid her antipathy for Millie, for she was perfectly aware that her mistress loved the young woman. If she were to alienate Millie, she'd also alienate Charlotte, which would inevitably lead to her own downfall. Although she worshipped her Master Sam with all her heart, and knew that he cared about her, she was acutely aware that Charlotte could easily turn him against her. Charlotte was his wife; she was merely his slave.

As the days passed, Della continued to harbor ill feelings for Millie. However, she sincerely tried to love her new mistress—but Charlotte seemed only vaguely aware of her existence. She seldom spoke to her unless it was about her duties as cook. She paid little heed to Della's supposed distinctive position and thought of her simply as one of several servants who made up the household. Della had always taken enormous pride in her status among the other slaves and was rankled by Charlotte's refusal to acknowledge her importance.

Dislike for her mistress soon took root, but she kept it carefully buried, along with her feelings for Millie. She bitterly resented both women's presence.

10

She wished her darling Master Sam had never taken that trip to New Orleans, where he had met Charlotte Blackburn and married her following a whirlwind courtship. Life at Cedarbrook had been much more pleasant for Della before Charlotte's and Millie's arrival.

Now, as Della's eyes swept over her mistress, concern registered in her gaze. Not only was Charlotte's fatigue evident—she looked as though she were about to collapse.

"Miz Charlotte, ma'am," Della began gently. "You is all tuckered out. Why don't you lie down for a spell? I'll watch over Millie." Charlotte was pregnant, and the servant's worry wasn't for her mistress, but for the baby. She didn't want anything to happen to Master Sam's child.

Sighing wearily, Charlotte agreed, "Yes, I think I'll rest a few minutes." She looked at Della, smiled her thanks, then crossed the room to her own fourposter bed. Her advanced pregnancy made her move awkwardly. She drew down the chenille spread, placed one pillow on top of the other then, carefully, she lay down.

The weather was unseasonably hot for Mississippi in early June, and the sun, now directly above, made the room uncomfortably warm.

Charlotte rubbed a hand across her perspiring brow and considered telling Della to draw the heavy drapes, to darken the room and block out the sun's rays. But a slight breeze was drifting in through the raised windows, and she decided to leave them open.

Hoping to have a few minutes of complete rest, she closed her eyes and tried to relax. A small,

11

gnawing ache emanated from her lower back. She couldn't remember when the pain had started or how long it had been there. If she rested for a while it would surely ease up and go away. Her baby wasn't due for another month, so the pain probably wasn't related to her condition.

Millie's cries had quieted and were now soft moans. Charlotte dreaded her own labor and hoped it wouldn't be so tortured as Millie's. She turned her thoughts away from childbirth, for if she kept thinking about it, she wouldn't be able to rest.

A fly had flown in through one of the open windows to rest upon the sunlit sill. Its constant buzzing was hypnotic, and listening vaguely, Charlotte drifted into a tranquil state somewhere between sleep and consciousness.

Her dream took her back in time, on a journey to the day Sam Warrington had brought her to Cedarbrook. Her first glimpse of her new home had been through the full branches of cedars which grew abundantly on both sides of a winding driveway that led to the columned mansion. Sitting in the brougham beside her husband, staring wide-eyed out the carriage window, she had barely been able to restrain her excitement. She had never seen a home more magnificent.

Cedarbrook was grand indeed, and she'd been so certain that she and Sam were destined to live happily ever after! Her life was a fairy tale come true!

For the first months of her marriage to the dashingly handsome and wealthy Sam Warrington, Charlotte had come very close to finding complete happiness. She loved her husband dearly and reveled in the way he doted on her. He had placed his beautiful young bride on a pedestal, and she was flattered to think Sam held her in such high regard. There was only one flaw in her marriage, and it was this one flaw that prevented her from achieving complete happiness.

Charlotte was by nature a passionate woman, and her husband's hasty fondling and unfulfilling sexual encounters had awakened this passion within her. Needing to appease the hungry longing Sam aroused but never sated, she decided to cast aside all modesty and respond wantonly.

Sam had been thoroughly shocked by what he considered rather brazen behavior. He believed firmly that a genteel lady should regard the sexual act as something she submitted to because it was her wifely duty.

Outraged, and abashed by his wife's wantonness, he explained heatedly that the "marriage bed" had only one purpose . . . to conceive children. He'd not tolerate his wife acting like a whore or a black wench. She was the mistress of Cedarbrook and would behave accordingly. A refined white lady responding to sex—why, the mere thought was absurd and inconceivable!

Properly chastised and inwardly ashamed, Charlotte had humbly apologized and had tried to cover her blunder with a lie, assuring her angry husband that he'd misconstrued her actions. She abhorred the intimacies of marriage but wanted desperately to give him children, especially sons.

He believed her, and so he promptly placed her

back on her pedestal. Thereafter, when he came to Charlotte's bed, she would submit docilely, and when he parted her legs and entered her, she would hold back the need to respond.

Remembering her humiliation and her husband's admonishments brought a warm flush to her cheeks. Her hands were at her sides, and knotting them into fists, she pressed them firmly against the feather mattress. Sometimes she almost wished she were one of her husband's slaves. At least as a slave she'd be free to express her passion, to love without inhibition.

She turned her head and looked at Millie. The woman was still in pain. Charlotte was usually a caring person, but for a moment, a vicious glare came to her eyes as she wondered bitterly if Sam had allowed Millie to respond ardently to his embraces. Had Millie's baby been conceived in the throes of ecstasy, while hers had been conceived in a merely stoical union? Had Sam demanded Millie's passion? Had she given it to him of her own accord? Had Millie been granted what she herself had been denied?

Charlotte moaned softly, rolled to her side, and turned her face away from Millie. She mustn't allow such bitter thoughts to plague her. Of course Millie hadn't responded! The man had forced himself on her, and Millie, a slave, had had no alternative but to submit.

With stark clarity, Charlotte remembered the day she had learned that Millie was with child. Millie had been unable to conceal her morning sickness from her mistress, and when Charlotte had con-

14

fronted her, the servant had admitted everything, confessing tearfully that the master had used her several times. Charlotte had begun to suspect that she herself was with child, and learning that Sam had gotten not just her pregnant, but Millie too, had infuriated her.

Charlotte, unable to forgive her husband's infidelity, had refused him entry to her bedroom. Henceforth they would be married in name only. She knew how badly he longed for a son, and she hoped spitefully that the child she carried was a girl. It'd serve him right! He'd never have a son, for she didn't intend to relent and permit him her bed. It was a severe punishment, but one she thought he justly deserved.

Realizing Charlotte might never forgive him, Sam had considered divorce, but had quickly discarded the possibility. Divorce was not only scandalous, but also degrading. Furthermore, and more importantly, he still loved his wife. He wanted her to remain the mistress of Cedarbrook and wanted her to be the mother of his children—preferably sons. If he were patient and remorseful, surely with time she'd concede and grant him his husbandly rights.

When Sam learned that his wife was with child, he was overjoyed. He was confident that following the birth of his son, Charlotte's anger would abate. Once her maternal love had been awakened, she'd long for more children; perhaps a daughter for her to dote on. In time, all would be resolved between them. His hopes were high, his mood optimistic.

Della, on the other hand, was more practical and pessimistic. The woman possessed incredible insight

15

and knew that the birth of Charlotte's child wouldn't make her forgiving. A large gap had opened between her Master Sam and his wife, and it would take more than a child's birth to close it. And as each day passed, the gap grew wider.

Della had been a young woman of eighteen when the senior Sam Warrington had purchased her and brought her to Cedarbrook. The cook, Abbie, was getting on in years, and Della was her apprentice. Sam had been a boy of two, and from the first moment he and Della had set eyes on each other, a warm relationship had developed. Sam's mother was an invalid, and longing for maternal affection, Sam found it in Della's loving presence. The boy lost his mother when he was six, and his father never remarried. Although Della didn't dare forget that she was a slave and had no legal rights, she nonetheless slipped into the role of mistress. She ran the house with the meticulous precision of a captain. Every room was spotlessly clean, and woe to any slave who shirked his or her duty! A shiftless household servant was a rarity, for if Della caught a servant doing a job haphazardly, she had no qualms about doubling her hand into a fist and sending it plunging into the unfortunate slave's face. If that didn't put vigor into the lazy servant, she'd complain to the master, and then the disobedient servant was sent to the barn, strung up, and cruelly whipped.

Sam was seventeen when his father passed away following a sudden illness. Cedarbrook suffered no hardships over the senior Warrington's untimely demise, for Sam and Della were indeed capable of running the mammoth plantation.

For thirteen years life passed pleasantly for Della.

She reveled in her position over the other slaves and virtually worshipped her Master Sam. Then, unexpectedly, her euphoria came to an abrupt end. Sam had taken the ill-fated trip to New Orleans and had returned with his bride.

Della knew of everything that went on at Cedarbrook, her master's and mistress's business included. Della greatly resented Charlotte for refusing Sam his husbandly rights. Why couldn't the woman understand that Sam had turned to Millie only to satisfy his male lust? A man's sexual drive was strong and demanding. If he used a wench, it spared his wife frequent trips to her bedroom. In Della's opinion, Sam's use of a wench was testimony of his deep love and respect for his wife.

Sam's misery and remorse were almost more than Della could bear. His unhappiness broke her heart. He loved his young wife, had done everything humanly possible to prove his devotion. Yet Charlotte had the audacity to coldly reject him! Della's loyalty lay blindly with her master, and her resentment for her mistress grew.

Now, as Della stood beside Millie's bed, her thoughts were about Charlotte's mistreatment of Master Sam. A slow-burning anger was welling within her when Millie's piercing scream suddenly penetrated the room. Sweeping all thoughts of her mistress aside, Della bent over Millie, lifted the bedcovers, and began examining her.

Rushing to the small bed while holding an arm supportively beneath her swollen stomach, Charlotte cried, "Della, we must send for Doctor Elliott!"

The servant gaped at her mistress as though the woman were out of her mind. "Miz Charlotte, ma'am, the doctah ain't gonna come out here to see no slave. He's a white doctah, and ain't no white doctah gonna help a colored wench."

"But Millie's almost all white!"

"Don't make no neverminds. As far as the doctah's concerned, she still colored even, if she is a high yella."

"But Millie might die without a doctor!" Charlotte declared. Her tone was now less demanding, for she knew Della was right. Doctor Elliott would consider tending a slave beneath his dignity. Furthermore, he'd take it as a personal insult if she were to ask him to help poor Millie.

Having finished her crude examination of Millie, Della said calmly, "The baby's a-comin'. I can see its head."

Another resounding scream tore from Millie's throat. Charlotte's face turned deathly pale, and Della, afraid her mistress might faint and endanger the master's child, said persuasively, "Miz Charlotte, you'd best go downstairs and wait in the parlah. I'll come and get you when the sucker's born."

Charlotte was feeling lightheaded and agreed to leave. She knew nothing about birthing and would be no help to Della. On her way to the door, she recalled the servant's last words and remarked with a note of exasperation, "Della, I do wish you'd stop referring to the baby as a sucker. The term is abhorrent."

"Yes'm," the woman mumbled, but her mistress's request made no impression on her.

18

Prologue

Part Two

Carefully Charlotte climbed the spiral staircase. She had done as Della had advised and had gone to the parlor to await the birth of Millie's child. But she had found the waiting unbearable and decided to return. She knew she wouldn't be any help to Della, but her presence might be a comfort to Millie.

As Charlotte entered her bedroom, Della was standing beside a wooden crib. Previously Charlotte had ordered Silas, the plantation carpenter, to build two cribs, one for Millie's baby and one for her own. Silas's workmanship was excellent and he had done a remarkable job.

Hearing her mistress, Della turned away from the crib and met Charlotte's questioning gaze.

"She's done had a girl," Della said softly.

"Is the baby all right?"

"Yes'm. She big and healthy."

19

"And Millie? How is she?"

Della shook her head, expressing sorrow. "Millie, she lost a lot of blood. I cain't stop the bleedin'. I think, mistress ma'am, that she a-dyin'."

"God, no!" Charlotte cried. Striving to control her emotions, she stepped to Millie's bed, drew up a chair, and sat down. Grasping the woman's hand, she cried, "Millie, you must get well!"

Millie's life was ebbing away, and mustering the last of her strength, she whispered, "I never wanted to have a baby."

Millie paused to catch her breath. Charlotte, tears flowing, waited for the dying woman to continue. Charlotte knew why Millie had never wanted to be a mother—Millie had hoped never to bring an innocent child into a life of slavery.

"Miss Charlotte," Millie began, her voice terribly weak, "Help my daughter . . . promise me that you'll help her."

"I promise," Charlotte answered with a sob.

Millie gasped. Then, as she drew her last breath, she managed to utter two final words: "Free her."

Charlotte placed her hands over her face. Deep sobs racked her body and she cried uncontrollably.

Della waited until her mistress's sobs abated somewhat before moving to her and gently placing a hand on her shoulder. Della said truthfully, "Miz Charlotte, ma'am, there weren't nothin' I could do to save her."

Controlling her grief, Charlotte replied, "I believe you." Then a hard, bitter glare came to her eyes. "But a doctor might have been able to save her. If I could've summoned Doctor Elliott, maybe Millie would still be alive!"

Although Della had disapproved of Millie, as she disapproved of all light-colored Negroes, there were times when she felt an undeniable camaraderie with them. In the eyes of the law, their drop of Negro blood made them just as black as their darkest brethren. Now, feeling a certain amount of pity for Millie, Della mumbled sadly, "You's right, Miz Charlotte. Doctah Elliott might've saved poor Millie."

Slowly Charlotte rose from her chair and walked to the crib. Leaning over, she picked up the newborn infant. Cradling the baby in her arms, Charlotte smiled wistfully as she remarked, "She looks white."

Joining her, Della agreed. "Yes'm, she sure do."

"She's a quadroon."

"Yes'm."

Della's eyes opened extraordinarily wide when, to her disbelief, Charlotte actually kissed Millie's daughter. Della had never seen a white woman kiss a Negro child. For a moment she was shocked speechless, then, finding her voice, she gasped, "Miz Charlotte, I don't believe what I seen!"

Returning the baby to its crib, Charlotte replied calmly, "Is it so surprising to see an aunt kiss her niece?"

"What you mean?" Della exclaimed.

"Millie was my half-sister. My father and Sam have a lot in common. They both prefer to bed Negro wenches over their wives."

"Is that why you and Millie was so close?"

"Yes. I'm a year older than Millie. My father gave her to me as a playmate. Then, when we grew older,

21

she became my personal maid. Millie was even educated. My tutor was a northerner and she never sent Millie away during my lessons. So as I learned, so did Millie."

Della's mouth dropped open. An educated slave was almost beyond her comprehension. "You mean Millie could read and write?"

Charlotte laughed—it was a sad, hollow sound. "She could read and write as well as I, maybe even better."

"Lawdy mercy!" Della declared. "I sure wish I could read and write. But, Masta Sam, he don't allow his slaves to learn any education. He say it against the law."

Suddenly a sharp pain shot through Charlotte, causing her to clutch at her stomach.

Moving quickly, Della soon had her mistress undressed and in bed. As Charlotte suffered another severe pain, Della said hastily, "I be right back, Miz Charlotte. I got to send someone for Doctah Elliott and Masta Sam."

"Where is my husband?" Charlotte asked.

"He went into town to bet on the rooster fights."

It was on the tip of Charlotte's tongue to utter a bitter remark about Sam being in town, gambling and drinking, while Millie died giving birth to his child. But, her words were cut off by another contraction.

Charlotte's twin daughters were born quickly and with relative ease. Only Della was in attendance, for the doctor and Sam hadn't arrived from town.

When her mistress gave birth to a small but apparently healthy baby girl, Della was disappointed that it wasn't a boy; however, her disappointment was suddenly supplanted by shock when she realized that Charlotte was about to give birth to the baby's twin. Charlotte's second daughter was tiny, fragile, and lived only a few minutes.

Della, being a slave, had trained herself to turn off her emotions, and when it suited her purpose, she could be as hard as stone and cold as ice. But beneath her stoic exterior lurked a caring heart, and it was with genuine tenderness that she told Charlotte that her secondborn had died.

Charlotte, devastated, had broken into heartrending tears. Della had taken her mistress into her arms and comforted her until her sobs had quieted.

Now, as Della gently eased Charlotte from her arms and urged her to lie back on the pillows, she murmured soothingly, "Miz Charlotte, you gotta be thankful that your first baby is all right."

"Yes, I know," the grieving woman whispered.

Della was sitting on the edge of the bed. As she started to rise, Charlotte's hand reached out and grasped her wrist. The servant was unnerved by the strange gleam in her mistress's eyes.

"Della," Charlotte began, her voice filled with excitement, "do you realize what God is telling us?"

Della was totally baffled. "No, ma'am."

"He wants me to replace the baby I lost with Millie's baby."

"He ain't tellin' you no such thing!" Della asserted, incredulous that a plan so devious had crossed Charlotte's mind.

Her mistress was not about to be dissuaded. She spoke briskly and with determination. "Della, you must move quickly before Sam and Doctor Elliott arrive. Place my poor dead baby on the bed beside Millie, then put Millie's baby in the crib next to my daughter. When the doctor and Sam get here, tell them that my twins and I are doing fine, then let them know that Millie and her baby are both dead."

It was a moment before Della could overcome her amazement and find her voice. "Miz Charlotte, ma'am, you's talkin' like a crazy woman! You cain't pass off Millie's baby as your own!"

"Yes, I can—and I will!" Charlotte's eyes glazed wildly.

"What you wantin' to do is wrong, and I ain't gonna let you do it."

A cold, calculating expression fell across Charlotte's face. "You and I will become conspirators, Della. I intend to go through with this to help Millie's daughter. Raising her child as my own is even better than setting her free. And you shall go through with our conspiracy for your Master Sam's sake."

"I ain't gonna agree to pass off a wench's git as Masta Sam's legal daughter." Della emphasized the word "git," a term commonly used to describe a slave child sired by its white master.

"Yes, you will agree," Charlotte remarked with certainty. "You love Sam very much, don't you?"

"Yes'm, you know I do."

"And you'd do anything to make him happy, wouldn't you?"

Della didn't answer.

24

"He hasn't been happy lately, has he? In fact, he's been downright miserable. And we both know why he's been so unhappy, don't we? It's because of me."

Charlotte paused intentionally, letting her words sink in before leading up to the finale. "I can make him happy again, Della. All I have to do is promise that we'll keep trying until we have a son."

"You mean you'd let Masta Sam have his husbandly rights again?"

"Yes, I would, and I'd do so willingly. If you'll agree to keep my secret. I'll assure Sam that I forgive him for what he did to Millie, and I'll become a wife to him in every sense of the word."

Della was uncertain. Slaves were never given the opportunity to make important decisions, and now one had suddenly been dropped into her lap. Her Master Sam's happiness depended on her, and she longed to see him happy again. But could she bring herself to deceive him in such a way . . . to pass off a quadroon baby as his white daughter . . . ? If he were to learn the truth, what would he do to her? Would he have her strung up and whipped? Or would he sell her to a cane plantation, where she'd be worked to death within a year?

Pressing her point, Charlotte said levelly, "Della, if you refuse to help me, I promise you that Sam will never share my bed. He'll never know the joy of a son. And he won't divorce me. He'd rather die than bring such shame on the Warrington name." Sitting up and taking both of Della's hands into hers, she continued desperately. "These two babies are girls, so where's the harm? They won't inherit Cedarbrook; Sam's son will be the heir."

25

Tentatively, Della bought her reasoning, and preferring to play along until she'd had more time to reconsider everything, Della moved away from the bed. Carrying out her mistress's instructions, she placed the dead infant beside Millie and covered them both with a sheet. Then, picking up Millie's baby, she took the child and laid it in the crib next to Charlotte's daughter.

Hovering over the crib, Della studied the two babies. Millie's child was larger than Charlotte's, and although her complexion was a shade darker, her hair was lighter. Both infants were strikingly beautiful, and even a casual observer would've been taken aback by their astounding beauty and perfection.

"They don't look like twins," Della remarked.

"They share a family resemblance," Charlotte replied. "After all, they are not only cousins, but also half-sisters."

"Yes'm, I reckon they is. Your pappy sired you and Millie, and Masta Sam is the pappy of these-here girls. These two share a lot of the same blood." Della placed a hand on Millie's daughter. "But this one here, she has Negro blood, and no matter how much you and me pretend that she's white, it ain't gonna make no neverminds. She still gonna be black."

"Honestly, Della! Must you sound so melodramatic?"

At that moment a loud, insistent rapping sounded at the door, followed by Sam's voice. "Della, Doctor Elliott is with me. Is it all right for us to come in?"

Charlotte's gaze flew to the servant. "Della,

please . . . please!"

Della didn't commit herself. Instead, she went to the door and opened it. As the two men hurried inside, the doctor asked anxiously, "Am I too late?" Both men were handsome and strongly built. Their presence seemed to fill the room.

"Yes, suh, Doctah Elliott," Della answered. "You's too late. The mistress done had her babies."

"Babies?" Sam spoke up."

"Yes, Masta Sam. You got twin daughters, and they both doin' fine."

Charlotte let out the breath she'd been holding and smiled inwardly.

"Daughters," Sam repeated, his disappointment obvious.

Della cast her mistress a meaningful glance. Understanding, Charlotte caught her husband's eye, held out her arms, and said cheerfully, "Darling, don't look so disappointed. We have two beautiful girls, and maybe our next child will be a boy."

His face alight with hope, Sam rushed to his wife, sat on the edge of the bed, and went into her outstretched arms. "Our next child? Charlotte, are you telling me . . . ?"

"Yes!" she exclaimed. "I want us to have a son." Holding him tightly, she whispered in his ear, "Sam, I'm sorry for the way I treated you. Please forgive me."

"I'm sorry too, darling. I promise I'll never touch Millie again." It was a promise he had every intention of observing. Hereafter, he'd keep his dalliances safely guarded from his wife and confine his sexual activities to the field wenches.

27

Leaving his embrace, Charlotte's eyes filled with tears as she murmured, "Millie also had her baby today. She and the child are dead." She nodded toward the bed in the corner.

Following her gaze, Doctor Elliott went over and drew down the sheet. Studying the baby girl, he said without emotion, "The sucker was too small to live. It's a shame it didn't survive. It's a light-colored wench and would've brought a good price someday." He drew up the sheet without giving Millie so much as a desultory glance and walked over to the crib to look at the babies. A large grin spread across his face as he observed, "Sam, you have two beautiful daughters—but they aren't identical twins. The small one's gonna have your black hair and blue eyes." He turned his perusal to Millie's baby. "This girl looks as though she's going to take after Charlotte. She'll have brown hair and green eyes."

Rising from his wife's bed and joining the doctor, Sam was in an apparent good mood as he remarked, "Josh, all newborn babies look alike. How can you tell what color hair or eyes they're gonna have?"

"Just a calculated guess. But I'll bet you a hundred dollars that I'm right."

As Sam took him up on his wager, Charlotte wondered how her husband could take Millie's death, and the loss of the baby he thought was his and Millie's, so lightly.

Doctor Elliott lifted the babies, and carrying them to Charlotte, he laid them on the bed, one on each side of her. Grinning, he remarked, "I don't suppose you and Sam picked out names for twins."

"No, we didn't," she replied, placing an arm about

each child and drawing them close.

Moving quietly, Della stood at the foot of the bed, and standing inconspicuously, she listened closely.

"May I name them, darling?" Sam asked.

"Yes, of course," Charlotte agreed.

Poised close to the bed, Sam reached down and placed a hand on Millie's baby. "This one will be called Johanna." He then moved his hand to the other baby. "This one's name is Jolene."

"Johanna and Jolene," his wife repeated. "Yes, I like those names."

"Then it's settled," Sam declared. He looked at the doctor. "This calls for a celebration. Will you join me in the study for a drink?"

"I'd be honored, but first I think I should earn my doctor's fee and examine your wife and daughters . . . although they appear to be perfectly fine."

Aware of Della's close presence, Sam smiled largely and moved over to the servant. Draping an arm about her shoulders, he said with praise, "Della, you've done a superb job. I owe my wife's and daughters' good health to you."

"Thank you, masta suh," she murmured respectfully. She lowered her gaze, for she couldn't bring herself to look him in the eye.

The dark shadows of night had fallen over the plantation, the field slaves were ensconced in their crude cabins, and the household servants had retired when Della knocked softly on the study door. She knew her master hadn't yet gone to bed.

"Come in," he called.

29

She entered hesitantly and closed the door behind her. Warrington was seated at his desk, and moving over to stand across from him, she said apologetically, "I's sorry to disturb you so late, Masta Sam."

He had been going over his ledgers, and closing the books, he leaned back in his chair and watched Della curiously. "I thought you went to bed a long time ago."

"Yes, suh, I did. But I couldn't fall asleep."

"Is something bothering you, Della?"

"Yes, suh, I's bothered somethin' terrible." She saw concern in his eyes. The expression causing her to break into heavy sobs.

Alarmed, Sam left his chair and hurried to Della's side. In all the years he'd known her, he couldn't remember having seen her cry. "Della, what's wrong?"

"Oh Masta Sam!" she bawled. "I cain't lie to you! No matter what Mistress Charlotte says!"

Firmly, he ordered, "Della, control yourself! What has Charlotte done to upset you?"

The woman exhaled deeply, calmed herself, then began, "This mornin' Millie gave birth to a baby girl."

"Yes, I know," he interrupted. "She and the baby died. Is that why you're upset?"

"But Masta Sam, the baby didn't die."

"What?" he exclaimed.

"Millie's baby is alive. Miz Charlotte, she passin' Millie's baby off as her own."

"What the hell are you saying?" he demanded angrily.

Revealing Charlotte's deceit, Della explained

everything as she uncovered the conspiracy in vivid detail.

Sam's first impulse was to strike out at Della for spouting such lies about her mistress, but in the next moment his better sense prevailed. He knew without a doubt that Della wasn't lying. Charlotte was guilty as charged.

Afraid of being severely punished, Della began crying again. "Forgive me, Masta Sam! I know what I done was terribly wrong, but Miz Charlotte, she had me all confused. After I went to bed tonight, I knew I couldn't keep Miz Charlotte's secret. I cain't let her pretend Millie's git is your white daughter."

A couple of minutes passed before Sam responded, but to Della the period seemed interminably long. "I don't blame you, Della. I'm sure Charlotte had you as confused as you claim. I'm just thankful that you finally came to your senses and confessed."

Grabbing his hand, she brought it to her lips and kissed it. "Thank you, Masta Sam."

He jerked his hand away, moved to the liquor cabinet, and poured himself a glass of bourbon, then downed it in a single gulp.

"What you gonna do, Masta Sam?"

He shrugged. "Nothing."

Astounded, Della cried, "What you mean? You got to do somethin'!"

He poured another drink, then returned to Della. "I intend to let my wife play her little game. In the long run, what difference will it make? The child's merely a girl. It's not as though I'm pretending a colored baby is my son. If it makes Charlotte happy to mother both babies, then I'll allow her to do so. I mustn't do anything to alienate my wife, for as soon as Charlotte is physically able, I plan to get her pregnant with my son."

"But Masta Sam, you's helpin' her pass a colored baby as white. What if someday Millie's daughter becomes engaged to a white gentleman?"

"That will never happen, for as soon as Millie's daughter comes of age, she'll be told the truth. In the meantime, she'll be raised alongside my daughter and given the same education and advantages. Then, when she's grown, I'll give her some money and send her up north to fend for herself. She'll be a refined, educated young lady and will have no problem snaring herself an eligible Yankee." He sighed deeply, then considering himself a man of nobility, added, "Besides, she's my own git through Millie, and it's the least I can do for her."

Della was impressed. "You's kind, Masta Sam."

"However," he continued, "in case I were to die unexpectedly, I must take special precautions. In the morning, I'll go into Natchez and see my lawyer, Mr. Holmes, and have papers drawn up stating that Millie's child is alive and is legally my slave. I can trust Mr. Holmes implicitly and will tell him everything. He'll know what kind of documents I'll need. I'll also write a letter to my brother in England and let him know the truth. Between my brother and Mr. Holmes, I can guarantee that Millie's git will never inherit any of my property."

"Or marry a southern gentleman," Della put in.

Neatly, he finished off his drink. Then, placing the glass on the desk, he asked, "Are the babies in the nursery?"

"Yes, suh."

"Let's go see them," he said, taking her arm and ushering her toward the door.

They quickly climbed the stairs and moved quietly down the hall and to the nursery door. Opening it, Sam stepped inside with Della close behind.

The room, lit by a soft-burning lamp, illuminated the two cribs that were placed side-by-side. Della followed Sam to the sleeping infants.

"Which one is my daughter?" he whispered.

"They's both your daughters."

Frowning, he demanded gruffly, "You know what I mean! Which one is my daughter and which one is my git?"

Della pointed to Jolene. "This one here belongs to you and Miz Charlotte." She pointed to Johanna. "That one is yours and Millie's git."

Sam studied the babies for a moment, then turned to leave, but changing his mind, he leaned over Jolene's crib and picked her up. She awoke, and although her little face wrinkled into a frown, she didn't cry. Smiling at his daughter, Sam commented, "She's beautiful, and someday she'll marry into a prominent southern family."

He returned the baby to its crib. Although Sam Warrington dreamed of a son, he felt a warm, paternal affection for Jolene. For the unfortunate Johanna, he felt nothing at all.

Chapter One

Jolene Warrington sat at her vanity and brushed her hair absently. Her gaze in the mirror was vacant, for her mind wasn't on what she was doing. Her shiny black tresses shone like ebony as she ran the brush through the long, straight locks.

At eighteen, she was a striking and attractive young woman. Her sky-blue eyes and light complexion contrasted beautifully with her black hair. Her small frame was softly curvaceous. She was shorter than average women and no taller than most girls of about thirteen. Her facial features were so perfectly formed that they could've been sculpted by an artist. Her high cheekbones and full lips gave her a sultry look that was enchanting.

However, Jolene didn't find herself especially pretty, for she thought she was too short and too small-breasted, and she wished her straight hair would curl naturally.

As a little girl she had once complained to her father about her hair, and he'd told her that his great-grandfather had married an Indian woman, and that he and Jolene had both inherited their straight black hair and high cheekbones.

Now, as she continued to brush her dark tresses, her thoughts were centered on her father. She could hardly believe that he was dead, that she'd never see him again, never hear his deep voice or see his endearing smile.

She laid down the brush, rose from the vanity stool, and moved slowly across her bedroom. Going to the large, canopied bed, she sat on the edge. It was early morning and she was still wearing her dressing gown. She started to undress, but got no further than releasing the first button before grief overtook her, and falling across the bed, she cried until there were no tears left to shed.

She rolled to her stomach and rested her head on her folded arms. She supposed her sorrow would be easier if it weren't doubled, for she had not only lost her father, but also her younger brother.

Now she had no family except for her twin sister Johanna, for their mother has passed away years ago. Their maternal and paternal grandparents had been dead for years.

Jolene's thoughts wandered back in time as she remembered that shortly following her mother's death, her father had sent her and Johanna, at the age of twelve, to a girls' boarding school in St. Louis. It had broken Jolene's heart to leave Cedarbrook. Johanna, on the other hand, had been glad to leave. Jolene understood why her sister was happy to move away from home, and she didn't blame her for wanting to leave. Whereas Cedarbrook held good memories for her, she knew that it was different with Johanna. For some reason which Jolene never understood, Sam Warrington had never shown Johanna love. Although he had showered Jolene with affection, he had acted as though his other daughter didn't even exist. Her father's mistreatment of Johanna had bothered Jolene, and a few times she had spoken to her father about his behavior. Each time he had cut her off abruptly, telling her that someday she'd understand. Understand? How could she conceivably understand why a father ignored his own child?

Johanna's mistreatment hadn't stopped with Sam Warrington but had extended to Della. The servant had virtually idolized Jolene but had seemed to resent Johanna. The girls had been away at school for a year when their father wrote to let them know that Della had died of scarlet fever. The servant's death had saddened Jolene, but Johanna had merely uttered, "good riddance." Jolene hadn't judged her sister, for she understood her coldness. Della had never shown Johanna any affection—why should Johanna grieve for a woman who'd never cared about her?

Although Johanna had never received love from her father or Della, her brother Carl had loved his sisters equally. Johanna had felt a strong sibling rivalry with Jolene, but toward Carl she harbored neither jealousy nor resentment.

On the sisters' eleventh birthday, Carl's feelings for Johanna changed dramatically. All at once he

36

started treating her coldly, even going so far as to give a birthday kiss to Jolene while flagrantly ignoring Johanna.

That same evening Jolene had gone to her mother's room to bid her goodnight, and as she started to knock on the door, she overheard Charlotte asking Carl, "Your father knows the truth about Johanna, doesn't he?"

Although Carl was only nine, he had answered with an arrogance beyond his years, "Of course he knows! He's always known and decided it was time I learned the truth!"

"He had no right to tell you!" Charlotte had cried harshly.

At that moment, Della, lumbering down the hallway, had caught her young mistress eavesdropping and had ushered her back to her own room. The next day Jolene had confronted her mother with what she'd overheard, but Charlotte had refused to explain.

What truth had her mother and Carl been discussing? What had her father told Carl about Johanna, and why did it change his feelings for his sister? There were no answers to these questions, and the more Jolene thought about them, the more confused she became. Finally, she had decided to cast them aside. However, now that Johanna had lost Carl's brotherly affection, Jolene tried twice as hard to show her sister how much she herself cared. Losing Carl's love had made Johanna more embittered, and outwardly she seemed to accept Jolene's love, but inwardly her malicious jealousy for her sister had grown even stronger.

Fortunately for Johanna, she wasn't robbed of a mother's love, for Charlotte loved her as much as she loved Jolene, and if she showed any preference, it was for Johanna . . . not that she actually loved Millie's daughter more, but because she knew that the girl needed her more.

Although Charlotte's death was devastating for Jolene, it was twice as tragic for Johanna, for she had lost the only person who loved her and whom she could love in return. She supposed that Jolene sincerely cared, but she harbored so much jealousy for her sister that it was impossible for her to feel anything for her but contempt.

After Charlotte passed away, it was understandable that Johanna was eager to leave Cedarbrook. Jolene, on the other hand, was reluctant to leave her beloved home.

The school allowed the girls to visit Cedarbrook twice a year, for three weeks at Christmas and for two months during the summer. Jolene looked forward to the visits; Johanna dreaded them.

Although the school granted parents unlimited visitation rights, Sam Warrington never went to St. Louis to see his daughters. In his letters, which were always addressed to Jolene, he'd explain that as a planter he was too busy to leave Cedarbrook.

The sisters were sixteen when Sam's lawyer, Mr. Holmes, due to illness, took on a young assistant who often went to St. Louis on business. While there he would always stop at the school and visit the Warrington sisters, return to Natchez, then send a written account to Sam.

The young lawyer, Robert Hawkins, soon developed a number of excuses to make even more trips to St. Louis, for he was hopelessly enamored to Johanna. She in turn found him terribly attractive and reveled in his attentions. Having received no love from her father, she was hungry for a man's affections.

Jolene began to suspect that Johanna and Robert Hawkins were having an affair, but she never confronted her sister with her suspicions. It wasn't any of her business. Furthermore, if she were wrong, Johanna might never forgive her for having thought such a thing.

At eighteen the sisters graduated, and it was on their graduation day that a telegram from Mr. Holmes arrived at the school, announcing that Sam Warrington and his son had been killed. It also stated that Robert Hawkins was on his way to St. Louis to escort the ladies home, and that upon his arrival, he'd explain what had happened.

Closeted in the head matron's office with the Warrington sisters, Hawkins told them their father and brother had been heading home from New Orleans when they were attacked and killed by a band of runaway slaves. The guilty men had been caught, hastily tried, and hanged.

During the long trip to Cedarbrook, Jolene, dressed in the customary black, had sincerely mourned her father and brother. Johanna, also wearing black, appeared bereaved as well, but inwardly she felt nothing. Why should she mourn their deaths? If it were the other way around, they certainly wouldn't mourn hers!

Now, as Jolene left the bed and removed her dressing gown, her thoughts were on her sister. She wasn't fooled by Johanna's pretenses and knew that her sister didn't truly share her grief. But as always, she understood Johanna's feelings.

While Jolene was thinking about her sister, the young woman was descending the spiral stairway. A loud rapping sounded at the door, and the Negro butler, Lazarus, hurried into the foyer to admit the caller. Pausing, Johanna waited to see who had arrived.

It was Robert Hawkins, and glad to see him, Johanna smiled warmly.

Robert kept his attaché case, but handed his hat and gloves to the servant. Then he watched as Johanna descended the remaining steps. She had discarded her mourning dress and was wearing a brightly colored gown. Her curly golden-brown hair was unbound, falling softly about her oval face. Her loveliness never failed to impress Robert, and as he admired her beauty, he said with a smile, "Johanna, forgive me for calling so early."

Taking his arm and leading him toward her father's study, she said gaily, "Nonsense—you don't owe me an apology. However, your visit comes as a surprise. I was expecting Mr. Holmes. He's supposed to read Papa's will this morning."

She opened the study door, and as he followed her inside, Robert said sadly, "Mr. Holmes died last night. He went peacefully in his sleep."

The lawyer had been ill for a long time and his passing came as no surprise to Johanna. "Does this mean that you'll read the will?"

Going to the massive oak desk, Robert put down his attaché case, returned to Johanna, and took her into his arms. "Darling!" he groaned. "God, how do I tell you?"

Gently but firmly she backed out of his clinging embrace. "Tell me what?"

"Now that Mr. Holmes is dead, I'm responsible for his legal affairs. I knew that this morning he planned to read your father's will. Before coming here, I looked over all your father's papers." Robert's face paled somewhat, and his dark eyes were clouded with pain.

Noting his consternation, Johanna sighed with disappointment and walked to the desk. Leaning against it, she folded her arms beneath her full breasts. Her eyes met Robert's. He was a tall, attractive young man. Johanna knew that he was hopelessly in love with her. She found his admiration flattering and enjoyed making love with him, but that was as far as her feelings went.

"Robert," she began, somewhat exasperated, "I can guess why you're so upset. Papa didn't leave me anything, did he? He left his entire estate to Jolene." A resentful expression hardened her features, and her green eyes shot daggers at him. "Damn!" she shouted. "I was afraid Papa would do this to me!"

She began to pace the room, raging, "Cedarbrook is worth a fortune! Why did Jolene have to inherit everything? She'll be rich while I . . . I'll be destitute!" Abruptly she whirled about, faced Robert, and said furiously, "I hate her! Do you hear me? I hate Jolene!"

He stepped to her quickly. "You don't mean that."

"Yes I do! I hate her, and I wish she were dead!"

Against her protests, he drew her back into his arms. "Darling, you are saying these things out of anger."

"Oh, Robert!" she cried brokenly. "I had hoped and prayed that Papa had left Cedarbrook to both of us!"

Since the day Johanna had learned of her father's and brother's deaths, she had envisioned herself reigning over Cedarbrook. Sharing it with Jolene hadn't dimmed her dream of glory, for she had planned to find a way to be rid of Jolene . . . permanently.

Holding her tight, Robert said sympathetically, "I understand how you feel, Darling." He did truly share her feelings. Robert had imagined himself married to Johanna and living at Cedarbrook in total luxury.

Extricating herself from his firm hold, she gazed into his eyes and asked tearfully, "Did Papa leave me anything at all?"

Robert groaned, and finding himself unable to meet her gaze, he glanced down at the floor. How was he to tell her the truth?

Sensing there was more than her father's will bothering him, she asked pressingly, "Robert, is something else wrong?"

He moved away and walked to the liquor cabinet.

"Isn't it a little early for a drink?" Johanna remarked.

He nodded. "Yes, but believe me, I need one." He quickly poured himself a tumbler of brandy, which he downed at once. He put down the glass, wheeled about, and meeting her gaze, said truthfully, "Johanna, before I tell you what I've learned, I want you to know that I love you. Nothing could ever change my feelings for you."

Impatient, Johanna demanded, "Robert, please! What is it?"

He went to her, took her arm, and led her to the sofa. Urging her to sit beside him, he took her hands into his. He began gently. "Along with your father's will and papers, there is an official document which states that he has only one legal daughter—Jolene."

"I don't understand!" she interrupted.

"Please, let me finish." He smiled plaintively, squeezed her hands, and continued. "Johanna, sweetheart, it's true that Sam Warrington is your biological father, but your mother was a mulatto slave."

"No!" she screeched. Jerking her hands free and leaping to her feet, she cried angrily, "I don't believe you! How dare you insinuate that . . . that I'm part Negro!"

He hurried to the desk, opened his attaché case and removed the document. Taking it to Johanna, he handed it to her. "This will explain everything about your birth."

She returned to the sofa and sat down. Robert watched her closely as she read the document. The horror on her lovely face cut painfully into his heart.

Her hands were trembling and she dropped the paper onto her lap. "My God! It's true!" she

43

moaned. "I'm a nigger!"

Going to her and kneeling at her feet, he pleaded, "Darling, don't call yourself that!"

Her expression verged on derangement. "Why not? It's the truth, isn't it?"

"You have only one-quarter Negro blood."

"Which makes me a quadroon," she uttered bitterly. "Legally, I'm a black slave. Since Papa is dead, I belong to Jolene. I'm her property. She can sell me if she chooses."

"Stop it!" Robert demanded. "You know damned well that Jolene won't sell you. She loves you."

"Does she?" Johanna challenged harshly. "When she learns I'm a black wench, she won't be so quick to love me!" Suddenly lifting the document and waving it in front of Robert's face, Johanna said eagerly, "All we have to do is destroy this paper and no one will ever know the truth about me!"

"It wouldn't do any good. In your father's will he mentions you as a slave. He's left you a thousand dollars and instructions for you to be set free and sent north."

"A thousand dollars!" she remarked caustically. "That was magnanimous of him!"

"I don't blame you for feeling bitter. But Darling, this isn't the end of the world. I'll go north with you and we'll be married."

"And live in poverty?" she exclaimed sharply. "You're a southerner. How many clients do you think you'll have in the north? When a Yankee needs professional help, he won't turn to you. He'll hire a Yankee lawyer."

"Then we'll stay in the south. We'll move to

Memphis, or some other city where no one knows you."

"When Papa's will becomes public, everyone in the county will know the truth. Even if we were to move to Memphis, eventually my past would catch up with me." She stared at him meaningfully, her face flushed. "It's against the law to marry a Negro. Do you want to go to prison?"

He didn't reply. Instead, he took the document from her hands and carried it back to his attaché case. He stood quietly as his thoughts ran turbulently.

Johanna's thoughts were also in turmoil then. All at once she hurried to Robert, grasped his arm, and urged him to face her. She had a tentative plan but wasn't sure if it could be carried out. What she had in mind might be impossible. Also, she'd need Robert's full cooperation.

"Robert, do you truly love me?" she asked, her growing excitement bringing an attractive sparkle to her emerald eyes.

"Yes, of course I do," he answered.

"I love you, too, Robert," she hastened to reply. Saying this when she knew it wasn't true, didn't faze her in the least. She needed Robert's help, and her whole future depended on his assistance.

She'd never before professed her love. Overjoyed, the young lawyer embraced her. Wrapping her arms about his neck, she offered him her lips, and lowering his mouth to hers, he kissed her passionately.

She pretended to respond wholeheartedly to his ardor. Then, feigning reluctance to leave his arms,

45

she drew away. The fear that he might refuse to help was causing her heart to pound rapidly, and using it to her advantage, she grasped his hand and placed it on her breast. "Feel how kissing you makes my heart race! That's because I love you so desperately."

She removed his hand, gazed helplessly into his eyes, and continued wretchedly, "Oh, Darling, we could've been so happy here at Cedarbrook! If only . . . if only Papa's will didn't mention the truth about me! Surely there's something we can do! Isn't there any way that you can erase that part of the will?"

"Johanna, my darling," he began, as though speaking to an overwrought child, "It can't possibly be erased."

"Can it be changed?" she questioned, holding her breath expectantly.

He was puzzled. "What exactly do you mean?"

"To explain, I need to see the will. Do you have it with you?"

"Yes, I do, but I can't let you read it. It would be unethical."

"Ethics be damned!" she cried. "I'm talking about my future! *Our* future!" When he showed no visible signs of relenting, she forced tears to surface and moaned desperately, "Robert, for God's sake, why are you worried about ethics at a time like this? I thought you loved me!"

"I do!" he swore.

"Then prove it and show me the will!"

"All right," he conceded. Turning to the attaché case, he withdrew the will and handed it to her.

Grasping it, she went to the chair behind the desk,

sat down, and began reading intently.

Robert returned to the liquor cabinet and poured himself another brandy. He sipped the drink, and as the clock over the mantle ticked away the minutes, Johanna continued perusing her father's last will and testament.

"Robert!" she suddenly exclaimed. "It can be changed!"

Putting down his glass, he moved quickly and stood beside her chair. "What do you mean?"

"I think if we're very careful and use the exact shade of ink, we can change all the Johannas to Jolenes, and the Jolenes to Johannas!"

"You can't be serious!" He was incredulous.

"I'm very serious, Robert!" she replied firmly. Opening a drawer and removing a sheet of paper, she placed it on the desk. Taking the ink pen, she dipped it into the well, then wrote her own name and Jolene's. Slowly and with precision, she proceeded to show him how easily the names could be changed. As she went along, she explained, "Look, Robert. In the name *Johanna,* all we have to do is change the 'h' to an 'l,' write an 'e' over the two 'a's, and remove one 'n.' With the name *Jolene,* we make the 'l' an 'h,' change the first 'e' to an 'a,' then trace an extra 'n' over the 'e' and add an 'a.'"

"It'd never work," he remarked. "If anyone were to examine it closely—"

She interrupted. "You're a reputable lawyer, and no one will question your integrity."

"Jolene might!" he pointed out.

"We won't give her a chance. I'll carry out Papa's instructions, give her money, and sent her north."

47

"Those instructions were for you, not Jolene."

"I'm also his daughter!" she declared, springing to her feet. "Why should I settle for nothing when I can have it all!" Clutching his shoulders, she continued rapidly, "Robert, I'll give Jolene more than a thousand dollars. There's no need for you to worry about her. She'll be financially independent. Oh, Darling, don't you understand? This is our only chance! If we don't grasp this opportunity, our future is doomed, our love hopeless!"

He was relenting. "What about the document?"

"You can destory it. Papa, Mr. Holmes, and probably my brother are the only people who knew of its existence."

"Johanna, do you realize how severe the consequences will be if we're caught?"

"Yes, of course I do! But Robert, what other choice to we have? Don't you want us to marry and live at Cedarbrook? Don't you want to be rich?"

He said nothing but turned and moved aimlessly to the window, parted the drapes, and gazed vacantly outside. Yes, he wanted to marry Johanna and live at Cedarbrook, and he also longed for wealth. But Robert Hawkins was basically an honest man. He had never committed an unlawful act. Johanna's deceitful ploy weighed heavily on his conscience. He had a depressing feeling, though, that if he refused to cooperate, he'd lose the woman he loved.

Furthermore, and more importantly, if he didn't change the will, Jolene might turn against Johanna and keep her a slave, or perhaps even sell her. After all, did he truly know Jolene? The times he had seen the two sisters together, he'd gotten the impression that Jolene cared very deeply for Johanna, but impressions could be deceiving. Suddenly, a vision of Johanna standing partially nude on a vendue block flashed before his eyes. The picture was horrifying and he quickly banished it.

He turned to position his back to the window and looked thoughtfully at Johanna. She was poised beside the desk, her eyes searching his, her expression frantic.

Her beauty struck him profoundly. In his opinion there was no woman more beautiful than she. His scrutiny intensifying, he tried to find a sign of her African ancestry, but there was none. In fact, if one were looking for a shade of Negro origin in the two sisters, Jolene's black hair would cause one to pick her over Johanna.

Then, without warning, Robert's southern upbringing intervened: he'd been raised to believe there was an uncrossable line between black and white. Could he actually bring himself to marry Johanna, knowing her mother was a mulatto slave, that his children would be one-eighth Negro?

Yes, he told himself firmly. *I love Johanna and I don't care about her ancestry!*

His mind made up, he returned to her, drew her close, reassured her, "I'll do as you want."

Clinging to him, she cried happily, "Thank you, Robert!"

Releasing her, and getting down to business, he remarked briskly, "First, I'll destroy the document, then forge the names in the will."

Taking the document from the attaché case,

he stepped to the fireplace, got a match from the mantel, lit it, and touched the flame to the paper. Dropping the burning document into the hearth, he watched until it was completely consumed.

As Johanna joined him, Robert murmured heavily, "I hope this is the only document."

She was confused. "I don't understand."

"Your father may have sent a duplicate to someone . . . a relative, perhaps."

"The only relative Papa had is a younger brother who now lives in England. He hasn't been stateside since he married an English woman, and that was twenty years ago."

A soft knock sounded on the door. "Johanna?" they heard Jolene call. "May I come in?"

Moving quickly, Robert dashed to the desk, grabbed the will, scooped up the sheet of paper that Johanna had written on, and shoved them in his attaché case. He stepped back to Johanna and said in a whisper, "In order to use the same color ink, I'll have to make the changes in Mr. Holmes's office. Then, to be on the safe side, we need to give the fresh ink a couple of days to dry completely. I'll use Mr. Holmes's death as a pretext to postpone the reading of the will."

She nodded, conveying her agreement. Then, forcing warmth into her voice, she invited Jolene to join them.

Entering, Jolene bade the young lawyer good morning, then asked when Mr. Holmes was due to read the will.

"Mr. Holmes died last night," Robert explained.

"I'm sorry to hear that," Jolene replied sincerely.

"Please give my condolences to his family."

"Yes, I will," he assured her, his heart suddenly pounding. Had Holmes said anything to his wife or children about Johanna? No, of course not, Robert quickly convinced himself. Holmes was trustworthy and wouldn't have betrayed what Warrington had told him in confidence.

"Robert is going to read the will," Johanna told her sister. "However, he'd like to wait a few days. You see, he's quite upset over Mr. Holmes passing away."

Jolene turned to Robert. "I understand, and there's no hurry in reading the will. Take all the time you need."

"Thank you, Jolene," he murmured. He studied her for a moment. He thought her very pretty and was amazed that her black mourning clothes couldn't dim her beauty.

Johanna, aware that Robert was staring strangely at her sister, quickly grasped his arm. She was afraid he might start feeling sorry for Jolene and abolish their deceptive scheme.

"I won't keep you any longer, Robert," Johanna remarked brightly. "I know you have pressing work back at the office."

"Yes, I do," he replied, going to the desk and picking up his attaché case. Assuring the women that they needn't show him out, he wished them a good day and left.

As Robert closed the door behind him, Jolene's gaze swept disapprovingly over Johanna's attire. "Isn't it a little early to discard your mourning clothes? What if we should have more company

51

besides Robert? What would they think, seeing you dressed this way?"

It was on the tip of Johanna's tongue to come back with a bitter retort, but suddenly, realizing she shouldn't arouse suspicion, especially from her father's neighbors and friends, she decided she should continue wearing her mourning dress.

Fibbing smoothly, she told her sister, "This morning I saw a stain on the dress and I'm having one of the servants remove it. As soon as it's cleaned, I intend to put it back on."

"I'm sorry," Jolene replied. "I shouldn't have jumped to conclusions." Absently she moved to the fireplace, and catching sight of the fresh ashes, she paused to look at them. It was early summer, and except for the burned document, the hearth was bare. "Did you burn some paper?" Jolene asked, turning her gaze to Johanna.

"Yes—but nothing important," she replied evasively. Then, quick to change the subject, she said heartily, "I don't know about you, but I'm famished. Let's have breakfast, shall we?"

"All right," Jolene agreed, and giving the ashes no further thought, she followed her sister out of the room.

Chapter Two

The young servant poured the last bucket of water into the marble tub, then turning to her mistress, said, "Your bath is ready, Miz Jolene."

Jolene was sitting on the bed daydreaming, and the servant's voice brought her back to reality. "Thank you, Patsy."

"You's welcome, ma'am," she replied with a wide grin. Patsy, at sixteen, was blooming into a lovely young woman. Her dark skin was smooth and flawless, her figure well endowed, and her pretty face framed by short, tightly curled hair.

Patsy's mood was chipper, for she knew this morning Mr. Hawkins was supposed to read Master Sam's will. Aware that her former master had always been distant with Johanna, Patsy was certain that Jolene had inherited control of the plantation and its slaves. She was also certain that Jolene would be a compassionate mistress, whereas she suspected Johanna would be a tyrant.

Removing her dressing gown, Jolene went to the

tub and lowered herself into the warm, perfume-scented water.

"Do you want me to wash you, mistress ma'am?" Patsy asked.

Jolene smiled tolerantly. "As I've told you before, I'm quite capable of washing myself, Patsy. You don't have to wait on me hand and foot."

"Yes'm," the servant mumbled. Her admiration for her mistress deepened.

"Why don't you sit down so we can talk," Jolene suggested.

Patsy's mouth dropped open. A slave sitting in the presence of white folks was unheard of.

The young woman laughed pleasantly at the servant's astonishment. "Get my vanity stool, bring it over here, sit on it, and talk to me."

When she was seated, Jolene asked, "Patsy, generally speaking, are my father's slaves happy and content?"

"Yes'm, I guess they is," she answered, her hesitation apparent.

"You don't have to be afraid to speak openly. Please be honest with me."

Encouraged, Patsy said in a lowered voice, "Well, Miz Jolene, we house servants got it better than most, but the field slaves, they's got it real hard. Mista Sullivan, the overseer, he powerful mean. He always a-whippin' the men, and the young women, he . . . he makin' 'em come to his house at night."

"Did my father know about this?" Jolene demanded.

Patsy dropped her gaze. "Yes'm," she admitted sheepishly. "Masta Sam, he gave Mista Sullivan full control. Since Mista Sullivan been overseer, Cedarbrook got more cotton than ever before. Masta Sam, he closed his mind to Mista Sullivan's meanness, 'cause Mista Sullivan makin' him a lot of money off the crops."

Her father's insensitivity cut her to the core. That he had allowed the overseer to treat the field slaves so cruelly sent a surge of anger through Jolene. She had disapproved of Sam's treatment of Johanna, but other than that, she had believed her father beyond reproach.

"Mr. Hawkins is due this morning to read Papa's will, but when he leaves, I'll send for Mr. Sullivan and dismiss him. There'll be no cruel overseers at Cedarbrook." For a short time Jolene remained deep in thought. Then, looking at Patsy, she said briskly, "I want you to make arrangements for me to speak to all the field workers. I'll give them my personal guarantee that the next overseer will be a fair and compassionate man."

Jolene sighed heavily. If it were possible she'd set all her father's slaves free and pay them wages to work at Cedarbrook, but the southern bureaucracy was too powerful and would intervene. There were nearly two hundred slaves at Cedarbrook, and the south's judicial system would never allow that many blacks freed at one time.

Well, Jolene mused with resignation, maybe I can't set my slaves free, but I can make their lives as pleasant as possible. Cedarbrook will be run like its own town and be governed by the same kind of laws. Also, there'll be no more "jumping the broom" when a couple want to marry . . . I'll send for a black preacher.

Her plans to better Cedarbrook began to fill her

head, and she was now anxious to finish her bath and write down some of her ideas on paper. Smiling radiantly, she looked at Patsy and remarked, "There are going to be a lot of changes at Cedarbrook, changes for the better!"

Smiling in return, Patsy said happily, "Yes'm, I's sure there is gonna be some changes. You's gonna be a good mistress, and I sure hope Masta Sam left Cedarbrook to you. Miz Johanna, she won't care 'bout us slaves, she don't care 'bout no one but herself."

Seated at her dresser, Johanna was studying her reflection. She looked pale and gaunt. The full impact of her ancestry hadn't hit her until hours after learning that her mother had been a mulatto slave. Since then she'd been so upset that sleep had been impossible. Plagued by insomnia, she'd tossed and turned as worrisome thoughts kept her awake. When she finally did fall asleep, she was haunted by troubled dreams. She had a couple of packets of sleeping powder that Robert had given her, but she hadn't used them for fear that the potent sedative might prevent her from waking and escaping one of her nightmares.

Opening a jar of rouge, she rubbed the red paste onto her pale cheeks, which brought color back to her face. Picking up the hairbrush, she began running it briskly through her long, golden-brown tresses.

Her thoughts ran as briskly as the brush. Now that she had learned the truth, she understood why her father had always treated her so coldly, while

56

showering Jolene with affection. Johanna, familiar with southern slang, realized bitterly that Sam had considered her his "git" and Jolene his daughter.

"We were both your daughters, damn you!" she raged, slamming down the brush against the dresser top. She rose quickly and began pacing the room with the restlessness of a caged lion.

She was wearing a dressing gown, and its long, silky folds billowed lightly about her legs as she continued to pace back and forth.

She was scared, confused, and unnerved. Robert would read the will this morning, and what if something went wrong? If she and Robert were caught, the repercussions would be severe. But if all went well and Cedarbrook became hers, could she adequately run an estate as large as this? She knew absolutely nothing about operating a plantation.

Although Johanna was scared that hers and Robert's deception might be uncovered, and was worried about running Cedarbrook, she was more concerned about Jolene. She knew her sister well and was perfectly aware that sending her north was not the solution. Jolene would suspect that she and Robert had changed the will, and even if she did go north, she'd return, hire a lawyer, and have the will examined. Johanna was acutely aware that the will wouldn't stand up under close perusal.

She must find a way to be rid of Jolene permanently, and she must do so without Robert's knowledge. She could inveigle the young lawyer into changing a will, but she knew she could never convince him to be a conspirator in murder.

Hoping to find a way to murder her own sister didn't touch Johanna's conscience. All her life her jealousy had caused her to hate Jolene. Her plan to destroy her sister was practical, though, more than revengeful. As long as Jolene was alive, there was a good chance that she and Robert would be caught.

Knowing there were no answers at the moment, Johanna stopped her pacing, went to her bedroom door, opened it, and looked down the hall. Seeing Patsy coming out of Jolene's room, she called sternly, "Get in here, you lazy wench! I need someone to help me dress!"

Obeying, the young servant moved quickly and followed Johanna into the bedroom.

"Where have you been?" Johanna demanded. "I told you last night that I wanted you to report to me this morning!"

"I was helpin' Miz Jolene with her bath," Patsy explained.

Placing her hands on her hips and eying the servant harshly, Johanna snapped, "Well, hereafter, you'll be my own personal maid! Do you understand?"

"Yes'm," she answered timidly. "But, Miz Jolene, she a-wantin' me to be her maid."

The slave's impertinence infuriated Johanna. "Don't you dare question my orders! Now, if you don't want to feel the back of my hand against your face, you'll fetch my mourning gown, brush it thoroughly, then help me dress!"

"Yes'm, Miz Johanna." Patsy complied hastily. As she carried out her mistress's instructions, Patsy was sure that this would be the last time she'd be forced to do maid service for Johanna.

"I's just sure *that* Miz Jolene will inherit control of Cedarbrook," Patsy thought. "Then, Miz Jolene will tell her ole mean sister that I's to be her own maid."

A shudder ran through the young slave as she imagined a life as Johanna's personal maid. The woman was overbearing, cruel, and short-tempered, and would undoubtedly make her servant's life a hell on earth!

Jolene and Johanna were having breakfast in the formal dining room when Lazarus interrupted to let them know that there was a slave trader out front wishing to speak to one of them. The butler spoke with disdain, for itinerant slave traders were looked down on by blacks as well as whites.

"I'll see what he wants," Johanna offered, rising from her chair.

Lazarus stepped aside for his mistress, then, following at a respectable distance, he accompanied her from the dining room, down the hall, and into the foyer.

Stepping out onto the white-pillared porch, Johanna's gaze traveled distastefully over the unkempt trader and his pitiful coffle gathered on the well tended lawn.

Lazarus stood a few steps behind his mistress. He had seen the trader several times and knew that his name was Cal Atkins. The man's circuit always brought him to Cedarbrook, where he hoped to make a purchase. Lazarus could recall Sam Warrington selling only twice to the trader. Both times, he had sold slaves who were "runners."

Now, as the butler studied the slaves belonging to the trader, he shook his head sympathetically. The blacks, old or maimed, were a pathetic lot.

Meanwhile, Atkins, hoping to buy a young, healthy buck who happened to be a "runner," made a feeble attempt to imitate a gentleman and removed his filthy, tattered, hat. Smiling congenially at Johanna, he bowed from the waist and paid his respects. "Good mornin', Miz Warrington. Ma'am, please accept my deepest condolences for your terrible loss. Mista Warrington was a fine man, and he's gonna be sorely missed."

"Thank you," Johanna said stiffly. "What can I do for you, sir?"

"Allow me to introduce myself. I'm Cal Atkins." He waved a hand tersely toward his coffle. "And these-here darkies are my slaves. I'm on my way to New Orleans to sell these nigras at the vendue block. In the past, I done some business with your pappy, and I was wonderin' if you might have a nigra you need to get shet of. Like maybe a 'runner,' or a troublemaker. I'll offer you a fair price, ma'am. Cal Atkins is an honest man. Ask anybody, they'll tell you it's true."

It was on the tip of Johanna's tongue to curtly dismiss the coarse man, but suddenly an imperceptible and calculating smile crossed her lips. She could hardly believe her good fortune! Cal Atkins might very well be the answer to her dilemma.

Feigning a friendly smile, Johanna descended the porch steps, went to the trader, and asked him sweetly, "Would you mind taking a stroll with me? I need to talk to you privately." She gestured toward the house. "I'd invite you inside, but with so many slaves moving about, the walls have ears."

"I know what ya mean, ma'am. Them darkies

know everything 'bout their owners' business."

Although Johanna continued to smile, she was finding it very difficult to do so. The man's foul odor was overwhelming, and she wondered if he ever took a bath. Beneath the dirt, grime, and straggly beard lurked a young man who, cleaned up, would be nice-looking.

"Will you come with me?" Johanna asked pleasantly, urging him to fall into step beside her. She didn't dare take his arm. The thought of touching him made her skin crawl.

He hesitated. "I don't like to leave my coffle untended. They might get it in their heads to run. I best chain 'em to my buckboard."

Anxious to put her hastily laid plan into motion, Johanna said firmly, "That isn't necessary. I'll have my butler do it for you." Quickly she ordered Lazarus to chain Mr. Atkins' slaves.

Grudgingly he complied, and as his mistress and the trader walked away, he mumbled beneath his breath, "I wonder what that woman is up to. Whatever it is, I bet it ain't no good."

Johanna and her companion strolled in silence as she led him leisurely down the cedar-bordered driveway. Then, glancing around and seeing no slaves in the vicinity, she brought their steps to a halt.

"Mr. Atkins, what I want to discuss with you is strictly confidential. Will you give me your word as a gentleman that you'll keep our conversation between the two of us?"

"Yes, ma'am," he was quick to agree, his curiosity killing him. What secret did this gorgeous woman wish to share? Cal began to fidget nervously. He

61

wasn't used to associating with southern ladies; usually they went out of their way to snub him.

"Mr. Atkins," she began levelly, "the other day my lawyer came to see me. He had a document with him that he thought I should read. This document, signed by my father, stated that my sister, Jolene, isn't white. Her mother was a mulatto slave, but for some unexplained reason, my parents decided to raise her as if she were truly their daughter." She lowered her eyes and pretended modesty. "Papa is her biological father."

"I understand, ma'am. You don't have to be embarrassed."

She smiled prettily and returned to meet his gaze. "When I learned the truth, I went to Jolene and told her. I wanted to spare her the embarrassment of learning about her ancestry at the reading of the will."

Pausing, Johanna managed successfully to appear frightened. "Mr. Atkins, Jolene turned on me viciously. She now hates me because I'm white and she isn't. She has even gone so far as to threaten me." Johanna looked at him as though, being white, the two of them shared a special bond.

He bestowed on her an understanding glance, then asked, "Miz Warrington, are you tellin' me that this wench actually threatened you with bodily harm?"

"She swore she's going to kill me!" Johanna gasped.

"Ma'am," he began, offering gentle advice, "You don't have to tolerate no slave a-threatenin' ya. All you gotta do is order a couple of your strong bucks to string her up and lash her with the whip. 'Bout a dozen lashes will make her docile."

"It isn't that simple. Since learning the truth about herself, Jolene has started inciting my slaves. If I order her whipped, I'm liable to have an uprising on my hands." She gazed at him helplessly, tears welling in her beautiful green eyes. "Oh, Mr. Atkins, I'm so afraid! Papa and my brother are gone, and I have no man to protect me! Jolene hates me so, and I'm scared that she'll turn all my slaves against me! I'll be murdered in my bed for sure!"

Touched, and responding gallantly, Cal said quickly, "Ma'am, you just tell me how I can help, and I'll do so gladly."

"I want you to sneak Jolene away from here. I'll pay you handsomely, of course."

His gallantry instantly replaced with financial gain, he replied, "I'll do what you want, ma'am. When I get her to New Orleans, I'll sell her on the vendue block. I'll send you half the money I get for her."

"No! I don't want you to sell her, I want you to kill her!"

He was taken aback. "Why do ya want me to do that? If she's a quadroon, she's worth a lot of money."

Johanna forced herself to speak evenly. "Mr. Atkins, if she's sold, she's liable to escape her new owner, return here, and murder me. As long as Jolene is alive, she remains a threat to my life. I must have her killed, but I must have it done without my slaves knowing about it. At present she has their blind loyalty. Once she's gone, they'll soon forget about her. You know how it is with them—out of sight, out of mind. I prefer that no one know about

63

this. I'll not only pay you for getting rid of her permanently, but I'll also see that you're rewarded for your silence in the matter."

Cal's thoughts were running greedily. He planned to take her up on her lucrative offer. However, he had no intentions of killing a quadroon wench and cheating himself out of her worth . . . she'd bring a high price in New Orleans.

Johanna continued, "Mr. Atkins, I want you to take her away from this plantation, kill her, then bury her body where it won't be found."

She waited, but when he made no reply, she pressed on, "Well, do we have a deal?"

He smiled. "Yes'm, we sure do."

Johanna sighed with relief. "Thank you, Mr. Atkins."

Knowing he'd need a bill of sale to put Jolene up for auction, he said, "I'll need papers on this wench."

"Why?" she questioned. "You aren't going to sell her, you're going to kill her."

"Ma'am, these roads are guarded by slave patrols, and they usually stop me and make me show 'em that I got legal papers on all my slaves. Just in case I'm stopped 'fore I get rid of your wench, I'll need proof of her ownership." Cal Atkins was just as calculating as his new partner.

"Very well," Johanna conceded. "I'll make you a bill of sale. I've never done this before. What exactly does a bill of sale include?"

"You just write the price I paid, her name, age, and general description. Also, bein' that she's a young wench, you'll have to state whether or not she's a virgin, and if she ain't, you gotta put down how many suckers she's had."

"Jolene is still a virgin," she said assuredly.

A quadroon who was a virgin brought an enormous price, and Cal smiled inwardly with greed.

"When I state the amount you supposedly paid for her, how much should it be?" Johanna was inexperienced in such matters.

"You'd best put down five hundred dollars, 'cause young quadroon wenches are kinda valuable. We don't want the slave patrol gettin' suspicious." Cal was certain that if he were stopped by the patrol, they'd accept the price. However, he knew in New Orleans she'd go for a thousand. Suddenly, though, he was struck with second thoughts: if this wench wasn't pretty, she wouldn't be all that valuable. Trying to sound only vaguely curious, he asked, "By the way, ma'am, is this wench good-lookin'?"

Johanna, her jealousy surging, answered disdainfully, "Yes. In fact, she's very beautiful."

Cal, concealing his relief, asked, "How much you plannin' to pay me to get rid of her?"

"I think two hundred dollars will be sufficient, don't you?" She gave him a level stare which seemed to say that that was her top dollar.

Cal was agreeable. He'd get two hundred dollars for doing nothing. Then, when he sold the wench, he'd make at least a thousand free and clear.

He offered her his hand. "Miz Warrington, shall we shake on our deal?"

Although she was reluctant to touch him, she accepted his handshake. Then, laying their plans, she said crisply, "Make camp a short distance from here. Tonight, I'll slip Jolene a potent sedative. At midnight, chain your coffle to some trees and return here with the buckboard. Come to the side door which leads into the study. I'll be waiting for you with your money and a bill of sale. Then I'll show you to Jolene's room. She'll be heavily sedated, so you'll have to carry her outside and to your buckboard."

Cal nodded. "All right, ma'am. I'll do just as you say."

"Good," she remarked. "I need to get back to the house before we arouse too much suspicion. And, Mr. Atkins, I think you should leave at once."

"Yes'm." He was more than willing to oblige.

She smiled secretively. "I'll see you at midnight." Without further ado, she turned about and walked swiftly toward the columned mansion. She looked like the cat who had swallowed the canary. Soon she's be permanently rid of Jolene, and then Cedarbrook would be all hers!

That Johanna had just ordered her own sister's murder didn't bother her in the least. Her emotional abuse at the hands of her father, her brother, and Della had helped to make her the cold, unfeeling woman that she was. However, Millie's daughter had been born with aggressive and self-centered traits, but due to her unfair upbringing, these bad characteristics had worsened. Furthermore, all her life she had maliciously despised her sister. Now, learning that Jolene was white, whereas she herself possessed Negro blood, had aroused her hate to the fullest.

Johanna Warrington was more dangerous than a black widow spider, and ordering Jolene's execution bothered her no more than swatting a fly.

66

Chapter Three

Jolene stepped out onto the porch, and the sight of Atkins' slaves shackled to the buckboard affected her profoundly. She disapproved of slave traders and thought them despicable, and the way they treated their coffles was, in most cases, inhumane.

She looked about for Lazarus or Johanna. The butler had apparently left, but she caught sight of her sister coming toward the house. Jolene was surprised to see the slave trader walking a short distance behind her. Evidently they had been talking together.

As Johanna climbed the porch steps, Cal went over to his slaves and undid their chains. Out of the corner of his eye, he discreetly examined Jolene from head to foot. She was indeed a beauty, and he was beginning to think that she might bring more than a thousand dollars. He looked away from the stunning woman and told his slaves to line up behind the wagon. As he climbed onto the seat and took up the reins, he smiled to himself. He had been somewhat suspicious of Johanna and had unknowingly suspected the truth. Now, after seeing Jolene's black hair, he was confident that Johanna had told the truth. If one of the sisters was a quadroon, it was obviously the one with the dark hair. He had seen dozens of quadroons in New Orleans, and the majority of them, regardless of their white skin, had ebony-colored hair.

Jolene waited until Atkins had slapped the reins against his team of horses and started down the driveway before turning to Johanna and demanding testily, "Why in the world were you talking to that dreadful man?"

Johanna's face revealed nothing. "I merely told him that he and his kind weren't welcome at Cedarbrook."

"You didn't have to take a walk with him to tell him that," Jolene retorted.

"Honestly!" Johanna spat angrily. "Must you make such a fuss?" Just then Robert's buggy approached the house. A man on horseback accompanied him, but she couldn't make out who it was.

As the visitors drew closer, Jolene recognized the horseman. "It's Marshall Walker."

"Marshall!" Johanna breathed. Her heart pounded and she suddenly felt as apprehensive as a schoolgirl. She hadn't seen Marshall in over four years, but her admiration for him hadn't dimmed with the passage of time.

Marshall, although still relatively young, owned an enormous and prosperous plantation a few miles from Cedarbrook. He had inherited it years before from his father. He was ten years older than the Warrington sisters, so when the girls were children, he had paid them little attention. Marshall had thought of Sam Warrington as an older brother. Sam, in turn, had been fond of Marshall and had always tried to help him.

As a child Johanna had developed a crush on Marshall, a crush that had lasted through puberty and was still evident. The last few times the sisters had been home from school, Marshall, for one reason or another, had been unable to pay his respects, causing four years to elapse since he had last seen them.

The two men drew up their horses and dismounted. Climbing the steps ahead of the lawyer, Marshall smiled charmingly as his gaze raked appreciatively over the sisters.

First he embraced Jolene, and she returned his hug warmly. She had always liked Marshall and found him quite irresistible. He then turned to Johanna and drew her against him. For years she had dreamed of being in his arms, and she clung tightly as she relished his closeness.

If the handsome planter was aware that Johanna's embrace had been more ardent than friendly, he didn't let on. Releasing her, he smiled down into her flushed face and said, "Johanna, you have grown into a lovely woman." His gaze now on Jolene, he continued, "You are both more beautiful than words."

"Thank you," the sisters murmured.

"I should've called sooner to pay my condolences, but my plantation demands so much of my time that

I can barely find time to get away. Please excuse my negligence, and, believe me, my thoughts have been with you both."

"You needn't apologize," Johanna replied. "You're here now, and that's what matters."

"Yes," he agreed, looking a little ashamed. "But I didn't come simply to express my condolences. I'm also here for the reading of the will. You see, before Mr. Holmes passed away, he told me that Sam remembered me in his will." He glanced at Robert. "Mr. Hawkins notified me that he planned to read the will this morning. I was on my way here when he and I happened to meet on the road."

Johanna, enraptured, was barely listening to Marshall's explanation. He was even more handsome than she remembered. His expensively tailored jacket and trousers fit his tall, slender frame perfectly. He removed his wide-brimmed panama hat, and the sun's rays made his golden hair shine radiantly. He apparently worked outdoors a great deal, for his clean-shaven face was tanned.

"Johanna," Robert spoke up, gaining her attention. "As we were arriving, we saw Cal Atkins leaving. Why was he here?"

"He wanted to know if we had any slaves for sale."

Marshall took it upon himself to give advice. "You and Jolene must avoid dealing with men like Atkins. His kind aren't gentlemen, nor can they be trusted."

Robert, anxious to read the will and get it over with, looked at Johanna and remarked, "Shall we all go into the study?"

"Yes, of course," she answered, her eyes communicating secretively with his. "The sooner we get Papa's will read, the sooner we can put it behind us."

Johanna had intended to escort Marshall inside, but before she could, he stepped to Jolene and offered her his arm. Taking his gesture as a sign that he had chosen Jolene over herself, Johanna's bitterness and jealousy surged so violently that she gasped aloud.

"Are you all right?" Robert asked, stepping quickly to her side.

Regaining her composure, Johanna answered, "Yes, I'm fine." As Marshall and Jolene entered the house, she moved closer to the lawyer and whispered, "Do you think we'll get away with it?"

He smiled reassuringly. "Yes, I do. My forgery was so good that I even impressed myself."

Johanna smiled triumphantly.

A short time later, Jolene flung open her bedroom door, rushed inside, and fell across the bed. Lying on her back, she stared vacantly up at the ceiling. Her face was deathly pale, and her eyes were glazed with shock. She felt as though she had just lived through a terrible nightmare.

Her muscles were taut, her body rigid. Inhaling deeply, then exhaling, she tried to relax.

It couldn't be true! It just couldn't! Charlotte had been her mother, not the slave called Millie!

Her eyes smarted with tears as she thought back to the reading of her father's last will and testament. Sam Warrington's disposition of his property had been short and straight to the point. His prize

71

Morgan had been left to Marshall, who shared his love for thoroughbreds. Except for the horse, his entire estate went to Carl, but in case of his son's death at the reading of the will, Cedarbrook and its assets belonged to his daughter.

Thinking back, Jolene remembered how Robert had paused at this point, looked from her to Johanna, then glancing down at the will to reread it: "Cedarbrook and its assets belong to my daughter . . . Johanna."

Jolene had been struck dumb. Papa had left everything to Johanna? No! No, it didn't make sense! He might leave Cedarbrook to them jointly, but he'd never completely cut her out of his will! Never!

Jolene barely had time to regain a semblance of composure before being hit with another shock, this one more formidable than the first.

Unable to look at Jolene, Robert had kept his eyes on the paper as he deceitfully revealed that Jolene's mother had been the mulatto slave called Millie.

Now, her thoughts centered on Johanna and Robert, Jolene rose from the bed and paced restlessly across the floor. Her shock was waning, and she was able to think more clearly.

Had Johanna and Robert changed her father's will? Yes! It was the only answer that made any sense! If her mother had been a mulatto slave, Sam Warrington would never have favored her over Johanna!

Abruptly her pacing ceased as she suddenly recalled the conversation she'd overheard between her brother and Charlotte. "Your father knows the truth about Johanna, doesn't he?" Now this "truth" that had always eluded her became crystal clear. Her father had told Carl the truth about Johanna, that Johanna's mother had been a slave.

"Johanna's mother—not mine!" Jolene exclaimed aloud.

Calming herself, she returned to her bed and sat down. Certain beyond all doubt that her father's will had been falsified, she considered what action she should take. It'd be best not to let Johanna and Robert know she was suspicious of them, for if they were capable of fraud, they might also be capable of silencing her permanently. For the remainder of the day, she'd be noncommital and withdrawn. Then, early in the morning, while Johanna was still in bed, she'd sneak away to Natchez. Her father had influential friends in the city and she'd turn to them for help.

As Jolene plotted, Johanna showed Marshall to the front door.

"I just can't believe it," Walker remarked. "Jolene's mother was a slave?"

Pausing at the door, Johanna lifted her gaze to his and said somberly, "I've never been so shocked. Poor Jolene. My heart aches for her."

Marshall seemed confused. "It doesn't make sense."

"What do you mean?" she asked, on her guard.

He answered somewhat hesitantly. "Between the two of you, Sam always favored Jolene. You'd think . . . ?"

"Yes, I know what you're trying to say," she cut in quickly, as she conjured up an excuse he'd accept. "But Marshall, maybe Papa truly loved Millie and was drawn to Jolene because she reminded him of her mother."

He was only half convinced. "Maybe . . . however, if that were true, you'd think he'd have left her more than a thousand dollars."

"Well, in a way he did. He gave her an education." Placing a hand on his arm, she said magnanimously, "I intend to give her much more than the thousand Papa requested. Once she's settled up north, I'm sure she'll be content."

Then, Johanna managed to force tears to well in her eyes, and pretending heartbreak, she sobbed heavily, "I'd keep her here with me if I thought she'd be happy! But when people learn the truth, they'll . . . they'll treat her like a Negro!"

Quickly he took her into his arms, as she'd known he would. Placing her head on his shoulder, and feigning sorrow, she clung to his strength.

Holding her close, he murmured, "Johanna, you're a very compassionate young woman, and apparently you love your sister very much."

"Oh, I do! I do!" she cried, her voice breaking.

As the couple embraced, Robert, having grown impatient waiting for Johanna's return, entered the foyer. He cleared his throat to make his presence known.

Releasing Johanna, Marshall looked at the lawyer and, with an undertone of praise, said, "Johanna plans to give Jolene much more than a thousand dollars before sending her north."

Robert's unscrutable gaze beheld Johanna. "Oh? That's very generous of you."

Johanna smiled sweetly. "It's the least I can do. After all, she is my sister."

Marshall quickly made his excuses and left, letting Johanna know that he'd return for the Morgan later in the week.

Now that they were alone, Robert stalked angrily to her side and grasped her arm. He spoke in a low, furious voice, demanding, "Why were you in Walker's arms?"

Pulling away, she replied petulantly, "Honestly, Robert! Your jealousy is not only disgusting but completely uncalled for! Marshall was merely consoling me."

"Consoling you?" he sneered. "Yes, we both know how upset you are."

Not wanting to incite her conspirator's wrath, she pouted prettily. "Robert, sometimes you can be such a silly goose. If I had acted overjoyed, don't you think Marshall would've thought it strange? I must be very careful not to do anything to arouse undue suspicion. When the will becomes public knowledge, there will be enough gossip without me attracting even more attention!"

Knowing she was right, Robert's anger faded. "I'm sorry, Darling. Please forgive me."

"Of course I forgive you," she quickly assured him. Taking his hands and holding them tightly, she looked into his eyes, pleading, "Sweetheart, I think you and I should be very cautious for the next few months. We must wait for the gossip to die down before we're seen together as a couple."

Reading objection in his eyes, she went on in a sugary tone, "I don't think it'd cause unnecessary gossip if you were to come here, say once a week or so, as though you were here on business. I can't bear the thought of going weeks on end without seeing you."

Again, he knew she was being sensible. He relented, albeit reluctantly. "Very well, Darling." He drew her into his embrace.

She slipped her arms about his neck and urged his lips to hers. Johanna, feeling victorious, smiled to herself. She had found a way to get rid of Jolene and had convinced Robert to limit his visits, which would of course leave her free to pursue Marshall Walker.

Jolene, avoiding her sister, had stayed in her room all day and into the night. It was late, and she was dressed for bed when a soft but insistent knock sounded at her door. Jolene was sitting at her vanity, brushing her hair. "Yes?"

"Jolene, may I come in?" Johanna requested, her tone as sweet as honey.

Jolene's brow furrowed. "What do you want?"

"I brought you a glass of sherry," Johanna explained, and without waiting to be invited in, she opened the door and entered.

Carrying a tray with two filled glasses, she went to her sister and placed their drinks on the dressing table. Picking up the glass laced with the potent sleeping powder, she offered it to Jolene. "Here; drink this. It'll make you feel better." Her sudden

76

smile was overly tender. "It'll also help you sleep. I remember Mama used to have a glass of sherry before bedtime."

Jolene accepted the wine. Turning her gaze from her sister, she stared thoughtfully at the drink. She'd never tasted sherry; but her nerves were on edge and she did need something to help her relax.

Lifting her own glass to her lips, Johanna said, "To your health."

Jolene took a sip. The beverage tasted somewhat bitter to her. If this hadn't been her first taste of sherry, she'd have known that Johanna had put something in it. But since she had no way of knowing this, Jolene drew a deep breath, lifted the glass, and drank its full contents.

Finishing her own drink, Johanna returned her glass to the silver tray, placing it beside Jolene's empty one.

Taking her sister's arm, Johanna encouraged, "Come; let me help you to bed."

Jolene drew back. "Please go away and leave me alone."

Whirling about, Johanna walked around the room, studying its huge size and elaborate decor. "I think I'll move into your bedroom," she announced. "It's larger and more elegant than mine." Her voice grew bitter. "Of course, that's because dear Papa decided which room was to be mine and which was to be yours. Naturally, he gave you the better one."

"I offered to change rooms with you years ago," Jolene murmured, feeling strangely lightheaded.

"Jolene, you are unbelievably sweet," she remarked tartly. "Sometimes you are so sweet that you make me sick!" Stalking to Jolene and leering down at her, Johanna sneered viciously, "I wonder if you have any idea how many times I've wished you were dead!"

Jolene wanted to respond, but she was now already growing too drowsy to sort out her thoughts. She tried to rise from the vanity stool, but her knees were too weak to support her. As the room began to spin before her eyes, she managed to groan, "You put something in my drink, didn't you?" Inwardly, she blamed her own stupidity. She should've suspected something like this!

"Only a sleeping powder," Johanna answered. Smiling coldly, she added, "A double dose, of course."

"Why?" Jolene choked out.

Grasping her sister's arms and leading her to the bed, Johanna replied, "I want you to sleep soundly. In the morning, when you awaken, you'll understand why."

Johanna forced Jolene to lie down. Jolene longed to fight against the woman's abuse, but she was too drugged to resist.

Remaining beside the bed, Johanna crossed her arms beneath her full bosom and eyed her helpless victim with a level, hateful stare. "I'll stay until you fall asleep."

"Why do you despise me so?" Jolene whispered feebly, trying in vain to stay awake.

"Need you ask?" Johanna demanded harshly. "I've hated you since we were children! Papa, Carl, and Della—they all loved you!" Her voice broke with emotion. "God, I wanted them to love me! I needed their love so desperately!"

Despite everything, Jolene felt a pang of pity for her sister. "It wasn't my fault," she moaned. She was drifting into unconsciousness. "I always wanted them to love you . . . Mama loved you . . . I loved you . . ."

"I never wanted your damned love!" Johanna snarled.

Jolene, now barely awake, finally made her accusation: "You and Robert changed Papa's will, didn't you?"

Johanna was quite proud of herself. "Yes, of course we did." She watched as Jolene's eyes closed, then waited a short time until she was sure that her sister was sound asleep.

Johanna left the room in a hurry, for it was late and Cal Atkins was due at midnight.

Chapter Four

As Jolene began to slowly awaken, she became aware of a rocking motion. It wasn't smooth but jolting, and it kept her body rolling back and forth against a hard upright structure. When she opened her eyes, she realized she was being tossed against the sideboard of a moving wagon.

Alarmed, she sat up with a start, and the sudden movement sent a pain throbbing in her temples. She massaged her head gingerly as she tried to reason where she was and how she'd gotten here.

She saw a coffle of slaves walking sluggishly behind the wagon. There were over a dozen of them, and most were either old or maimed. The men were manacled, but the women were unfettered. The slaves at the front of the weary procession noticed that she was awake. They looked at her blankly, without emotion.

Jolene's eyes turned from their hopeless gazes to scan the countryside. The group was apparently traveling through a rural area, for the dirt road was bordered on both sides by full-branched billowing trees and thick shrubbery interspersed with prickly brambles.

She glanced cautiously over her shoulder to see who was driving the wagon. Although the man's back was turned, she still recognized him—it was the slave trader, Cal Atkins!

Jolene gasped softly. Dear God, what had Johanna done to her? Had she actually sold her to this horrible man?

In an effort to calm herself, Jolene inhaled deeply. She mustn't panic! She had to be in complete control of her emotions when she talked to Mr. Atkins, for she must make him believe that she was not merely a slave to be purchased.

Her throat was extremely dry and she looked around, hoping to find water. She became aware of her new attire: a plain butternut dress and worn, scuffed slippers. She'd never seen these clothes before, but she didn't question why she was dressed this way. Obviously Johanna had put her in the type of clothing that slaves wore. She wondered what she was wearing beneath the simple dress, but with the coffle walking behind the wagon, she couldn't very well lift her skirt to find out.

She mentally prepared herself to speak to Atkins, then moved to face him. She was surprised to see him turned in the seat, regarding her with a level stare.

A cold, cruel grin spread his tobacco-stained lips. "Howdy, little gal. How ya feelin'? You slept all night and all mornin'. It's 'most lunchtime."

He patted the wagon seat. "Why don't ya climb up

81

here and sit next to your new masta? We need to get acquainted, don't we, Sugar Babe?"

Complying, she stepped a little awkwardly over the back of the seat and sat beside him. "Mr. Atkins," she said carefully, "I must talk to you. I am not—"

He cut in sharply. "Now, you better listen to me, Miss Uppity! Don't call me 'Mis-ter'—you gotta address me respectfully. I'm *Masta Atkins.*"

"But you don't understand!" she began desperately.

He slapped her soundly across the cheek, the sharp blow jerking her head to the side. "You watch how you talk to me, you damned wench! If you wanna speak to me, you do it right. You say 'Masta Atkins, suh,' or you don't say nothin'!"

Her cheek stung and her eyes smarted with tears. Knowing it was futile to argue, she said between gritted teeth, "Master Atkins, sir—"

Again he interrupted her forcefully. "Damn you! I won't tolerate no wench a-talkin' like a refined white lady. You say 'Masta suh'! Do you understand? Ain't no nigra gal gonna talk highfalutin' in my presence!"

Highfalutin'? Jolene cringed inwardly. How was she to reason with such an ignorant man?

"Masta Atkins, suh," she said stiffly, "I am not a quadroon. My sister deceived you."

He lifted a hand, warding off her words. "Don't start spoutin' lies. Miz Warrington, she done warned me 'bout you. Last night when I come to fetch you, she told me what to expect. She said you'd try to tell me that she's the sister with the nigra mama."

"It's true!" Jolene insisted. "I swear it!"

He eyed her shrewdly. "What's your name, gal?"

"Jolene," she answered, finding his question perplexing.

"If your name is Jolene, then you're the quadroon sister."

"Why do you say that?"

"'Cause Miz Warrington done showed me her papa's will—that's how I know. It was right there on paper, just as clear as day. Sam Warrington done pronounced you a slave."

"But my sister and her lawyer changed the names."

He shook his head, heaved a deep sigh, then pulled back on the reins. As the pair of horses came to a stop, he turned in the seat and looked Jolene straight in the eye. He spoke unyieldingly. "Miz Warrington told me you'd swear up and down that she and Mr. Hawkins changed the will. Let's get one thing straight here and now. I think you're a colored wench, and there ain't nothin' ya can say to change my mind. I also know you're a troublemaker. Miz Warrington told me all 'bout how ya been incitin' her slaves, tryin' to get 'em to join ya in an uprisin'. She paid me to kill ya, but I got a hankerin' to take ya to New Orleans and sell ya. You're a damned good-lookin' gal and you'll bring a good price."

He reached over and grasped her arm roughly. His eyes narrowed into angry slits and his grasp tightened painfully. "But regardless of how much money you're worth, I'll kill ya if ya keep tellin' me lies 'bout Miz Warrington. She's a real sweet lady, and I won't tolerate no wench a-sayin' mean things 'bout her. You be a good little gal, and I'll treat you real nice-like. You get me mad, though, and I'd just as soon paddle your ass as look at ya. And I'll paddle it till it bleeds. Now, do we understand each other?"

Jolene could barely believe this was happening to her. Surely it was a nightmare and she'd soon awaken. Johanna's maliciousness was shocking and frightening; but Cal Atkins was terrifying! Oh God, was she truly at the mercy of such a cruel man?

Cal, losing patience, wrapped his fingers more tightly about her arm and shook her roughly. "Answer me, ya damned wench! Do we have an understandin'?"

Knowing she had no alternative but to pretend submissiveness, she nodded.

"Don't you nod when I ask you a question. You answer me more respectful-like!"

Jolene swallowed heavily, and although it galled her to do so, she replied, "Yes, Masta Atkins, suh."

"That's better," he remarked, releasing his brutal grip. He glanced quickly around and, spotting a patch of grassy land, decided, "We'll stop here for lunch."

Securing the brake, he jumped down and went to Jolene. "Get down from there and plant your pretty ass under that oak. Don't ya dare make a move while I'm tendin' to my darkies, 'cause if ya do, I'll see ya. And then I'll be forced to punish ya."

Without answering, Jolene climbed down and did as she'd been told. Sitting, she drew up her legs, tucked the long folds of her skirt about them, and crossing her arms on her raised knees, rested her head.

This couldn't be happening to her—it just couldn't! It was too ironic . . . too impossible . . . too *horrifying!*

But it is happening, Jolene told herself firmly. *And sitting here feeling sorry for myself isn't going to help.*

With a calmness that hung by a thread, she considered her options: she could attempt an escape, and if successful, find her way to Natchez, where she could ask her father's friends for help. Her heart sank, for she seriously doubted she could escape Cal Atkins. She wondered if perhaps she should continue to pretend submissiveness, travel to New Orleans with Atkins and his coffle, and once there, seek help. Surely she could get someone to listen to her! Or should she try again to persuade Atkins to believe the truth? She could promise him a large reward for his cooperation.

As she pondered her options, Cal saw to his coffle. The slaves, seated on the ground, were eating cold corn pone when the trader ambled over to Jolene.

"Ya hungry?" he asked her, grinning.

"No," she answered. Her stomach was tied in knots, and even the mere thought of food nauseated her.

At Cal's feet was a large stone partially buried, the top protruding obliquely. Resting his foot on the sharp-edged rock, Cal placed an arm on his knee and studied Jolene with an expression that she couldn't discern. Then, suddenly, a lewd glint came to his watery, washed-out eyes.

Recognizing the look, Jolene shuddered.

"You sure are a pretty little gal," he said thickly. "Last night when I was helpin' Miz Warrington dress ya in them clothes you're a-wearin', I seen everything you got." He licked his lips. "Yes sirree, you're a fine-lookin' wench."

85

Jolene was aghast. Johanna had actually allowed this man to see her unclothed! She began to shudder in horror.

Cal laughed heartily. "Don't look so insulted. You ain't no refined southern lady no more—you're just a high-yella and ya ain't got nothin' a white man ain't got a right to see."

He drew closer. "And I got a hankerin' to see it all again. Why don't you be sweet, Sugar Babe, and strip off that dress? All you got under it is a pair of cotton bloomers, and they come off real easy. You don't have to be scared 'bout losin' your maidenhead, 'cause I ain't gonna poke ya. A quadroon who's a virgin is worth too much money, and I ain't about to lower your value. But there's ways a man can pleasure himself with a woman without penetratin' her."

Cal's voice was loud and his slaves, listening, stopped eating their skimpy meals to watch. They felt little pity for Jolene, for they envied her her ivory skin and her rare beauty. They knew she'd most likely be sold to a rich gentleman who would pamper and spoil her, whereas they would probably be sold to poor farmers who'd work them hard without so much as even meager comforts. Or worse, they'd be sold to cane plantations, where they'd be worked to death within a couple of years.

Cal knelt in front of Jolene. "Just relax, Sweetie Pie, 'cause your new masta's gonna give you pleasure like you ain't never had before."

Stiffening, Jolene braced herself against the wide trunk of the oak. "Don't touch me!" she cried angrily.

The trader sneered. "I reckon I got to teach ya

some manners. You don't have the right to tell me what to do. You don't have no rights at all."

Jolene knew she'd rather die than submit. Cal reached for her, and reacting alertly, she avoided his touch and sprang catlike to her feet. Kneeling, he was in a vulnerable position, and using it to her advantage, she kicked him under the chin, sending him sprawling. Moving speedily, she darted around him and was about to make for the surrounding shrubbery when unexpectedly his hand snaked out and grabbed her about the ankle. He jerked forcefully, causing her to lose her balance. Her arms flailed wildly as she tried vainly to regain her momentum. Suddenly, Cal's firm hold jerked her foot out from beneath her, and as she plunged to the ground, her head struck a solid blow against the protruding rock. Stars swam before her eyes until she sank endlessly into a bottomless void.

Cal, afraid she might be dead, crawled to her side. Carefully he lifted her head. He cringed at the sight of the blood oozing from a deep, jagged cut across her forehead. *Damn it!* he swore to himself. It she died, he'd be out a thousand dollars or more!

"Wake up, you damned wench!" he ordered desperately, shaking her. There was no response, for Jolene was unconscious.

The sound of approaching horses arrested Cal's attention, and easing Jolene back to the ground, he glanced quickly over his shoulder. There were two riders on the road, who'd seen him and were stopping.

He watched the men as they dismounted and hurried in his direction. One was white, the other a Negro. Quickly Cal's experienced eyes appraised the latter. He'd never seen a more superb specimen. He was indeed a fancy, and on a vendue block, he'd go for at least three thousand dollars.

Turning his scrutiny to the white gentleman, Cal noticed that both he and his servant wore western attire. In this part of the country, such garb looked out of place.

"Has there been a accident?" the white man inquired, gesturing toward Jolene.

"She fell and hit her head on this-here rock," Cal answered.

Kneeling, the man gently examined the girl's injury. "It looks serious," he murmured. Taking a handkerchief from his pocket, he bound it about her bleeding head.

"How did she fall?" the Negro asked.

Cal bristled: he thought the man impudent. How dare he speak to him like an equal? He waited for the white man to chastise the servant, but when no reprimand seemed forthcoming, he decided simply to ignore the question.

"You need to get her to a doctor immediately," the white man remarked.

"There's a town about two miles up the road," Cal replied. "But I can't travel very fast, what with my nigras on foot."

The man glanced at Atkins's pitiful coffle, shook his head sympathetically, then turned back to the matter at hand. "If you don't get your wife to a doctor as quick as possible, she's liable to die."

At first Cal was offended that the man had mistaken a wench as his wife. Then, realizing Jolene showed no physical resemblance to her colored kinsmen, he excused the man for his erroneous assumption.

He responded hesitantly. "Well, I can't go no faster than my darkies can walk." But he didn't want to lose his most valuable slave, and taking advantage of the man's mistake, he asked, "Suh, would you mind deliverin' my wife to the doctor? Travelin' horseback, you can get there a lot faster than I can." Cal smiled to himself. If this stranger was a gentleman, he couldn't very well refuse to help a white lady, whereas if he knew she was a quadroon, he'd most likely refuse.

The man was eying Atkins scornfully. He despised slave traders.

"I'd appreciate it, suh," Cal went on. "And I'd be forever beholdin' to you, Mista . . . ?"

"Spencer's the name. Kurt Spencer."

"I'm Cal Atkins," the trader said, offering his hand. Spencer hesitated, then shook hands with him. "Well, Mista Spencer? Will you offer me your help?"

Kurt thoughtfully gazed down at Jolene. He was amazed that this coarse, evil man had such a pretty wife. He wondered if this fragile woman was as depraved as her husband. Could such a beautiful lady be cold and cruel? He already knew the answer, for he'd lived in the south long enough to know that some of the most heartless slave owners were women.

Meanwhile, as Kurt mused on this, Cal watched him curiously. Spencer was a striking figure—his tall, well-developed frame exuded a masculine aura that women were sure to find irresistible. Now, as he pushed his wide-brimmed hat back from his brow, Cal could see that his sandy hair matched his well-groomed moustache.

Slowly, Cal turned his attention to the black. The tall, muscular man stood leisurely with his hands on his hips.

Becoming aware of the trader's scrutiny, he lowered his gaze to meet Cal's level stare.

The Negro's audacity infuriated Cal. Never in his life had a black man looked him directly in the eye. But despite these feelings he couldn't help but admire the man: his flawless skin was light brown, and his narrow nose and firm lips revealed his white origin. Probably had a white pappy, Cal surmised, his eyes traveling admiringly over the man's strong physique.

Spencer's deep voice interrupted the trader's thoughts. "I'll take your wife to the doctor."

"Thank you, suh. I sure do appreciate your help."

The man lifted the unconscious Jolene as though she weighed no more than a feather. "By the way, how did she fall?" He hadn't forgotten that Atkins had avoided answering this particular question before.

Thinking quickly, Cal replied, "She was frightened by a snake, took off runnin', tripped, and hit her head on the rock."

Kurt believed him; he had no reason to doubt the man's story. He nodded for his companion to follow, and carrying Jolene with ease, he took her to his horse. Carefully he handed her to his companion, mounted, then reached down and lifted her into his arms.

As the other man mounted his horse, Kurt looked at Cal, who had moved over to stand close to his chained slaves. "I'll tell the doctor he can expect you within the hour."

Cal nodded agreeably, although he doubted he could encourage his sluggish coffle to move so quickly. It'd be closer to two hours before he reached town.

Kurt spoke to his companion. "It's a good thing we rested the horses a couple of miles back, otherwise they'd be too tired to run all the way to town."

The large Negro smiled, his eyes twinkling mischievously. "I certainly didn't think we'd be spending this afternoon saving a beautiful damsel in distress."

"Neither did I, Daniel," Spencer answered, gazing down into Jolene's pretty face. "Sleeping Beauty, I hope you recover," he murmured softly, taking time to admire her lovely features. He was wondering about the color of her eyes when suddenly her lids fluttered open. He found himself gazing into the bluest eyes he'd ever seen. "You are indeed a beauty," he whispered, smiling tenderly.

For a fleeting moment she saw the handsome stranger clearly. Then her eyes closed and she drifted back into unconsciousness. But the man's face was forever etched in her mind, and in her heart as well.

Cal was looking on. He watched as the men suddenly spurred their mounts into a loping gallop and disappeared down the road, leaving a trail of dust in their wake.

Chapter Five

Seated at her father's desk, Johanna closely observed the huge man Lazarus was showing into the study. Removing his weathered hat, the man said tersely, "Afternoon, ma'am."

"Good afternoon, Mr. Sullivan," she replied, feigning a warm smile. She turned to the servant. "That will be all, Lazarus."

"Yes'm, Miz Johanna," he muttered, leaving the room. He was about to close the door, but driven by curiosity, he merely pretended to shut it. Leaving it open a mere crack, he decided to eavesdrop. The servant's curiosity wasn't petty, but grave. Johanna was his new mistress, and he didn't trust her any more than he trusted the overseer. Now the two were conferring, and Lazarus knew that the fate of all the slaves at Cedarbrook depended on the outcome. He felt some foreboding, for he was aware of the evil that lurked in Johanna as well as in Sullivan. He could foresee only trials and tribulations for the slaves at Cedarbrook.

He sighed. If only Miz Jolene were running the

plantation! He believed Jolene would be a kind, understanding mistress. He still found it hard to accept that she was Millie's daughter. He'd been at Cedarbrook for over thirty years, and he remembered Millie well. He also knew that Sam Warrington had been very distant toward Johanna, whereas his affection for Jolene seemed boundless.

Lazarus suspected Johanna and Robert had somehow changed Sam's will, but as a slave, there was nothing he could do about it. If he went to one of Sam's friends and voiced his suspicion, he'd most likely be strung up and whipped.

The butler couldn't recite all the laws which referred to a slave as property under the twelve propositions, but he was familiar with most of them. One in particular crossed his mind: a slave cannot be a witness against a white person. Although he longed to help Jolene, his hands were tied by the laws of property.

The night Atkins had come to the house for Jolene, Lazarus, hidden in the corridor, had seen the trader carry Jolene to his buckboard. Lazarus had always known that Johanna was jealous of her sister, but he'd never imagined that she hated her enough to sell her to a slave trader.

Now, as he pressed his ear against the door to the study, he prayed that Jolene was well and that someday soon, justice would prevail and bring Johanna's reign to an end.

Meanwhile, inside, Johanna was pouring the overseer a glass of bourbon. He sat across from the desk. She cast him her sweetest smile. "Mr. Sullivan, I feel that I must be completely honest with you. I know absolutely nothing about operating this plantation." She waved her dainty hands in a helpless fashion. "I'm at a loss, and I don't know what to do. I sent for you because . . ." She purposefully let her voice fade as though she was suddenly a little shy. Her green eyes opened wide, their expression innocent and trusting. "You're so knowledgeable and such a strong, dependable man, that I must implore you to help me!"

Sullivan was hopelessly enamored of her, as she'd been certain he would be. He found her touching and beautiful and was flattered by her dependence on him. When he'd received word that she wished to see him, he'd been worried that he was about to be dismissed. He was a harsh, demanding overseer, and he was certain one of the house servants had notified Miss Warrington that he'd mistreated her field slaves.

Johanna had indeed been so informed, for Lazarus had taken it upon himself to tell his mistress of the man's cruelty. Johanna had quickly told him to mind his own business. She didn't care how cruelly Mr. Sullivan treated the field slaves as long as he got a full day's work out of them.

Taking a liberal swallow of his bourbon, the burly man's beady eyes scanned Johanna's lovely form. Despite her mourning dress, she was a stunning beauty and he found himself totally bewitched.

Quaffing down the rest of his drink, he placed the empty glass on the desk, looked adoringly at Johanna, and said gallantly, "Miss Warrington, I'm at your beck and call."

She gloated. Men were such silly fools! A woman as beautiful as herself had no problem wrapping them around her little finger. She sighed as though

94

greatly relieved. "Mr. Sullivan, you have eased my mind tremendously."

"Together, you and I will make Cedarbrook the most prosperous plantation in Mississippi." He watched her expectantly. "But in order to do so, you must give me full rein."

"Oh, I intend to," she declared. "If you'll run the plantation, I'll run the house. There are going to be some drastic changes made. My house servants are terribly spoiled. They are also quite outspoken—especially Lazarus. He actually had the gall to complain to me about the way you treat the field workers."

Wanting to exert her power and prove to Sullivan that she had the grit to properly operate a plantation, she continued, "When we're finished here, I want you to take Lazarus to the barn and have a couple of our strongest bucks string him up. He is to be thoroughly whipped for daring to degrade a white man's behavior."

"Yes'm. I'll see to it personally that the meat's stripped right off his back. I'll order twenty lashes."

Lazarus, poised outside the door, heard his punishment, Perspiration beaded his brow. He had been whipped only once in his life. At the time he'd been a young man, but the thirty lashes had nearly killed him. He wondered if he would survive the twenty he was soon to receive.

Continuing, Johanna said briskly, "Since you'll now have more responsibilities, I'll raise your wages."

Sullivan was pleased. "That's right generous of you, ma'am!"

"Nonsense," she remarked. She returned to the

95

liquor cabinet, where she refilled his glass and poured some sherry for herself.

She gave him his bourbon, and when she was again seated, she bestowed upon him a commending glance. "Your firmness with my slaves has my complete approval. Their care is now solely in your hands. I'll not interfere so long as Cedarbrook continues to prosper."

"Ma'am, can I give you some advice?"

"Yes, of course."

"You got a lot of old field slaves who ain't earnin' their keep. They're a worthless lot and should be gotten rid of. These slaves are just costin' you money to feed."

"But how can I dispose of old slaves? Who'd want to buy them?"

"Some of these itinerant slave traders might. They can sell 'em to cane plantations."

She thought for a moment. Although the horror of condemning older slaves to cane plantations didn't penetrate her conscience, it did make an impression on her better judgment. If Marshall were to find out, he'd be shocked. She knew that he was most kind and lenient with his own slaves and would be mortified to learn that she had disposed of hers in such a thoughtless fashion.

"Mr. Sullivan, I'll not give permission to send my elderly slaves to such a fate."

He conceded reluctantly. "All right, ma'am . . . have it your way. But I must say that I thought you had better business sense."

She didn't like his belittling her, and it led her to confess candidly, "I do have business sense, Mr. Sullivan. I'm not keeping my old slaves because I have a soft heart . . . quite the contrary. I hope to marry Marshall Walker, and when I do I'll be twice as rich, for I'll have two plantations. But Mr. Walker is very compassionate toward his slaves. If he were to learn that I had disposed of my elderly slaves, he might turn against me." She smiled complacently. "So you see, I am acting in a businesslike manner after all."

"So you intend to snare Walker, do you?"

"Yes I do—but I don't like the term 'snare.' I happen to be in love with Marshall. His wealth is merely the icing on my cake."

Lazarus, still listening, decided he had heard enough and turned from the door. As he lumbered toward the kitchen, his mood was sober. Johanna had given Sullivan free rein. He felt a deep sympathy for the field workers, for their lives would undoubtedly be hell. The elderly ones crossed his mind, and he thanked God that his mistress had her cap set for Master Walker; otherwise she would have granted Sullivan permission to sell them.

Lazarus was in his mid-fifties, but his strong build belied his years, and he normally moved with a youthful vitality. But today the man's shoulders drooped beneath his foreboding burden and his steps were sluggish. His impending whipping had shattered his spirit.

The hope that someday Jolene would return and take over Cedarbrook was all that prevented him from going to his former master's gun cabinet, taking a rifle, and ending his enslavement.

The laudanum that Dixie, the cook, had given

Lazarus didn't completely obliterate the pain, but it did help the butler to drift into somnolence.

However, he slept only a short time, for the pain was too severe to allow a deep, forgetful sleep. Now, as his aching, burning back roused him from slumber, a moan sounded deep within his throat. He was lying on his stomach, and lifting his head slightly, he saw that Dixie was sitting beside his bed.

Lazarus and Dixie shared a small bedroom off the kitchen. They'd been together for five years. Shortly following Della's death, Sam Warrington had bought Dixie to replace the cook he had lost. Lazarus and Dixie didn't become a couple by choice. The butler and cook were expected to share the bedroom adjacent to the kitchen. Whether or not the two liked each other or thought each other attractive was not taken into account. As far as Sam Warrington was concerned, they could sleep together, or one could sleep on the floor. It made no difference to him, for there was only one bedroom and he wasn't about to order another built simply to accommodate a slave.

Lazarus had shared the small bed with Della as he now did with Dixie. He had not been in love with Della, nor was he in love with her replacement. He knew Della's feelings were the same as his, but he suspected Dixie felt a strong affection for him. He respected her and liked her a lot, but all the same, he coupled with her for the same reason he had with Della: it was better than sleeping alone. A warm body to cuddle with at night was about the only pleasure a slave could hope for.

Lazarus was not incapable of love. He had merely hardened his heart to the emotion. As a young man he had known love. At the time he had lived on the plantation where he was raised. The senior Sam Warrington had paid a visit to this plantation and had been quite taken with the young Lazarus. When he offered to buy him, the offer was accepted. Lazarus, knowing he'd never see his love again, had convinced her to run away with him. They were caught, and Lazarus was strung up and given thirty lashes. But Warrington didn't consider Lazarus a habitual runner, and he honored his agreement to buy the slave. A couple of days after the whipping, Lazarus, heavily sedated, was placed in a buckboard, and driven away, still unconscious, from the only home he'd ever known.

His new home in Mississippi was similar to the one in Alabama, and he made the change with relative ease. But losing the woman he loved had broken Lazarus' heart, and when it finally healed, he swore that it'd never be broken again. Love was an emotion he cast out of his life. In his opinion love was a luxury white folks reserved for themselves; for slaves it was self-destructive.

Now, as another moan sounded deep in Lazarus' throat, Dixie asked, "Is you in terrible pain?"

He tried to give her an encouraging smile, but the effort proved too much. "I's hurtin' bad, but I be all right in a couple a days."

She broke into heaving sobs. "I just cain't believe Miz Johanna ordered you to be whipped! You's the bestest slave at Cedarbrook! She mean, that Miz Johanna! She terrible mean!"

In spite of the pain it cost him, Lazarus reached out and patted her hand. "Don't get yourself all upset."

She nodded feebly, then wiped at her tears. Dixie was a big woman, and heaving her large frame from the chair, she stepped into the kitchen and returned with a basin of warm water and dressing for Lazarus' cuts.

"I'm gonna wash your back, then put some mutton taller on it. It'll take out some of the sting."

Gently she sponged his back with a soft cloth before generously applying the dressing. The muttony odor was strong and its pungent stench filled the small room. Although the smell was distasteful, the results were rewarding, and Lazarus began to feel better.

He closed his eyes, and as he welcomed Dixie's ministrations, he thought about the cruel whipping he'd been forced to endure. Cringing, he remembered that first, biting sting of the lash. It had felt like a red-hot iron branding his flesh. He had promised himself he wouldn't cry out, but by the fifth lash the pain had grown too intense and he was screaming in agony.

Dixie had just finished doctoring Lazarus' back when the bedroom door swung open. Startled, the woman whirled about, and the sight of her mistress set her heart thumping with fear.

Johanna went to the bed and looked down at Lazarus. "How do you feel?"

"I feel all right, Mistress ma'am," he uttered.

"Nonsense! Don't lie to me! You feel terrible, don't you?"

Lazarus groaned inwardly. What the hell did she want from him? Wasn't the whipping enough? Did she now want him to grovel at her feet?

"Yes'm," he conceded. "I feel terrible."

She turned a sharp eye on Dixie. "Leave us alone!"

"Yes, Miz Johanna," the servant replied, leaving quickly.

Placing the hard-backed chair close to the butler's bed, Johanna sat down. She leaned so close that Lazarus could smell the sherry on her breath. "I didn't want to have you whipped, but I had to make an example of you."

She waited for a reply, but none came. Lazarus had nothing to say to her.

"Hereafter, you must learn to keep your place," she went on. "You're a slave, and you must never speak badly about a white person. Do you understand?"

"Yes'm," he murmured, fighting the urge to wrap his fingers about her neck and squeeze.

"Good!" she replied. She left the room quickly. As she entered the kitchen, she saw Dixie standing at the stove.

"I'm going to lie down. Wake me when dinner is ready," she ordered. She massaged her temples. "It's been a trying day, and I have a dreadful headache."

The sun dipping into the west cast a reddish glow over the countryside as the two riders loped down the narrow dirt road.

Daniel, growing impatient with his companion's silence, said testily, "You haven't spoken two words since we left the doctor's house."

Kurt shook himself free of his thoughts. "I'm sorry . . . I keep thinking about Atkins' wife. I hope she'll be all right."

Daniel frowned. "If you knew the woman, you probably wouldn't even like her. Just because she's beautiful on the outside doesn't mean she's beautiful on the inside. And considering the kind of a man she married, she's likely to be as bad as he is."

Kurt chuckled. "You're probably right." Not entirely convinced, he added, "Maybe we should have stayed until Atkins got there. We simply dropped her at the doctor's house, then left."

"Atkins asked you to deliver his wife. He didn't expect you to stay and hold her hand until he arrived."

"You're right—but there's something about Atkins and his wife that bothers me . . . I just can't figure out what it is. I feel like I should turn my horse around, ride back, and wait for the woman to regain consciousness."

Daniel grinned teasingly. "You're just a sucker for a pretty face."

Ridding himself of his bothersome thoughts, Kurt said briskly, "If I remember correctly, there's an inn about ten miles up the road. If it's still there, we can get us a couple of rooms for the night."

Sighing with fatigue, Daniel agreed silently. It had been a long, tiring trip from Texas. Though he felt uneasy about returning to the south and was eager to get back to his ranch, he had considered this journey essential. His mother was still a slave at the Willow Hill plantation, and he was determined to buy her freedom and take her back to Texas with him.

Thirty-one years ago, Daniel had been born at Willow Hill, and when he was eight, he was sold to Kurt's father, Edward Spencer. Spencer gave young Daniel to his son for his eighth birthday. The two boys liked each other and got on well. But Daniel missed his mother and grieved over their separation. Kurt understood and was sympathetic. He considered asking his father to take Daniel back to Willow Hill, but afraid Daniel would only be sold again, he decided it was best for Daniel to stay where he was.

Edward Spencer visited Willow Hill frequently, and Kurt, knowing how much Daniel enjoyed seeing his mother, always made sure that he and Daniel accompanied his father on these visits. Although Daniel was separated from his mother, he nonetheless got to see her fairly often. On one occasion, Spencer, wanting to please his son, had offered to buy the woman, but the master of Willow Hill had refused to sell. Daniel's mother, Lucy, was the best cook in the county, and the family at Willow Hill was not about to part with her.

The years rolled by pleasantly for Daniel and Kurt as they indulged in the usual mischievous scrapes common to boys their age. When Kurt reached puberty and was sent away to school, he took Daniel with him. It was a northern school, and when Kurt requested that Daniel be allowed to sit in on his studies, the schoolmaster saw no reason to deny the request. As Kurt learned, so did Daniel.

When Daniel and Kurt were twenty-one, their education was completed and they returned home to Heritage Manor. Spencer now expected Kurt, his oldest son, to take over most of the responsibilities involved in running the mammoth plantation. He was shocked and disappointed when Kurt informed him that he had no intention of living at Heritage Manor and was planning to move to Texas.

Although he loved his father, mother, and younger brother, he knew that he didn't belong on a southern plantation.

Daniel was legally Kurt's slave, and before they left for Texas, Kurt had manumission papers drawn up which set Daniel free.

The adventurous young men were no longer master and slave, but simply two friends who gladly left the south to go west and sow their wild oats.

After a couple of years of carousing, womanizing, gambling, and taking odd jobs, they decided it was time to start thinking about secure futures. Sticking to their resolve, they worked hard, saved their money, and within a few years were both able to buy their own spread of land in northern Texas. Although Daniel was still treated with a certain amount of bigotry, it was mild compared to what he'd dealt with in the South. Most Texans living in the northern region were too concerned about the Comanches to worry about Daniel's race. In several Indian conflicts Daniel had fought heroically alongside his neighbors, earning their respect and admiration.

When Kurt received a letter from his father asking him to come home for his younger brother's wedding, Daniel decided to accompany him. He was sure he had enough money saved to buy his mother from Willow Hill; if not, he planned to steal her!

Now, as the two Texas-toughened cowboys galloped up to the roadside inn, the sun had made its full descent and darkness shrouded the land.

Dismounting, they flung their reins over a dilapidated hitching post. The inn was rundown and in dire need of repair. An elderly Negro sitting on the deteriorating porch leaped to his feet as fast as his tired legs could manage. Stepping to Kurt, he bowed respectfully. "Evenin', masta, suh. You want me to take your hosses to the barn?"

"Yes, thank you."

The slave lowered his eyes humbly, but the stranger's politeness made him forget his manners and he raised his gaze in surprise. In all his sixty-odd years, he'd never received a "thank you" from a white man.

Kurt and Daniel entered the inn. The interior wasn't in much better shape than the exterior.

An obese, unshaven man at the door welcomed Kurt: "Come on in, stranger!" He gestured to a dusty counter filled with papers and ledgers. "Step right over here and I'll get you registered. I suppose you're wantin' a room for the night."

Kurt, experiencing second thoughts, debated whether to ride a piece down the road and camp out for the night; but by this time the landlord had his register open and was pointing at it.

"Sign right here, suh," he said heartily. He didn't get too many customers who seemed like aristocrats, and although Kurt was dressed in western attire, the man was sure he was southern nobility.

Kurt picked up the pen and wrote, "Kurt Spencer of Heritage Manor."

The owner was impressed. "Heard of Heritage Manor, I have. It's in Alabama, ain't it?"

Kurt said that it was indeed.

"It's a pleasure and an honor to have you here, Mr. Spencer. Supper's served in the dinin' room at eight o'clock sharp, and breakfast is at seven."

"That'll be fine," Kurt assured him.

Turning his huge frame about, the man yelled loudly, "Missy, get in here!"

Within moments a young colored girl appeared. Kurt figured she'd been in the kitchen, for she was wearing an apron and she smelled of fresh baked bread.

The landlord winked at Kurt. "Kinda pretty, ain't she?"

Kurt merely nodded.

"Your room and meals come to ten bucks, but if you want this-here wench to warm your bed, it'll be five dollars more."

"No, thank you. I need only a room and meals."

The landlord shrugged. "If that's what you want. But I thought a young, healthy man like yourself would be wantin' some pleasurin'." He looked sternly at Missy as though it were her fault Kurt had turned her down. "Get back to the kitchen!" he ordered.

As she hurried away, the owner handed over a key. "Your room is at the top of the stairs, second from the right."

"I'll need two rooms," Kurt replied.

The man's eyes swept over Daniel. Then, turning back to Kurt, he remarked, "You mean you're a-wantin' accommodations for your servant?" He shook his head emphatically. "Sorry, but I don't allow no bucks a-sleepin' inside my establishment. He'll have to stay in the barn."

Daniel cringed. How could he and Kurt have been so stupid? Had ten years in Texas completely wiped out their memories? This landlord saw him as a slave, and traveling servants were supposed to sleep

106

in barns, not in beds!

Kurt was seething, but, the landlord was too interested in Daniel to notice his customer's anger. Raking his gaze over Daniel, he continued admirably, "Mr. Spencer, you've got a fine-lookin' boy. I bet he's worth at least, two, three thousand dollars. I'd buy him if I could, but I ain't got that kind a money."

Daniel had heard all he could stomach, and as he whirled about to leave, Kurt, moving with lightning speed, reached across the counter and grabbed the owner by the front of his soiled shirt. Seeing this, Daniel broke Kirt's hold, and leading him forcefully to the door, remarked strongly, "He's not worth it! Do you want to get thrown in jail?"

As they stepped outside, Kurt groaned, "Damn it, Daniel, we should've known that would happen!"

"Well, we'd have encountered it sooner if we hadn't been camping outdoors. We're in the deep south now, and we'd best remember it." He forced a smile. "The next time we stop at an inn, I'll just go on to the barn. If all the places are as bad as this one, the barn will probably be a hell of a lot cleaner!"

As they headed toward the livery to retrieve their horses, Kurt acted as though his good mood was restored. But deep inside he was gravely worried. He had tried to talk Daniel out of making this trip, assuring him that he'd buy Lucy and bring her back to Texas, but Daniel had been determined to come along, regardless of Kurt's objections.

Kurt's worries were well justified, for the south was a dangerous place for a free man of color.

Chapter Six

"What do you mean, Jolene's got amnesia?" Cal demanded.

Dr. Mayfield had taken Atkins into his parlor where, gently, he had told the young man that his wife was suffering from loss of memory. Jolene had been unconscious for two days, during which time Cal had taken a room at the hotel while keeping his slaves chained in the livery stable.

Patiently the doctor explained, "Your wife received a minor concussion, and the injury has brought on amnesia. However, there's no reason for undue alarm. In such cases the loss of memory is usually only temporary."

"Are you sure she ain't fakin' it?" Cal asked.

The question took the doctor by surprise. "Why would she do a thing like that?"

Cal, wishing he hadn't spoken so rashly, mumbled, "Sometimes Mrs. Atkins will do things to get attention." He swallowed nervously. If Dr. Mayfield were to learn that his patient was a quadroon slave, he could legally bring charges against the trader, for the Hippocratic Oath he'd taken as a physician didn't extend to slaves.

"There's no way I can be a hundred percent sure, but it's my medical opinion that your wife has amnesia. I don't believe she's pretending."

Damn! Cal thought to himself. Why did the wench have to get amnesia and lower her value? Well, I'll just make damned sure that the buyers don't know about it! To bring the highest price, she's got to appear healthy mentally as well as physically!

"Doctor, I appreciate all you've done. If you'll tell me how much I owe you, I'll pay up, get my wife, and be on my way."

"Mrs. Atkins should rest a few more days," the doctor advised. He was in his late forties, his goatee streaked with gray, and his waistline beginning to bulge.

"I can't stay around here no longer. I'm already two days behind schedule. I gotta get my coffle to New Orleans."

"Mr. Atkins," Mayfield began hesitantly, "Since you're in the business of buying and selling slaves . . ." His voice drifted.

Cal eyed him speculatively. "You got a slave you wanna sell?" He knew southern aristocrats like the doctor found dealing with slave traders degrading.

Uneasily he stammered, "Well . . . yes, I have. I've been a widower for two years, but next month I plan to remarry. My fiancée lives in Natchez, but after we're married she'll reside here." Embarrassed, he blushed. "I have a young colored woman as my housekeeper, but I'm sure my future wife will be offended by her presence. If she were an older servant, there'd be no problem."

"You don't have to explain, Doctor. I understand . . . you're wantin' to sell your bedwench, right?"

The physician's blush deepened.

Cal guffawed. "You don't have to be embarrassed. I like wenches, too."

Smiling tentatively, the doctor excused his own behavior. "She's very pretty, and too tempting for any man to refuse. I'm quite fond of her, though— and if you buy her, promise you'll make sure that her new owner will treat her compassionately."

"Sure, Doc, I promise," Cal assured him, knowing perfectly well he'd do nothing of the kind. He'd sell her to whoever was the highest bidder, compassionate or not.

"Thank you," Mayfield murmured.

"Let me see the gal, and I'll give you my price."

The doctor went and opened the parlor door and called loudly, "Mary Jane—come here."

The young woman was exceptionally beautiful. Cal examined her keenly, grinning inwardly, for he doubted the doctor was aware that his wench was a prize. He'd offer the man five hundred, then sell her in New Orleans for a thousand or more. He could hardly believe his good luck! If he bought this lovely creature, he'd own two wenches who were fancies. Never in his career had he had two such valuable slaves in his possession.

Continuing his visual examination, Cal tried to guess her origin. He decided she was a mixture of Hausa and American Indian, with a touch of white blood thrown in. In his business he'd bought and sold enough slaves to recognize their breeding.

Although Mary Jane stood unflinching beneath the trader's keen scrutiny, she was uneasy. From the day the doctor had told her he was getting married, she had known this moment was inevitable.

"I never buy a pig in a poke," Atkins remarked. "She'll have to shuck down."

"That won't be necessary!" Mayfield yelled. "I give you *my word* that she's in perfect health and has no unbecoming blemishes or deformities."

Atkins was in a hurry and decided to believe the doctor. He didn't have time to argue. "I'll give you five hundred for her."

Mayfield accepted the price, went to his desk, pulled out the secretary drawer, removed a sheet of paper, and wrote up a bill of sale.

"Mary Jane," the doctor said, somewhat remorsefully, "go to your room and pack your belongings."

"Yes, masta," she replied in a soft voice.

He touched her arm fondly. "You've been a good servant, and I regret that I must sell you. But, considering. . . ."

Mayfield longed for Mary Jane's forgiveness, for his conscience was bothering him. She understood her master well and knew he was waiting for her to ease his troubled mind. Well, she'd be damned if she'd cooperate! In his own arrogant way, he'd been a good master, but she felt no loyalty toward him. At the tender age of thirteen, she had learned to be true only to herself!

Refusing to say anything to assuage his guilt, she turned and left the parlor.

*   *   *

Jolene was staying in the doctor's guest room, and as Mayfield and Atkins entered, she looked strangely at the unkempt man who accompanied the physician.

The men came to Jolene's bedside. Speaking to Cal as if Jolene weren't there, Mayfield said, "Your wife has been conscious only a short time. She's very confused, but understandably so."

Jolene's blue eyes opened wide. Wife! Surely this dreadful-looking man wasn't her husband!

They were staring at her. Turning from their steady scrutiny, she rolled over on her side. She fought back the tears that were now threatening to overflow.

Jolene was terribly frightened. A couple of hours ago when she had regained consciousness, she had awakened to a life she didn't recognize. She had no memory—she couldn't even recall her name.

She had panicked, and it had taken the doctor quite a while to calm her. Once he had her relatively composed, he'd told her that her name was Jolene Atkins and that her husband was staying at the hotel. He then suggested she try to remember her husband.

She had concentrated deeply, and when a man's face flashed before her vividly, she was certain that her memory had been triggered. But the man she remembered wasn't the person who was now in her room! The face in her mind held no resemblance to the man now with Dr. Mayfield.

She closed her eyes and the image came back. She saw a pair of brown eyes, and their expression was tender. She remembered sandy-colored hair showing beneath a wide-brimmed hat and a trim moustache over well-shaped lips. Suddenly, to her amazement, she could remember the man speaking to her. What exactly had he said? Yes! Yes, she remembered . . . he had said, "You are indeed a beauty." Who was he? Why did she remember him, when she couldn't even remember her own name?

"Mrs. Atkins," Dr. Mayfield began, interrupting her reverie. "Turn back over and look closely at your husband. Seeing him might revive your memory."

Heistantly she complied. She preferred not to look at this man who was supposedly her husband. God, why would she have married someone like him? And who was the stranger who kept flashing across her mind? If only . . . if only he'd been her husband! If she were married to him, she wouldn't feel quite so frightened.

She forced herself to look closely at Cal, but his face was unfamiliar. "I'm sorry," she murmured to the doctor. "I don't remember this man."

Cal was growing impatient, for he was anxious to start for New Orleans. "It don't make no neverminds whether she remembers me or not. We gotta get goin'. I got a coffle to deliver. Like you said, Doc, in time her memory'll come back. She'll probably be fully recovered by the time we reach New Orleans." Leaning over the bed, he smiled at Jolene. "You'll soon remember me, won't you, Sugar Babe?"

Atkins' closeness made her cringe, and aware of her reaction, his grin broadened. Standing upright he asked briskly, "Where's her clothes, Doc?"

Mayfield went to the wardrobe and handed the garments to Cal, who pitched them onto the bed.

"Get dressed," he ordered shortly. "Time's a-wastin'."

When she made no move to obey, he flung off the bedcovers. She had on a plain white gown that belonged to Mary Jane.

Harshly, Cal demanded, "I told you to get dressed, damn it!"

Excusing himself, the doctor turned to leave, but was detained by Cal, who asked, "With that bandage on her head, I can't see how bad her cut is. Will it leave a scar?"

"It might leave a small one," he replied.

As Mayfield left them alone, Cal cursed to himself. Even a small scar was liable to lower her value. Eying Jolene darkly, he threatened, "Woman, if ya don't get out of that bed and put on them clothes, I'm gonna dress ya myself!"

She sat up and reached for her garments. The thought of him dressing her was repulsive. Imagining his hands on her flesh made her skin crawl. "Would you mind turning your back?" she asked.

He laughed coldly. "You ain't got nothin' I ain't seen before." But he had more on his mind than watching Jolene dress. He began to move around the room, opening drawers and examining the contents.

Taking advantage of his preoccupation, Jolene hastily removed her gown and donned her simple attire.

Finding what he wanted, Cal took a pair of scissors and slipped them into his pocket. Stepping to Jolene and grabbing her arm, he said, "Let's go."

She tried to draw away from his touch, but his hold was too firm. Still finding it incredible that she was married to this uncouth man, she questioned,

114

"Mr. Atkins, are you sure I'm your wife?"

"Why would you ask me that?"

"I may have amnesia, but I didn't lose my reasoning. There's no way on God's earth that I'd marry soneone like you."

"Still uppity, ain't ya? I always heard that amnesia don't change a person's character." Increasing his grip on her arm, he ushered her out of the room, down the hall, and outside.

The doctor was on the front porch with Mary Jane, who had her few belongings packed in a carpetbag.

The few times Mary Jane had tended to her, Jolene had been unconscious, so she was seeing the young woman for the first time.

"How you feelin', Mrs. Atkins, ma'am?" Mary Jane inquired politely.

Cal, impatient to leave, didn't give Jolene time to answer. Locking her arm in his strong grasp, he led her down the porch steps as he commanded, "Mary Jane, there's no time for chitchat. We're leavin', Gal, 'cause we still got four or five hours of daylight left."

Mary Jane picked up her bag, and as she started to follow the trader, the doctor detained her. "Mr. Atkins promised me your new owner would be kind."

She wanted to laugh in his face, but fearing Atkins would punish her for it, she simply turned away from her former master and followed her new one across the street and to the livery stable.

Dr. Mayfield had told Jolene that her husband was a slave trader, so the chained slaves came as no surprise. As he paid his bill and saw to his coffle, Atkins left Jolene standing with Mary Jane.

"Did Mr. Atkins buy you from the doctor?" Jolene asked the servant.

"Yes, ma'am," she replied. Although she knew she was overstepping her bounds, her curiosity prompted her to question, "Why do you call your husband 'Mr. Atkins'?"

"Didn't Dr. Mayfield tell you that I have amnesia?"

Mary Jane was amazed—she'd never met anyone suffering from amnesia. "No, ma'am, he didn't."

She nodded toward Cal, who was busy harnessing a pair of horses to the buckboard. "That man isn't my husband. Don't ask me how I know, but I do. It's just a feeling I have."

Mary Jane agreed. "I believe you, ma'am. You talk like an educated, refined lady, and there ain't no way your kind is gonna marry-up with white trash."

Unconsciously Jolene grasped the other woman's arm. "Then why am I here with him? How did I come to be in his company?"

Mary Jane shook her head sympathetically. "I ain't got no idea."

"Dr. Mayfield said that amnesia like mine is usually temporary. Hopefully, I'll soon remember everything." To herself, she added, *Then I'll know why I'm traveling with this foul creature. And I'll remember whose face keeps torturing my mind and pulling at my heartstrings. Who is the handsome stranger who once called me a beauty? Was I in love with him? I must've been, otherwise, why would I remember his face so clearly?*

* * *

Cal allowed Jolene and Mary Jane to ride in the back of the buckboard. They were valuable cargo, and he wanted to keep them fit.

As they traveled slowly down the dirt road which led toward the Mississippi-Louisiana line, Jolene, leaning back against the sideboard, tried in vain to recall at least part of her past. She was beginning to feel frustrated, and seeing this, Mary Jane moved over and sat beside her.

"You're tryin' to remember, ain't you?"

"Yes, but I can't recall anything."

"Maybe you're tryin' too hard. Why don't you relax and think about something else for a while?"

Jolene smiled warmly at the other woman. "I'll try to." Turning her thoughts away from herself, she asked, "Are you going to miss Dr. Mayfield?"

"No, ma'am, I ain't gonna miss him as a person, but I reckon I might miss the way he treated me."

"What do you mean?"

"He was a good masta. He never beat me or nothin' like that. He just expected me to keep his house clean, cook his meals, and when he got the urge, he expected me to come to his bed." A tiny smile touched her lips. "That part wasn't so bad. He was always gentle, and it was over real quick."

Cal, driving the team, could hear what the women were saying. Since he had nothing else to occupy his mind, he continued to listen.

"How long were you with the doctor?" Jolene queried.

"'Bout a year," she answered.

Becoming very interested in the woman who had befriended her, Jolene asked, "Would you mind

117

telling me about your life?"

"I guess not," Mary Jane answered hesitantly. She'd never had a friend to confide in and was somewhat leery. Moreover, this woman wasn't truly her peer; she was white.

"Please?" Jolene encouraged, her curiosity sincere.

Mary Jane went on with some reservation. "I don't remember my mama, but I was told she was a prostitute in New Orleans. I don't reckon she was a whore by choice, for she was a slave. The madam who owned my mama also owned me, and when I was two years old, she sold me to one of her customers. He had a slave-breedin' farm, and he liked to buy youngsters, raise them, then sell them at a large profit."

"Slave-breeding farm?" Jolene asked, perplexed.

"Yes'm. He raised slaves for the market, like some men raise cattle." A forlorn expression shadowed her face. "Growing up on a slave farm was awful lonely. The masta didn't allow none of us slaves to love each other. He didn't want us to have no emotional attachments. He said it made it easier when it came time to sell us away from each other.

"When I was about ten, a family stopped at the masta's place to water their horses. They was travelin' in a covered wagon and was on their way to a farm they had inherited. Their name was Donaldson, and Mrs. Donaldson, she happened to catch a glimpse of me. I was standin' off a piece, watchin' her and her family. She took a likin' to me at first sight and asked the masta if he'd sell me. She told him that she had two teenage sons, but no daughters, and needed a girl to help her with the household chores. She said she wanted a young one, so's she could raise her to suit herself.

"The masta sold me, and before I even had time to know what was happenin', I was inside the wagon travelin' with the Donaldson family.

"The farm they'd inherited wasn't much, but they was able to scrape a livin' out of it. Mrs. Donaldson was a good, kind woman, and we got along just fine. I ain't never loved nobody, but I guess I came awful close to lovin' her. When I was thirteen, she come down with a fever and died."

Mary Jane fell silent. When she started to speak again, her voice was intense. "At thirteen, I was maturin' and I'd had my time of the month. I was no longer a girl. The mistress had only been dead a few days when her sons dragged me to the barn. They was about to force themselves on me when their papa showed up. When he told them to stand back, I thought he was goin' to save me."

"He didn't?" Jolene questioned.

"He told his sons to stand back, 'cause it'd been years since he'd had a virgin and he wanted to be the one to bust me."

"Good God!" Jolene cried.

"I reckon him and his sons had been wantin' me for quite a spell but were afraid to touch me as long as the mistress was alive. I stayed with the Donaldsons for two more years, then Mista Donaldson decided to get married. The same as Doctah Mayfield, he didn't want me around his new wife. He told me he was goin' to sell me, and I was glad—I was sick of him and his sons. They were worse than

119

animals. He took me to town and sold me to Mista Brownlee, the blacksmith. Mista Brownlee was married, but his wife had run off with a travelin' man, leavin' him and their three small sons. Mista Brownlee bought me to take care of his house and his boys and to share his bed. He was full of anger 'cause his wife had left him, and he took pleasure in takin' out his anger on me. 'Bout a year after he bought me, his wife came back. He forgave her for leavin' him. Of course, she insisted he get rid of me. This time I was sold to a slave trader. He weren't no different than the Donaldson men or Mista Brownlee. We was on our way to New Orleans when the trader took sick. We stopped at Doctah Mayfield's house. The doctah offered a good price for me, and I was sold."

Mary Jane looked at Jolene somberly. "That's my life story, ma'am. It ain't very pretty, I reckon."

"A few minutes ago I was feeling sorry for myself because I couldn't remember my past. If it's anything like yours, I hope I never do remember."

"You don't have to worry none. Your past can't be nothin' like mine. You're a white lady."

"No she ain't!" Cal spoke up suddenly.

"What?" Jolene exclaimed.

He twisted around in the seat so he could face her. "You heard me—you ain't white. And you ain't my wife. You're a quadroon wench, and I'm takin' you to New Orleans to sell ya." He cackled. "Think maybe I'll sell you at a private auction. That way I can put you on the vendue block butt-naked!"

Chapter Seven

Since the day Cal Atkins had told Jolene that she was a quadroon slave, she had withdrawn into a protective cocoon. The shock of who she was, coupled with her amnesia, had been too much to bear.

Now, lying in the back of the buckboard, she listened vaguely to the sounds of the Louisiana night as she gazed upward at the myriad stars etched across the dark sky.

They were camped a short distance outside New Orleans and would enter the city early in the morning. The long journey had been difficult and tiring; but as Jolene continued to gaze up at the stars, she realized the journey had given her time to come to terms with her life.

She must crawl out of her invisible cocoon and start concentrating on self-preservation. Her memory hadn't returned, but she still believed her amnesia was temporary and she'd soon recall her past.

Atkins had told her about Cedarbrook and that she and Johanna had been raised as twins until Sam Warrington's document revealed the truth; that Jolene's mother had been a mulatto slave. He explained that she and Johanna shared the same father, but that Johanna's mother had been the white mistress of Cedarbrook. He elaborated further, letting Jolene know that when she learned her own mother had been a mulatto, she had rebelled and started inciting the slaves at Cedarbrook, going so far as to threaten Johanna's life. Because of her vicious behavior, Johanna had had no alternative but to sell her away from Cedarbrook.

As Cal had been telling Jolene about herself, she had listened closely and had seemed to accept everything he was saying. But somehow she didn't quite believe him. She didn't know why she doubted his story, for she couldn't remember anything about her past; but for some reason she sensed it hadn't happened as Cal had said.

Now, closing her eyes, Jolene murmured intensely, "Cedarbrook . . . Cedarbrook. . . ." She waited, hoping the name would spark a memory. Nothing! The name was as foreign to her as her own.

Hearing Mary Jane coming toward the buckboard, Jolene sat up and greeted her with a smile. Climbing in, Mary Jane asked, "Are you nervous 'bout reachin' New Orleans?"

"Yes," she answered honestly. Standing on a vendue block as buyers bid on her had Jolene terrified. She'd be purchased as if she were a piece of property!

"It won't be all that bad," Mary Jane lied in an

effort to soothe her friend. She knew that for a well-bred woman like Jolene, the slave auction would be horribly degrading. She wished she could help her, but there was nothing she could do.

Jolene's small hands knotted into fists as she said desperately, "If only I could remember!"

"What good would that do you?"

"Then I'd know for sure if I'm really a quadroon slave."

"You think maybe you ain't?" Mary Jane questioned.

Jolene, relaxing, expelled a heavy sigh. "I don't know. It's a feeling I have, just like I knew I wasn't married to Atkins."

Mary Jane started to reply, but as she caught sight of Cal sauntering toward the wagon, she fell silent.

The trader's gaze swept appreciatively over the two women. They were indeed beauties. In some ways they were very similar, for they both had straight black hair, high cheekbones, and delicately carved features. However, Jolene's complexion was ivory white, whereas Mary Jane's was a golden bronze. Also, Mary Jane was at least a head taller than Jolene, and her frame was more fully endowed.

Continuing his persual, Cal decided he found Jolene the prettier. Her petite frame and alabaster flesh appealed to him.

Several times he'd considered using the women for his own entertainment. He could fondle Jolene, then fully appease himself with Mary Jane, for she wasn't a virgin. But he suspected that Jolene would persuade Mary Jane to join forces with her and fight him off. Then he'd be compelled to make them submit by physical force, and in the process they could be injured, which would lower their value. Cal's greed was much stronger than his desire.

Reaching the wagon, the trader leaned against it and handed Mary Jane the pair of scissors he'd swiped from Dr. Mayfield's guest room.

Accepting them, she asked, "What you want me to do with these, Masta Atkins?"

"Take that bandage off Jolene's head and cut out the stitches. When you finish, cut her hair so it covers her forehead."

"You mean you want me to give her bangs?"

"Bangs?" The word confused him. "Just cut her hair so that it hides the scar!"

Turning to Jolene, Mary Jane removed the bandage. "It's gonna hurt some when I take out the stitches."

"That's all right," she murmured.

As Mary Jane carefully snipped at the stitches, Jolene held still and didn't flinch, though the procedure was painful.

When Mary Jane was finished, Jolene asked, "How bad is the scar?"

"It's still kinda red and puffy, but in a few more days it'll hardly be noticeable."

"Do you think it's permanent?"

She shrugged. "I can't tell yet."

Cal mumbled gruffly, "Stop yer damned chatterin' and get to cuttin her hair!"

Mary Jane removed a comb from her carpetbag, then, despite her inexperience, did a remarkable job cutting Jolene's hair. The straight bangs, falling neatly across her forehead, completely hid the small scar.

Eying her workmanship, Mary Jane decided the bangs, though unstylish, were rather becoming on Jolene.

Cal, taking this in, said sternly, "I got some things to say, and I want ya to listen closely. When we get to New Orleans and buyers start lookin' at you and talkin' to you, don't you tell 'em that you got amnesia! Now, I'm tellin' you this for your own good. 'Cause ain't no smart buyer gonna purchase a wench who's addle-headed, which means you'll get bought by someone who ain't all that smart. Then you'll end up belongin' to a poor farmer or some stupid cracker. So for your own well-bein', you'd better act like there ain't nothin' wrong with ya. Also, I want you to keep your hair to where it hides that scar. Scars lower a slave's value, and it's in your own best interest to have rich buyers biddin' for ya. Do ya understand what I'm sayin', gal?"

"Explicitly, Masta Atkins," she replied, her mood spiteful.

"*Explicitly?*" Cal muttered angrily, knowing she had intentionally used a word he wouldn't understand. "That education you got ain't gonna do you no good when your new masta'a a-partin' your legs, rammin' you full a his own kind of knowledge!" With that, Cal grabbed the scissors and walked away from the wagon.

"He was right 'bout you not tellin' anyone you got amnesia," Mary Jane remarked. "You don't wanna be bought by a poor masta."

Jolene nodded. "Yes, I know." She looked pleadingly at her friend. "I hope we're purchased by the same buyer!"

"It'd be nice," Mary Jane agreed. "But it's unlikely." Stretching tiredly while repressing a yawn, she suggested, "I guess we might as well get some sleep. Tomorrow's gonna be a busy day."

Mary Jane picked up her blanket and spread it beside Jolene's. "Goodnight," she murmured.

"Goodnight," Jolene replied.

Atkins returned, and carrying out his nightly ritual, he placed manacles about the women's ankles and shackled them to the wagon. He wasn't about to take a chance on his most valuable cargo escaping.

When the trader left to see about the rest of his coffle, Jolene lay down, closed her eyes, and waited for sleep. Vividly the image of a man's face flashed across her mind. *Who is he?* her heart cried. *Why do I remember his features with such clarity?* If only she knew what part he played in her past. She thought deeply, but to no avail, for she couldn't remember; but she now began to believe that she must've been in love with him.

New Orleans, known as the "queen city of the Mississippi" ranked fourth in population in United States cities, had the first railroad west of the Alleghenies, and rivaled New York for first place among American ports. It was a major national market for cotton, sugar, and slaves. The Creole culture that flavored New Orleans' activities contributed to its reputation as an enticingly wicked city.

Kurt and Daniel had decided to visit New Orleans

126

for a few days, and while there, to purchase themselves new wardrobes. Their western clothing was out of place here; furthermore, Kurt needed a suit for his brother's wedding.

The two friends had parted company upon their arrival, for Daniel had gone to the colored section of town, where he could find accommodations and a tailor. Kurt had taken a room at the Hotel St. Louis.

Kurt, accustomed to waking early, was up and dressed before the sun had risen above the horizon. Knowing the dining room wouldn't be serving breakfast for another hour, Kurt paced his room restlessly. He wasn't used to having idle time on his hands. Ranch life kept him busy from sun-up to sundown, but he found the work invigorating. He was anxious to return to Texas, for he missed his ranch and the wide-open spaces.

Although Kurt was wearing a new set of clothes tailored for an aristocrat, it seemed as if his muscular frame didn't belong in the trim linen suit. The light gray jacket was drawn tightly across the width of his broad, sinewy shoulders, and the dark gray trousers fit a little too snugly.

However, Kurt's thoughts weren't on clothes as he continued to pace across the blue carpet. His troubled thoughts were on his friend Daniel. He had an uneasy feeling about Daniel coming back to the South. Several times he had tried to shake the feeling, but it held steadfast. Kurt knew he wouldn't rest easy until he and Daniel were back in Texas; and hopefully, Daniel's mother would be with them. Kurt knew how badly Daniel wanted to free Lucy from slavery.

127

Pausing, Kurt checked his pocket watch. He still had thirty more minutes before breakfast. Impatient with the way time seemed to be crawling along, he sighed testily, placed his hands on his hips, and looked distractedly about the room.

The Hotel St. Louis was, in most people's opinion, the grandest hotel in New Orleans, and its elegant rooms attested to its grandeur. A huge, carved mahogany bed with a white counterpane occupied the far end of the room, and the matching bureau supported an elongated mirror. Two large armchairs were placed near the windows, and they were upholstered in the same powder-blue material as the draperies. There was a crystal chandelier which boasted whale-oil lamps in lieu of candles.

Deciding to get a breath of fresh morning air, Kurt stepped out onto the terrace. Standing at the intricate railing, he looked down at the street below. He watched with interest as vendors paced up and down, calling out their wares in lilting cadences. Suddenly Kurt's attention was drawn to a slow-moving buckboard followed by a straggling, shuffling procession of slaves.

Looking more closely, he recognized the slave trader, Cal Atkins. Cal had ordered Jolene to ride on the seat beside him, and as Kurt continued to observe them, he studied the lovely woman he thought must be Atkins' wife. He was glad to see that she had apparently made a complete recovery. He kept them in view until they moved out of sight. Then, turning about, he went back into his room.

The royal-blue carpet reminded him of Jolene's eyes. He'd never seen eyes so brilliantly blue, and they contrasted beautifully with her jet-black hair. Atkins' wife was indeed a rare beauty.

He shrugged his strong shoulders as if to dismiss her from his mind. But to his dismay, her image lingered: she hadn't completely left his thoughts since the moment he'd seen her open her eyes and look up at him. Her eyes had been enchanting, yet he'd detected a note of sadness that had deeply touched his heart.

Smiling a bit ruefully, he murmured, "Sleeping Beauty, why does your image torture me so?"

Kurt, his mind on a hearty breakfast, was descending the marble staircase when he happened to catch a glimpse of the man registering at the front desk. He paused for a moment—he could hardly believe that the master of Willow Hill was here at the Hotel St. Louis! Although Kurt hadn't seen the man for over ten years, he had no problem recognizing him, for he had changed very little.

Hurrying to the desk, Kurt said heartily, "John! John Delmar! It's good to see you again."

The middle-aged man hesitated as he tried to recall this young, handsome man who had greeted him so warmly. Then, recognition setting in, he grinned broadly. "Kurt Spencer? Well, I'll be damned!"

He shook Kurt's outstretched hand before embracing him fondly. Holding him at arms' length and admiring his good looks, Delmar's words raced, "Texas seems to have agreed with you. What are you doing here in New Orleans? Have you been home

129

yet? I suppose you came back for your brother's wedding."

Chuckling softly, Kurt answered, "I stopped in New Orleans to buy a new wardrobe. And, no, I haven't been home yet. And, yes, I came back for Richard's wedding. However, before returning home, I was planning to stop at Willow Hill."

"Oh?" John questioned.

"I need to discuss a personal matter with you."

"Why don't we go into the dining room and talk over breakfast?"

Spencer agreed, and John asked the desk clerk to have his bags delivered to his room.

When the two men were seated and their coffee had been served, John looked warmly at Kurt and queried, "Son, what's on your mind? How can I help you?"

"Do you remember Daniel?"

Delmar thought for a moment. "Daniel? I'm not sure. What's the chap's last name?"

"I'm talking about Lucy's son."

"Lucy? My cook?"

Kurt nodded.

"Sure—I remember her boy. I sold him to your father, and he gave him to you for your eighth birthday. Thereafter, when your father visited Willow Hill, you and Daniel came with him."

"Lucy is still with you, isn't she?"

"Of course she is." He patted his expanding waistline. "She's the best cook in Alabama. But speaking of Daniel, didn't you take him to Texas with you?"

"Yes, I did. I also set him free."

130

Delmar frowned slightly. "What you do is your own business but personally, I don't hold with freeing nigras."

"Daniel came back with me. He's here in New Orleans. He's staying in the colored section of town. We're supposed to meet the day after tomorrow, and then our plans were to visit Willow Hill."

"Were?" John questioned. "Well, I hope you haven't changed your mind. I'm only staying in New Orleans for one day. I'll be leaving in the morning, but I'd be honored to have you as a guest at Willow Hill. You be sure and pay me a visit before going to Heritage Manor." He smiled widely. "I want you to see my son and daughter. They were still children when you left for Texas, but Alan and Sabrina are grown now." His gray eyes twinkled. "Sabrina is a lovely young woman, and although she's received numerous marriage proposals, she still hasn't found the man she wants to marry."

The waiter brought their breakfast, and Kurt waited until they had been served before saying, "John, Daniel wants to buy his mother."

The older man looked at him with surprise. "You can't be serious!"

"I'm quite serious. He intends to offer you a fair price."

"The price be damned! Lucy's not for sale!"

"For God's sake, John! Lucy is Daniel's mother!"

Anger sparked in Delmar's eyes. "Now you listen to me! Your father is my closest friend, and out of respect for him I'll refrain from losing my temper. I will say this once and only once. Lucy is my property, and she's *not for sale.*"

Kurt started to speak, but John held up his hands. "The subject is closed!"

The younger man relented, but only temporarily. He didn't intend to give up quite so easily. But he knew that at present there was nothing he could do.

Changing the subject, Kurt asked, "Why are you in New Orleans?"

"I came here to buy a couple of wenches, one to help Lucy in the kitchen and one to be a maid for Sabrina."

"Are you traveling alone?" Kurt asked.

"No. The rural roads between here and Willow Hill can be dangerous, so I brought a couple of strong bucks with me. I taught these two nigras to shoot, and when we're traveling, I arm them with rifles."

Delmar, generously spreading butter on a biscuit, continued, "As soon as I finish eating and freshen up, I'll go down to the slave jail and pick out a couple of wenches. That is, if there's any there worth buying. Would you like to join me?"

"Sorry, but I have an early appointment at the tailor's." Kurt's answer had been vague, for his thoughts were on Daniel. He dreaded telling his friend that Delmar was dead-set on keeping Lucy.

Chapter Eight

Delmar, followed by his two man servants, entered the two-story frame building known as the slave jail. The door opened into a small, stuffy office where an unkempt man was seated behind a desk. He was smoking a cigar and talking to Atkins, seated across from him.

John knew the jailkeep and greeted him politely.

Putting out his cigar in an overflowing ashtray, the man got to his feet. "Howdy, Mista Delmar. This-here is Cal Atkins, a slave trader. This mornin' he delivered a coffle for the auction day after tomorrow."

Delmar nodded curtly in Cal's direction, then turned back to the jailkeep. "I need to purchase a couple of wenches for house servants. Do you have any who qualify?"

The man beamed. "As a matter of fact, Mista Delmar, I do . . . Cal brought in a couple of prime wenches. They's real pretty little gals, and both of 'em qualify for workin' in the house." He winked at

Delmar. "Qualify for pleasurin' a man, too."

"I'm not looking for a bed wench," the planter replied, offended. "I need one woman who can be trained for the kitchen, and one to be a maid for my daughter."

"Would you like to see these two?"

"Yes I would," he answered.

Cal decided to speak up. "My wenches are fancies, and they're gonna cost you plenty."

Delmar detested doing business with men like Atkins and the jailkeep, but concealing his feelings, he said briskly, "Mr. Atkins, why don't I look at them before we start talking price?"

"Sure," Cal agreed. "They're upstairs. I'll take you to 'em."

John followed him. They walked upstairs, then past a long row of cells until they reached the last one.

There was no furniture in the small prison and only straw on the floor. As John looked through the bars at the two women, he was stunned by their beauty.

Cal introduced them: "This one is Jolene, and this here is Mary Jane."

Delmar's gaze lingered on Jolene, and he said hesitantly, "This one doesn't look like a Negro."

"She's a quadroon," Cal explained. The women were sitting on the floor, and seeing that they hadn't gotten respectfully to their feet, the trader ordered gruffly, "You two get up off your butts so this gentleman can see you better."

As they obeyed, John motioned to Jolene. "Come closer, girl."

134

Apprehensively she stepped forward.

"Have you ever worked as a lady's maid?" he asked.

Before she could reply, Cal spoke up, "Mista Delmar, this wench was raised as though she was white."

John was dumbstruck. "What?"

"It's a complicated story."

"You can tell me when we go back downstairs. The smell up here is unbearable. Good God, isn't this place ever cleaned?"

"Not too often, I reckon," Cal mumbled.

"Mr. Atkins, your wenches are high-quality, and I'm willing to discuss your price."

"Do you want me to have 'em shuck down for you?"

"No, that is not necessary. I'm sure they're both in good health."

As Delmar moved away brusquely, Cal eyed Jolene with a warning glance and whispered, "Gal, you remember what I told ya. Don't say nothin' about havin' amnesia." He left quickly and caught up with his prospective buyer.

Going to a corner of the cell, Jolene sat down, and looking at Mary Jane, she asked, "Well, what do you think?"

"'Bout what?"

"About the man who is considering buying us?"

Mary Jane shrugged, then went over to sit beside her friend. "He acts like him and his kind are better than anyone else."

Jolene smiled. "That's my impression, too."

"But we could do a lot worse. 'Sides, if he buys us

135

we won't have to stand on no vendue block. Also, he's thinkin' 'bout buyin' us both. We could be together."

Jolene sighed hopefully. If she and Mary Jane were sold together, at least she wouldn't feel so alone.

It was almost an hour before Cal returned to notify the women that they now belonged to John Delmar. The man had paid a thousand for Mary Jane and fifteen hundred for Jolene. Again Atkins made a point of reminding Jolene to keep her amnesia a secret. If Delmar were to find out, he'd bring her back and demand a refund.

Jolene had no intention of telling Delmar . . . she wasn't about to take a chance on the man returning her to this cell, where she could end up being bought by someone much worse. At least this man wanted her for a lady's maid; the next one might be looking for a bed wench!

Jolene and Mary Jane had just finished eating their supper, which consisted of cold corn pone sweetened with molasses, when the jailkeep came to their cell.

The man's narrow eyes swept lewdly over the two women. They were indeed prime wenches, and just looking at them stirred his desire. As he continued to ogle them, he decided Jolene was the more tempting. Her black hair, ivory complexion, and dark-blue eyes were enchanting, and her small frame was perfectly proportioned. The longer he studied her, the more he wanted her.

Finally, deciding to state his reason for coming to their cell, he said gruffly, "Your new masta wants you gals to bathe. He also sent over some new clothes for ya." He pointed to Jolene. "You can take the first bath." Quickly he unlocked the door, then motioned for her to step out.

Mary Jane reached into her carpetbag and removed a brush, which she handed to Jolene. "Here; after you wash your hair, you'll want to brush it."

Taking the hairbrush, Jolene followed the jailkeep past the other cells, down the stairs, and into the cramped office. He led her to a side door, opened it, and stepped back.

"There's a filled tub in there for your bath. The clothes Delmar sent are folded on a chair. When you finish, I'll take you back and the other gal can wash."

She went inside the room and glancing about, saw that she was in the jailkeep's bedroom. The large tub was in the middle of the floor, and walking over to it, she dipped her hand into the water. It was cold.

The man laughed shortly. "Delmar said he wanted you clean, he didn't say you had to wash in warm water."

Jolene felt filthy and was glad for a chance to bathe, even in unheated water. "Would you mind closing the door behind you?"

He hesitated, then complied.

Alone, Jolene quickly shed her dirty clothes and entered the tub. The cold water was chilling, but invigorating. Using the soap, she sudsed her hair, then submerged herself until her hair was well rinsed. That done, she set about washing her body thoroughly and was tempted to soak for a while, but knowing Mary Jane must be waiting anxiously to bathe, she climbed out of the tub.

She picked up a towel and dried herself briskly, then ran the brush vigorously through her hair until her dark locks were tangle-free. Looking over the clothes Delmar had sent, she saw that the dresses were two different sizes. The garments were plain, the type worn by the poor or by slaves. She took the smaller for herself. The two pair of cotton bloomers were identical.

A sudden draft caused Jolene to whirl about, and the sight of the jailkeep sent her heart pounding.

He shut the door behind him, and as his eyes drank in her naked body, he murmured thickly, "You sure don't look like no wench. You're just as light-colored as a white lady."

Jolene grabbed for the towel to cover herself, but the man lunged forward and grasped her about the waist. Lifting her into his arms, he carried her to his bed.

"Put me down or I'll scream!" Jolene shrieked.

"Scream all you want, gal. There ain't nobody around to hear ya except for some darkies, and they're locked up."

He dropped her onto the lumpy mattress, then falling atop her, pinned her beneath him as his wet mouth came down on hers.

Jolene fought with all her might, and although she struggled wildly, her strength was no match for his. Freeing her arms, she pushed in vain against his chest, but she couldn't budge him. He was much too heavy.

Taking his mouth from hers, he uttered gruffly, "Stop fightin' me, you damned wench."

He started to kiss her again, and seeing his intent, she turned her head to the side. She caught sight of a brass candlestick on the bedside table before he forced her face back to his. This time, when his mouth pressed against hers, she pretended to submit. As his lips continued their sickening assault, Jolene reached cautiously for the candlestick. Her fingers wrapped around its base, and lifting it, she brought it down heavily against the back of her attacker's head.

His body slumped and lay still. Managing to shove his limp form aside, she sprung to her feet. The sight of the blood now flowing profusely from his wound caused her to cringe. She was beginning to wonder if she'd killed him when to her relief she saw that he was breathing. Nevertheless she knew that she was in terrible trouble.

On the verge of panicking, she darted to the chair, grabbed her new clothes, and put them on, then slipped her feet into her old, scuffed slippers. What should she do? Should she wait and try to explain to Mr. Delmar that she had merely been defending herself? Would he believe her? What if the jailkeep was seriously hurt, or worse, what if he were to die? Would Mr. Delmar hand her over to the law so that she could be executed? Jolene decided quickly that she had only one choice—*she had to escape!*

As she hurried to the door, she glanced back at the jailkeep. His keys were on a belt about his waist. Should she free Mary Jane? No, she decided . . . if Mary Jane escaped with her and they were caught,

139

her friend would also be in deep trouble.

Opening the door, Jolene moved quickly across the small office to the outside. The night air was cool, and she breathed deeply. She paused for a moment, wondering which direction she should take. What was she to do? She considered going back inside to search for money, but afraid the jailkeep would regain consciousness, she dismissed the idea right away.

Running with no fixed route in mind, she soon put some distance between herself and the slave jail. By the time she felt it was safe to slow her pace, she was in the heart of town. She didn't know the street, but it was apparently a major one, for the sidewalks were crowded.

She was approaching the Hotel St. Louis when she suddenly saw John Delmar coming in her direction, accompanied by two male servants. She looked about frantically for a means of escape, and seeing an alleyway, darted into the dark passage. It ran alongside the hotel, and hastening to the back of the building, she scurried around it. She thought she was safe when, to her horror, she detected Delmar's voice. He and his men were coming down the alley and would soon be rounding the corner of the hotel.

Again she sought an escape route. Her eyes darted toward the hotel's crude quarters for their patrons' servants, then to the stables. She was considering running to the stables when she saw what looked like a back door. Praying it would be unlocked, she turned the knob and was thankful to find it open. She dashed inside, closing it mere seconds before Delmar and his men emerged from the alley.

Jolene found herself in a dimly lit cubbyhole adjacent to a narrow flight of stairs. She supposed she was in the servants' entrance. Uncertain of her next move, she remained hidden for a long time before deciding to venture up the steps. They led into a long, carpeted hall. There were rooms on both sides with gold-plated numbers on the doors.

She was near the end of the corridor and was about to descend the stairway when she heard a man's voice. It wasn't very distinctive, and she couldn't be sure if it was Delmar's, but not waiting to find out, she turned and rushed back down the hall. But before she could reach safety, the voice grew louder, and this time she recognized it as her new master's. Grabbing the closest doorknob, she hoped it'd be unlocked and the room unoccupied. She was in luck, and as the door swung open, she stepped into the dark room. Feeling her way, she managed to find an oil lamp on the bedside table. Fumbling, she located matches and lit the lamp. She adjusted the wick so that the flame gave off only the barest amount of light.

She went back to the door and opened it a crack. Peering out, she was appalled to see that Delmar's room was across from hers. His door was open, and he was talking to another man. She couldn't see the other man very well, for the back of his chair faced her. However, Delmar was seated so that he had a clear view of where she was hiding. If she were to step into the hall, he'd spot her right away.

She closed the door quietly and moved back to the bed. Glancing about, she saw belongings and realized someone was staying here. She hoped whoever was using it wouldn't return soon. Noticing a bottle of bourbon on the dresser, she walked over and picked it up. She was so frightened that she was trembling. Returning to the bed, she uncapped the bottle, and hoping the liquor would help her relax, she took a large swallow. The potent brew burned her throat, and for a moment she thought she might be sick. Then, as the initial nausea passed, the bourbon did indeed have a calming affect. She took another drink, but this time the brew went down much more smoothly.

Thereafter, Jolene made frequent trips to the door, only to hear that Delmar was still entertaining his guest. Each time she would return to the bed and have another drink of bourbon. The liquor continued to soothe her and made her present circumstances much less frightening.

Unaccustomed to alcohol, Jolene was soon rather tipsy. As drowsiness overcame her, she lay down on the bed and placed her head on the pillow. She told herself that she'd rest for only a minute, then check again on Delmar. She was strangely lightheaded, and the bed beneath her felt as though it were moving back and forth. She closed her eyes and drifted into a deep, bourbon-induced sleep.

Kurt bade John goodnight, and promising to visit Willow Hill before going to Heritage Manor, he left the planter's room and stepped across the hall to his own.

He was tired and looking forward to going to bed. Earlier, while leaving the dining room, he'd seen

Delmar returning from taking his men to the servants' quarters. The two had met in the lobby, and Delmar had insisted that Kurt join him in his room for brandy and conversation. During their lengthy talk, Kurt had indulged in several drinks, and he realized that he was now feeling them.

Remembering that he'd left his room unlocked, he turned the knob and stepped inside. The low-burning lamp immediately caught his attention, and his first thought was of Daniel: had he slipped up the back stairs and come to his room? He glanced about quickly, and as his gaze fell across Jolene, he shook his head as though his eyes were deceiving him.

Slowly he crossed the carpeted floor, paused beside the bed, and studied the beautiful woman, who was now sleeping soundly. A tender smile touched his lips as he took her in. She was lovely beyond words, and sitting gently on the edge of the bed, he reached over and lifted a lock of her soft, dark hair. He caressed the silky tresses, admiring their deep ebony color. Then he traced her facial features with a feather-light touch. The tips of his fingers played across her eyebrows, down to her high cheekbones, then to her sultry lips.

Noticing the half-empty bottle on the bedside table, he grinned wryly. Apparently Mrs. Atkins was far from temperance. Continuing to observe her, he became aware of her bangs—they hadn't been there the first time he had seen her. He supposed she'd cut her hair to conceal her injury. Leaning back a little so that he could get a full view of her face, he decided that he liked the bangs. They gave her an innocent but provocative look that was enchanting.

Enjoying himself thoroughly, he allowed his gaze to roam from her lovely face down to the slight swell of her breasts. Her simple, colorless dress was pulled taut, defining the shape of her small but firm bosom. Taking his time, he lowered his vision to her delicately rounded hips.

Suddenly realizing that his manhood was beginning to respond to his visual examination, he decided it was time to wake Mrs. Atkins and ask her to leave. Although he found her enticing, as far as he was concerned, married women were taboo.

A puzzled frown furrowed his brow. What the hell was she doing in his room? He shrugged his strong shoulders. Well, there was one way to find out; he'd wake her and demand an explanation.

He leaned closer. Her lips were so inviting that he was tempted to wake her with a kiss. Reminding himself that she was Atkins' wife, he held back the urge and murmured softly, "Open your eyes, Sleeping Beauty."

Hearing his voice, Jolene roused from her sleep, her lids fluttering open. The bourbon was still affecting her, and as her eyes took in the man's handsome face, her sight was blurry. But she was still able to recognize his features. His image had pulled at her heart for days!

Her intoxication gave her the courage to slip her arms about his neck and draw him closer. She felt strangely content, for the man she loved had finally rescued her! She longed to speak to him, but she couldn't find her voice. If only she wasn't so muddled! Why had she drunk so much bourbon?

As she tried to sort out her thoughts, Kurt, finding

144

himself in her arms, lost his self-restraint. His lips descended to hers, and their initial touch was gentle, but as a flame took hold within him, his kiss deepened fiercely.

Responding, Jolene's flimsy hold on reality was completely swept away as she became lost in a world where only she and her dream lover existed. Forgotten was the slave jail, the man who had attacked her, and the fact that she herself was a runaway slave. She had no life outside this room. Destiny had brought her to the arms of the one she loved. Here, in his warm embrace, she would stay . . . forever!

Kurt's feelings were just as intense. For some inexplicable reason, this lovely woman had tortured his mind, and her memory had penetrated his heart to the core. Now, unbelievably, Fate had brought her to his bed.

With his lips still on hers, he murmured hoarsely, "Sleeping Beauty, you have bewitched me." His sudden kiss was so passionate that it verged on brutality. "I want you! God, I can't help myself! I must make you mine!"

"Yes!" she cried, consumed by the deep longing within her.

He rose up and his dark eyes probed hers. "What we're about to do is wrong. But I can no more turn away from you than I can stop breathing. You're forbidden fruit, my love, but too tempting for a man to refuse." And he let himself give in to his desire.

Chapter Nine

"Forbidden fruit?" Jolene pondered. Why did he use such a phrase? She was about to question him, but before she could, his lips were again on hers, his demanding, heart-stopping kiss obliterating her thoughts.

Jolene, surrendering breathlessly, returned his ardor to the fullest and welcomed his probing tongue with a passion that belied her innocence.

Kurt desired her so powerfully that his hands trembled as he released the tiny buttons at her bodice. As he pushed aside the material, freeing her soft breasts, Jolene gasped aloud.

She was somewhat frightened; but Kurt, mistaking her gasp as one of passion, bent his head and caressed her ivory breasts with butterfly kisses. As his warm tongue flickered lightly over the taut nipples, his touch sent delightful shivers through Jolene, and she laced her fingers through his hair and arched beneath his stimulating fondling.

Kurt responded to her willingness and abandoned

her lovely breasts to press a hungry, fervent kiss on her pliable mouth.

Jolene's emotions swirled as, driven by a force that defied logic, she urged him onward with throaty impassioned moans.

"My beauty," Kurt murmured thickly. "You have the power to drive me beyond reason. I've never wanted a woman as desperately as I want you! I'm possessed!" He groaned deeply. "Damn! I wish you didn't belong to another man!"

"But I don't belong—" Jolene began, but Kurt's lips were suddenly on hers, silencing her words.

His passion was now fully aroused, and mistaking Jolene for an experienced woman, he took for granted that she was as eager as he to consummate their fiery, illicit union.

However, realizing he was angry with himself for wanting another man's wife, Kurt sat up abruptly and took off his shoes and jacket. Cursing silently, he quickly undid his trousers and moved so that he knelt on the bed at Jolene's side. Driven by unquenched desire, he lifted her skirt, drew down her cotton bloomers, and pitched the undergarment to the floor. Then, parting her legs brusquely, he positioned himself for entry.

Meanwhile, his curt treatment brought a semblance of sanity to Jolene, and she tried vainly to roll away from him.

Restraining her, Kurt chuckled gruffly. "Are you a tease, my forbidden beauty? Well, you have tempted the wrong man. I don't play games."

"But you don't understand. . . ." she stammered.

A devilish, unrelenting gleam flickered in his dark

147

eyes. "But I do understand, you unfaithful little vixen." His unexpected smile was cold and threatening. "You're an unfulfilled wife who thinks the grass is greener in another man's bed."

Jolene was baffled. Why did this man think she was married? If she only knew what part he had played in her past!

"I should toss you out of my bed and send you on your way," Kurt went on. "But I'll be damned if I will!"

Consumed by passion, Kurt slipped his trousers past his muscular hips. Then, wrapping an arm about Jolene's waist, he brought her thighs up to his.

She wondered somewhat frightfully if she was still a virgin. God, if only she could remember! Nevertheless, Jolene sensed that she had never known a man's love.

"No!" she cried helplessly. "Please!"

But Kurt was beyond listening; he was too angry with his weakness for this married woman. Well, by God, he'd take her and then cure himself of her once and for all!

Lunging forward, he achieved penetration, and as he robbed Jolene of her virginity, she cried out in pain.

Kurt froze! He lay on top of her without moving as his mind tried to grasp the startling realization that he'd just taken a virgin. But, damn it, she was married to Atkins! Then how . . . ? Why . . . ?

Jolene lay stiffly beneath him, but as her initial discomfort was gradually replaced by a feeling of rapture, she entwined her arms about his neck. Her legs relaxed and parted wider, allowing Kurt's hardness to dip even farther into her warm depths. Instinctively she arched her hips, searching, longing for appeasement.

Her sweet response brought a tender smile to Kurt's lips. "My deceitful beauty," he whispered huskily, "when we're finished, you have some explaining to do."

His words barely registered with Jolene, for she was too caught up in a wonderful, awakening ecstasy.

Planting a demanding kiss on her lips, Kurt slipped her legs about his waist and thrust deeply into her enfolding warmth.

Now that the shock of her virginity had waned, Kurt was overjoyed to know that this beautiful woman was truly his. Impelled by happiness and by Jolene's uninhibited surrender, Kurt made love to her tenderly, but with a passion so fervent that Jolene felt herself spiral upward to erotic heights she had never known. Then their fulfillment surged, bringing them total release, and their lips met in a sensual, breathtaking exchange.

Kurt moved so that he lay at her side. He wanted to question her but decided to wait and give her the opportunity to explain.

Meanwhile, Jolene's thoughts were swirling: why had this man taken for granted that she was married? She knew he had been a part of her past, for his face was her only memory. She sighed. Apparently he hadn't played an important role in her life; if he had, he'd certainly know she wasn't a married woman. Then why? Why had his image been locked away in her heart?

She rolled to her side, and rising on one elbow, she gazed thoughtfully at his handsome face. His eyes met hers, and their expression was undeniably tender. If she were to be completely honest with him, would he help her?

As her gaze came to rest on his sandy hair, she suddenly remembered the man in John Delmar's room: he had been seated with his back facing her, but she had seen the color of his hair. Good Lord, this man and Delmar's guest were one and the same! She couldn't possibly tell him the truth . . . he was Delmar's friend and would most assuredly turn her over to her new master!

Leaving the bed, she picked up her cotton undergarment and slipped it on. She had to get out of the room right away.

Reading her intent, Kurt drew up his trousers, and in a flash he was standing at her side. Grasping her arm, he uttered firmly, "You aren't leaving, my beauty, until you do some explaining." He forced her to sit beside him on the bed.

"Wh-what do you want to know?" she stammered, wishing her heart weren't pounding so fearfully.

"Why did Atkins tell me you were his wife?"

She looked at him blankly.

He smiled. "Maybe you don't remember. You, Atkins, and his coffle had stopped for lunch. You had just fallen and hit your head when Daniel and I happened by. Atkins told me you were his wife and asked me to take you to the doctor. He knew you needed medical attention as quickly as possible. Since I was traveling on horseback, I was able to make faster time. You regained consciousness for a moment and looked at me."

Jolene could hardly believe that this man had played such a small part in her past . . . why had a stranger's image been etched so permanently in her mind and in her heart?

"You didn't say anything," Kurt continued. "But you were lucid when you looked at me. Don't you remember?"

"Yes, I remember," she whispered.

His tone became more forthright. "You owe me an explanation. Why was Atkins pretending that you were his wife? And don't try to tell me that you two are married, because I know damned good and well that you were a virgin!"

Jolene swallowed nervously. She didn't know why Cal had lied, but she could venture an accurate guess. If the doctor had known she was a slave, he most likely would have refused to see her. And if this man had known the truth, he probably wouldn't have offered his assistance.

She remained silent . . . what should she say? Should she answer honestly? If she were to be candid, what would the man do to her? Would he take her to Delmar? Afraid that he'd return her to her master, she decided she had no choice but to think up a plausible lie.

Her thoughts raced as she conjured up a story.

"I'm waiting for your explanation," Kurt said impatiently.

She started to speak as she normally would, but catching herself, she copied Atkins' way of talking as she answered, "Cal's my brother. Sometimes he lets me go with him when he's deliverin' a coffle here to New Orleans. When we're a-travelin' and men he don't know come 'round, he always tells 'em I'm his

151

wife. He reckons that'll keep these men from tryin' anything with me." She looked Kurt in the eye and smiled shyly. "Cal, he thinks I'm kinda pretty, and he's afraid some man might find me too temptin'. You know how big brothers are; they're always protectin' their little sisters."

Kurt bought her story. "Your brother's right— you're a very beautiful temptation." He paused, then asked, "Why were you in my room?"

Jolene's story continued to flow. "I ain't never been in a hotel as grand as this one, and I wanted to see what it was like. I slipped in the back entrance and was walkin' down the hall when I heard voices. I was afraid to be seen, so I tried your door. It was unlocked and I snuck in here."

Kurt's eyes twinkled as he finished her explanation, "You found my bottle of bourbon, drank too much, and fell asleep—is that about right?"

"I hope you ain't mad at me for drinkin' your bourbon. But I was scared, and drinkin' seemed to help."

"Of course I'm not angry," he answered quickly. Placing a hand beneath her chin, he turned her face to his. "Tell me, Sleeping Beauty, why did you let me seduce you? You should've saved your innocence for the man you'll marry."

She shrugged, trying to appear unconcerned. "I reckon I was kinda muddled by the bourbon. 'Sides, been curious about lovin' for a long time, I have. But, Cal, he watches me like a hawk. He don't even allow me to have no beaux."

As she got abruptly to her feet, he asked, "Are you leaving?"

"I gotta go. Cal will be lookin' for me."

"You shouldn't be out at night alone. I'll go with you. Where are you and your brother staying?"

"You cain't go with me!" she insisted. "If Cal was to see us together, he'd be powerful mad. Scared of him, I am! Please let me go alone!"

"All right," he answered, "but you be careful."

"I will," she assured him.

Standing, he drew her gently into his arms. "I'm sorry about what happened tonight. You weren't the only one who had too much to drink. While I was visiting my friend, John Delmar, I indulged in too much brandy. It seems we were both a little intoxicated. However, that's no excuse for what I did to you. I only wish there was some way I could make amends."

Relishing the feel of his strong arms, she leaned into his embrace. Again she considered telling him the truth. He seemed kind, but would he be quite so compassionate if he knew she was a runaway slave who belonged to John Delmar? It was a chance she couldn't afford to take.

She was reluctant to leave the comfort of his arms, but stepping back, she looked up into his face and murmured, "You don't have to feel bad 'bout what happened tonight. I wanted it to happen, and if it hadn't been you, it'd have been somebody else." She thought she saw a look of hurt come into his eyes, but it was gone so fast she couldn't be sure. She fought back the urge to tell him that she didn't feel as cold as she sounded. But she knew she had to make him believe that she wasn't upset; otherwise he might take it upon himself to try and see her again.

Taking him unawares, she turned and fled the room, closing the door soundly behind her. Tears blurred her vision as she hurried down the hall and to the rear entrance. She descended the back stairway, and when she reached the dimly lit cubbyhole, she gave in to her heartache. She cried so hard that her shoulders shook with her sobs.

Finally her tears abated. Forcing thoughts of the handsome stranger from her mind, she concentrated fully on her perilous flight: where should she go? Cedarbrook! Yes . . . she'd find her way to the plantation where she was born. Surely the sight of Cedarbrook would revive her memory.

She groaned aloud. With no money how could she possibly get home? If only she weren't completely penniless!

As an idea suddenly occurred to her, she hurried up the narrow flight of steps. Swiftly she returned to Kurt's door and knocked on it.

He responded almost immediately.

"Excuse me," Jolene began shakily, for seeing him again tore into her heart. "Could I borrow some money?"

He had been surprised to see Jolene, but he was more surprised by her request.

She carried on excitedly. "I reckon you think I'm bein' awful forward, but I need money real bad. I spent some of Cal's money, and when he finds out, he's gonna be as mad as a hornet."

"Do you want me to replace what you spent?"

"If you don't mind," she answered.

Kurt smiled indulgently. "How much do you need?"

She gulped. "I . . . I think I spent 'bout twenty dollars."

He went to where his jacket was draped over a

chair, reached into the pocket, withdrew a wallet, and took out a few bills. He handed Jolene the money. "Here's twenty-five."

"Mighty beholdin' to you, I am," she replied with a smile. Then, before he could say anything, she whirled about and retraced her steps down the hall. She could feel his eyes on her until she turned the corner that led to the back stairway.

Holding the bills firmly, she fled down the steps and out the rear entrance. A night breeze was blowing refreshingly, and its softness caressed her long black hair as she headed into the dark alley only to come face to face with Cal Atkins.

A wicked grin crossed his face and his hand snaked out, capturing her wrist. "Well, well—if it ain't Miss Uppity. Been lookin' all over town for you, I have. A couple hours ago, I went down to the slave jail and learned you done escaped. I was thinkin' 'bout reportin' your escape to Mista Delmar when I decided to check back here. Good thing I did, ain't it? Now the jailkeep and me won't have to tell Mista Delmar that he bought a 'runner,' and you won't have to be strung up and whipped." Noticing she had money, he jerked the bills from her hand. "A slave don't need no money, so I reckon I'll keep this for myself. Where'd you get it, gal? Been sellin' your favors? Your papers say you're a virgin. Mista Delmar ain't gonna like it if he finds out you done been busted."

"I stole the money," Jolene blurted.

"You better not be lyin'."

"I'm telling the truth!"

He believed her. "Why did you knock the jailkeep on the head?"

"He was trying to rape me."

"That ain't what he said, but I'm inclined to believe you over him. I was worried 'bout you—that's why I came back to the slave jail. Had a feelin' that horny bastard would try somethin'. I swore to Mista Delmar that you was a virgin, and I got a reputation to uphold. Man of my word, I am." He tugged at her arm. "Come on, gal, I'm takin' you back to your cell."

Trying to pull away, she pleaded, "Please don't take me back! That man will try to force himself on me again!"

"No, he won't, 'cause I'm gonna stay there all night and make sure that in the mornin' when Mista Delmar picks you up, you're still a virgin."

Increasing his hold on her wrist, he forced her to fall into step beside him. As they emerged from the alley and to the front of the Hotel St. Louis, Jolene glanced up and was startled to see Kurt standing outside on his terrace.

Looking down, he caught sight of her and Atkins.

She gave him a timid smile. Then, turning away, she kept her stride even with Atkins'. She wondered if she'd ever see the handsome stranger again. He was friends with John Delmar, so she knew there was some chance their paths would cross. She hoped not, for she didn't want him to learn she was a slave. She was finding it hard to believe that she had actually made love to the man.

The mere touch of his lips on hers had completely destroyed her defenses. Was she in love with him? Is that why she'd surrendered so easily? *Yes,* she thought depressingly . . . *I love him. I've loved him since the first moment I gazed into his face.* Does he love me in return? No, of course he doesn't. He thinks I'm white trash, and it's quite apparent that he's an aristocrat. Aristocrats don't fall in love with white trash! Furthermore, if he knew I was a quadroon slave, he'd think even less of me. For my own sake, I must find a way to dismiss him from my mind as well as my heart.

As Jolene wondered about him, Kurt, watching her and Atkins, was involved in musings of his own. He hoped her brother wasn't too angry with her. He wondered what excuse she'd given him for being out this time of night. He didn't blame Atkins for keeping such a close eye on his sister. After all, her brother was only trying to protect her from men like himself.

A deep frown crossed Kurt's brow. He felt terrible about the way he'd seduced her. But, damn it, he hadn't known she was a virgin! Why the hell hadn't she stopped him? Suddenly her explanation came back to him, "If it hadn't been you, it'd been some other man." The little vixen had been bound and determined to lose her innocence.

By now Jolene and Atkins had walked out of sight, and Kurt left the terrace and went back into his room. Going to the bedside table, he opened the bottle of bourbon and took a large swallow. "Sleeping Beauty," he murmured as though Jolene were present. "Now that I've sampled your charms, maybe you'll stop pulling at my heartstrings." But even as he uttered the words, Kurt had a depressing feeling that he'd not find her so easy to forget.

Chapter Ten

Jolene, lying on a bed of straw, was awakened by sounds of the jailkeep opening the cell door. He was carrying two tin bowls filled with sweetened corn mush. As he entered, Jolene sat up and watched him warily.

As he handed her one of the bowls, his small eyes glared into hers. "You damned wench!" he grumbled. "My head still hurts like hell. I oughta teach you a lesson you'll never forget." But his threat was hollow, for he knew he'd have to answer to Atkins if he marred the wench, and he wasn't about to anger the slave trader. The man brought him too much business.

He gave Mary Jane the other bowl and left the cell without making any further comment.

Jolene had no appetite and set aside her meager breakfast.

Watching her, Mary Jane remarked, "You should eat. You'll need your strength."

Jolene knew she was right, but the sight of the

runny mush hardly whet her appetite. "The food here isn't fit for pigs," she complained.

"Better than nothin'," Mary Jane replied.

Jolene lay back on her straw pallet, and rolling to her side, she studied her friend. She supposed Mary Jane was a little upset with her. Last night, when Cal had returned her to the cell, Mary Jane had flooded her with questions that she'd declined to answer.

Sighing unhappily, Jolene closed her eyes and allowed the image of her lover to materialize. He was so handsome, the man she adored. Vividly she envisioned his dreamy brown eyes, his full lips, and his well-trimmed moustache. A warm tingle ran through her as she recalled the thrill of being held tight in his strong arms. The memory of their passionate union brought a vivid blush to her pale cheeks. She wondered if she'd ever be in his wonderful embrace again. She doubted she would, and the thought was disheartening. However, remembering her vow to dismiss him from her mind and heart, she cast all thoughts of him aside. Filled with resolve, she opened her eyes and sat upright.

Her gaze went to the bowl of mush. Mary Jane was right—she must eat to keep her strength. She didn't want to get sick. Last night, before she had finally fallen asleep, she had decided that when the time was right, she'd run away and find her way back to Cedarbrook. She believed returning to her former home would restore her memory. She hadn't blindly accepted everything Cal had told her about her life. Just because he claimed she was a quadroon didn't make it so. The man wasn't above deceit.

Picking up the bowl, Jolene began eating her

breakfast with determination. She could feel Mary Jane's eyes on her, but she waited until she had finished before meeting the other woman's gaze. "You're angry with me, aren't you?"

"No, not really. But I don't understand why you won't tell me what happened last night."

Could she bring herself to tell Mary Jane about her encounter with the handsome stranger? No! It was a memory she wished to hoard and not share with anyone. Talking about it might cheapen it and take away its enchantment.

"I can't tell you . . . not now. Maybe later. Please try to understand."

Mary Jane relented. "All right—I won't keep askin' you what happened." She had spoken sincerely, for she'd never had a good friend before Jolene, and she didn't want to say or do anything to lose her friendship.

The jailkeep returned, unlocked their cell door, and told them it was time to leave. Not wanting to keep Delmar waiting, he ushered them past the other cells, down the stairs, through his small office and outside.

Jolene's eyes were accustomed to the dusky interior of the jail, and the bright morning sunlight was blinding. Shading her eyes with her hand, she spotted two large Negro men seated on a buckboard. One held the horses' reins, the other had a rifle resting across his folded arms. As Delmar walked up to her, she turned to look at him.

Speaking crisply, the man ordered, "You wenches get in the back of the buckboard. We have a long way to travel, and I don't intend to waste any time."

160

"How far is it to your plantation?" Jolene queried, forgetting that a slave is not supposed to speak without asking permission. Furthermore, a slave always addressed his or her master respectfully, never as an equal.

Delmar was outraged by her insolence. "Girl, this time I'm going to let you get by with a warning! Don't you *ever* speak to me without asking permission, and when you talk to me, you address me properly! Do you understand?"

"Yes, Master Delmar," she answered between gritted teeth.

"You'll be a house servant, so you may address me as Master John."

Biting back a sarcastic retort, Jolene murmured with feigned humility, "Yes, Master John."

His arms akimbo, Delmar looked steadily into her large blue eyes, which met his without wavering. "I'm going to give you some good advice, girl. That education you received is no longer worth a damn. It'll alienate you from the other slaves. Also, I find your education irritating, and my son and daughter will feel as I do. A slave speaking like white folks goes against my grain. Hereafter, I want you to start talking like the rest of my house servants."

She lowered her gaze, not because she was humbled, but because she was afraid he'd see the resentment in her eyes. "Yes, Masta John," she murmured, fuming to herself.

"Good!" he remarked arrogantly. "All you have to do is learn your place, and you and I will get along just fine. Now, you two gals get in the buckboard."

At that moment, Cal Atkins arrived, driving his

old, rickety wagon. He had spent the night at the slave jail, but had left early to get his buckboard and horses from the livery stable. Without bothering to get down, he called to John, "Howdy, Mista Delmar. Hope your wenches make good servants, I do."

"I'm sure they'll be quite satisfactory," the planter called back, annoyed with the trader's interruption.

Atkins slapped the reins against his team, then waving to the jailkeep, he yelled, "I'm headin' home. See you in a couple of months when I bring in another coffle." He glanced at Jolene and Mary Jane. "You gals be good to your new masta!"

The women watched him as he rode away. "I hope I never see his face again for as long as I live," Jolene whispered to Mary Jane.

Tugging at her friend's hand, Mary Jane encouraged, "Let's go to the buckboard. We don't wanna anger Masta John. When he tells us to do somethin', it's in our own best interest to do it quickly."

Agreeing, Jolene followed the other woman over to the wagon. The Negro man holding the rifle placed it on the seat, jumped to the ground, then stepped to the rear of the buckboard to assist the women.

Jolene studied the big man as he lifted Mary Jane into the bed of the wagon. His complexion was extremely dark and his hair was tightly curled. He appeared to be in his late twenties, and his muscular build exuded enormous strength. He turned to Jolene, placed his powerful hands on her waist, and lifted her into the buckboard with incredible ease.

He smiled congenially, revealing straight white

162

teeth. "My name's Samson."

"I don't wonder," Jolene answered, somewhat in awe of his huge build.

"What's your name, gal?"

"Jolene, and this is Mary Jane."

The driver, twisting about in the seat so that he could face the women, said, "I'm George."

Although George's frame wasn't quite as muscular as Samson's, Jolene could see a stark resemblance between the men. "Are you two brothers?" she asked.

"We sure is," George answered. He looked fondly at Samson, leaving no doubt in Jolene's mind that the two brothers were apparently very close.

Mary Jane glanced over her shoulder to check on Delmar. The jailkeep had the planter involved in deep conversation, and taking advantage of her master's preoccupation, she asked Samson, "What kind of masta is Mista Delmar?"

"He can be a hard masta, but his son, Masta Alan, he's meaner than the devil. You gals best keep away from him. He likes pretty wenches."

"How far do we have to travel?" Jolene inquired.

"It'll take 'most a week to reach Willow Hill," George told her.

"A week!" Jolene exclaimed. She hadn't thought Delmar's home would be so far away.

"Willow Hill's in Alabama," Samson explained.

Jolene wanted to question the brothers more, but John's sharp command prevented further discussion. "Samson, stop talking to the women and get back up on the seat. We're leaving."

Obeying his master, the large man moved quickly.

As he took his place beside his brother, George laid the reins against the horses and the buckboard began to roll. Delmar, mounted on his roan stallion, rode a short way in front of his servants.

The jailkeep remained outside and watched them until they rounded the corner of the street and were out of view. He started to go back inside, but catching sight of a well-dressed gentleman arriving from the opposite direction, he waited to see what he wanted.

The man used long, swift strides and the jailkeep didn't have long to wait. Walking up to him, the gentleman nodded politely. "How do you do?"

"I'm fine, thank you."

"My name is Kurt Spencer, and I'm looking for Cal Atkins. Is he here by any chance?"

"Atkins left a short time ago."

"Did he say where he was going?"

"Yep, said he was headin' home."

"Was his sister with him?"

The jailkeep looked at him as though he were daft. "Atkins ain't got no sister."

"Of course he has. I've seen her."

"You might've seen a woman with Atkins, but she sure as hell weren't no sister. I've known Cal for years, and believe me, he ain't got no sister. Ain't got no kin at all."

A low-burning anger had begun to simmer within Kurt. So his Sleeping Beauty had lied to him! "When Atkins left, was he alone?"

"Yep, he sure was." The jailkeep paused and spat a stream of tobacco juice onto the ground. "'Cept for a couple of prime wenches, Atkins' coffle ain't worth

164

much. So he didn't stick around for the auction. Gonna sell the nigras myself and split fifty-fifty with Cal."

Kurt didn't want to be drawn into a lengthy conversation, and touching the brim of his hat, he said tersely, "Sorry to have bothered you. Good day, sir."

Leaving abruptly, Kurt headed back toward the hotel. Why had the woman lied to him? Damn her for the deceitful little vixen that she was!

This morning when Kurt had awakened, his thoughts had turned immediately to Jolene, and he had found himself longing to see her again. He had been forced to admit to himself, goodnaturedly, that his Sleeping Beauty had him completely bewitched. He'd never imagined himself falling for a woman like Atkins' sister. On the contrary, he had always thought he'd fall in love with a woman who was more educated and refined. As he'd compared his country-raised vixen to a cultured lady, Kurt had laughed aloud. She might not be cultured, but, by God, she had stolen his heart!

Determined to see her again, Kurt decided to talk to Atkins and ask his permission to take his sister to dinner. Anxious, he had dressed hastily, skipped breakfast, and hurried to the slave jail, where he hoped to find the trader, or at least learn where he was staying.

Now, as Kurt walked back toward the hotel, his anger was still smoldering. The country chit had made a fool of him! He smirked bitterly. She had even taken him for twenty-five dollars! Losing the money didn't bother him, but the fact that she had lied to get it made his blood boil.

His anger began to cool somewhat and Kurt stopped thinking about Jolene's deceit as his thoughts turned to the woman herself. Who was she? He didn't even know her name. What was her relationship with Atkins? She sure as hell wasn't his wife, and apparently she wasn't his sister. Why had the two of them been traveling together, and why did Atkins leave without her? Was she still in New Orleans? Kurt seriously doubted it. She had probably used his twenty-five dollars to leave town. Would he ever see her again? He decided it would be advantageous to her if their paths never crossed, for he might be tempted to break her beautiful neck.

Kurt Spencer had no patience with deceit and resolved to chalk up his escapade with Jolene to experience.

Delmar and his servants spent their first night at a rundown inn on a rural road between New Orleans and Willow Hill.

The planter had a room inside the public house, but custom dictated that his slaves sleep in the barn.

John trusted George and Samson implicitly and didn't manacle them for the night, but afraid his new wenches might run, he shackled them to one of the beams in the roomy barn.

It never crossed his mind to offer even a halfhearted apology to the women, for he considered them his chattel, which meant they had no rights; nor did they deserve common courtesy.

The women were seated on a bed of straw, and as

166

Jolene moved her leg, searching for a more comfortable position, the heavy manacle cut painfully into her flesh. The unexpected pain caused her to cry out.

Delmar had ordered Samson and George to sleep across the barn from the women, but hearing Jolene's cry, Samson came over to check on her.

"Did you hurt yourself?" he asked.

"Yes . . . I moved my ankle the wrong way, and the manacle cut into my flesh."

"You gotta be more careful."

"I will. Thank you for caring."

He sat down at her side. Samson was quite taken with Jolene. He thought her beautiful, but since she was a light-colored wench, he didn't think she'd be interested in him. The few quadroons he'd met in his life had found his dark skin and Negro features unattractive. Although he hoped Jolene would think differently, he wasn't about to get his hopes up.

"Which one of you did Masta John buy to be Miz Sabrina's maid?" he asked the women.

Mary Jane told him that it was Jolene.

He shook his head sympathetically. "That Miz Sabrina, she almost as mean as her brother." He looked at Jolene. "She gonna work you hard."

"I'm not afraid of hard work."

"She also got a sharp tongue."

"What is Mrs. Delmar like?" Jolene asked.

"She dead, been dead a long time. Miz Sabrina, she the mistress of Willow Hill." He eyed Jolene a little strangely. "Gal, you don't talk like no wench. You talk as good as Miz Sabrina."

"I was educated," she answered, offering no

167

further explanation.

"You mean you can read and write?" he exclaimed, astounded.

"Yes, I can."

He studied her thoughtfully.

Jolene was on the verge of asking him his thoughts when the innkeeper's servant entered with their supper. The elderly man carried a tray laden with tin plates filled with beans and cornbread.

Samson returned to his brother's side and told George in a low voice, "That wench Jolene can read and write. She's educated and can talk just as good as a white lady. We got to tell her what we're plannin' and ask her to join up with us. Her bein' able to read and write, and talk refined-like, might be a big help when we're on the run."

George, more conservative, was undecided. "We got to wait awhile. We don't know her good enough to tell her no secrets. First, we got to see if she can be trusted. We got plenty of time 'fore we make our break, so don't say nothin' to her yet."

"All right," Samson agreed. A hard, hateful glare glazed his eyes. "Sometimes when Masta John hands me that rifle I's suppose to protect him with, I gets a hankerin' to cock it, aim it at his smug face, and pull the trigger."

"You cain't do no such thing!" George whispered firmly. "When we run, we gots to do it right! If you was to get trigger-happy and shoot Masta John, the slave patrol would capture you for sure. Then they'd string you up and hang you by the neck 'til you's dead."

"Don't worry none," Samson replied. "I ain't

gonna do nothin' crazy. That northern abolitionist, he told us to sit tight and wait for him to contact us, and that's exactly what I aims to do. But just the same, I think maybe that Jolene might be helpful."

"You sure you ain't just fallin' for her?"

"Reckon maybe I find her real pretty, but she not only talks white, she also looks white. When we're runnin', she might be real useful." Catching sight of the innkeeper's servant coming toward them, Samson leaned closer to his brother and said in a serious whisper, "When it's time for us to run, I'm gonna kill Masta John, then I'm gonna kill Masta Alan. Kill 'em with my bare hands, I will."

A cold, foreboding chill ran down George's spine, for he knew that Samson's threat was real.

"I'm sorry, Daniel," Kurt said, "but John was adamant about not selling Lucy."

The two men were ensconced in Kurt's room. Daniel had slipped into the hotel by the back entrance.

"Damn his soul to hell!" Daniel raged. "Well, if he won't sell her, I'll steal her!"

"Don't do anything rash," Kurt advised. "Give me some time to change Delmar's mind. We'll stop at Willow Hill on our way to Heritage Manor. You can see your mother, and I'll try again to convince John to let her go."

Daniel agreed, for he knew at present he had no other choice. However, he was dead-set on taking his mother back with him to Texas.

Kurt poured them both glasses of bourbon, and

handing Daniel his drink, he said, "The tailor will have my clothes ready the day after tomorrow. We'll leave then, if you want."

"We can't leave too soon to suit me." Thinking of his mother brought a smile to his face. "I haven't seen Mama in over ten years. God, it's going to be good to see her again! I wonder if she's changed much."

Kurt was also eager to see Lucy, for he had loved her since boyhood. "I imagine ten years'll make a difference, but there's one thing for certain."

"What's that?"

"She'll still be beautiful. Beauty like Lucy's doesn't fade with time; it merely matures."

"I'll drink to that," Daniel declared, holding up his glass.

Toasting, Kurt replied, "Here's to Lucy."

"The only woman we've ever loved," Daniel added.

Kurt hesitated, then downed his bourbon.

His hesitation didn't escape Daniel. "Was I wrong about Mama being the only woman we've ever loved?" He watched his good friend closely.

"No, you weren't wrong," Kurt was quick to reply. He carried their empty glasses to the dresser. Then, turning back to face Daniel, he told him about finding Jolene asleep on his bed. He didn't tell his friend that they had made love, but it hadn't been necessary, for Daniel was able to figure that out for himself. The tortured look of love in Kurt's eyes revealed everything. Kurt finished by explaining his visit this morning to the slave jail.

"So she isn't Atkins' wife or his sister?" Daniel remarked.

170

Spencer, frustrated, said testily, "I have no idea who she is or where she's gone. I'll probably never see her again, which is just as well, for I'd most likely turn her over my knee and spank her bottom till she cried."

Daniel laughed heartily. "Sounds to me like this little gal has you flustered. When I think of all the women, some refined, others experienced, who've tried their damnedest to snare you but failed miserably, then the way this country girl comes along and traps you is almost comical."

Kurt arched a brow. "So you find it humorous, do you?"

Taking his hat from the chair and placing it on his head, Daniel answered, "We all have to lose our hearts sooner or later. Along with yours, you just happened to lose twenty-five dollars." Going to the door, he chuckled, "I thought you were too smart to be taken in, especially by such a country bumpkin."

"Your sarcasm isn't appreciated," Kurt grumbled.

"See you day after tomorrow," Daniel remarked, opening the door and leaving.

Kurt poured himself another drink before getting ready for bed. Though he was tired, it was a long time before he fell asleep, and when he finally drifted into slumber, his dreams were of Jolene.

Chapter Eleven

Johanna paced the parlor with the restlessness of a caged animal. She hadn't been away from Cedarbrook since the day she and Jolene had arrived from St. Louis. For the first few days friends and neighbors had stopped by to pay their condolences, but the visits soon dwindled. Days had passed without a single guest. The isolated country life didn't agree with Johanna, and she was beside herself with boredom. She had considered giving a party, but if she were to plan any form of festivity this soon after her father's and brother's deaths, society would be shocked. She was sure there were any number of barbeques and balls taking place, but she supposed that because she was in mourning, her name was respectfully omitted from the guest lists.

Now, ceasing her pacing, Johanna moved across the room to a table beside the open window. The table, made of fine-grained cherry, held a crystal decanter and goblets. As Johanna poured herself a glass of sherry, she wondered bitterly how she'd get through these days without wine to help her endure the lonely hours.

Taking her drink with her, she went to the large walnut desk and picked up an envelope, opened it, and removed a sheet of paper. Quickly her eyes scanned the short note. She didn't know why she bothered to read it. She had read it so many times that she had it memorized. It was a message from Marshall Walker notifying her that he'd be delayed in picking up the Morgan that Sam Warrington had left him.

As anger surged within her, she crumbled the piece of paper and stuffed it back into the envelope. Marshall hadn't said how long he expected to be delayed, but Johanna had received the letter days ago and she was growing impatient waiting for him to show up. If he didn't arrive soon, she'd find some excuse to visit him.

Lifting her glass, she took a large drink. Johanna had confidence in her charms and knew how to use them to her advantage, but she couldn't shake the gnawing feeling that she'd failed in her attempt to enchant Marshall Walker. The day that Robert had read Sam's will, she'd discreetly tried to lure Marshall, but apparently she hadn't been successful. Otherwise, he wouldn't have postponed his visit to Cedarbrook.

"Miz Johanna," Lazarus began, entering the parlor quietly.

His voice startled his mistress. "Honestly, Lazarus! Must you sneak up on me?"

"I's sorry, Miz Johanna," he mumbled.

"What do you want?" she asked.

"Mista Walker is here."

"Marshall!" she exclaimed. "I didn't hear anyone at the door."

"I saw him arrivin' and opened the door 'fore he could knock."

"Show him into the parlor. And hurry!"

Nervously Johanna patted her hair, hoping it was in place. She glanced distastefully at her mourning dress; if only she could wear bright colors—black was *so* unbecoming on her!

Lazarus led Marshall into the parlor, then asked his mistress if she wanted him to serve tea. She looked questioningly at her guest, but he quickly declined.

Dismissing the butler, Johanna smiled sweetly as she went and offered Marshall her hand.

"Johanna, I hope you're well," he said, placing a light kiss upon her soft skin.

"I'm fine, thank you."

"I'm sorry I wasn't able to come sooner for the Morgan, but work at my plantation held me up."

Placing her hand in the crook of his arm and leading him to the sofa, she urged him to sit beside her. "Honestly, Marshall!" she said, her tone sugar-coated. "You work too hard. Why don't you let your overseer take care of things so you'll have more free time?"

"I don't have an overseer. I've had a few over the years, but they didn't work out. I always find that they're mistreating my people." He paused, looking at her seriously. "Speaking of overseers, I've met Sullivan a couple of times, and I think you should keep a close watch on him. There's something about that man I don't trust. He strikes me as the type of overseer who could be quite cruel."

"Oh?" Johanna remarked innocently. "I didn't know. Of course, I'll keep an eye on him. But I'm sure he's treating my field workers fairly. Otherwise my house servants would know and one of them would certainly have informed me."

"If you learn that Sullivan is being brutal, as I suspect, you should dismiss him at once."

"I will," she hastened to reply.

Changing the subject, he asked, "Have you heard from Jolene?"

"No . . . no, I haven't," she stammered. "But I'm sure I'll hear from her soon."

"Where did she go?"

"Boston," Johanna lied smoothly. "We have a good friend there. We went to school with her, and Jolene plans to stay with her and her family."

"I'm glad she isn't alone."

"Yes, so am I."

He stood. "I hate to rush off, but I must go."

"No!" she objected, bounding to her feet. "Please don't leave so soon!"

He smiled warmly. "I'm sorry, Johanna. Please pardon my rudeness, but there's work waiting for me at home."

She frowned sullenly. "I was hoping you'd stay for dinner. I'm so lonely now. I have no one to talk to except for my nigras and Mr. Sullivan. The servants are no company whatsoever, and Mr. Sullivan . . . well, I very seldom talk to him, and when I do it's strictly business. He certainly isn't the kind of gentleman a lady asks to dinner."

Gently he placed his hands on her shoulders and gazed tenderly down into her emerald-green eyes. "I can well imagine how lonely you are. And I'm sure you miss your sister very much. I wish I could stay, but it's quite impossible."

"Can't your work wait till tomorrow?" she implored.

"Yes, I suppose it could—but I must be home for dinner, because I'm expecting company. Do you remember the Mitchell family?"

"I think so. Isn't Mr. Mitchell a merchant in Natchez?"

"Yes. He and his wife and daughter are my dinner guests." He smiled shyly. "His daughter, Amanda, and I are engaged."

"Engaged!" she exclaimed.

Marshall chuckled goodnaturedly. "Why do you sound so surprised? Did you think I was a confirmed bachelor?"

Johanna turned away so he wouldn't see her disappointment. She could hardly believe he was betrothed! For years she had dreamed of marrying Marshall, and she wasn't about to lose him to Amanda Mitchell! The last time she'd seen Amanda, they'd both been girls of thirteen. Johanna remembered that Amanda had been a little plain, but she might have grown into a beautiful woman.

Mustering a semblance of composure, Johanna faced Marshall and asked with a feigned smile, "When do you plan to marry?"

"We haven't set a date yet. In fact, we aren't even officially engaged. I'm giving a dinner party next week to announce our engagement." He appeared apologetic. "I didn't sent you an invitation because I realize you're still in mourning."

Johanna, determined to attend the party and evaluate her rival, said pressingly, "Marshall, please let me come. Papa would want me to go. It's your engagement party, and I should be there to represent Cedarbrook. You know how fond Papa was of you."

"Some people will question your presence. After all, you're still in mourning."

She lifted her chin defiantly. "I don't care if they do. Papa loved you like a son, and since he can't be there with you to share in your happiness, I shall take his place."

"Johanna, you are indeed a remarkable lady." He grinned suggestively. "If I weren't already in love, I'd most assuredly fall in love with you."

Johanna gloated inwardly, confident now that he'd soon be in love with her. She wouldn't let another woman stand in her way. She was determined to have Marshall Walker, and Amanda Mitchell and Robert Hawkins were merely obstacles to get rid of, one way or another.

His mood sobering, Marshall reminded her, "Also, it's now public knowledge that Jolene's mother was a mulatto slave. At times, people can be very rude and unfeeling. They are liable to talk about her in your presence. Considering how much you love your sister, the things they say might be painful."

"Yes—I know," she said sadly. "But I can't hide from the public indefinitely. Sooner or later I'll have to face their cutting remarks. I may as well get it over with."

His admiration for Johanna grew. He wondered why Sam Warrington had been cold and distant with Johanna when she was obviously both compassionate and courageous. Why had he favored Jolene over Johanna?

Smiling brightly, Johanna suggested, "I'll walk to the stables with you. I know you're eager to return home and get ready for your company. When you see Amanda, please give her my best. I don't remember her all that well, but I do remember that she was a very sweet girl."

"She still is, only now she's a sweet young lady."

Going to him and taking his arm, Johanna replied, "Yes, I'm sure she is. I'm looking forward to seeing her at your engagement party."

"I have a feeling you two will become good friends," he remarked, placing his hand over hers and leading the way out of the parlor.

Friends? Johanna wondered to herself. She hardly thought so!

Johanna was standing on the front porch watching Marshall leave. He had mounted his favorite horse, a magnificent black stallion. Walker's male servant, riding a short distance behind his master, was leading the spirited Morgan.

Johanna's gaze remained on the handsome planter as he rode farther down the long, meandering driveway. Angry tears smarted in her eyes as she thought about his involvement with Amanda Mitchell. All her life the people Johanna had loved most had denied their love in return: Sam Warrington,

Della, and eventually her brother. And now, Marshall Walker was infatuated with Amanda Mitchell! Again her love had been rejected. Well, she thought inflexibly, this time I'll not be denied. Marshall will fall in love with me. He will. I'll win his love one way or another, and I don't care who gets hurt in the process! Someday, Marshall will be mine!

Her determined thoughts were swept away as she suddenly caught sight of Robert's buggy entering the lane. She looked on as he and Marshall pulled up and exchanged a few words.

The lawyer waved goodbye to Walker. Then, slapping the reins against his horse, he continued his approach to the house.

Johanna was pleased to see Robert. She was lonely and also starved for a man's sexual advances. A passionate woman, she'd found abstaining from sex difficult indeed. Although she wasn't in love with Robert, she enjoyed going to bed with him. A small, dubious frown crossed her face. She couldn't be sure if the lawyer was a superb lover, for she had no one to compare him with. She had never been intimate with any man but Robert. She wondered about Marshall: was he a more proficient lover than Robert? She imagined herself naked in Marshall's arms, and the image aroused her deepest passion. Oh yes, she was sure making love with Marshall would be heaven, and he'd most certainly be the better lover!

As the lawyer reached the house, a young stablehand raced across the yard to take the gentleman's buggy and horse.

As he walked up the steps, Robert's eyes traveled hungrily over Johanna. Keeping to their plans, he had limited his visits to Cedarbrook and hadn't seen her in over a week. The young attorney was hopelessly in love with Johanna and had sincerely missed her.

Johanna hadn't especially missed him but she had missed his fawning. She loved attention and reveled in the way he doted on her.

Famished for attention and sex, Johanna barely gave Robert time to say hello before she ushered him into the house, up the stairs, and into her bedroom.

Hawkins, mistaking her anxiety for love, was deeply flattered and overjoyed to think that she desired him so intensely.

Johanna made love to Robert fervently and with a passion that sent his blood racing; however, her ardent response was deceptive, for as she made love to Robert, she imagined herself with Marshall.

Unlike at most plantation homes, the kitchen at Cedarbrook was an integral part of the house. Lazarus, sitting at the well-scrubbed table, watched Dixie absently as she stood at the cast-iron stove cooking dinner.

He glanced at the ceiling as though by looking up he could see through to the floor above. He knew his mistress was entertaining Mr. Hawkins in her bedroom. He was somewhat puzzled by her behavior. He'd heard her conversation with the overseer and knew that she had her cap set for Marshall Walker. Why then, was she in bed with the lawyer?

He smiled humorlessly. The woman was playing with fire, and he hoped she'd get burned. She intended to marry Walker, but in the meantime, she apparently planned to carry on her affair with Hawkins. Lazarus had no way of knowing if Marshall was succumbing to her charms, but he was positive that Robert was helplessly infatuated. And he still suspected that she and the lawyer had changed Warrington's will. He was sure Hawkins had agreed to be her partner in crime because he planned to marry her and live comfortably at Cedarbrook.

Lazarus' mirthless smile turned spiteful. If Johanna's intent to snare Walker was successful, how did she plan to get rid of Hawkins? After all, the lawyer had committed fraud to marry her. The mistress of Cedarbrook had indeed weaved herself a tangled web, and Lazarus prayed she'd get caught in the deceitful trap.

Dixie had turned away from the stove and was watching Lazarus thoughtfully. "What you thinkin' 'bout?" she asked curiously.

"Thinkin' 'bout Miz Johanna," he answered.

Dixie humphed. "Why you got her on your mind? Ain't you got nothin' better to think 'bout?"

Before Lazarus could reply, a loud, anxious knock sounded at the back door of the kitchen. Getting up, he went and answered it.

An elderly slave rushed inside. Her name was Ruby and she was the plantation's head laundress. As the woman broke into uncontrollable sobs, Dixie hurried to her, and taking her into her arms, asked, "What's wrong?"

Between heartrending cries, Ruby explained, "It's

181

my daughter Ida. She dead! Mista Sullivan, he come to my cabin last night and made her go with him to his house. Ida, she in love with Lucas, and she fought Mista Sullivan. Raped her, he did! Then he beat her 'fore he brought her back to me. She was hurtin' somethin' terrible. She died 'bout an hour ago. Lucas, he sayin' as how he gonna kill Mista Sullivan!"

Lazarus felt as if he'd aged ten years. He knew what was coming next and wasn't surprised when Ruby pushed away from Dixie's arms and turned to him. "Lazarus, you got to do somethin'! You got to talk to Miz Warrington and tell her what that overseer done to my little girl, then you got to tell her to get shet of Sullivan 'fore Lucas kills him! She listen to you, Lazarus. You a house servant and been here over thirty years!"

"I cain't do it," he moaned.

"What you mean, you cain't?" she exclaimed.

It was Dixie who answered. "The last time Lazarus tried to tell Miz Johanna 'bout Sullivan's meanness, she ordered him whipped."

"Is that why you was strung up?" Ruby asked Lazarus.

He nodded.

"You got to try again!" she insisted. "Maybe this time she listen to you. Mista Sullivan, he done killed my daughter! Miz Warrington, she'll care 'cause she done lost a valuable slave!"

"You might be right," Lazarus agreed uncertainly. "Miz Johanna, she ain't got no compassion, but she care 'bout her property. I talk to her when Mista Hawkins leaves."

"Promise?" Ruby pressed him.

"I promise," he mumbled, almost wishing he hadn't volunteered to help. He knew the chances were good that he'd be rewarded with another whipping. He wasn't a young man and doubted if he could now survive twenty lashes.

The moment Ruby left, Dixie turned on him anxiously. "Lazarus, is you crazy? That Miz Johanna, she liable to have you strung up for talkin' to her 'bout Mista Sullivan!"

Lazarus answered more curtly than he had intended, "Dixie, I know what I'm doin'! I gotta try and help our people! Mista Sullivan, if he get by with murderin' Ida, then what's gonna stop him from killin' again?"

Dixie, afraid for Lazarus, broke into heavy sobs. He drew her into his embrace and tried unsuccessfully to console her.

Lazarus waited until Robert left. Then, as Johanna went to the study, he followed and knocked on the door.

"Come in," she called.

Entering, the butler saw that she was pouring herself a glass of sherry.

"Is it time for dinner?" she asked, assuming that was why he'd come to her.

"No, mistress, ma'am," he replied.

Her brow furrowed testily. "That Dixie is too slothful! Can't she get dinner ready on time?"

"It still thirty more minutes 'fore dinner time."

"How dare you correct me?" she stormed. "If you aren't here to announce dinner, then what do you want?"

183

He swallowed heavily and perspiration beaded his forehead. "Miz Johanna, ma'am, Ruby's daughter is dead."

"Ruby? The laundress?" she asked sharply.

"Yes'm," he answered.

"How did her daughter die?"

"Ida, she was only 'bout fifteen, and she was a real pretty gal. Last night, Mista Sullivan, he take Ida to his house, where he rape her, then beat her real bad. Ruby, she come to the kitchen while Mista Hawkins still here and tell me and Dixie that Ida just died. I thought that you would want to know." Knowing it'd be useless to count on her compassion, he pressed the slave's value. "Ida, she was a prime wench, and you done lost a valuable slave."

At that moment a loud rapping sounded at the side door, and without invitation Sullivan barged in.

The burly overseer's eyes swept fleetingly over the pair, and ascertaining what was taking place, he said to Johanna, "Ma'am, I know what this nigra is tellin' you, but it is a bunch of lies. I didn't kill that gal—it was her boyfriend Lucas. Ida begged me to take her to my bed, and bein' a man, I didn't have the willpower to refuse. Lucas, he got all mad 'cause she came to me, and when she left my house and was on her way home, he beat her up. Now, these nigras are tryin' to put the blame on me. They're hopin' you'll dismiss me."

He pointed at Lazarus. "This-here nigra is the one who put the idea in their heads! He don't want me here at Cedarbrook."

Lazarus wanted to plead his innocence, but he knew there was nothing he could do. A Negro never openly contradicted a white person. His only chance

184

was to wait until Sullivan left, then try to convince his mistress that he wasn't guilty.

Johanna, remaining coldly calm, finished her glass of sherry before moving to the desk and sitting down. She didn't doubt that Lazarus told the truth and that Sullivan had indeed killed the young woman. But she didn't want to lose the overseer. Under his supervision Cedarbrook was turning a great profit. But she couldn't afford to lose prime slaves and wasn't about to allow the overseer to destroy valuable property.

She looked meaningfully at Sullivan. "Hereafter, I expect you to see to it personally that no more of my slaves are murdered. Do we understand each other, Mr. Sullivan?"

He understood only too well. She knew he was guilty as charged but was willing, this time, to overlook what he'd done. In the future he'd have to be more careful, for if it happened again, she'd not hesitate to fire him.

"Yes, ma'am," he replied. "I understand perfectly."

"Good!" she remarked haughtily. "I want Lucas put in chains, taken to the shack we use as a jail, and kept there until a slave trader passes by. Then I want him sold." She turned her stoic gaze upon the butler. "Lazarus, you haven't completely recovered from your last whipping, and yet you're already asking for another one. Considering your age, I seriously doubt you could live through it. Since you've been at Cedarbrook for so long, I've decided to show you leniency." Her gaze returned to Sullivan. "Lock Lazarus up in the jail with Lucas. He will stay there one week, and during that time he's to have nothing but bread and water."

"Yes'm," the overseer answered. He gestured to Lazarus. "Come on, you insolent nigger!"

Lazarus obediently followed the man through the door and outside. Although he dreaded his confinement, it was better than a whipping. He could survive a week's diet of bread and water; the lashing would most certainly have killed him.

The jail was located far from the house, and it took several minutes for them to reach the isolated shack. Quickly Sullivan locked Lazarus inside, then left to get Lucas.

Night had fallen and the jail was pitch-black, but finding his way to a corner, Lazarus sat down on the dirt floor. He leaned against the wall and his thoughts were soon drifting back over the years. It seemed that lately he was spending much of his time remembering the past. He supposed reminiscing went hand-in-hand with old age.

Staring into the dark, he conjured up the image of the woman he'd loved so many years ago. Time hadn't dimmed his memory, and he could visualize her as plainly as if only minutes had passed since he'd last seen her. He couldn't help but ponder why, after all these years, his thoughts now turned so often to the beautiful young woman he'd loved and lost. He wondered if she were still alive and if life had been relatively kind to her.

He sighed plaintively, and as her image remained in his mind, he murmured her name with deep, unforgotten love: "Lucy . . . Lucy."

Chapter Twelve

Lucy, standing on the front porch, watched the master of Willow Hill charging up the driveway on his roan. The slower moving buckboard was following, and she could make out two women sitting in the back of it. Apparently the master's trip to New Orleans had been successful, and she now had an assistant in the kitchen and Sabrina had a new maid.

Lucy was poised a respectful distance behind Sabrina and Alan, who were waiting dutifully to welcome their father home.

A slave boy had spotted Delmar and his servants before they'd turned into the drive that led to the main house. The youngster had raced up the lane shouting excitedly, "The masta's home! The masta's home!"

The boy's voice had carried into the house and Sabrina and Alan had stepped out onto the porch. The siblings weren't overly eager to greet their father, but because his arrival had been announced, they had no excuse not to welcome him.

Lucy's reason for joining them was routine, a perfunctory courtesy to her master.

Delmar, drawing closer, was pleased to see that his children were waiting. The sight of them lifted his spirits and made him feel proud. Although John was somewhat disappointed in his son's temperament, he thought him handsome; and in his opinion, his daughter, the apple of her father's eye, was more lovely than words could describe.

Delmar's gaze shifted to Lucy. He couldn't see her too well, for she was still poised behind Sabrina and Alan. Nonetheless his heart raced as he caught a glimpse of her. He wondered why, after all these years, she still had such a breathless effect on him. Why hadn't the passage of time cooled his passion for this beautiful, statuesque woman? His thoughts fled to Daniel: hell would freeze over before he'd sell Lucy. She'd remain his property until the day he died. Maybe he couldn't own her heart, but, by God, he owned her body!

Pulling up the stallion, Delmar dismounted, handed the reins to a stable boy, leaped the steps, and embraced his daughter. Turning to Alan, he asked anxiously, "Son, did everything go well during my absence?"

"Yes, Papa," he replied, hiding his resentment. He knew his father believed him too incompetent to run Willow Hill properly.

John looked at Lucy. Speaking crisply, he said, "I found a wench to assist you. You'll start training her immediately." He longed to take Lucy into his arms but couldn't very well do so in front of his children.

"Yes, masta, suh," she answered deferentially.

His eyes, communicating secretively with hers,

promised that later he'd receive her more warmly.

His visual message made no impression on Lucy. Years before she'd resigned herself to submitting to her master, and she accepted his fervent advances with little emotion. Her body was his to do with as he pleased; but her heart was her own.

George guided the buckboard to the house, and as he brought the conveyance to a stop, Delmar told Jolene and Mary Jane to come onto the porch.

They did so, pausing on the top step to await further instructions.

Surreptitiously, Jolene regarded the people standing before her. She looked first at Alan and was unnerved to find that his raking gaze was undressing her. Quickly she glanced away and set her vision upon his sister. Sabrina was perusing her, and the malicious jealousy Jolene saw in the woman's glare was more unnerving than Alan's lustful scrutiny. She turned her gaze cautiously to Lucy and found that the woman was studying her. A warm smile touched the servant's lips, and Jolene knew at once that this woman was her friend.

Delmar gestured toward Mary Jane. "This wench's name is Mary Jane, and she'll help Lucy in the kitchen. The other one is Jolene." He spoke to Sabrina. "She's your new maid."

Pouting, his daughter answered, "But Papa, she looks white. I don't like white nigras. They're an abomination."

"Nonsense," John disagreed. "She's that white because she's a quadroon."

"I don't want a maid who's as white as I am," was Sabrina's surly reply.

Alan chuckled. "Why don't you tell the truth?" he

189

baited his sister. "You don't want a maid who's prettier than you are."

"How dare you insinuate that a nigra is prettier than I am!" she snapped petulantly.

"Why not? It's the truth, isn't it?" he came back.

"That will be enough!" their father shouted. "Alan, apologize to your sister!"

Alan apologized, albeit reluctantly.

"Sabrina," Delmar began evenly, "I want you to give Jolene a chance. If her services displease you, I'll find you another maid."

Sabrina cast Jolene a catty glance. Then, bestowing a sweet smile upon her father, she answered pleasantly, "Very well, Papa. I'll give her a chance."

Jolene's face was inscrutable, but inwardly she was bristling. The Delmars' arrogance infuriated her. How dare they stand here and talk about her as if she weren't even present, or else too stupid to understand what they were saying? Suddenly remembering Cal had said that she'd been raised white, she wondered if she'd treated her slaves as shallowly as the Delmars. She hoped not.

Speaking to his son, John remarked sternly, "Alan, I want you to give me your word that you'll leave Jolene alone. If you hadn't gotten your sister's maid pregnant, it wouldn't have been necessary for me to find a wench to replace her."

"I won't bother her, Papa . . . I promise," Alan said insincerely.

"Lucy," John said, "take these wenches to the kitchen and give them something to eat, then see to it that they both bathe. Afterward, please show Jolene upstairs to Sabrina's room."

"Yes, Masta John." She motioned for Jolene and

190

Mary Jane to follow her. The kitchen was separated from the house, but a covered passageway joined the two structures. Lucy, however, chose to take the girls to the kitchen by way of the back door.

She walked briskly, forcing the women to pick up their pace in order to stay close.

Lucy opened the screen door, stepped back, and signaled for the girls to precede her inside.

Jolene, giving the huge kitchen a desultory glance, saw that it was meticulously clean.

"Sit yourselves down and I'll get you somethin' to eat," Lucy said. Placing an iron skillet on the stove, she continued, "My name's Lucy. Where you gals from?"

Mary Jane answered, "I used to belong to Mista Mayfield. He a doctor in Mississippi. Jolene's from a plantation called Cedarbrook."

Lucy whirled about. "Did you say Cedarbrook?"

"Yes'm," Mary Jane replied.

The woman gasped sharply, and for a moment the girls thought she might pass out.

"Are you all right?" Jolene asked, concerned.

Going to sit beside Jolene, Lucy asked breathlessly, "Is Lazarus still at Cedarbrook?" Large tears filled her eyes as she whispered almost inaudibly, "He's still alive, ain't he?"

Jolene was at a loss. Lazarus? Who was Lazarus?

Impatient with Jolene's blank expression, Lucy declared, "Gal, why are you lookin' at me like you're daft? Ain't there a Lazarus at Cedarbrook? Lord, I bet that Mista Warrington sold him! How long was you there?"

Jolene turned to Mary Jane, her eyes beseeching her for help.

"She cain't answer your questions," Mary Jane

191

told Lucy.

"What you mean? Why cain't she answer?"

"She don't remember."

"Don't remember what?"

Jolene explained, "I have amnesia." Deciding she had no other choice but to trust Delmar's cook to guard her secret, she told her everything.

Lucy listened intently. She believed Jolene but was heartsick to learn that this young woman could give her no information concerning Lazarus.

Finishing her revelation, Jolene said, "So I don't know if this man called Lazarus is at Cedarbrook or not. His name seems vaguely familiar to me, but I don't know if it's because I knew him, or if it's merely because his name is biblical."

Lucy sighed despondently. "Maybe it's best that I don't hear nothin' 'bout Lazarus. He part of my past, and that's where he oughta stay."

"Was you in love with 'im?" Mary Jane asked.

"I sure was." She shrugged. "But that was a long time ago."

"Did Lazarus live here at Willow Hill?" Jolene queried.

"He did 'til Masta John sell 'im to Mista Warrington."

Jolene said encouragingly, "Doctor Mayfield said that amnesia like mine is usually temporary. Soon I'll probably remember everything, and then I'll be able to let you know if Lazarus is still at Cedarbrook."

Lucy looked closely at Jolene. "I don't think you got colored blood in you."

"Why do you think that?"

"I know quadroons when I see one, and you ain't

no quadroon."

Desperately, Jolene cried, "Then why was I part of Atkins' coffle? He swore to me that my father's will pronounced me a slave!"

Slowly Lucy got up from her chair and returned to the stove. "Honey, I ain't got reply to that. You got to get your memory back, then you'll know all the answers." She turned and faced Jolene. "Will you take some advice?"

"Yes, of course."

"When you 'round others, don't talk so refined-like. The other slaves, they gonna feel intimidated, and the Delmars, they ain't gonna approve of you talkin' like a white lady."

"Mr. Delmar gave me the same advice, but I keep forgetting to change."

"You best start rememberin'," Lucy pressed.

"I will," Jolene replied. "Lucy?"

"Yes?"

"When I get my memory back, I hope I'll have good news about Lazarus."

"So do I," the woman answered. "And you needn't worry, I won't say nothin' to no one 'bout you havin' amnesia."

John waited until after dinner before sending a servant to the kitchen with a message that he wished to see Lucy. When she arrived in the study, Delmar was seated at his desk, sipping a glass of brandy.

"Did you want to see me, Masta John?"

"Yes. Close the door."

She complied and he put down his drink, leaned back in his chair, and looked appreciatively at the woman who, after thirty-odd years, still stirred his desire.

Lucy's beauty was classical, and at the age of forty-eight she was still striking. Her flawless skin was tobacco-brown, and her silky black hair fell to her shoulders in soft waves. She had a high forehead, a slightly aquiline nose, and finely shaped lips. She was tall for a woman, and her statuesque frame was well developed. Despite her plain butternut dress, she exuded an aura of grace and beauty.

John Delmar was in love with Lucy. It was an emotion that he himself was not aware of, for he believed unalterably that a white man couldn't love a colored wench. He could desire her and be fond of her, but he couldn't possibly feel any emotion so strong as love. That blacks were inferior to whites had been deeply inbred in Delmar, and he held so tenaciously to his conviction that he was unaware that his feelings toward Lucy were governed by love. He believed emphatically that he was merely fond of her because she had been his bed wench and a loyal servant for so many years.

Placing his glass on the desk, John stood and walked over to Lucy. Delmar was quite distinguished looking. His dark hair and full moustache were streaked with silver, and his build, although it showed signs of middle age, was for the most part still firm and muscular. Dressed in gray trousers, a rose-colored smoking jacket, and a ruffled white shirt, he was elegant and handsome.

"Lucy, I have some good news for you: Kurt and Daniel have returned."

"My boy's come home?" she gasped, her alarm evident.

"I saw Kurt in New Orleans. He and Daniel plan to stop at Willow Hill on their way to Heritage Manor. They should be here tomorrow, or the day after, at the latest."

John had expected Lucy to be overjoyed, and her apparent consternation puzzled him.

"What's wrong?" he asked. "Don't you want to see Daniel?"

"He shouldn't have come back!" she cried. "The south no place for him! He's free!"

She was trembling. Placing his hands on her shoulders, John said anxiously, "Lucy, I don't understand why you're so upset."

There were times when Lucy disregarded their master-slave relationship, and this was one of those times. "There's many whites in the south who resent a nigra who's been set free! Daniel's safer in Texas surrounded by wild Indians than he is here in the midst of white men who consider themselves civilized."

"As long as Daniel remembers his place and behaves himself, he'll be in no danger."

Lucy turned away and went to the door. She couldn't continue discussing her son with John Delmar; the man's stoic attitude toward Daniel was too infuriating, and she was afraid she might say or do something she'd later regret.

"I didn't give you permission to leave!" John grumbled angrily.

Unintimidated, Lucy opened the door before looking back at him. "I cain't stay, masta, suh. I want to be alone so's I can think 'bout my boy comin' home."

Delmar acquiesced. "Very well, Lucy—I understand. Tonight when everyone has retired, I want

195

you to come to my room."

Sharing her master's bed was the last thing she wanted to do. "Yes, Masta John," she answered softly. Then with a proud lift to her chin, she left the room with quiet dignity.

It had been a long, exhausting day for Jolene. She and the others hadn't reached Willow Hill until early afternoon, and she'd been fairly tired from the trip. But Sabrina hadn't taken that into account. Quite the contrary, the young woman had piled several chores on Jolene, demanding that she finish them before bedtime. In order to complete her work on schedule, Jolene had worked nonstop without even having supper.

Pampered and spoiled, Sabrina Delmar refused to do anything for herself, and Jolene had to wait on her hand and foot. Her new mistress was not only unbelievably lazy, but also overbearing. She issued orders and expected to have them carried out immediately.

By the time Sabrina had dismissed Jolene for the night, she was so worn-out that she was too tired to even go to the kitchen and fix herself a bite to eat.

She and Mary Jane were to share a small cabin situated a short distance behind the kitchen. Moving sluggishly, Jolene went out the back door and headed for the isolated shack. The night air was refreshing, and Jolene welcomed the cool breeze on her face.

The full moon, resplendent in a cloudless sky, shone down, casting dull shadows across the land. The chirping of crickets was so loud that their shrill music seemed to come from every direction, and in

the distance the soft neighing of horses inter-
mittently mingled with the insect sounds.

As Jolene entered the cabin, she was grateful that
she didn't have to sleep in a bedroom adjacent to
Sabrina's. She was thankful for the small, crude
shack where she could get away from her domineer-
ing mistress.

The interior was dark, but the moon shining
through the open window gave her enough light to
see. The cabin was furnished with a double bed and
chest of drawers. Mary Jane was asleep, but Jolene
didn't have to worry about waking her, for the cabin
had a dirt floor.

Quickly Jolene slipped out of her dress and shoes,
then lay down carefully on her side of the bed.

Sleepy, she closed her eyes. But as she did, Kurt's
image came back to haunt her: if he were to visit
Willow Hill, would it be possible for her to avoid
him? Delmar's home was huge, but Jolene knew that
practically speaking, it was unlikely that she could
stay hidden from Kurt if he were at Willow Hill. She
hoped he wouldn't visit, for she didn't want him to
see her as a slave. She'd rather he'd remember her as
Atkins' sister and as the woman who shared a special
moment in time with him.

To keep from crying she directed her thoughts
away from Kurt and concentrated instead on
escaping. She'd wait for the right opportunity to
present itself, then run away and return to Cedarbrook. She still believed that the sight of her former
home would revive her memory.

She was so fatigued that her thoughts of escape
quickly gave way to drowsiness. Exhausted, she
slept soundly through the night.

Chapter Thirteen

Jolene, sitting in a chair in her mistress's bedroom, was busy mending a formal gown when Sabrina entered.

"Put your sewing away for now," Sabrina ordered. "I want you to help me undress. I take a nap this time every day. While I'm resting, you may go to your cabin and rest also, or you may use your leisure time to visit with the other servants. I don't care how you spend your time as long as you return *here* in two hours to wake me."

"Yes, Miz Sabrina," Jolene answered respectfully. She was finding it hard to stay subdued, for she was elated by the possibility of having two hours to do with as she pleased. She helped the other woman undress, then handed her a dressing gown.

Slipping into the sheer garment, Sabrina sat down at her dressing table and ordered, "Brush my hair."

As Jolene did so, Sabrina admired her reflection in the mirror. She was proud of her beauty, and she used it effectively to manipulate men. Although she'd received numerous marriage proposals, she hadn't found the man she wanted to marry. A small, distasteful frown crossed her face as she thought about all the beaux who had practically begged for her hand. None of them had measured up to her ideal. Her future husband, besides being wealthy, must be extraordinarily handsome, possess an aura of mystery, and be ultra virile. So far she hadn't found a suitor who met these qualifications.

Sabrina Delmar was as beautiful as she was selfish. Her flaming red hair shone with radiant highlights and cascaded to her waist. Her graceful frame was voluptuous, and her smooth complexion was blemish-free.

As she continued to study her reflection, Sabrina happened to glance at Jolene, who stood behind her briskly brushing her mistress's hair. Taking a moment to regard her new maid, Sabrina found herself resenting Jolene's astounding beauty. Furthermore, Jolene didn't look like a Negro—her skin was too pale.

Delmar's daughter was always jealous of other women's beauty, and she disliked having a maid who was not only exceptionally lovely, but who also appeared to be white. She compared her own beauty to Jolene's and realized that some men might find Jolene the more attractive. Anger welled within her. But though the wench might be beautiful, she was just a slave, despite her ivory complexion!

Sabrina looked away from Jolene and returned to admiring her own reflection. Comparing herself to a quadroon was foolish. The woman was no threat to her! She was the mistress, Jolene the slave. If the wench displeased her or angered her, she had the power to order her strung up and whipped.

"That will be enough!" Sabrina snapped, ordering Jolene to stop brushing. Standing, she continued sharply, "The next time you brush my hair, do it more gently! My scalp is tingling from your abuse!"

"Yes, ma'am," Jolene replied softly, gritting her teeth to hold back a retort.

"After you turn back the covers, you may leave," Sabrina remarked.

Jolene went and drew back the spread of the large mahogany bed, and she couldn't help noticing what an exquisite piece of furniture it was. It had been ordered specially from Charleston. The intricate posts supported a wide canopy, and the inlaid cornice with finials was proof the bed was expensive.

Jolene left the room quickly, closing the door behind her. She had started down the long hall toward the servants' stairway when suddenly Alan Delmar seemed to appear out of thin air. The unexpected sight brought her to an abrupt halt.

Smiling shrewdly, he said quietly, "I've been waiting for Sabrina to dismiss you. I know she takes a nap this time every day, and I also know that you have two hours to pass. I've decided how you're going to spend those two hours: I want you to come with me to my room."

He reached for her arm, bur avoiding his touch, Jolene said firmly, "Masta John, he says you ain't supposed to bother me."

"What Papa doesn't know won't anger him."

Lurching incredibly quickly, he caught her by the wrist. Twisting free and forgetting to use her slave dialect, Jolene screamed, "Don't touch me! If you dare accost me again, I'll report your conduct to your father!"

Alan, gaping, was too flabbergasted to stop her from rushing past him and onward to the servants' stairs. He'd never heard a colored wench speak in such a way. Apparently she had received some form of education, and when she wanted to, she could speak as properly as a lady. He wondered if his father knew he'd purchased a slave who wasn't an illiterate. He debated telling Delmar, then decided against it. He smiled slyly—it'd be best not to say anything to cause his father to suspect he might be taking an interest in Sabrina's new maid; for Alan had every intention of getting Jolene into his bed.

It was a warm, pleasant day and Jolene decided to spend her leisure time outdoors. She hurried from the house, crossed the fields, and headed toward the fertile meadow that was lcoated on Delmar property.

The summer breeze caressed her unbound hair as she moved gracefully through the glade, and when she came to a brook, she gratefully sat down on the bank.

The warm day was a bit overcast, and as the sun hid behind a cloud, Jolene lay back on the grass and gazed upward at the brilliant blue sky. She sighed disconsolately as she thought about her amnesia. If only she could remember! Doctor Mayfield said her loss of memory was only temporary, so why hadn't she recovered yet?

Lucy had said that she wasn't a quadroon. Could the woman be right? Remembering everything Cal had told her about her life at Cedarbrook and her sister Johanna, Jolene wondered if she were white—and perhaps the true mistress of Cedarbrook. Had Atkins and her half-sister somehow tricked her?

She frowned impatiently. Of course the two hadn't performed any trickery—if she were white, and Sam Warrington's legal daughter, how could they manage to pass her as a slave? Such a thing was incomprehensible.

Jolene turned her thoughts to escape. She saw no reason to procrastinate. Tomorrow, while Sabrina was napping, she'd sneak away from Willow Hill. That way she'd have a two-hour head start before she was missed.

She knew she had to make a more detailed plan, but at the moment she was too tired to concentrate. Clearing her mind, she closed her eyes and was soon sound asleep.

Kurt had bought a buckboard in New Orleans and two horses. Now, as he traveled toward Willow Hill, Daniel was driving the wagon and he sat beside him. Their two saddle ponies were tied at the rear.

"Aren't we on Delmar's property?" Daniel asked, finding the terrain familiar.

Kurt nodded. "We've been on his land for the past couple of miles."

"Delmar has a spread so large most Texans would envy it."

Restless from riding in the slow-moving buck-

202

board, Kurt said, "I think I'll ride horseback and cut through the woods to Willow Hill. Do you mind?"

"No. Go ahead. I'll see you later."

Daniel stopped the wagon and Kurt jumped to the ground, walked back to his hourse, untied it, and mounted. Waving to his friend, he urged his steed off the main road and into the surrounding woodlands.

Kurt had ridden only a short distance when he came to the peaceful meadow where Jolene, still asleep, lay beside the brook.

Kurt drew up his horse abruptly. Dismounting, he walked stealthily toward Jolene. What was she doing here? He had believed he'd never see her again, and coming upon her *so* unexpectedly had his head spinning.

Moving silently, he knelt at her side. Seeing that she slept soundly, he felt a smile tug at his lips. He started to waken her but decided instead to enjoy the luxury of admiring her loveliness. Captivated by her beauty, he studied her high cheekbones, exquisitely dainty nose, and full, kissable lips. Her bangs fell impishly across her forehead and enhanced her guileless beauty. Unable to resist such a beautiful vision, he bent his head and pressed his mouth to hers. "Wake up, Sleeping Beauty."

She awoke instantly, and as she gazed into the eyes of the man she loved, she whispered, "I must be dreaming."

"If you're dreaming, then so am I," he replied huskily, lying beside her and taking her into his arms.

Jolene's better judgment warned her to push

203

away, get to her feet, and run. She was sure her lover was on his way to Willow Hill, where he'd certainly learn that she wasn't Atkins' sister, but a slave. But as Kurt pressed a hungry, heart-stopping kiss to her lips, all her sanity seemed to desert her. Lacing her arms about his neck, she fervently returned his ardor.

Meanwhile, Kurt knew that he should break their embrace and demand an explanation. She had lied to him about being Atkins' sister, and he deserved the truth. However, as her lips continued to respond sweetly, he decided his questions could wait.

Her kiss set him on fire and her closeness inflamed him. He was amazed that a woman he'd known such a short time could so easily arouse his deepest passion. Where this lovely vixen was concerned, he had no self-restraint, no will power. He was putty in her hands.

When he lifted her dress, she didn't object, for she wanted him as desperately as he wanted her. It pleased him when she offered no protest as he removed her undergarment. His fiery little country chit was indeed a woman after his heart. God, he loved her passion!

Tantalizingly his fingers played along the inside of her legs before moving upward to cup the dark triangle between her delicate thighs.

Finding his touch thrilling, Jolene arched as his probing finger sent her passion swirling to ecstatic heights of sensation and plumbing her to new depths of rapture.

Rising up, Kurt looked adoringly at her, admiring the cascade of black hair on the grass, the prominence of her delicate cheekbones, and the deep blue of her eyes.

"Love me," she whispered throatily. "I need you to love me."

"I know, my beauty, for I also need your love." He lowered his head and covered her mouth with his. Her hand went to the nape of his neck, pressing him ever closer.

Consumed with desire, Kurt hastily removed his boots and loosened his trousers. Kneeling between her parted legs, he murmured shakily, "One of these days, Sweetheart, we're going to make love more properly. The first time, I thought you were a married woman and took you out of anger as well as passion. This time, I feel we must hurry before we're discovered. But someday. . . ."

Jolene was sure that that "someday" would never come, for if things went as planned, she'd never see him again. Certain that he was visiting Willow Hill, she hoped to avoid him for the remainder of the day. Then, tomorrow, when Sabrina was taking her customary nap, she'd run away.

She watched through love-glazed eyes as Kurt slipped his trousers past his muscular hips, and the sight of his hard desire sent her heart pounding with anticipation.

He entered her slowly, pressing himself into her warm depths and as she moaned aloud with pleasure, he lunged forward, sinking deep within her.

Her legs wrapped about his waist, and he drove into her wildly, demandingly. Equaling his passion, she met each exciting thrust until their mutual climax emerged swiftly, overwhelming them with blinding, sweet release.

Kurt kissed her endearingly before moving to stretch out at her side. His breathing was labored and it took a moment for it to slow back to normal. Then, sitting upright, he drew on his trousers. Handing Jolene her undergarment, he said, "You'd better put these back on before someone comes along."

As she took his advice, her thoughts ran turbulently. She knew he'd now start flooding her with questions. He'd want to know why she was here on John Delmar's property and would probably ask about Atkins.

Deciding her best recourse was to offer an explanation before he could begin questioning her, she reverted to Cal's dialect and said, "I guess you're a-wonderin' what I'm doin' here. My brother and me, we live close by, and. . . ."

"Tell me, my beauty," he interrupted forcefully. "Are you a habitual liar, or do you only lie to me?"

"Wh-what?" she stammered.

"The morning after you visited my hotel room, I went to the slave jail looking for Atkins. I wanted his permission to take you to dinner. I learned from the jailkeep that Atkins had left, and I also learned that he doesn't have a sister."

Flustered, Jolene looked away. What was she to do now? Should she tell him the truth? No . . . no! Her better judgment cried. *If I tell him I'm a slave, he'll think even less of me! Furthermore, he'll probably be so angry that he'll report everything I've done to Delmar!*

Grabbing his boots and slipping them on, Kurt asked testily, "Why did you lie to me?"

Thinking quickly, Jolene answered, "I'm sorry I lied—I am. But I was ashamed to tell you the truth."

"Why?" he asked, watching her closely.

"Cal and me, we was goin' to New Orleans to get married. I changed my mind 'bout marryin' him, and I was runnin' away from him when I slipped into the hotel. Cal, he's got a terrible temper, and I was afraid of him. When I left the hotel, he caught up to me. He took me back to the hotel where we was stayin', and 'cause he was mad at me, he went to a saloon. While he was gone, I snuck out of town. I hitched a ride with the money you gave me."

"Why didn't you tell me you were supposed to marry Atkins?"

She shrugged. "Thought you might think bad of me 'cause I was runnin' out on him. Men always stick together."

Kurt wasn't sure he believed her, but he decided for now to take her at her word. "What are you doing here?"

"Live close by, I do. My family has a farm up the road a piece. I come here all the time."

Kurt and Daniel had passed quite a few rundown, poverty-stricken farms on the road to Willow Hill, and Kurt supposed she and her family lived on one of them. "What is your name?" he asked.

"Jo—" She caught herself. She couldn't tell him her name! He might mention it to Delmar.

"Jo?" he asked archly. "Is that short for Josephine?"

"Yes," she replied unhesitatingly.

He smiled. "That's a big name for such a small lady."

"Reckon that's why my Ma and Pa call me Jo.

What's your name?"

"Kurt Spencer."

"Kurt," she repeated. "I like your name. It seems to fit you." She got quickly to her feet. "I gotta go. My Ma's expectin' me back to help with supper."

"When will I see you again?" he asked, standing.

"I don't know," she mumbled.

"How about tomorrow? We can meet here, or I can go to your home."

"I reckon I can meet you." Jolene hated lying to him, but what else could she do?

"Good. We'll meet here . . . same time?"

"Sure, that'll be fine. Are you visitin' Mista Delmar?"

"Yes, I am."

"Don't say nothin' to him 'bout seein' me here. He might get mad 'bout me bein' on his property. Rich planters like Mista Delmar ain't got no use for us poor folks."

"I won't say anything."

She was reluctant to leave him, but knowing it'd soon be time to awaken Sabrina, she had no choice but to go.

He held out his arms to her, and she went into his embrace. She snuggled intimately, wishing she could stay this way forever. If only she were free to love him!

Relishing her nearness, Kurt drew her closer. Finding her again had lifted his spirits, and this time he was determined not to lose her. He didn't understand why this country chit had stolen his heart, but for some unexplained reason, she'd come to mean everything to him. He was eager to know her better and to make love to her again.

Stepping back and placing a hand under her chin, he tilted her face up to his. "You won't stand me up tomorrow, will you?"

"Of course not," she fibbed.

He studied her thoughtfully. "I wish I could believe you, but I have a feeling that you might vanish from my life like an apparition."

She smiled, and it was such a beautiful smile that it went straight to Kurt's heart. "Kiss me good-bye?" she whispered.

"I'll gladly kiss you, but it won't be good-bye. That word will never be used between us."

He kissed her deeply; then, twisting out of his arms, Jolene lifted the hem of her long skirt and ran gracefully toward the main road. As soon as she was out of his sight, she circled about and headed back in the direction of Willow Hill.

Chapter Fourteen

Daniel drove the buckboard down the long, mean-dering lane that led to the Willow Hill mansion. The stillness that hung over the place came as no surprise to him, for he remembered that the Delmars, following the noonday meal, always rested for a few hours. During this time the yard slaves and house servants were extra quiet so they'd not disturb their owners.

Guiding the wagon to the back of the house, Daniel pulled up the horses, secured the brake, and jumped to the ground. His heart beat faster at the thought of seeing his mother. He could hardly believe ten years had passed! He felt uneasy that he had been so long in returning, but it had taken him all this time to save enough money to buy Lucy's freedom.

Anxious to see his mother, Daniel swiftly walked to the back door, opened it, and stepped into the kitchen.

Lucy was standing with her back to the door,

drying the lunch dishes.

For a moment Daniel looked lovingly at his mother. He noticed that she'd put on some weight since he'd last seen her, but she carried the extra pounds well and her tall, graceful frame was still beautiful.

"Mama?" he said, his deep voice breaking with emotion.

She froze at the sound of it.

"Mama?" he called again.

Slowly Lucy put down the plate she was drying. Then, turning about, she looked at him through tear-glazed eyes. A sob caught in her throat. "Daniel! Thank the good Lord you alive and well! But you shouldn't a come back!"

Crossing the floor in two long strides, he took his mother into his arms. "Mama, didn't you know that someday I'd come back?"

Clinging to her son, Lucy cried, "It dangerous for you here in the south!"

"Nonsense, Mama," he replied lightly, hugging her close.

Stepping out of his embrace, Lucy held him at arms' length as she admired the man her son had become. Daniel was superbly handsome. His tall, muscular physique was well-proportioned, his features were finely defined, and his dark hair fell across his brow in soft ringlets. Her son's good looks heightened Lucy's fears for his safety, for she knew if he were a slave, he'd be called a "fancy," and on a vendue block he'd be worth three or four thousand dollars. Slave stealers frequented the rural roads in Alabama, and if they were to come upon

211

Daniel, they'd certainly seize him. His freedom papers would be worthless, for these thieves would destroy the manumission document.

Leading his mother to the kitchen table, Daniel seated her, then took a chair for himself. The minutes ticked away as he talked about his life in Texas and about his ranch. In turn, she told him that her life had changed little since she'd last seen him.

"Is Delmar good to you?" he now asked.

"Masta John treats me like he always did."

Daniel frowned. "Do you mean he still expects you to share his bed?"

She didn't answer, but her silence told him it was true.

"I should think by now he'd have a much younger woman. Don't misunderstand what I'm implying. You're still very lovely, but. . . ."

"I know what you mean," she interrupted. "Most mastas want young wenches in their beds." She shrugged. "But Masta John, he ain't never wanted no woman but me."

Daniel's brow furrowed in deep thought. "Mama, is Delmar in love with you?"

She stared at him as if he'd lost his mind. "White mastas don't fall in love with their bed wenches!"

"I wish you wouldn't refer to yourself as a bed wench! The term is degrading!"

Sighing heavily, Lucy reached across the table and placed a hand over Daniel's. "Son, that education you got liberated you, and Masta Kurt, he freed you all legal-like. But I ain't emancipated; I been a slave all my life. I cain't think like you do."

Her hand tightened on his. "Daniel, don't you see that the south's no place for you? You got to go back to Texas!"

"I'm not leaving without you," he declared.

Lucy was incredulous. "I cain't go back with you! Masta John, he won't let me!"

"I hope to buy your freedom, but if Delmar refuses to cooperate, I'll find a way to steal you."

"No!" she objected. "I cain't let you take such a risk! Daniel, Honey, don't you realize it'd be impossible for us to get away? We get caught for sure, then you get thrown in jail. You a colored man, and the white judge, he send you to prison for life!"

"Mama, I'm willing to take my chances!"

"Well, I ain't willin'! I won't let you risk your own freedom to try and gain mine! Son, you cain't make me run away with you." She leaned back in her chair, crossed her arms over her chest, and uttered emphatically, "I won't go!"

"Mama, please!" he implored.

"My answer is 'no.' and you cain't say or do nothin' to change my mind."

A trace of tears came to his eyes. "But Mama, don't you want to be free?"

Swallowing back the lump that had risen in her throat, Lucy replied with dignity, "Of course I longs for freedom. But I ain't gonna get that freedom till the day I die and go to heaven. Then I be free."

At that moment the back door opened and Mary Jane came into the kitchen. The day that Kurt and Daniel had taken Jolene to Doctor Mayfield's house, Mary Jane hadn't been home, so Daniel was seeing her for the first time.

Getting to his feet, Daniel swept his gaze appreciatively over the young woman. Then, as their eyes met, he was disappointed to see that she was watching him with indifference.

"Mary Jane," Lucy began, "this is my son Daniel. He lives in Texas." She added with pride, "He's not only free—he's educated, too."

Mary Jane went to the stove and poured herself a cup of coffee. "His education didn't make him too smart; otherwise, he wouldn't have come back to Alabama."

Daniel chuckled. "Why do you say that?"

She turned to face him. "You stay 'round these parts, and you'll lose your freedom. White mastas, they don't hanker to free nigras, especially when they's prime bucks."

"That's exactly what I've been tryin' to tell 'im." Lucy remarked with a harrumph.

Daniel returned to his chair. He was finding his homecoming more and more disappointing; he had thought Lucy would be overjoyed to see him, but he knew that worry for his safety was taking priority over any happiness she might be feeling.

"Has you had your lunch yet?" Lucy asked him.

He shook his head, his jovial mood plunging.

Standing, Lucy said briskly, "I'll go to the smokehouse and get a slice of ham, then come back and fix you somethin' to eat."

"I'll go for you," Mary Jane offered.

"Thanks, Honey, but you stay here and keep Daniel company." Lucy stepped to the pantry and picked up a basket. "I also need to gather up some vegetables for supper."

214

The moment Lucy was gone, Daniel gave in to his sadness. Placing his elbows on the table, he leaned his head into his hands. "God!" he groaned. "Was I wrong to come back?"

Mary Jane watched him uncertainly. She didn't trust men; it seemed they'd always used her, or else mistreated her. But they'd all been white whereas this man was a Negro. Nonetheless, Mary Jane held herself at bay and offered Daniel no sympathy or support.

Leaning back in his chair, he turned to look at her. She was startled to see that his face was streaked with tears.

"I thought Mama would be happy to see me," he said brokenly. "I've been gone ten years. I'd have come back sooner, but I wanted to make enough money to buy her from Delmar. I want to take Mama to Texas. I have a ranch. It's not too prosperous right now, but someday it will be."

Mary Jane took a sip of her coffee. She wasn't sure what she should say. The man's consternation was evident, and he seemed to want her opinion. "I reckon Lucy's happy to see you again. But she's probably afraid somethin' bad will happen to you. The South's full of evil men who hate free nigras. Don't you realize you in danger?"

"I'm not exactly alone. My friend and former master, Kurt Spencer, is traveling with me. His name and white skin afford me all the protection I need."

"Then you best stick close to 'im, or else you might get in trouble."

Putting thoughts of his mother aside, Daniel

suggested with a smile, "Mary Jane, come sit down and tell me about yourself."

She shook her head. "I don't wanna talk 'bout myself."

"All right," he relented. "Then we'll talk about something else."

She eyed him suspiciously. "What you wantin' from me?"

"Only your company," he answered.

Conceding with reservations, she went to the table and sat down. Smiling tentatively, she admitted, "I didn't even know that Lucy had a son."

He was surprised. "She's never spoken to you about me?"

"No—but I ain't been here very long. Only a couple of days." Recognizing his white origin, she asked, "Has you got a white pappy?"

He nodded affirmatively. "I've never seen my father, though. He was an overseer here at Willow Hill. From what I understand, Delmar's wife dismissed him before I was born. I used to ask my mother about him, but she always avoided my questions. For some reason she preferred not to talk about the man who sired me." He expelled a deep sigh. "I imagine the man forced himself on her, and Mama probably found talking about him unpleasant, so I let the subject rest and stopped probing her for answers she didn't seem to want to give."

Mary Jane asked him about his life in Texas, and the time passed pleasantly as he described some of his and Kurt's western escapades, plus an account of how they had come to own their ranches.

Mary Jane listened with fascination. She could

216

barely grasp the wonders that came with freedom. This man who had been a slave now owned property, and more stupendously, he was free to make his own decisions! As Daniel told her about his life, Mary Jane's heart filled with envy.

Lucy returned, and with Mary Jane's assistance, Daniel's meal was soon prepared. He had just finished eating when Delmar came into the kitchen.

Lucy and Mary Jane got respectfully to their feet, and Delmar waited for Daniel to do likewise. When it became apparent that he wasn't about to, Delmar told him irritably, "This is my house, and I demand proper courtesy. Stand up!"

Reluctantly Daniel pushed back his chair and got to his feet.

Speaking to Lucy, Delmar remarked, "I suppose this is Daniel."

"Yes, Masta John," she replied.

Admiring Daniel's good looks, John continued, "He's changed a lot in the past ten years—filled out into a prime buck."

"Man," Daniel corrected, his voice barely above a whisper.

"What did you say?" Delmar snapped.

"I'm not a buck, I'm a *man.*"

Daniel's curt remark shocked Mary Jane, for she'd never heard a Negro talk back to a white person.

Lucy, seeing her master's smoldering rage, said quickly, "Masta John, Daniel didn't mean no disrespect. He's been away too long, and he's forgot his manners." She turned to her son, her eyes pleading with him. "Daniel, you apologize to

217

Masta John!" She grasped his arm, her fingers digging into his flesh. "Please!"

For his mother's sake, he grudgingly apologized.

Delmar, still perturbed, asked gruffly, "Where's Kurt?"

"You mean he isn't here?" Daniel asked, surprised.

"Address me respectfully!" the planter demanded.

Swallowing his pride, Daniel repeated with a bitter undertone, "You mean he isn't here, Mista Delmar, suh?"

"If I had seen him, I wouldn't be asking about him, would I?"

"He was tired of traveling in the buckboard and decided to ride horseback. He cut through the woods, Mista Delmar, suh."

"Well, if he isn't here soon, I'll go look for him." John wondered why Kurt was so late arriving. Surely nothing had happened to him. "Daniel, you may take your buckboard and horses to the stables. Do you remember Abe?"

"Yes, suh," he answered. Daniel and Abe had been boyhood playmates until Delmar had sold Daniel to Kurt's father.

"Abe is now in charge of the stables, and he has his own cabin. You can stay with him until you and Kurt leave."

Opening the door to the covered passageway between the kitchen and the house, Delmar left.

"Daniel," Lucy began anxiously, "you got to remember you in Alabama now. You cain't talk to white people like you's their equal."

"Your mama's right," Mary Jane said. "If you get

white gentlemens angry, they liable to string you up and whip you, or else tar and feather you. When I belonged to Mista Brownlee, I saw a Negro man tarred and feathered. It was an ugly sight."

"I'll try and remember to keep my place," Daniel replied. He drew his mother into his arms. "Don't worry, Mama. Nothing's going to happen to me."

"Lord, I wish I could believe that!" she moaned. "But I know I ain't gonna rest till you's back in Texas."

And you'll be there with me, Daniel swore silently. He was still determined to free his mother, or die trying.

Sabrina, wanting to look especially pretty for dinner, stood at her armoire, trying to decide which gown she should wear. There were dozens of evening dresses from which to choose, and after discarding several, she finally made her choice and placed it carefully on the bed.

Turning to look at Jolene, she remarked haughtily, "This gown is exquisite, don't you think? Papa bought it for me last year in St. Louis."

Jolene put away the last of Sabrina's clean laundry, then going to admire the gown, she answered, "Yes, ma'am. It's very lovely." Tentatively she reached down to run her fingers across its silky softness. The sea-green dress was made with gauffered flounces around the hem, and a heavily fringed white sash was tied about its waist. It had been designed to be worn with the hoops that were now so popular.

"I want to look ravishing tonight," Sabrina said. "Kurt Spencer arrived this afternoon and is planning to stay for a couple of days." Her gray eyes sparkled. "He's a very handsome bachelor."

Going to the armoire, Jolene began picking up Sabrina's discarded gowns and hanging them neatly.

After leaving the meadow Jolene had managed to slip into the house through the back door and return in time to awaken her mistress. She knew Kurt had arrived a short time later, for Delmar had sent Mary Jane to Sabrina with a message that she was to come downstairs and greet their guest.

Jolene wasn't surprised that Kurt had apparently made quite an impression on Sabrina. He was an exceptionally handsome man, and she was sure most women would find him irresistible.

Sabrina went to the dressing table, sat down, and as she absently brushed her hair, turned her thoughts to the past. The last time she'd seen Kurt before he'd left for Texas, she had been nine years old and he had been twenty-one. Kurt and Daniel had visited Willow Hill so Daniel could say goodbye to Lucy. Although Sabrina had been a child, she had thought Kurt extremely handsome and debonair. Through the years her thoughts had often returned to Kurt, and she had hoped that someday he'd come back home.

However, this afternoon Kurt had informed her that he planned to leave for Texas following his brother's wedding, and Sabrina had found the information disappointing. She didn't want Kurt to leave. She wanted him to stay in Alabama, fall in love with her, and ask her to be his wife. She had visited

Heritage Manor on several occasions, and she now felt she'd be perfectly content to live there with Kurt. But living in Texas was out of the question. She had no intention of enduring all the hardships that faced a rancher's wife.

Well, she though firmly, I'll persuade Kurt to give up his ranch and remain at Heritage Manor. Looking into the mirror and appraising her own beauty, she was confident that she'd encounter no problems changing Kurt's mind. She'd soon have him at her beck and call and anxious to do her bidding.

"Jolene!" she said sharply. "You can put away those dresses later. Come help me get ready. I don't want to be late for supper."

Jolene was on her way to the servants' back stairway to go to the kitchen for the evening meal when she met Mary Jane coming down the hall.

"I was on my way to get you," Mary Jane said, falling into stride beside Jolene. "Lucy's got supper ready. She's real anxious to see you."

"Oh? Why?" Jolene asked.

"Her son Daniel is visitin', and she wants you to meet him. He lives in Texas and is travelin' with Mista Spencer."

Jolene stopped suddenly. She couldn't meet this Daniel! If he was traveling with Kurt, then he was with Kurt when she was taken to Dr. Mayfield. He'd certainly remember her! Thinking back to that night in Kurt's room, she remembered his mentioning Daniel. Her eyes probed Mary Jane's. "Did you ever

221

see Daniel before today?"

"No, of course not."

Jolene's thoughts raced. Apparently, Mary Jane had missed Kurt and Daniel the day they had brought her to the doctor's house.

"Mary Jane," she began nervously, "I can't meet Daniel . . . not tonight. Tell Lucy that I'm sorry."

"Why cain't you meet 'im?"

"I . . . I have too much work to do. Sabrina has some dresses that need mending. Would you mind bringing my dinner to me on a tray?"

"But wasn't you on your way to the kitchen?"

"Yes, to get a tray—but now you can get it for me. I'm sorry, truly I am." She turned about sharply and headed back to Sabrina's bedroom. Opening the door, she rushed inside. Would the lies never end? She hated being dishonest! Perhaps she should have told Kurt the truth from the beginning and spared herself all the lying that had followed.

Her deceit weighed heavily on her conscience as she walked over to the window that overlooked the flower garden. Pulling aside the curtain, she stared thoughtfully into the moonlit night. Lying to Kurt was bad enough, but now she'd been forced to lie to her good friend. As she thought about Lucy, she was racked with guilt. Her refusal to meet Daniel would hurt Lucy very deeply.

Jolene was near tears when suddenly she spotted Sabrina and Kurt walking in the garden. Startled, she stepped a little to the side so they couldn't see her. However, she didn't want to spy on them. She started to move away, but the sight that confronted her rendered her immobile. She looked on wide-eyed as the man she loved kissed another woman.

Anger surged within her, giving her the initiative to move from the window. Oh, she had been a fool to think she was special to Kurt! Obviously he wanted her in the same way a man wanted a prostitute or a bed wench! She was nothing more to him than a plaything! He needed her to satisfy his lust while, in the meantime, he intended to court Sabrina Delmar!

"Kurt Spencer!" she raged quietly. "You'll never take advantage of me again! Tomorrow I'm leaving Willow Hill, and then I'll leave Alabama! And I hope I never see you again for as long as I live!"

Her thoughts turning to her plans for escape, she stepped to Sabrina's dressing table, pulled out a drawer, and removed a pearl brooch. On their trip to Willow Hill, they had passed though Mobile, and she knew the city was only a few miles away. Tomorrow she'd walk to Mobile, then sell the brooch and use the money to travel to Cedarbrook.

Staring guiltily at the piece of jewelry clutched in her hand, she wondered if this was the first time she'd ever stolen. She had a feeling that it was.

Desperately, she moaned, "I'm not only a liar, but now I'm also a thief! God, what's next?"

Chapter Fifteen

Kurt allowed Sabrina's kiss to linger before he gently broke their embrace by taking her arms from around his neck and stepping back. Her sudden kiss had taken him by surprise.

Following dinner, Sabrina had asked Kurt to join her for a walk, and from the moment they had entered the garden, she had started flirting. Although Kurt had sensed that she was the type who might fling herself into a man's arms and boldly kiss him, his thoughts had been on Jolene and Sabrina had taken him unawares.

Her aggressive designs left him cold, but he didn't want to do or say anything to hurt her feelings, so with a somewhat devilish smile, he said lightly, "If your father were to catch us kissing, he might be upset. He trusts me to act like a gentleman and not make advances to his daughter."

Lifting her hand, he placed a kiss upon it, bowed from the waist, and continued, "You're a lovely temptation, but as a gentleman, I must hold my feelings in check. Now if you'll excuse me, I promised Lucy I'd go to the kitchen and visit with her."

Sabrina, thinking herself too beautiful for a man to reject, believed Kurt was merely practicing southern chivalry, and that in truth, he was hopelessly infatuated. She was sure he intended to maintain proper deportment, which meant he'd asked her father's permission to pay court.

Smiling sweetly, Sabrina answered "Please don't let me keep you. I'm sure Lucy is anxious to talk with you. Although I was only a child when you and Daniel used to visit, I remember Lucy was very fond of you."

Kurt bid her a quick goodnight, then went around the side of the house and knocked on the kitchen door.

"Come in," Lucy called.

Daniel's mother was sitting at the table, but at Spencer's entry, she got to her feet. Stepping to Kurt, she enfolded him in her arms and hugged him affectionately, and he wholeheartedly returned her warm greeting. Earlier they had seen each other briefly, but they'd barely had time to exchange a few words, let alone embrace.

Lucy poured two cups of coffee, and when they were seated at the table, she looked at Kurt and said fondly, "Masta Kurt, you sure are a handsome man."

"Thank you, Lucy." He didn't ask her not to call him "masta," for he knew she'd be uncomfortable addressing him any other way. She'd been a slave all her life, and speaking deferentially to whites was

225

deeply ingrained.

In a grave tone, Lucy said, "I needs to talk to you 'bout Daniel. I'm terribly worried. He shouldn't have come back here. The south's no place for him."

"I agree. I didn't want Daniel to accompany me, and I tried to talk him into staying in Texas, but he was determined to see you."

"I suppose you know that he wants to buy me from Masta John."

"Yes, and I also know that Delmar has no intention of selling you."

"Did you talk to Masta John 'bout it?"

"When I saw him in New Orleans, I told him what Daniel wanted, and he said that you weren't for sale. He sounded quite adamant."

"Masta John, he won't never sell me," Lucy murmured, defeated.

"Why is he so determined to keep you?"

She shrugged. "I reckon he don't want no other cook."

"I don't believe it's strictly your cooking. Delmar's in love with you, isn't he?"

"Why, Masta Kurt, you know white gentlemens don't fall in love with colored wenches!" Lucy spoke candidly, for she wasn't aware that her master had fallen in love with her. Just like John Delmar, she believed emphatically that such a situation was impossible.

Kurt wasn't convinced. "You can believe what you want, but I have a feeling that Delmar's feelings for you run deeper that you realize."

Lucy found the possibility too outrageous to consider. "Speakin' of love, has you got someone special? You been a bachelor long enough, and it's time for you to settle down. Do you have a girl back in Texas?"

"No," he answered. "But there is someone special. Only I'm not free to talk about her yet."

"She live 'round these parts?"

"I'm not sure just where she lives, but it's one of the farms close to Willow Hill."

"Farm?" Lucy questioned, astounded. She knew all the farmers in the immediate area were destitute and were commonly called "poor white trash." "Is you sayin' her folks are poor?"

Kurt chuckled good-naturedly. "Do you think a lady has to be rich for me to care about her?"

"In the south, aristocrats marry aristocrats."

"Well, I don't live in the south any longer, and 'aristocrat' is simply a word rich southerners bestow upon themselves so they can feel superior to others who are less fortunate."

Lucy, inquisitive about Kurt's love, was about to question him further, but at that moment Daniel came into the kitchen. Her son joined them at the table, and as the two men started talking to her about Texas, her curiosity concerning Kurt's romance drifted from her thoughts.

Jolene was so restless she was unable to fall asleep, and afraid her tossing would awaken Mary Jane, she got out of bed, slipped into her dress, and stepped outside. The rustic cabin had two steps that led to the door, and sitting on the top one, Jolene cupped her chin in her hands and stared vacantly into the dark night.

She frowned as she thought about tomorrow's perilous flight. If she were caught, she'd be severely punished. Would John Delmar order her strung up and whipped? The possibility was so real that she felt as though she could actually hear the sound of the lash whizzing though the air. As she imagined the whip landing painfully against her bare back, she shuddered.

I must think about something else! she told herself firmly. *If I keep thinking about getting caught and being punished, I'll lose what little courage I have and then I'll be too scared to run away.*

Filled with resolve, she wiped all thoughts of escape from her mind; however, as the memory of Kurt kissing Sabrina returned to haunt her, she grew angry with herself. Couldn't she find something pleasant to dwell on?

She tried to recall a pleasant memory but couldn't remember any except for the wonderful moments that she had shared with Kurt. Now his dalliance with Sabrina had cast a dark shadow over the memories she'd treasured.

Her mind lingered on thoughts of Kurt. He was a two-timing, despicable cad! If she never saw him again, it'd be too soon. Recalling their encounter at the brook. she remembered his telling her that the word "good-bye" would never be used between them. *He's a lying scoundrel!* she fumed inwardly. *If he married Sabrina Delmar, he'd have no qualms about telling me "good-bye!"*

She gritted her teeth. Damn! She shouldn't let Kurt's interest in Sabrina infuriate her. After all, she hadn't planned ever to see him again, for she was returning to Cedarbrook, where, with luck, the closed door to her past would be opened. She must concentrate fully on regaining her memories and forget that Kurt Spencer had trifled with her affections.

But it hurts so terribly! she cried silently. *It hurts to know that Kurt merely used me as he would use a prostitute! Or a woman of color,* her thoughts added quickly. *Does he know the truth? Could he possibly have guessed that I'm a quadroon? Was my black hair a dead giveaway? No!* she argued. *A lot of white women have hair as dark as mine.*

Tears welled in her eyes, but determined not to cry over Kurt Spencer, she went back inside the cabin. Removing her dress, she gently slipped into bed.

Clearing her trouble mind of Kurt and of tomorrow's escape, she closed her eyes and waited for sleep. But it was a long time before she finally drifted into a fitful, dream-filled slumber.

Jolene was apprehensive. Her heart hammered quickly as she put on one of Sabrina's gowns. While her mistress was having lunch, Jolene had taken the dress, a petticoat, and a pair of shoes, and sneaked downstairs and out the back door to store the stolen goods in her cabin. She had returned to Sabrina's room to await her mistress so she could help her get ready for her customary nap. As soon as Sabrina had been tended to, Jolene had rushed back to the cabin and was now dressing.

There was no mirror and Jolene couldn't see her

full appearance, but she was confident she looked acceptable. The dress and shoes were a little too large for her small frame, but no one would notice.

For her escape to work, stealing the clothes had been essential. It was important for her not to draw any unnecessary attention to herself, and if she were dressed poorly, she might attract people's interest. To mingle inconspicuously in Mobile, she must give the impression that she was a middle-class lady. Also, when she sold the pearl brooch, she didn't want the pawnbroker to suspect it had been stolen. If she were wearing a slave dress, he'd certainly be suspicious; furthermore, when she bought passage to Natchez, she wanted to look like she could afford the ticket.

Jolene had chosen a summer traveling dress from Sabrina's abundant wardrobe. The mauve garment had a simple lace design with a matching fringed shawl. After she sold the brooch, she planned to buy the remaining articles that she'd need and a reticule to carry them in. Then she'd certainly look as though she were a lady of moderate means traveling from Mobile to Natchez. She had already decided that, if anyone were to ask, she'd say that she had been visiting her sister and was now on her way home.

Jolene went to the door, opened it, and peeked out cautiously. She was sure that the most dangerous part of her flight would be getting safely away from Willow Hill. Someone could spot her so easily!

There was no one about, and as she hurried from the cabin, Jolene wrapped the shawl tightly about her shoulders. Lifting the hem of her long dress, she fled toward the vast fields. Without daring to look back to see if she was being watched, she ran as fast as her legs could carry her, and by the time she reached the wooded area that led to the main road, she was out of breath. Stopping, and breathing laboriously, she wondered if she should go on to the road and try to get a ride into town. Afraid that it was too risky, she decided instead to walk through the woods but stay close to the main road.

She moved onward at a slower pace, for she knew if she kept pushing herself, she'd soon be too exhausted to reach Mobile.

As she passed the trees, bushes and protruding roots that grew thickly in her path, her thoughts went to Kurt. Had he gone to the brook to meet her? Yes, she mused, bristling. I'm sure he's there waiting for his country bumpkin to arrive so he can take advantage of her innocence! Well, hereafter, if he wants a woman to satisfy his physical needs, he can use Sabrina Delmar! They're both contemptible skunks, and they deserve each other!

When Sabrina had awakened to find Jolene gone, she had been enraged. Forced to dress herself, she stormed out of the room and went straight to the kitchen, where she ordered Mary Jane to find Jolene and tell her to report to her mistress at once.

Failing to locate Jolene, Mary Jane was certain she'd run away. Reluctantly she went to Sabrina and shocked her with the news of Jolene's disappearance.

Outraged, Sabrina had gone running to her father. Thereafter the entire house was in an uproar.

Over a year had passed since a slave had dared to run away from Willow Hill, and Delmar's wrath was at fever pitch. He quickly sent for Samson and George and told them to round up the dogs, then saddle his horse and Alan's, plus two mounts for themselves.

Delmar and Alan, flanked by Sabrina and Lucy, were going out onto the front porch when Kurt rode up to the house. He had been at the brook, and believing the little chit had stood him up intentionally, he was in a foul temper.

As Kurt reined in, George and Samson arrived. George was leading four saddled horses, and his brother was holding onto three leashed hounds that barked excitedly.

Dismounting, and walking up to the porch, Kurt asked Delmar, "What's going on?"

"One of those new wenches I bought in New Orleans has run away. She's only been gone a little over two hours, so we shouldn't have any trouble catching her."

Kurt eyed the rambunctious dogs disapprovingly. "Are they necessary?" he asked.

Knowing what he was thinking, John answered, "These hounds are trained to track, not attack. I use my vicious dogs only when I'm hunting a runaway buck." Hurrying down the steps, he said over his shoulder, "Mount up, Kurt, and come with us."

Kurt declined. He didn't want to chase after a helpless woman. Besides, he didn't blame her for running. He believed every human being, regardless of color or creed, had the right to freedom.

John handed Jolene's nightgown to Samson, telling him to let the dogs get a good whiff of it so

232

they'd know the wench's scent.

Meanwhile, Lucy, wringing her hands nervously, called softly to Kurt, "Masta, may I talk to you for a minute?"

The servant's request irritated Sabrina, for she wanted to monopolize Kurt's attention. She placed a hand on his arm, turned to Lucy, and said firmly, "You can talk to Kurt later. Now I want you to fix us some cool lemonade. I'm sure Kurt could use a refreshing drink after his ride."

By now the hunters had mounted, and as Samson released the dogs, Delmar waved to Sabrina, saying loudly, "I'll be back for supper, and I'll have that insolent wench with me."

"Good luck, Papa!" she yelled as he and the others rode away.

Kurt watched as they followed the dogs toward the fields, then turning back to Sabrina, he removed her hand from his arm and said curtly, "Excuse me."

He went quickly to Lucy. Having disobeyed her mistress, she was still on the porch, instead of in the kitchen preparing lemonade. "What do you want, Lucy?" he asked kindly.

She motioned for him to follow her to the far end of the porch, then in a lowered voice said anxiously, "Masta Kurt, you got to catch up to Masta John and the others."

He frowned. "I'd rather not."

"But you got to be with 'em when they find that poor girl. She gonna be scared to death of them dogs, and the masta's so mad that he's liable to order Samson or George to whip her. If you're with Masta John, maybe you can stop him from hurtin' her."

233

"Why are you so concerned about this girl?"

"She's different from most slaves."

"What do you mean?" he questioned, confused.

"I ain't got time to explain. They gettin' too far ahead of you, and you got to leave now!"

Kurt was still reluctant to join in the hunt, but realizing how much it meant to Lucy, he agreed to go. "All right, I'll catch up to them. But I can't promise that I can keep Delmar from punishing her."

She understood. "Just promise me that you'll try."

He smiled reassuringly. "I'll try my damnedest." Whirling about and heading for his horse, he told Sabrina, "I changed my mind about not joining your father."

As he swung lithely into the saddle, she called, "Kurt, there's no reason for you to go along."

"See you later," he said tersely, slapping the reins against the neck of the stud.

Sabrina watched until horse and rider had disappeared. Then, glaring at Lucy, she spat petulantly, "You sent him after Jolene, didn't you?"

"Yes'm," she answered.

The young mistress stamped her foot. "Oh if you weren't Papa's pet, I'd take a buggy whip to you!"

Lucy was not intimidated. Smiling to herself, she went into the house and to the kitchen. Although she was still concerned about Jolene, she felt better knowing Kurt would be there when she was caught. That Jolene might get away never entered Lucy's mind, for no slave had ever escaped Willow Hill, though several had tried.

Chapter Sixteen

Jolene continued walking in the general direction of Mobile, but the woods became so dense that she lost sight of the road. It was impossible for her to follow a straight path, and her meandering course gradually took her farther and farther into the heavy thicket.

It was cool within the solid shade afforded by the billowing, full-branched trees, and sitting beneath a tall oak, Jolene decided to rest for a few minutes. That she had wandered from her original course didn't concern her, for she was confident about finding her way back. She knew it was vitally important that she stay within sight of the rural road because it would eventually lead her to Mobile.

Removing the fringed shawl from her shoulders, Jolene folded it, then placed it on the high grass to use as a pillow. Relaxing, she lay down and gazed upward through the branches of the oak. The vast sky appeared as tiny blue specks between the leaves.

Despite her fear of being caught and taken back to Willow Hill, she enjoyed basking in her newborn freedom. For the first time since Cal Atkins had told her that she was a slave, she felt vitally, wonderfully alive!

As her thoughts centered on slavery and the bigoted south, she was repelled by the wicked system that ruled her homeland. She sighed plaintively; the slaves had lost their freedom, but masters like John Delmar would lose their souls! The Day of Judgment would right all wrongs!

Clearing her mind, Jolene closed her eyes, gave in to her weariness, and drifted serenely into a dreamlike state. Suddenly, she heard the distant but unmistakable baying of hounds. She sat up with a start, her eyes open wide and glazed with fright.

Delmar! she thought fearfully. *He was using dogs to track her!*

As Jolene leapt to her feet, the futility of her escape struck her full-force. She had been a fool to think she could run away. Why hadn't she realized that Delmar would come after her with dogs?

Forgetting the shawl, Jolene turned and ran blindly, her flight taking her deeper into the forest. The dogs' excited barks grew steadily louder. Panicking, Jolene fled wildly. The congested vegetation slowed her progress as low tree branches blocked her way and prickly bushes snagged at her dress.

For a moment she considered giving up and waiting for Delmar, but afraid the dogs would arrive first and tear her to pieces, she continued her reckless flight.

Kurt's heart wasn't in the chase as he rode

alongside the master of Willow Hill. Running down a helpless, frightened woman wasn't his idea of sport, but he suspected Delmar and Alan were enjoying themselves. Kurt knew that the slave's escape had aroused Delmar's wrath to its zenith; nonetheless he seemed to find the hunt exhilarating.

Kurt realized that he'd been away from the deep south too long and had forgotten how masters like Delmar relished their imperial reign. He was beginning to suspect there was a sadistic streak in Delmar, and the feral, vicious glare he now saw in the man's eyes justified his suspicion.

He felt a twinge of pity for the young woman they were chasing, for her master would most assuredly punish her severely.

Recalling both Lucy's plea that he help the runaway slave and his promise to try, Kurt groaned. He was beginning to doubt he could say anything to mellow Delmar's rage or lighten the slave's impending punishment. However, for Lucy's sake as well as the girl's, he'd give it his best effort.

The hounds' constant barking changed suddenly to ferocious, jaw-snapping growls. For a split-second, Kurt's eyes met John's; then, urging their horses into a full gallop, they headed toward the vicious sounds. Alan, Samson, and George followed close behind.

The dogs, having found Jolene's abandoned shawl, were fiercely ripping the garment to shreds as the hunters arrived. Reining in, Kurt looked at Delmar and bellowed testily, "I thought you said these dogs weren't vicious!"

"They usually aren't," he answered quickly. John was concerned. He'd paid fifteen hundred dollars for the wench, and he wasn't about to take unnecessary chances on losing his investment. As the three hounds deserted the shredded garment to bound further into the woods, Delmar yelled to Samson and George, "Stay with those hounds and don't let them harm the woman!"

"Yes, suh, masta," the brothers said in unison. They immediately slapped the reins against their horses and bolted after the baying hounds.

Delmar's concern for the woman came as a pleasant surprise to Kurt. Maybe he'd been mistaken and the man wasn't as unfeeling as he thought.

"John," he began evenly, "I'm glad to hear you don't want the girl harmed."

"Of course I don't want my valuable property destroyed!" Delmar spat impatiently. "I paid fifteen hundred for the damned wench!"

Spencer's worry for the runaway slave resurfaced. Apparently he hadn't been mistaken and Delmar was as unfeeling as he had originally suspected.

The man's all heart, Kurt mused caustically before asking, "You don't plan to have her whipped, do you?"

John answered crisply, "The whip leaves scars, and she's too much of a fancy to be marred. I'll have Samson lay the paddle on her pretty ass." He turned and spoke to Alan, "Son, did you remember to bring the paddle?"

"Yes, Papa," he replied. He had the leather paddle attached behind his saddle, and he glanced back to make sure that it was still there.

"A good paddling will cure her insolence, but it won't leave any scars," John went on. Then, before Kurt could say anything, he sent his roan stallion into a loping gallop.

Quickly Spencer and Alan followed suit, and as Kurt caught up to Delmar, his thoughts wandered from the matter at hand and traveled to his beautiful country chit. A deep frown furrowed his brow as he reflected on her failure to meet him at the brook. He didn't understand why her absence had shattered him, for he had sensed that she'd once again disappear from his life. What kind of game was she playing? Twice now she had appeared unexpectedly, welcoming him with open arms and uninhibited passion, only to vanish afterward.

He shook his head as though by doing so he could just as easily shake her from his mind. Well, if he never saw her again, it would suit him just fine! He had no patience with deceit, and the little vixen lied constantly.

Jolene, running blindly, didn't see the protruding root in her path, and as the toe of her shoe struck against it, she lost her balance and fell heavily to the ground. The dogs were now dangerously close, and before she could get up, the snarling hounds were upon her.

Jolene rolled over quickly and lay on her stomach. Instinctively she knew she must remain perfectly still, for if she were to move, the excited animals would certainly attack. They had caught their prey and were anxious to end the chase with a kill. The dogs, stalking, sniffed at their victim, waiting for her to get up and run so they could bring her down.

Jolene's heart was thumping, and she barely dared to breathe for fear that the dogs would pounce.

When she heard riders arriving, she was so relieved that she thanked God for their presence, even though it meant returning to Willow Hill. She'd survive a lashing, but the dogs would suredly have killed her!

The two men dismounted swiftly, and as George called off the dogs, Samson rushed to Jolene. Sitting, he lifted her from the ground and placed her on his lap. "Is you all right?" he asked urgently.

Relieved to find herself in his strong, protective arms, she placed her head against his shoulder and cried, "Yes, I'm fine, thanks to you!"

Samson chided her gently. "You shouldn't have run away. Didn't you know that the masta would get the dogs after you? If you decide to run again, you gots to do it right."

"Wh-what do you mean?" she stammered. She hadn't completely recovered from her frightening ordeal, and her heart was still pounding. Finding a feeling of security in Samson's closeness, she remained cradled in his comforting arms.

George, having tethered the dogs, walked over to them. At his approach Samson cast his brother a determined look. He knew George was opposed to taking Jolene into their confidence, but Samson still believed she should be included.

Defying his brother's wishes, he asked Jolene, "Ain't you ever heard of the underground railroad?"

George's eyes warned Samson to say no more, but longing to convince Jolene to run away with them, Samson continued, "They's southerners who's willin' to help runaway slaves. Northern abolitionists, they knows these people, and when one of these abolitionists convinces a slave to escape, he gives 'im directions to these southern peoples' houses so they can hide 'im out and help 'im get up north."

"Do you know an abolitionist?" Jolene asked, her interest piqued.

Samson nodded. "He contacted me and George when we was in New Orleans. He said for me and George to get 'bout five of Masta John's slaves willin' to run, and then he'd get word to us when it was time for us to escape."

"It sounds dangerous. Please be careful," she said sincerely.

Samson didn't have time to ask her to join them, for they could hear the others approaching.

Jolene, postponing the moment when she'd have to look into Delmar's condemning eyes, snuggled closer to Samson and hid her face in his strong shoulder. "Will Delmar have me whipped?" she asked shakily.

Samson had seen the paddle on Alan's horse. He saw no reason to lie to her; to give her false hope would be cruel. "The masta will most likely order you paddled." In an effort to give her a little comfort, regardless of how small, he added, "A paddling ain't nearly as bad as a lashin', and it don't leave no scars."

Jolene feared the paddling, and as her tears overflowed, she clung to Samson and sobbed brokenly.

Coming upon the scene, the three men drew up their horses. Kurt, his gaze centered on the woman in Samson's arms, was startled by her ivory skin. Her face was turned away, and at first he didn't realize who she was, but as recognition set in, he could barely believe his own eyes.

Remaining mounted, Delmar ordered sharply, "Samson, move away from the wench!"

"Yes, masta," he replied as he reluctantly released Jolene, got to his feet, and stepped aside.

Remaining seated, Jolene bowed her head and stared down at her lap. Her whole body was trembling, and it took all the will power she possessed to keep from begging Delmar for mercy. Despite her fear, her pride and dignity surged suddenly, and with intrepid courage, she raised her face and looked squarely at her master.

His heated gaze was unnerving, and glancing away from the fire in his stoic eyes, she turned her vision to Alan and then to the third man. The sight of Kurt hit her with shocking force, and she cried out as though she had been physically struck.

Kurt, eying her unwaveringly, smoldered with rage. That she was apparently a slave wasn't the fuel igniting his anger; it was the outrageous lies she'd told him.

"Samson!" Delmar shouted. "I want you to strip that wench, then paddle her ass! Twelve slaps of the paddle should cure her rebellious nature!"

"Wait, Papa!" Alan interjected. "Let me paddle her." The mere thought of lashing Jolene's bare buttocks aroused young Delmar's passion. Yes, he'd spank her thoroughly. Then, tonight, he'd go to her cabin and caress the whelps on her pretty little behind before turning her over and ramming his hard erection deep within her. As he envisioned such pleasure, Alan actually licked his lips in anticipation.

Delmar had no objections to his son carrying out Jolene's punishment. "If you want to whip her, go ahead. But be fast about it. I want to get home in time for supper."

Before Alan could dismount, Kurt swung down from his horse. Jolene was still sitting on the ground, and he stepped to her side. Moving with an air of nochalance, Kurt picked her up and carried her back to his horse. Placing her in the saddle, he said levelly, "No one is going to whip this woman."

John, outraged, bellowed, "Kurt, damn your insolence! This wench is my property and I'll decide whether or not she's whipped!"

Meanwhile, Jolene was afraid to believe that Kurt could save her. If she let her hopes rise, Delmar's despotic authority might send them plunging. She gazed deeply into Kurt's dark eyes, praying she'd detect a look of encouragement, but she read only anger in his cold scrutiny. Her heart sank. She not only had Delmar's wrath to face, but also Kurt's.

Drawing his heated perusal from Jolene, Spencer turned and faced the Master of Willow Hill. Delmar was taken aback by the burning fury in Kurt's steady gaze. The younger man's glare was murderous.

Kurt, taking control of his emotions, chose to try and reason with John; if diplomacy failed, he'd resort to violence.

"John," he began evenly, "I'm considering buying this woman from you, and I don't want her harmed."

Jolene gasped, and her cheeks flushed at the thought of belonging to Kurt. Then, slowly, resentment set it. If he could coldly buy a human being as though he were purchasing an animal, he was no better than Atkins or Delmar!

Kurt had offered to buy Jolene without forethought, for he didn't believe in slavery. Well, he mused, if Delmar agrees to a sale, I'll buy her, then set her free.

"You can't have her," Alan finally spoke up.

Ignoring young Delmar, Kurt said to John, "You don't have to decide this very moment. Why don't we wait and discuss the transaction after dinner?"

Delmar had no intention of selling Jolene, but in order to pacify Kurt, he pretended to mull it over. Kurt's father was his best friend, and he didn't want this incident to interfere with their long-term friendship. Following dinner, he'd flatly refuse to sell the wench but smooth over the matter by promising not to have her paddled. His promise should appease Kurt. Then, tomorrow morning, as soon as Spencer left for Heritage Manor, he'd tell Alan to use the paddle on the wench. He'd not allow a runaway slave to escape punishment!

Delmar glanced quickly at Jolene, and seeing that she was wearing one of Sabrina's gowns, his irritation deepened. For stealing her mistress's dress, he'd add three more slaps of the paddle.

"Well?" Kurt asked, impatient with Delmar's silence.

"All right, Kurt," he answered. "I'll think over your proposition, and we'll discuss it after dinner."

"Papa, no!" Alan opposed angrily. Believing Spencer was buying Jolene for a bed wench, young Delmar was consumed with jealousy. He wanted her for himself!

Answering his son curtly, John replied, "We'll talk about this later." He switched his attention to George and Samson. "You two ride in the rear, and don't let those dogs get loose!"

Delmar urged his horse into a gallop, and Alan

244

quickly caught up and rode alongside his father so that he could continue voicing his objections.

Mounting, Kurt swung up into the saddle and positioned himself behind Jolene. His arms went about her as he reached for the reins. Stiffening, Jolene sat ramrod straight.

Knowing she was avoiding leaning back against him, Kurt purposefully encouraged his steed to take off with a sudden lurch, which successfully sent Jolene falling back into the circle of his arms.

As Kurt slowed the horse into a steady walk, she attempted to resume her rigid seat, but he wouldn't allow it. Placing his lips close to her ear, he murmured softly, "Tell me, my deceitful little beauty, where do your lies stop and the truth begin?"

"The truth begins right now," she replied tartly. "I'm a quadroon slave!"

"Since you're a slave, how did you manage to slip into my hotel room?"

"I escaped from the slave jail."

He arched a brow. "You expect me to believe that a snip of a girl like yourself managed to escape a barred cell?"

"I don't care what you believe!" she spat sharply. "And I wasn't in a cell, I was in the jailkeep's bedroom, taking a bath."

"I'm intrigued," he remarked sarcastically. "Tell me more."

She snapped petulantly, "I'm not telling you anything! Why should I? You'd just think I was lying!"

"I wonder why," he retorted. His anger was still smoldering. "I'm impressed with your new diction. Did you learn it overnight?" Receiving no answer, he continued, "Why do you speak as though you were educated?"

"The answer to your question is self-explanatory!"

"Where did you go to school?"

"St. Louis," she answered. Her eyes widened with suprise. How did she know that she'd gone to school in St. Louis? Was her memory coming back?

Although Kurt intended to question her more about her schooling, he decided it could wait until later. "Is your name really Josephine?"

"No," she answered guiltily. "It's Jolene."

"Jolene?" he repeated.

"Yes, but it's spelled J-o-l-e-n-e instead of J-o-l-e-e-n." She inhaled sharply. Good Lord, she remembered her name had an unusual spelling. Her memory was indeed returning! Oh, thank God. *Thank God!*

Kurt, unaware of Jolene's excitement, proceeded with his interrogation. "When I found you with Atkins, were you part of his coffle?"

"Yes. He was taking me to New Orleans to sell me."

"Who did Atkins buy you from?"

"My sister. She and I were raised as twins. Then, after our father died, his will revealed that my mother was a mulatto slave." Jolene wished he'd stop bombarding her with questions. If she could concentrate without interruptions, she might recall more of her past.

Since she had lied so often, Kurt was hesitant to believe her. Returning to her education, he asked, "What school did you attend in St. Louis?"

"Miss Rawlins' School for Young Ladies. The

woman was a tyrant." Her spirits soaring, Jolene beamed. Her memories were starting to flow. She not only remembered her school, but also Miss Rawlins!

"Why did your sister sell you to Cal Atkins?"

"Supposedly, I was inciting the slaves and had threatened my sister's life."

"What do you mean, 'supposedly?'"

"I can't remember my past because I'm suffering from amnesia."

Incredulous, Kurt remarked, "Now I've heard everything!"

"But it's true!" she insisted. "All I know about my past and my life at Cedarbrook is what Atkins told me!"

Kurt's mouth twisted into a surly grin. "I suppose Atkins also told you how to spell your name, the school you attended, and that Miss Rawlins was a tyrant. My God, woman, don't you ever run out of lies?"

"I'm not lying!" she cried. "I just now remembered the things you mentioned. Apparently my memory *is* returning, Dr. Mayfield said the amnesia would be temporary."

"Are you about to tell me that when you fell and hit your head, the blow caused amnesia?"

"Yes! But it's true!" she declared firmly. "When I regained consciousness—"

He interrupted forcefully. "Shut up! I can't tolerate any more of your fabricated stories. My patience is at an end. So help me God, if you utter one more damned lie, I'll place a gag over your beautiful, dishonest little mouth. This evening when I discuss buying you, I'll find out the truth about you from John."

"But he doesn't know," she said quickly. "Atkins told me not to tell Mr. Delmar that I had amnesia."

"Damn it, Jolene!" he raged. "Don't push me too far, or I'll carry out my threat to gag you!"

Oh, the man was insufferable! Her temper flaring, she spat, "You pompous, arrogant cad! If you don't want to hear my answers, then stop giving me the third degree!"

"Gladly!" he responded heatedly. He withdrew into a sizzling silence. The woman was exasperating. First she pretended to be Atkins' sister, then his fiancée! Now she expected him to believe that she had amnesia! What kind of outrageous lie would she tell next? Fuming, Kurt felt his explosive temper hanging by a mere thread.

As they rode without speaking, Jolene's anger began to abate. Although Kurt's refusal to accept her amnesia was irritating, she nonetheless understood his reluctance to believe her. She had lied to him too often. Wanting to make amends, she said softly, "Thank you for saving me from a whipping."

"Don't be so hasty with your thanks," he growled. "You're still liable to get a thorough whipping. When I become your master, I might sling you over my lap and spank your bare bottom until you're sore for a week! I'll give you a resounding whack for every lie you've told!"

Kurt's threat revived her temper, and she no longer cared to patch up their differences. "If you lay a hand on me, I'll kill you, you damned bully!"

"That kind of talk can get a slave in serious trouble. Slaves have been hung for less."

"I'd rather be dead than belong to you!" she came

back, angry tears smarting in her eyes. "I hate you!"

Pulling her flush to his chest, he said with certainty, "You'll soon belong to me, and when you do, I'll make you retract those words."

The feel of his hard chest, and the strength in his arms, was provoking a feverish feeling within her. Her brow broke out in perspiration as her heart picked up speed. Knowing she was succumbing to his masculine closeness, and determined not to surrender, she uttered fiercely, "I want to ride with Samson!" She must get away from him before she made a fool of herself by throwing her arms about his neck and begging him to love her! Oh God, she felt so alone, so confused! If only she had Kurt's devotion and protection! She sighed dejectedly. Now that Kurt knew she was a quadroon, she'd never have his love. White men didn't fall in love with colored wenches!

Her request to ride with Samson took Kurt by surprise. Then, remembering she had been in the man's arms when he, John, and Alan had found them, he wondered if she and Samson were somehow involved. Jealousy was an alien emotion to Kurt and he didn't know how to deal with it. Reacting irrationally, he slowed his horse until Samson and George caught up, then reining in abruptly, he lifted Jolene from the saddle and placed her roughly on the ground.

His rough treatment caused her to lose her balance, and as she landed solidly on her rear, he grumbled, "If you want to ride with Samson, then be my guest!" With that, he urged his horse forward, leaving her glaring murderously at his departing back.

Chapter Seventeen

By the time Delmar and the others reached Willow Hill, the sun was low in the sky. Abe, who was in charge of the stables, hurried to the house to take the gentlemen's horses. As the three men were dismounting, George, Samson, and Jolene arrived.

"Return the dogs to their pen," John told George. While the servant quickly obeyed, Samson jumped down from his horse. Reaching up, he lifted Jolene from the saddle and placed her on her feet.

Kurt looked on, his face inscrutable, but inwardly he was furious. His fury was aimed at himself more than at Jolene, for he had no patience with this weakness she stirred within him. He knew her for the deceitful little vixen that she was, yet for some inexplicable reason, she touched his heart.

"Come here, girl!" Delmar called to Jolene.

Complying, she moved toward her master, who was poised at the bottom of the steps. Kurt was standing beside him, but she avoided looking into his eyes.

"I want you to go to your cabin and stay there," Delmar began firmly. "Don't try to run away again, because if you do—" Hiw words halted abruptly. Although he had noticed earlier that Jolene was wearing Sabrina's dress, he hadn't spotted the pearl brooch pinned to the garment. Now, as he stared at the piece of jewelry, his eyes bulged with rage.

Following his angry gaze, Jolene gasped. Oh, why hadn't she remembered to remove the brooch? Stealing the expensive brooch was probably a worse offense than running away! She knew she was in grave trouble.

Delmar's hand shot out, grabbed the brooch, and ripped it free. "So you're not just a runaway, but also a thief!" The irate man's face turned beet red as he thundered, "You thieving, insolent wench! I'll teach you a lesson you'll never forget! How dare you steal from me and my family! Being a woman isn't going to save you!" He glared at Samson. "Take this thief to the barn and chain her! After I've had my dinner, she's to be strung up and given twenty lashes with the whip!"

Every muscle in Kurt's body grew taut. She couldn't possibly survive so many lashes!

Samson, hesitating, murmured piteously, "But, Masta John, that kind of punishment will kill her for sure."

Delmar was enraged. "Goddamn you, Samson! I should peel the meat off your back for questioning my orders!"

Kurt quickly intervened. "John, you can't—"

Delmar, beyond listening, cut in sharply, "Stay out of this! It's none of your business!" He was so

251

upset that he no longer cared about pacifying Kurt.

"But, Papa," Alan whined, "if you kill the wench, we're gonna be out fifteen hundred dollars." He was using her value as a ploy to get through to his father. The money meant nothing to Alan. He didn't want Jolene dead before he had time to get his fill of her.

Striving to control his ire, John answered with a semblance of calm, "Alan, I regret wasting fifteen hundred dollars, but I must make an example of her. If she gets by with stealing, what's to stop the other slaves from trying it as well?"

His father's reasoning made sense. Nonetheless, knowing he'd never enjoy Jolene's lovely body was depressing.

As Alan sulked, Kurt gathered his thoughts. He knew it'd be useless to try and change Delmar's mind until the man's temper had time to cool. He had no intention of standing by and doing nothing to save Jolene. After dinner, he'd offer John a generous price for the woman, but if that failed, he'd find a way to steal her. Jolene would suffer the whip over his dead body!

Turning to Kurt, Delmar said somewhat apologetically, "I understand how you feel. But the wench must pay for her crime."

"With her life?" Kurt responded bitterly, unable to repress his vexation.

The man shrugged unfeelingly. "Maybe she'll survive the lashing."

Jolene's fear had rendered her riveted to the spot, and she had been unable to move, even when Samson had taken her arm to assist her to the barn. Her gaze turned frantically to Kurt. Oh, surely he'd make an attempt to save her! She waited breathlessly for him to come to her defense. When he made no move to do so, Jolene, giving up, leaned weakly against Samson's brawny frame. She was going to die! Only Kurt had a chance to save her, and he didn't care enough to even try!

As resentment washed over her, drowning her fear, she moved away from Samson, straightened her posture, and looked unwaveringly at the three men poised before her. Her eyes roamed from Alan to Delmar and then to Kurt, and she was startled by the intense hatred that filled her heart. She despised them, and if she'd had a gun, she'd have shot the arrogant bastards without blinking an eye!

If she had to die, she'd do so with her dignity intact. She'd not give them the perverted pleasure of watching her grovel at their feet!

With a defiant lift to her chin, she turned to Samson and placed her hand in the crook of his arm. "Shall we?" she asked, as though he were about to escort her onto a dance floor instead of into the barn to await her doom.

Kurt's eyes shone with admiration for Jolene as he watched them walk away. He'd read of gallant men walking to the gallows with the same kind of dignity and courage.

Delmar's mood was cranky as he preceded Kurt into the room he used as an office. The moment they'd finished with dinner, Spencer had insisted they talk privately. John had been hesitant to agree, for he was sure the man hadn't changed his mind about buying Jolene. Why he would want to own such a rebellious, untrustworthy slave was beyond his comprehension.

Going to his massive oak desk, John sat down and gestured for Kurt to do likewise.

Kurt didn't mince words but got straight to the point. "I want to buy Jolene."

John frowned. "She's not for sale."

"I intend to offer you a generous amount."

Delmar studied the younger man thoughtfully, then sounding paternal, asked, "Son, why do you want this particular wench so badly! I've other pretty wenches on the plantation. You can take your pick. I'll sell you the one of your choice."

"Jolene's my choice," he answered.

John didn't want to be rude, so he acted as if he were willing to hear Kurt's price. "How much are you prepared to pay?"

"You gave fifteen hundred for her, is that correct?"

Delmar said that it was.

"I'll give you three thousand. You'll double your money."

Astounded, the man stared at Kurt in disbelief. "That's too much to pay for a wench, even one as pretty as Jolene. Surely you aren't serious!"

"I'm dead serious."

John contemplated the offer. It was tempting, but the wench had stolen from him and he felt he owed it to himself to see her severely disciplined. "Sorry, Kurt, as I said before, she's not for sale."

Kurt was determined. "I'll up it to four thousand." Although he was willing to go even higher, to sign over his ranch if necessary, he thought it best to force John to play his hand. "That's my top bid."

Delmar's head shook with amazement. "Damn!

I've never seen a man so hungry for a wench." He smiled somewhat hesitantly. "Although I'd love to see that damned gal strung up and whipped, I can't refuse four thousand dollars. There are times when profit comes before pleasure." He offered his hand to Kurt. "We'll shake on the deal."

Reaching across the desk top, Kurt accepted the man's handshake.

"Do you want her kept in the barn for the night?" John inquired.

"No. I'll ask Lucy to bring her into the house."

"The wench doesn't sleep in the house. She has a cabin out back."

"If you have no objections, tonight she'll stay in my room." Kurt wasn't about to give her a chance to run away again. Also, there was Alan to consider: if Jolene was left alone, he wouldn't put it past the man to force himself on her. He had seen the lustful way Alan had looked at her.

Mistaking Kurt's reason for wanting Jolene in his room, John chuckled amusedly. "You can't wait to get her in your bed, can you? Can't say that I blame you. She's enticing. Sobering, he added, "Take my advice, son, and break that rebellious spirit of hers. If you don't, she'll give you trouble."

It wasn't her spirit he intended to break, but her habitual lying. Standing to push back his chair, Kurt said, "If you'll excuse me, I'll go to the kitchen and send Lucy to the barn for Jolene."

"Sure, go right ahead. While you're tending to that, I'll write out a bill of sale."

Lucy, sitting at the kitchen table between Daniel

255

and Mary Jane, was trying desperately to hold back her tears. By now every slave on the plantation knew that Jolene had been sentenced to receive twenty lashes of the whip. Twenty lashes could kill a healthy man, and Lucy knew a woman as fragile as Jolene couldn't possibly survive such a punishment.

"I cain't just sit here and do nothin' to help that poor girl," Lucy remarked. "I'm gonna go to Masta John, get down on my knees, and beg 'im to spare her!"

Daniel placed his hand on her arm, detaining her. "Mama, wait. I think Kurt's talking to Delmar."

"'Bout Jolene?" she queried.

"I have a feeling he's trying to buy her."

Lucy expelled a heavy sigh. "If Masta John got his mind set on keepin' Jolene, I doubt if Masta Kurt can convince 'im to change it."

"Money has a way of changing a person's mind," Daniel replied. He smiled introspectively.

Reading his thoughts, Lucy said gently, "Honey, I know what you're thinkin', but Masta John ain't gonna sell me, no matter how much money you offer." However, she was hopeful for Jolene. "But I pray Masta Kurt can get 'im to sell Jolene."

Mary Jane, unable to keep her tears in check, broke into deep, heaving sobs. Crying convulsively, she moaned, "God's got to help Jolene; He's just got to!"

At that moment Kurt entered the kitchen. Mary Jane's sobs subsided at once, and three pairs of eyes looked at Kurt questioningly.

His grin was askew. "Lucy, will you go to the barn and bring Jolene to her brand new master?" His eyes twinkled mischievously.

ACCEPT YOUR **FREE GIFT** AND EXPERIENCE MORE OF THE PASSION AND ADVENTURE YOU LIKE IN A HISTORICAL ROMANCE

Zebra Romances are the finest novels of their kind and are written with the adult woman in mind. All of our books are written by authors who really know how to weave tales of romantic adventure in the historical settings you love.

Because our readers tell us these books sell out very fast in the stores, Zebra has made arrangements for you to receive at home the four newest titles published each month. You'll never miss a title and home delivery is so convenient. With your first shipment we'll even send you a **FREE** Zebra Historical Romance as our gift just for trying our home subscription service. No obligation.

BIG SAVINGS AND **FREE** *HOME DELIVERY*

Each month, the Zebra Home Subscription Service will send you the four newest titles as soon as they are published. (We ship these books to our subscribers even before we send them to the stores.) You may preview them *Free* for 10 days. If you like them as much as we think you will, you'll pay just $3.50 each and *save $1.80 each month* off the cover price. *AND you'll also get FREE HOME DELIVERY.* There is never a charge for shipping, handling or postage and there is no minimum you must buy. If you decide not to keep any shipment, simply return it within 10 days, no questions asked, and owe nothing.

MAIL IN THE COUPON BELOW TODAY

To get your Free **ZEBRA HISTORICAL ROMANCE** fill out the coupon below and send it in today. As soon as we receive the coupon, we'll send your first month's books to preview Free for 10 days along with your **FREE NOVEL**.

─── F R E E ───

B O O K C E R T I F I C A T E

ZEBRA HOME SUBSCRIPTION SERVICE, INC.

YES! Please start my subscription to Zebra Historical Romances and send me my free Zebra Novel along with my first month's Romances. I understand that I may preview these four new Zebra Historical Romances Free for 10 days. If I'm not satisfied with them I may return the four books within 10 days and owe nothing. Otherwise I will pay just $3.50 each; a total of $14.00 (a $15.80 value—I save $1.80). Then each month I will receive the 4 newest titles as soon as they come off the press for the same 10 day Free preview and low price. I may return any shipment and I may cancel this arrangement at any time. There is no minimum number of books to buy and there are no shipping, handling or postage charges. **Regardless of what I do, the FREE book is mine to keep.**

Name _____
                          (Please Print)

Address _____ Apt. # _____

City _____ State _____ Zip _____

Telephone ( ) _____

Signature _____
              (if under 18, parent or guardian must sign)

Terms and offer subject to change without notice.

11-88

Overjoyed, Lucy leapt to her feet. "I sure will, Masta Kurt!"

Going to Spencer, Mary Jane grabbed his hands and squeezed them tightly. "Thank you, masta, for savin' Jolene!"

"I thank you too, Masta Kurt," Lucy added.

Kurt was a little embarrassed by their demonstrative gratitude. But he appreciated their warmth, for he doubted he'd receive a thank you from Jolene. She'd probably tell him she'd rather die under the whip than belong to him.

He looked at Lucy. "Bring Jolene back to the house. I'm sure she'd like a bath, so help her bathe, then show her upstairs to my room."

Lucy was stunned to find Kurt treating Jolene like a bed wench. Before she could voice her opinion, he said impatiently, "Go do as I said!"

"Yes, Masta Kurt," she replied, heading toward the back door. "But I just got to say that I'm ashamed of you. I never thought you'd buy a gal for a bed wench."

"She's not my bed wench," Kurt assured her. "And I plan to set her free."

Whirling about to face him, she asked, "When?"

"When I'm damned good and ready," he remarked with a devilish grin.

"And when might that be?"

"That's none of your business. Now get the hell out of here." He spoke without anger.

"I'll go with you," Mary Jane offered, following Lucy out the door.

As Kurt sat down at the table, Daniel asked, "How much did she cost you?"

"Four thousand," he answered quietly.

Daniel whistled softly. "That's a hell of a lot of money."

"You're telling me." Kurt sounded unconcerned, but he had labored hard for that four thousand dollars, and it was going to take a lot of work to replace it.

Daniel went to the stove and poured two cups of coffee. Returning, he said, "I'm not leaving with you in the morning. I plan to stay here and visit with Mama a while longer. I've already talked it over with Delmar, and he has no objections. I'll come to Heritage Manor in a few days."

"It's not safe for you to travel these roads alone."

"I won't be alone. The Delmars are coming to your brother's wedding, and I'll travel with them."

Kurt was relieved. "In that case, I don't see any reason why you shouldn't stay. Have you said anything to John about buying Lucy?"

"Not yet, but I will soon." He paused for a moment. "Kurt, what do you think of Mary Jane?"

"I don't really know her, but she's very pretty." A sparkle came to Kurt's eyes. "I have a feeling Lucy isn't your only reason for staying at Willow Hill."

"I admit that I find Mary Jane very attractive, but she doesn't share my feelings. I don't think she wants to become involved. I'm not sure if it's just me, or if she tries to avoid men in general."

"Why don't you ask her?"

"Maybe I will."

Kurt finished his coffee. Getting to his feet, he said, "I need to get back to John's office so we can finalize the sale." He went to the door that led into the covered passageway. "Good luck with Mary Jane."

"Thanks. I have a feeling I'll need it."

There was a lone lantern hanging from one of the barn's high beams, and its soft, luminous glow shone on Lucy and Mary Jane as they hurried inside.

Jolene, sitting on a bed of straw, watched as Lucy grabbed the key from the peg. Then, with large smiles on their faces, she and Mary Jane rushed to their friend.

As Lucy unlocked the heavy manacles, Jolene exclaimed, "What are you doing? You can't help me escape! Delmar will find out and punish you both!"

"You ain't escapin', honey!" Lucy remarked. "You bein' set free!"

"Wh-what?" she stammered, finding the news too miraculous to believe.

"Masta Kurt, he done bought you!" Mary Jane declared, kneeling beside her.

Removing the manacles from Jolene's ankles and wrists, Lucy set them aside. Then, sitting on the prickly straw, she explained, "Somehow he convinced Masta John to sell you. But Masta Kurt's gonna set you free!"

"Did he say that?" Jolene questioned anxiously.

"He sure did," the woman replied.

"When does he intend to let me go?"

Lucy answered, "He didn't give no specific time."

Mary Jane, seeing no reason to hedge with Jolene, remarked, "Masta Kurt said he'd set you free when he was damned good and ready."

Jolene's blue eyes flashed angrily. Seeing this, Lucy spoke in Kurt's favor. "Honey, don't you pay no mind to what Mary Jane said. Masta Kurt's a good man, and he'll set you free real soon." Suddenly, remembering Kurt telling her that there was a special woman in his life, she began to put two and two together. Watching Jolene closely, she asked, "Today ain't the first time you and Masta Kurt seen each other, is it?"

"No," she answered honestly, determined to put an end to the lies.

"Where did you meet Masta Kurt?" Lucy pried.

"Right after I fell and hit my head, Kurt happened by on his way to New Orleans. Because he was on horseback, he took me to Dr. Mayfield's house. Atkins had told him that I was his wife."

It wasn't necessary for Jolene to go into details as her story unfolded, for she had already told Lucy parts of it.

"When I was running away from the slave jail, I spotted Delmar. I slipped into the hotel and by chance hid in Kurt's room. Later he found me asleep on his bed. I told him I was Atkins' sister."

"Why did you tell 'im that?" Lucy wanted to know.

"Well . . . you see, he knew I wasn't Atkins' wife." She blushed blatantly.

Lucy raised her eyebrows knowingly.

Smiling timidly, Jolene continued, "Lucy, you have extraordinary insight. As you have already surmised, Kurt and I made love, and he knew I was a virgin." She looked at Mary Jane apologetically. "That's why when I was returned to our cell, I couldn't tell you what had happened. It was too private . . . too special."

"I understand," she said softly.

"Yesterday, while Sabrina was napping, I went to

the meadow. Kurt was on his way to Willow Hill, and he found me sleeping beside the brook. Before leaving New Orleans, he learned Atkins didn't have a sister. He demanded an explanation from me. I just couldn't bring myself to tell him I was a slave, so I told him Atkins and I had been engaged and that I'd decided not to marry him. Kurt wanted to know what I was doing in these parts, so I said I lived on a nearby farm."

Lucy's eyes twinkled. "I wish I could've seen the look on Masta Kurt's face when he found out who you really was. Bet he was fit to be tied!" Her mood sobering, she placed her hand over Jolene's. "Honey, will you take some good advice?"

"I'll try," she answered.

"When Masta Kurt sets you free, you get 'im to put a weddin' ring on your finger. Then you can start a brand new life in Texas."

"I can't go to Texas!" Jolene exclaimed. "I must return to Cedarbrook!"

"Why do you want to go back there?" Lucy asked, her tone disapproving. "You should just forget about that place."

"But you don't understand. My memory has returned. I remember everything. At first it came to me in spurts. Then, as I was sitting here alone, my complete past suddenly came back. It was like a dam had burst inside my head, releasing my memories in a gushing flood."

Jolene leapt to her feet, and as she looked at her two good friends, her eyes shone radiantly. "I'm not a quadroon slave! I'm the true mistress of Cedarbrook!"

Chapter Eighteen

Stunned silence followed Jolene's declaration. Mary Jane and Lucy merely stared at her, their mouths agape, as though they had found her words too incredible to grasp. Then, regaining her composure, Lucy mumbled, "I don't know why I feel surprised. I knew all along that you don't have no colored blood."

"If you's the true mistress of Cedarbrook," Mary Jane began, "then how come you was with Atkins?"

Quickly, Jolene told the women how Johanna and Robert had changed Sam Warrington's will, that Johanna had laced her sherry with a sleeping powder, and that she had awakened the next day to find herself a part of Atkins' coffle.

When her friends offered no reply, she exclaimed, "You believe me, don't you?"

"Yes," Mary Jane was quick to answer. "I believe you."

Jolene turned to Lucy, but the look of anxiety on the woman's face told Jolene that she hadn't even heard her question.

"If your memory's returned," Lucy murmured apprehensively, "then you should know if Lazarus is still at Cedarbrook."

Jolene smiled, happy that she had good news to report. "Yes, he's still there."

"How . . . how is he?"

"When I left, he was fine. And I'm sure he still is. Johanna wouldn't let any harm come to Lazarus."

Lucy tried to hold back her tears but failed miserably. Crying openly, she sobbed, "Thank the good Lord that Lazarus is alive and well!"

Kneeling in front of Lucy, Jolene took the woman's hands and held them tightly. "When I return to Cedarbrook, I intend to prove that Johanna and Robert forged Papa's will. Then, as soon as I have that taken care of, I'll bring Lazarus to Willow Hill so you can see him."

"No! Don't do that!" Lucy cried in panic.

"But why not?"

Lucy didn't answer right away, and when she did reply, her voice choked up. "Over thirty years done passed since I last saw Lazarus. When he thinks 'bout me, that is, if he ever does, he remembers me as I was at sixteen. I want 'im to go on rememberin' me that way." Her eyes looked sadly into Jolene's. "Honey, some things are better left in the past."

"But you still love him!"

"Do I?" she questioned. "How can I love the man Lazarus is now, when I don't even know 'im? No, honey, I loved the young Lazarus, but I don't love 'im no more."

Jolene was about to argue the point, but seeing

263

this, Lucy said briskly, "We got to get back to the house." Standing, she continued, "While you takin' a nice hot bath, I'll fix you somethin' to eat. Then Masta Kurt wants me to take you to his room."

"What! Jolene exclaimed, grasping Lucy's arm and urging the woman to face her. "Now that he owns me, does he expect me to share his bed?"

"When you tell 'im who you really is, he won't 'spect you to do nothin' of the kind."

Infuriated with Kurt's arrogance, she raged, "Oh, that contemptible cad! So he bought me for a bed wench, did he?"

Soothing Jolene, Lucy said, "There ain't no reason for you to get all upset. 'Sides, Masta Kurt said he wasn't buying you for a bed wench but so he could set you free."

"Yes, and I know when he plans to give me my freedom!" Jolene steamed. "He plans for me to warm his bed until he and Sabrina are married. After that, he'll get around to setting me free!"

"What you talkin' 'bout?" Lucy demanded, surprised.

"Sabrina Delmar has her cap set for Kurt, and I have a feeling that what Sabrina wants, Sabrina gets!" Jolene looked anxiously at Lucy. "You've known Sabrina all her life. Have you ever known her not to get what she wanted?"

"No," she replied, "that gal ain't never been denied anything. But—"

Interrupting, Jolene added, "Mark my word, she'll not be denied Kurt Spencer!"

"You didn't let me finish," Lucy went on. "I was 'bout to say that Miz Sabrina ain't never been denied anything money could buy. Masta Kurt ain't for sale."

"Sabrina has other assets besides money," Jolene answered, her meaning clear.

Lucy, thinking of Sabrina's beauty, was suddenly worried that Jolene might be right . . . Kurt could very easily succumb to Sabrina's wicked charms. She found the possiblity depressing, and eager to change the subject, she said briskly, "Come on; let's get back to the house."

Longing for a hot, relaxing bath, Jolene didn't resist.

Kurt had remained in the office with John for quite some time, closing their deal, conversing, and drinking brandy. Now, finishing his last drink, Kurt thanked John for the brandy and was on his way out of the room when all at once he stopped. Turning about, he stepped back to the desk, looked at Delmar, and asked, "Did Atkins say anything to you about Jolene having amnesia?"

The man stared at him as though he were daft. "Of course not! Amnesia? That's absurd! Why would you ask me such a thing?"

"Jolene claims to have amnesia."

Delmar laughed shortly. "I told you that gal was trouble. There's nothing wrong with her memory. On the trip from New Orleans, I asked her about her life at Cedarbrook, and she answered my questions without a moment's hesitation."

A part of Kurt agreed with John. Jolene was indeed trouble, and there was probably nothing

265

wrong with her memory—she had merely lied to him again. Yet another part of him wasn't so sure. Could she possibly be telling the truth?

Continuing, Delmar said "The gal was raised to believe she was white until her father's will was found to state that she was a quadroon slave. She's intelligent, and that makes her dangerous. She'll not submissively accept her bondage until you break her rebellious spirit."

"If you feel that way about her, why did you buy her?"

"I admit it was a mistake. I never bought an educated slave before, let alone one with so much white blood. We learn from our mistakes, though."

Kurt bid John goodnight, left the office, hurried up the marble staircase, and was heading down the hall when Sabrina stepped out of her bedroom and blocked his path.

She was wearing a sheer blue dressing gown which silhouetted her supple curves temptingly. Her long, flaming hair cascaded over her shoulders in lustrous softness. She was the picture of seduction, and for a moment her beauty captivated Kurt. But he was anxious to see Jolene, and Sabrina's wanton maneuver failed.

Brushing past her, he said with a smile, "Sabrina, what would your father say if he knew you were standing in the hall half-dressed?"

She grabbed his arm, detaining him. "I don't care what Papa would say. I'm a grown woman now."

His dark eyes, twinkling, raked over her desirable form. "You are indeed a woman."

She moved closer, daringly wrapping her arms

266

about his neck. "Do you find me attractive, Kurt?"

"Of course. You're a very beautiful young lady." He was about to pry her arms loose, but reading his intent, she brought her lips to his, kissing him with determination.

As Kurt was attempting to break her clinging embrace, he heard Lucy's soft, astonished gasp.

Sabrina was also aware of the servant's presence, and she stepped back quickly.

However, Lucy was not alone. Jolene was with her. Having entered the hall by the servants' back stairway, they had been on their way to Kurt's room when they'd come upon the embracing couple.

Lucy eyed Kurt sharply. Then, pointing to his room, she said to Jolene, "This where Masta Kurt's stayin'." She made a point of casting another harsh squint in Spencer's direction before turning about and leaving.

"Jolene," Kurt uttered uncomfortably, clearing his throat. "What are you doing here? You're supposed to be in my room." His gaze swept intensely over her delicate frame. Her loveliness struck him profoundly. Jolene, dressed in a plain nightgown, was more enticing than Sabrina in her expensive negligee.

"Sorry, Masta Kurt," she said mockingly. "Lucy fixed me somethin' to eat, and I was delayed gettin' up here. Go to your room now and I will warm your bed." She sent him a refractory glare, then stepped to his room, went inside, and shut the door with a solid bang.

"Kurt, surely you don't intend to keep that wench in your bedroom!" Sabrina remarked, anger underscoring each word. "I won't have it! I realize a man enjoys a lustful dalliance with a pretty wench, but I'll not tolerate that kind of thing under my roof!" She inhaled weakly as though she were about to swoon. "Especially this close to my own bedroom!

Kurt wasn't sure which angered him more, Jolene's insolence or Sabrina's demands. "I have your father's permission to keep Jolene in my room. You don't have to worry. It'll only be for one night. I'll be leaving in the morning."

"I thought you had too much class to buy a wench for . . . for carnal pleasure." Imagining Jolene in Kurt's bed aroused in Sabrina not just jealousy, but also feelings of insecurity. For the first time since she'd decided to marry Kurt, Sabrina wondered if she would fail. With a woman as pretty as Jolene sharing his bed, it might be impossible for her to tempt him with her own charms. She had planned to tease him, and when his passion was fully blazing, she'd remind him that she was a lady of virtue. He'd soon want her so desperately that he'd ask her to be his wife. But now that that damned wench was appeasing his male desires, her scheme to entrap him might be hopeless.

Meanwhile, Kurt was finding Sabrina's views annoying. He felt all this was none of her business. He answered curtly, "I didn't buy Jolene for carnal pleasure. I bought her so that I could set her free."

With that he walked away, leaving Sabrina staring at him in disbelief. Why would he pay out money for a slave merely to set her free? To Sabrina, it was illogical and made no sense whatsoever.

Going to his room, Kurt opened the door, stepped

268

inside, then turned about and pushed in the bolt.

Jolene was sitting in the corner of the room in a large, overstuffed chair. Her legs curled up beneath her, she refused to look at Kurt and kept her gaze glued to the throw rug next to the bed.

The room was lit by a single lamp, and its golden glow fell across Jolene. She was strikingly sensual in the saffron lamplight. Enchanted, Kurt stood silently as his eyes drank in her beauty. Her jet-black hair fell about her face and shoulders, its darkness accentuating the clear blue of her eyes. The thin gown defined her ivory breasts and outlined her delicate thighs.

Kurt wanted her. His desire was so powerful that he had to force himself not to go to her, take her into his arms, and carry her to his bed.

He turned away, afraid that if he didn't, he'd lose his self-control and ravish her, with or without her consent. He went and sat on the edge of the bed. He inhaled deeply, trying to quell his passion. When at last he felt he was master of his emotions once more, he looked at her and said, "I suppose you're wondering why I bought you from Delmar."

"I never wonder about the obvious," she remarked tartly, her gaze still withdrawn.

Kurt looked at her questioningly. "The obvious?"

Her gaze rose to meet his, and his masculine physique made her heart skip a beat. The top two buttons on his beige shirt were undone, revealing the curly hair that grew thickly across his muscular chest. His dark brown eyes were watching her, hawklike, and his full lips were on the verge of a crooked grin, causing one side of his trim moustache to lift wryly.

He's such a good-looking devil! she mused. Even her amnesia failed to block his handsome image from her mind.

Kurt waited patiently for her to respond to his query, and she began to grow uncomfortable beneath his unwavering scrutiny.

Stammering self-consciously, she mumbled, "It's . . . it's quite obvious to me that you bought me for a bed wench."

"Why do you think that?"

She waved a dainty hand toward the large bed. "Why else would I be in your room?"

"Maybe I just want to keep you safe."

She frowned. Did he take her for a fool? Keep her safe? She was in no danger! Her thoughts suddenly went to Sabrina, and a wicked smile crossed her pretty mouth. She could well imagine how much her former mistress must resent her presence in Kurt's room.

Wondering the reason behind her intriguing smile, he said, "A penny for your thoughts."

Dismissing Sabrina from her mind, she answered with a scornful glare.

He shrugged insouciantly. "Sorry I can't offer more than a penny, but you cost me a bundle, and my finances are dangerously low."

Impatient with his toying, she changed the subject. "Now that I'm your slave, what do you intend to do with me?"

"Take you with me to Heritage Manor. We'll leave in the morning. If we get an early start, we can be there by nightfall."

"Heritage Manor?"

"My parents' home."

She watched him guardedly. "Lucy told me you plan to set me free."

"That's right."

"When?" she asked at once.

"As soon as I can arrange it," he answered evasively.

"But you must set me free immediately!"

"It takes time to draw up legal manumission papers."

Bolstered by her eagerness, she bounded from the chair. Hands on hips, she said testily, "I don't need manumission papers! I'm not a slave! I'm the mistress of Cedarbrook!"

Kurt groaned. What outlandish lie was she now about to invent to astound him? He got to his feet and towered over her. Looking down into her shining blue eyes, he muttered dryly, "The mistress of Cedarbrook? That's quite a proclamation from someone who's suffering from amnesia."

"But I no longer have amnesia!"

"How nice that you made such a miraculous recovery." His tone was sarcastic.

"You don't believe me, do you?" she asked irritably.

He grinned without mirth. "Lying is your forte, is it not?"

"This time I'm telling the truth! I *did* have amnesia!"

"What happened to your amnesia on the trip to Willow Hill? John claims he questioned you about your past and that you answered his queries

271

without hesitation."

"But don't you understand? I answered him with lies!"

"Lies?" he repeated harshly. His patience depleted, he grasped her shoulders and stared darkly into her flushed face. "Of course you answered him with lies! You don't know how to do anything else!"

"Kurt," she began desperately, "you must listen to me—I'm not a slave. My sister Johanna is the one who's a quadroon! She and our lawyer, Robert Hawkins, changed Papa's will. They swapped my name with Johanna's."

Kurt, finding her story implausible, released his hold on her shoulders, stepped back, and laughed dryly. "What kind of fool do you take me for?"

"An arrogant, despicable one!" Her temper was raging. "And how dare you laugh at me!"

"Your tale is so outlandish that it's laughable."

"It's not a tale, it's the gospel truth!" she insisted.

His face was implacable. "The first time I saw you, I was told you were Atkins' wife—"

"That's right," she interrupted. "But *I* didn't tell you that lie—*Atkins* did."

"Granted," he replied. "Now may I continue without interruption?"

She nodded, her heart pounding.

"In my hotel room you informed me that you were Atkins' sister. But yesterday at the meadow, you admitted that you'd lied and were, in truth, Atkins' ex-fiancée. Then, today, I find out you're a slave, a slave with amnesia who can ironically remember the school she attended, among other things. Now it seems your amnesia is gone, and you remember that you're the mistress of Cedarbrook, a title out of which you were cheated by your sister. She and her lawyer robbed you of your birthright by changing your father's last will and testament. How convenient for them that no one suspected foul play. Otherwise, an investigation would surely have ensued."

Jolene, thinking he was beginning to believe her, was too overcome with anxiety to detect his sarcastic undertone.

"I suspected them," she said hastily. "I planned to go to Natchez and ask some of my father's friends for help, but before I had a chance to, Johanna slipped me a sleeping powder. Before I fell asleep she even admitted that she and Robert had tampered with the will. It was the next day before I woke, and by then I was a part of Atkins' coffle. I tried to tell him that Johanna had deceived him, but he wouldn't believe me."

"Nor do I!" he shouted. He wanted to believe her . . . God, how he wished he could accept everything she had said! But she'd lied to him too many times, and he couldn't trust her any more.

Enraged, Jolene screamed, "You hateful bastard!"

He reached her in two quick strides. His hand shot out with the swiftness of a snake and captured her arm in a viselike grip. "Let's not resort to name-calling, for you'd only lose!"

Jolene had been hoping and praying that Kurt would help her get back to Cedarbrook. She had believed him compassionate, but he was just as unfeeling as Delmar. In her blinding rage she kicked out at him, and her bare foot landed harmlessly against his shin.

He quickly twisted her arm behind her back and drew her flush to his hard frame. "Let's not resort to violence, either, for you'd lose again."

"Isn't there any way I can win with you?" she spat, trying vainly to escape his grip.

"Of course not," he replied. "I'm the master and you're the slave, remember?"

"You'll never master me, Kurt Spencer!" she swore.

"We'll see about that." Lifting her into his arms, he carried her to the bed. The covers had been drawn back, and as he placed her on the sheets, his conscience reminded him that he hadn't planned for this to happen. He had wanted her in his room so he could keep her safe, not so he could take advantage of her.

Standing back, he looked down at the lovely woman lying upon his bed. Her ebony hair spread across the pillow like silky damask, and her eyes were as blue as the ocean; he felt as though he were drowning in their bottomless pools.

As she returned his passionate gaze, Jolene felt her desire for Kurt race through her veins with a force so demanding that, forgetting her anger, she held out her arms to him. "I want you," she murmured raspingly. All of her craved his magical touch.

His self-control stripped away, Kurt went into her welcoming embrace, and as he lay beside her, she turned intimately to him. Their lips met in a fiery exchange which left them trembling with breathtaking passion.

After a flurry of more fervent, uninhibited kisses, Kurt removed Jolene's cotton gown. As he dropped the garment to the floor, he rose upon an elbow to study her in the lamplight. His eyes raked hungrily over her firm breasts, then down to her tiny waist and flat stomach. Continuing his perusal, he gazed longingly on the dark vee between her tempting thighs before admiring her delicately sculptured legs. Her beauty was an aphrodesiac, and driven now by a need to possess her totally, he got up to undress.

Jolene, wanting him just as desperately, watched as he hastily disrobed. When he stood before her unclothed, she drew in her breath admiringly at the sight of his perfect masculine build. Oh, he was handsome, this man who had such unlimited control over her body, heart, and emotions!

She reached up and pulled him to her. His strong frame hovered above her as his lips captured hers in a long, blazing kiss which sent her senses reeling.

She opened her legs to receive him and was a little disappointed when he moved to lie at her side.

"Not so fast, my beauty," he murmured huskily. "This time it'll be different. I've made love to you twice, and both times, I did so hurriedly." He smiled tenderly. "There's no reason to rush, so I intend to enjoy you thoroughly and at my leisure. You're the most desirable woman I've ever known, and I'm going to relish every inch of your delectable body."

Expertly, Kurt's hands and lips awoke such passion in Jolene that she writhed and moaned with unbearable ecstasy. Just when she thought she could take no more of this wonderful torment, he leaned over her, lifted her thighs to his, and entered her quickly.

She gasped as his throbbing manhood filled her with rapture, and wrapping her legs about his waist, she drew him in even deeper.

Kurt moved against her, and matching his demanding rhythm, she equalled his hard thrusting until urgently their love climaxed, spiraling them upward to passion's glorious apex.

He rested on her for a moment, then placed a light kiss upon her mouth before moving to rest at her side. Draping an arm about her small shoulders, he drew her close.

Nestling her head on his wide chest, she sighed deeply. She couldn't fight Kurt, for he was indeed the master. She was helpless against him, for she loved him too desperately.

As Jolene lay quiet, inwardly defeated, Kurt's thoughts were swirling. Had she told him the truth? Was she truly the mistress of Cedarbrook? Had her sister and the lawyer committed fraud? He wanted to believe Jolene's story, as incredible as it was, but part of him refused to give in. He knew firsthand that Jolene was capable of lying.

Clearing the doubt from his mind, he decided to turn off the lamp and get some sleep. Tomorrow he and Jolene would be faced with a tiring journey. He turned to her, and seeing that she'd fallen asleep, a gentle, love-filled smile curled his lips.

Moving carefully so he wouldn't wake her, he got up and extinguished the lamp. The silver moonlight filtering in through the open window lit his way back to the bed. Standing, he looked thoughtfully down at Jolene. He smiled as he studied her small frame and pretty face: she looked so innocent and helpless, yet he knew she was quite capable of deceit and had more courage than most men. No, she was neither innocent nor helpless! Again his musings wandered to her sister and the lawyer: if the pair were guilty of fraud, they should be exposed.

As Kurt lay down, drawing Jolene snugly against him, he considered visiting Cedarbrook and doing a little investigating of his own. A stubborn frown crossed his brow. He wouldn't let Jolene know what he was planning, for he wasn't convinced that she hadn't lied. After his brother's wedding, he'd postpone freeing Jolene and pay an unexpected call at Cedarbrook.

His mind made up, Kurt set all thoughts of these things aside and went to sleep.

Chapter Nineteen

"Jolene, it's time to wake up," Kurt said softly. Her head was nestled on his shoulder, and he fought the temptation to place his hand under her chin and tilt her lips up to his. Gently he brushed aside her bangs. The scar was barely noticable and would be completely gone in a couple of weeks. When she didn't stir, he said again, "Wake up, Jolene."

Stretching catlike, she moaned sleepily and opened her eyes. "I slept so soundly," she murmured, repressing a yawn. "I didn't even dream. I haven't had such a good night's sleep since this whole nightmare began." Contented, she snuggled closer to his warm, strong body. She wondered if Kurt's protective presence was why she'd slept so peacefully.

Her cuddling was stimulating, and it was an effort for Kurt to control his passion. His need to make love to her was pressing.

Throwing back the covers, Kurt swung his long legs over the side of the bed. His clothes still lay on the floor, and reaching for them, he mumbled,

"You'd better get dressed. We have a long trip facing us, and we need to get an early start."

"I can't get dressed," she answered. "Unless you want me to wear my nightgown to Heritage Manor."

He seemed bemused. "Nightgown?"

"I don't have any other clothes with me. If you'll recall, when I came to your room, all I brought was myself and a nightgown."

"I'll have Lucy bring you your clothes," he replied.

Leaving the bed, Kurt dressed with haste. God, it was tempting to crawl back into bed with the enticing vixen!

This morning, before awakening Jolene, Kurt had made a solemn vow to himself. He'd sworn emphatically to cease using her as a bed wench. He didn't believe in slavery, nor did he approve of white men taking advantage of their female slaves. Yet he had done just that.

Now, as he finished dressing, Kurt reminded himself that he hadn't exactly used Jolene . . . he hadn't taken her lustfully and without feeling, he'd made love to her tenderly and with all his heart. His conscience intervened; she was legally his slave and he had taken her to his bed. He was guilty as charged! A man had to live by his own code of honor, and last night he had defied his convictions.

Once dressed, Kurt headed for the door without giving Jolene a backward glance. Damn, if he were to turn and look at her lying there in bed, so beautiful and so innocently provocative, he might lose what little control he still had.

"Kurt?" she called. Surely he wasn't leaving so abruptly!

He didn't stop . . . he couldn't. His will-power

was too shaky.

Jolene watched him leave her room, and as he closed the door behind him, her brown knitted petulantly. When he needed her to satisfy his sexual desires, he treated her as though she were special, but now that his lust was temporarily appeased, he couldn't care less about her feelings. She was merely his slave, his bed wench, and he owed her no respect. Respect? Ha! In his opinion, she was his chattel and had no rights whatsoever!

Angry tears filled her eyes, and for the first time since she'd awakened in Atkins' buckboard to find herself a slave, Jolene gave in to her bottled-up pain. Burying her face in the pillow, she cried until, at last, her tears ran dry.

Jolene was sitting at the table with Lucy and Mary Jane when Kurt and Daniel brought the buckboard to the back door.

Daniel entered the kitchen and asked Jolene, "Are you ready to leave?"

"As ready as I'll ever be," she mumbled despondently.

Lucy took a straw bonnet from a peg on the wall and handed it to Jolene. "Here, you gonna need some protection from the sun." Then, placing her arm about Jolene's shoulders, she led her through the door. Daniel and Mary Jane followed close behind.

Kurt was sitting in the buckboard, his saddle pony tied behind. Patiently he waited for Jolene to exchange farewells with her two friends.

Holding the wide-brimmed bonnet in one hand, Jolene turned to Lucy and hugged her. "I'll miss you." Her voice wavered.

"I'm gonna miss you too, honey." Placing her lips close to Jolene's ear, she whispered secretively, "You take my advice and marry Masta Kurt."

"I'd rather marry a polecat!" she remarked more loudly than she'd intended.

Kurt, hearing, couldn't help but grin.

Stepping to Mary Jane, Jolene embraced her tightly. "You've been a good friend. I don't know what I'd have done without you."

Tears forming in her eyes, Mary Jane murmured, "I sure hope we'll see each other again."

"We will," Jolene said with certainty. For a long moment she gazed at the two women. God, how she was going to miss them! They were true friends, and she knew she'd be lost without them.

With Daniel's assistance Jolene climbed into the buckboard and positioned herself as far from Kurt as the seat allowed. Keeping her eyes straight ahead, she put on the bonnet and tied the ribbons beneath her chin.

Spencer gave her a sidelong glance. She was wearing the simple, drab dress that Delmar had bought her in New Orleans, but despite its shapelessness, she looked beautiful beyond words. "Don't you have a bag?"

"All I own are the clothes on my back," she answered.

"There's a small town between here and Heritage Manor. We can stop and buy you an extra dress and whatever else you'll need."

281

"Thanks, masta, suh!" she snapped.

Preferring not to banter with the exasperting chit, Kurt said good-bye to Daniel. Then, with a wave to Lucy and Mary Jane, he slapped the reins against the horses and guided the buckboard toward the front of the house.

Daniel and the women trailed behind the wagon so they could watch Kurt and Jolene's departure.

Delmar and his children were standing on the pillared porch to bid their guest good-bye.

Pulling up, Kurt secured the brake and jumped to the ground. Going to the Delmars, he said politely, "Thanks for your hospitality."

John, shaking Spencer's hand, replied heartily, "We enjoyed your visit. Give your father my best regards."

"I will," he answered.

Kurt turned to Alan to pay his respects, but the man's attention was on Jolene alone. Recognizing the hungry, lustful expression in Alan's eyes, Kurt was relieved to be taking Jolene away from Willow Hill. Taking his gaze from young Delmar, he smiled at Sabrina and told her good-bye.

"It's not good-bye, Kurt," she declared, her eyes shining brightly. "Papa, Alan and I will be coming to Heritage Manor for Richard's wedding."

"Of course," he replied. His eyes swept the threesome. "I'll see you soon." His farewells complete, Kurt joined Jolene, laid the reins against the horses, and started down the winding lane.

Sabrina was consumed with jealousy, and her heated glare remained on Jolene's back as the buckboard drew farther away.

282

Becoming aware of his daughter's surly mood, John asked, "Are you upset?"

Trying to cover her jealousy, she answered peevishly, "Of course I'm upset. You sold my servant right out from under me, and this morning I had to dress myself."

"I'm sorry, Sweetie. I'll find you another maid."

"When?" she insisted, pouting.

Catching sight of Daniel and the women returning to the kitchen, John called, "Lucy, Mary Jane— come here."

They obeyed quickly, and pausing at the bottom of the porch steps, they choruched, "Yes, masta?"

"Lucy," Delmar began, his tone almost apologetic, "can you manage for a while longer without an assistant?"

"Yes, suh, I reckon I can," she mumbled.

"Good!" John remarked. He looked at Mary Jane. "Girl, I've decided to make you a lady's maid." Delmar smiled complacently at his daughter, waved a hand in Mary Jane's direction, and said, "Now you have a maid."

Turning to Mary Jane, Sabrina appraised her with a cold, superior perusal. "Come with me to my room" she demanded haughtily.

As the servant obeyed her mistress, Lucy left to return to the sanctuary of her kitchen. She felt sorry for Mary Jane. If she herself were given a choice, she knew she'd rather pick cotton in the fields than be Sabrina's personal maid . . . the woman was a tyrant.

Alone with his son, John noticed that the young man's face was sullen. Delmar emitted a long sigh.

Why were his children so temperamental? "Is something bothering you?" he asked Alan.

Alan shook his head. "Nothing you'd want to hear."

"Tell me," his father urged gently.

Deciding to speak to him man-to-man, Alan began pressingly, "Papa, I'm twenty years old, but you still treat me as though I were a boy."

"What exactly do you mean?"

"I'm a man now, and I have certain desires and needs." He grew flustered. "Damn it, Papa, do you expect me to remain celibate until I get married? When you were my age, you probably had *your* share of wenches."

"So that's what's ailing you," John said. "Son, there are whorehouses in Mobile. I've never forbidden you to visit them."

"How often do I get into Mobile?" he questioned, sounding desperate. "Besides, why should I pay for a whore who's liable to give me some contagious disease when this plantation is overrun with clean wenches?"

"You know how I feel about you crawling into bed with our wenches. I don't want any of your offspring running around this plantation as pickaninnies. That's why I had to get rid of your sister's maid and buy Jolene to replace her."

"But, Papa, other plantation owners and their sons do it all the time. If I get a wench pregnant, when the sucker's born you've got a slave, free of charge."

"What other planters do with their wenches is their own business, but personally, I don't hold with mixing white blood and colored blood."

Alan's voice began to whine. "How can you say that when you've been sleeping with Lucy for years?"

"I never got her pregnant," he remarked. "She had a very difficult time giving birth to Daniel. She was damaged so badly that she became barren."

"If you're so dead set against me knocking up a wench, then give me one who can't conceive."

"Who, for instance?"

"I read the papers on Mary Jane, and she hasn't been a virgin for years, but she's never gotten pregnant. She probably can't have babies."

Seeing instant refusal on his father's face, Alan continued harshly, "Damn it, Papa! By the time one of your bucks become my age, you make damned sure that he's paired off with a wench! You claim a horny nigger is a dangerous one! Well, what about your own son? Don't you think I've got feelings?"

John gave the situation serious consideration. Perhaps he had neglected his son's needs. Furthermore, if Alan had a woman at his disposal, maybe he'd start acting more mature. John supposed it was difficult for Alan to grow up when his young, healthy body kept demanding release . . . and got none. Thinking back, he remembered that at Alan's age, he'd had more than his share of whores and wenches. John's father hadn't cared if his son got one or more of their wenches pregnant. Young and virile, John had planted his seed in quite a few women slaves before his first offspring was born. But he hadn't been prepared for the repulsion he'd felt at the sight of his firstborn. There was something about his own flesh and blood being a Negro slave that had turned his stomach. Thereafter he had refrained from sleeping with his father's slaves and had limited his sexual attentions to whores. Then, following his father's demise, he sold every child he'd sired, turning a deaf ear to the heartbroken pleas of their mothers.

Now, thinking about Alan's needs, he had to admit that his son had made a valid point: apparently, Mary Jane was incapable of bearing children.

John yielded. "Very well, Alan. You may have Mary Jane for a bed wench. However, I forbid you to sleep with her here in the house. We must consider your sister. I don't want her exposed to this kind of indelicate situation. When you get the urge to lie with the wench, do so in her cabin."

Alan was ebullient. "I will, Papa! And thank you for understanding!"

Pleased over their newfound camaraderie. John draped his arm about Alan's shoulders in a friendly fashion. "That Mary Jane is a fine-looking woman. I almost envy you."

"I'll have her buckin' and beggin' me for more," Alan boasted.

"You're quite a stud, eh?" he asked good-naturedly.

"You just wait, Papa. Tomorrow, Mary Jane will be walking straddled-legged. But she'll have a big, contented smile on her face!"

John laughed. "Son, you must be a chip off the old block!"

*   *   *

The trip to Heritage Manor seemed interminable to Kurt and Jolene, for the strain and tension between them were nerve wracking and depressing. Their conversations were short and impersonal, and by the time Kurt turned the buckboard onto the driveway of his parents' home, he and Jolene were relieved to find the journey over.

Dusk cloaked the land as the tall-pillared colonial house came into full view. The mansion was pretentious, the lawns manicured. The horses, probably sensing the end to their tiring haul, broke into a trot as they pulled the wagon up the long, tree-bordered lane.

"You home is very impressive," Jolene said sincerely.

"Not my home; my parents'," Kurt clarified. "I lay no claim to Heritage Manor. When my father passes on, everything will go to my brother, Richard."

"This place must be worth a fortune. How can you turn your back on such wealth?"

"My values are more important to me than money. Besides, I'm making my own fortune in Texas."

"Then you're doing quite well?" she queried.

He grinned teasingly. "I was, until I paid out four thousand dollars for an ungrateful wench."

"Four thousand!" Jolene gasped, finding the amount unbelievable.

Kurt toyed with her. "If I set you free, I'm out a lot of money. Maybe I'll keep you and let you work off the four thousand. My ranch house could use a woman to keep it clean, and after a long day on the range, I'd sure enjoy a good home-cooked meal." He arched a brow. "You can cook and clean, can't you?"

Her eyes flashed angrily. "You arrogant devil! If you'll take me to Cedarbrook, I'll return your four thousand dollars, plus another thousand for your trouble."

"Don't you think your sister might object?"

"Damn it! Cedarbrook isn't hers—it's mine!"

They had reached the house, and Kurt let the matter rest. Alighting, he reached up, wrapped an arm about Jolene's waist, and lifted her from the buckboard. Placing a hand on her arm, he led her up the steps to the front door. Opening it, he stepped back for Jolene to precede him. Then, entering the huge foyer, he yelled loudly, "Anybody home?"

Removing her bonnet, Jolene swept her eyes over what she could see of the house. A winding marble stairway led upstairs, and a tall mahogany Roxbury clock stood in one corner. The walls were papered in a bright pattern, and a framed mirror stood out stunningly against the colorful design. The mirror was bordered with flowers and leaves painted white, with gilt highlights. Glancing over her shoulder, she saw an intricately carved coat rack, its bare limbs awaiting winter.

"Is anybody home?" Kurt called again.

They heard the scurrying of feet. Then, suddenly, three people arrived in the foyer at once, all of them trying to hug Kurt simultaneously as they exclaimed over his presence.

Standing back, Jolene watched as Kurt's family made a fuss over him. She looked first at the man who was apparently his father, and she could see a stark resemblance to Kurt. She sensed intuitively that under different circumstances she and Edward

Spencer would be friends. She turned her perusal to Richard—there was little similarity between the two brothers. Richard's frame was the smaller, and his blond hair had a reddish cast.

Slowly she looked at Kurt's mother. Katherine Spencer had become aware of Jolene's presence and was staring at the young woman with obvious distaste. Jolene took an instant dislike to the mistress of Heritage Manor, and she sensed that the feeling was mutual.

Katherine was a tall, heavy-set woman, and her strawberry-blond hair, piled on top of her head in an abundance of curls, made her look even taller. Her angular face was cold, and her eyes held no compassion.

Turning to her son, Katherine demanded curtly, "Who is this . . . this woman?" She studied Jolene disparagingly.

By now the two men had also become aware of their silent guest. Richard, eyeing Jolene's modest wardrobe, looked down his nose at her. Why in the world did Kurt bring such white trash home with him?

Jolene, resenting Richard's smug scrutiny, silently called him a stuck-up bastard, Then, lifting her proud chin ever so slightly, she looked at Edward. Recognizing genuine warmth in his curious gaze, she smiled at him tentatively.

Stepping to Jolene, Kurt wrapped an arm protectively about her waist and drew her to his side. "Mother," he began haltingly, "this is Jolene."

"But why is she here?" the woman insisted. "Where did you meet her, and why is she accompanying you?"

Kurt, uncertain of how to break the news to his

family, cleared his throat hesitantly. He hated the idea of introducing Jolene as his slave, but he couldn't very well avoid the truth. When the Delmars arrived for Richard's wedding, they would most assuredly mention his buying Jolene.

Losing her patience, Kurt's mother insisted pettishly, "Answer me! Why did you bring this piece of white trash into my home?"

Jolene didn't give Kurt time to respond, and letting her temper get the better of her, she said spitefully, "I ain't white trash! I's a quadroon!"

"Wh . . . what?" the woman choked out, paling.

"I's Masta Kurt's brand new bed wench, mistress, ma'am!" Jolene blue eyes gleamed wickedly.

Swooning, Katherine leaned into Richard's outstretched arms. As he helped his mother into the drawing room, she pleaded weakly, "Get my smelling salts."

Folding his arms across his chest and holding back an urge to laugh, Kurt eyed Jolene with feigned ire. "When you want, you can be quite a hellion!"

Refusing to apologize for her behavior, she remarked nastily, "Your mother is a snob! And she got what she deserved!"

Edward Spencer had been listening, and his unexpected jovial laughter startled Jolene. Patting his son on the back, he asked cheerfully, "Son, where did you find this delightful minx?"

"I bought her from John Delmar."

Edward looked at him peculiarly. "I thought you opposed slavery?"

"I do," he answered.

"Then why did you buy the girl?"

"I aim to set her free." He cast Jolene a piercing glare. "That is, I'll set her free when I'm damned good and ready."

Frowning, she wished she could stick her tongue out at him without looking ridiculous.

Edward studied the pair, his curiosity aroused. "Kurt, later you and I have some talking to do. But now I think you should take Jolene to the overseer's house. It's empty—my overseer quit last week, and I haven't had time to replace him."

"Thanks," Kurt replied, relieved that there was a comfortable place for Jolene to stay.

Moving readily, he took Jolene outside. Going to the buckboard, he grabbed the carpetbag which held the articles he had bought for Jolene on their way to Heritage Manor.

Taking her by the arm, he led her along the short path to the overseer's home. The square structure resembled a back-country farmhouse. Leading Jolene up to the porch, Kurt explained, "My grandfather built this house. It was his home until he became rich and had that monstrosity erected." He gestured tersely toward the manor house.

He opened the door, and following him inside, Jolene asked, "Don't you like your parents' home?"

Finding a lamp and lighting it, Kurt replied dryly, "It's too ostentatious for my taste."

The door opened into a roomy parlor, and looking about, Jolene was pleased to find the decor cozy and comfortable. The furniture was old, but in good condition. She supposed most of the pieces were cast-offs from the big house.

Kurt went into the kitchen, returning momentarily. "The overseer must have left in a hurry, for there's plenty of food, so you'll be all right for the night. I'll come back and check on you in the morning. You'll be safe here, and you won't be bothered by me or anyone else." He raised a brow questioningly, "I hope you understand what I'm trying to say."

Needling him, Jolene remarked saucily, "Of course I understand. You're afraid your mother will have a tantrum if you share this house with your bed wench."

Jolene's referring to herself as his bed wench made Kurt cringe. "What I do is none of my mother's business," he replied.

"I don't see any likeness between you and your mother."

"That's because she's my stepmother."

"Oh?" Jolene questioned. She was somehow relieved Kurt wasn't Katherine's natural son.

"My mother died in childbirth."

"Having Richard?"

"No, she died giving birth to me. Richard was born about a year after my father married Katherine."

Kurt's gaze met and held Jolene's for a tense moment. Then, conquering an overwhelming need to take her into his arms, he went to the door, opened it, bid her a pleasant goodnight, and left.

Stepping to the parlor window, Jolene watched as Kurt's long strides carried him out of her sight. Her brow furrowed: if lust was Kurt's reason for buying her, then why was he allowing her to stay in this house alone? She found his behavior perplexing.

She'd been certain that he was an unfeeling cad, but now she wasn't so sure.

Sighing heavily, she turned from the window. The quiet, empty house was depressing. She heard singing coming from the slave cabins, and the plaintive melody went with her melancholy mood. Going to a pine rocker by the unlit hearth, she sat down and, rocking gently, she thought about Lucy and Mary Jane. She missed them so terribly that her heart ached.

Although she loved Lucy, it was Mary Jane whom she missed more. When they had been a part of Cal Atkins' coffle, a special friendship had developed between them.

Speaking aloud, Jolene said to herself, "As soon as I prove I'm Papa's legal daughter, I'll return to Willow Hill and buy Mary Jane. Then I'll set her free, and she can live at Cedarbrook for as long as she wants."

She rested her head on the back of the chair. "I can only hope that, in the meantime, she'll be safe at Willow Hill."

Chapter Twenty

Mary Jane moved slowly through the dark kitchen. She considered going to Lucy's room to see if she were still up so they could talk for a while. Lucy's small quarters were adjacent to the kitchen, but Mary Jane saw no light shining under the closed door, so she went on outside.

The night air was refreshingly cool, and as she walked toward her isolated cabin, Mary Jane found the brisk air rejuvenating. She was tired, for Sabrina had worked her hard.

She was close to her cabin when suddenly a man stepped out of the shadows. Startled, Mary Jane's heart lurched. Then, recognizing Daniel, she smiled shakily. "You scared me half to death!"

"I'm sorry," he quickly apologized. "I've been waiting for you."

"Why?" she asked, on her guard.

Seeing distrust on her pretty face, he said gently, "I only want to talk to you."

Mary Jane, still uneasy, replied candidly, "No man has ever wanted simply to talk to me."

Daniel knew of Mary Jane's oppressive past, for she had told Lucy and he had persuaded Lucy to tell him. "I'm not like all the men who abused you," he said tenderly.

"How did you know 'bout them?" She was surprised.

"Lucy told me." He placed a hand lightly on her arm and led her to the cabin steps. "Let's sit down and talk."

His touch evoked strange feelings in Mary Jane, feelings she couldn't understand. The sensation was pleasing, though, and she let his hand remain as he urged her to sit beside him.

Ill at ease, Mary Jane waited nervously for Daniel to start talking. Although she had been abused by men for years, her heart was entirely innocent: she knew nothing about love between a man and a woman. She didn't even know how to carry on a conversation with a gentleman.

Daniel, understanding her insecurity, was overwhelmed with compassion for this beautiful young lady who through no fault of her own had suffered such mistreatment.

"How was your first day as Sabrina's maid?" he asked.

Mary Jane smiled without mirth. "How do you think?"

"Pretty bad, eh?"

"She's the most demandin' woman I've ever worked for. I did everything she told me, but she wasn't satisfied and made me do it all again."

Daniel frowned. "The damned bitch!"

"Don't talk 'bout Miz Sabrina like that! What if Masta John was to hear you? He'd whip you for sure!"

"I'm not his slave . . . he can't order *me* lashed."

"Don't be so sure. He'd find a way."

The soft moonlight shining on Mary Jane's face revealed the fright in her large eyes. Touched by her concern, Daniel murmured, "Very well—I'll watch what I say."

"Lucy's right. You oughta go back to Texas. You liable to get in trouble if you stay in these parts."

He groaned sorrowfully. "How can I leave without my mother?"

"You got to do it, for your own sake as well as Lucy's. Since you done come back, she been terribly worried 'bout you. If you really love your mama, you'll return to your ranch so she can have peace of mind."

"I guess you're right." He sounded defeated.

Impulsively she placed her hand over his. "I reckon it hurts to leave someone you love."

Entwining their fingers and holding her hand snugly, he whispered, "It hurts like hell. I don't suppose *you've* ever left a loved one."

"I never had nobody to love 'til I met Jolene." Tears came to Mary Jane's eyes. "I'm gonna miss her a lot. I reckon it's best if a slave never finds anyone to care 'bout, 'cause chances are good that they'll only be separated."

A lump rose in his throat. "God, Mary Jane! You've had a hard life."

She shrugged. "It could've been a lot worse."

"Worse?" he questioned. "What could be worse than being used and defiled by your white masters?"

Sympathizing with other women slaves that she'd met or known about, she answered with feeling, "I ain't never had my own baby sold away from me.

That would be worse." She looked meaningfully at Daniel. "Your own mama went through that."

"But we were lucky that I was sold to the Spencers. I got to come back here often and visit with Mama."

"You must've been born under a lucky star. You had a good life even when you was still a slave. You got to be educated, then set free, and now you have your own ranch." She sighed deeply. "I sure wish I had an education. It must be nice to read and write and know how to talk proper-like."

An idea suddenly occurred to him, and Daniel grinned widely. "Mary Jane," he began, excitement in his voice. "This afternoon I talked to Delmar about buying Mama, and he flatly refused to consider selling her. I know he's not going to change his mind, and I know that Mama won't relent and run away with me." His smile grew even larger, and as his hand tightened over hers, he continued, "I have the money that I saved to buy Mama, but now why don't I use it to buy you? I'll set you free, then take you to Texas with me. And if you want to learn to read and write, I'll teach you." He met her incredulous gaze. "There'll be no strings attached. My ranch house has two bedrooms, and you can have the extra one."

Astounded, she stammered, "But—I don't understand. Why would you do this for me and not expect me to sleep with you?"

He answered honestly. "My reason for wanting to help you isn't entirely unselfish. I've grown very fond of you. I think I'm falling in love. I hope that in time you'll share my feelings. If I take you with me when I leave, maybe you'll eventually learn to love me.

However, if you don't, you'll still be free to do whatever you want."

Mary Jane wasn't sure which shocked her more—the thought of being free, or Daniel's declaration of love.

When she remained silent, Daniel urged, "Well, what do you say? Do you want me to ask Delmar if he'll sell you?"

"He won't wanna sell me to you 'cause you're a colored man."

"I'll offer him a price so generous that he'll set aside his bigotry."

"You got that much money?" she asked, amazed.

"I brought five thousand dollars with me. I knew in order to buy Mama, I'd need a tidy sum. Of course, I'm not stupid. My first offer for you won't be that high, but I'll keep raising it until he gives in. I think he'll settle somewhere between two and three thousand."

"Where'd you get all this money? Ain't you afraid someone will steal it?"

"I have it hidden in Abe's cabin. He has an old chest of drawers, and I buried my money three feet in front of it." He sounded unconcerned. "Besides, who's going to try and steal it? Slaves don't need money, and the Delmars have more than they need."

"The Delmars are greedy enough to want more."

He chuckled. "You're probably right, but they don't know where it's hidden." Placing a hand beneath her chin, he tilted her face up to his. "Mary Jane, will you come with me to Texas?"

"How can you want someone like me for . . . for your woman? I ain't smart, and I been used over and over again."

"In the first place, I don't want you as my woman, I want you as my wife. And in the second place, I happen to think you're very smart. As for being used—my God, Mary Jane, don't you realize that you're as pure as the newfallen snow?"

"How can you say that when you know I ain't no virgin?"

"Maybe you aren't a virgin technically, but in your heart you are. You have no idea how beautiful the love between a man and woman can be."

"If you's talkin' 'bout pesterin', I hate it!"

"I wouldn't call what your white masters did to you pestering. It was rape. I'm talking about love, and love is as far removed from rape as night is from day. Don't confuse the two, Mary Jane."

"I wish I knew a little more 'bout love, then maybe I'd understand what you's tryin' to say."

Smiling tenderly, he stood, then drew her to her feet and into his arms. Holding her close, he whispered, "I'm going to kiss you. Do you mind?"

"I don't like kissin' either," she answered straightforwardly.

He wasn't dissuaded. "While I'm kissing you, I want you to forget about those men who've abused you. Concentate fully on the feel of my lips on yours. And remember that I'm kissing you because I care very deeply for you."

Tentatively he pressed his mouth to hers, drawing her snugly against his strong frame. She leaned into his embrace, wiping all thought from her mind except for the pleasant touch of his lips.

"How do you feel?" he whispered in her ear.

"I feel all warm inside," she answered somewhat breathlessly.

"So do I," he admitted. Again he placed his mouth over hers, but this time he intensified their kiss and was pleased when she returned his ardor.

Her sweet response aroused his passion, and releasing her reluctantly, he stepped back. It was too soon to teach her the art of love—he didn't want to rush her. "I'd better let you go inside and get some sleep, but I'll see you in the morning. After Delmar has had his breakfast, I'll talk to him about buying you."

"Oh God! God!" she cried desperately. "Please, please let Masta John sell me!"

Daniel felt pangs of dread. What if Delmar refused to cooperate? Had he elevated Mary Jane's hopes for nothing? Would Delmar send them plunging? He found himself silently uttering his own prayer.

Overcome with worry, and filled with love, he suddenly brought Mary Jane back into his arms and kissed her daringly, passionately. "I love you!" he declared forcefully before letting her go, turning about and walking away quickly.

Mary Jane's eyes followed him until he was enveloped by the darkness of night. Gingerly, she ran her fingertips across her lips which still tingled from his ardent caress. She tried to understand this exciting, warm feeling that Daniel had awakened within her. Was she experiencing love? Was it love that was making her heart beat faster, and her body ache for a release that went beyond her comprehension? Had Daniel been right? Could a relationship between a man and woman be truly beautiful? If only she had an older woman to talk to, someone who would understand her confusion and explain what she was feeling. Maybe in the morning she'd talk to Lucy. After all, Lucy had been in love with Lazarus, so she'd understand.

A radiant smile crossed Mary Jane's face, and hugging herself happily, she murmured, "I guess I'm fallin' in love. And it makes me feel good." She looked up at the dark heavens dotted with twinkling stars. "For the first time in my life, I feel really good 'bout myself and 'bout life. Thank you, God. Even if things don't work out and Masta John won't let me go, I's still grateful that I know what it's like to feel good—and—and truly alive!"

Her spirits soaring, Mary Jane opened the door and went inside her dark cabin. The moonlight that shone through the bare window outlined the form of the man lying on her bed. Her elation tumbled as fear and dread welled within her. As she realized Alan Delmar was the intruder, tears flooded her eyes and pain shot through her heart. How could God be so cruel as to give her a taste of heaven one minute, only to sentence her to hell the next? Maybe there was no God, or if He did exist, he was the white man's Lord!

Fluffing up the pillows and leaning back against them, Alan said huskily, "I've got some good news for you, gal. You're gonna be my bed wench." He had overheard Mary Jane's and Daniel's conversation. He smiled smugly. Lucy's uppity son would never own Mary Jane!

"You be good to me," Alan continued, his eyes raking Mary Jane's ripe curves, "and we'll get along just fine. But if you're insolent, I'll lay my belt across your bare ass. Do you understand me, girl?"

"Yes, masta," she murmured, her submissive reply

stemming from a lifetime of servility.

Alan was nude, and he reached down and lifted his erect manhood. "Look what your masta's got for you. Shed your clothes, then come over here and slide down on your new toy."

From habit Mary Jane started to remove her shapeless dress, but all at once her newborn pride surfaced. No, she'd not submit! Daniel had shown her the meaning of dignity, and she'd not relinquish it without a struggle. If Alan wanted her, he'd have to take her by force! She knew that he'd punish her severely for disobeying, but she no longer cared. She owed it to herself and to her love for Daniel to fight for her self-respect!

Taking Alan totally unaware, she whirled about and ran from the cabin.

"Come back here, you damned wench!" she heard him rage as she fled down the steps. Mary Jane had no conscious thought as to where she was heading, but her desperate flight took her to the back door of the kitchen, and swinging it open, she darted inside.

Rushing to Lucy's room, she pounded wildly on the door. "Lucy! . . . Lucy, let me in! . . . You got to help me!"

Getting out of bed, Lucy quickly lit the lamp. Then, as she admitted Mary Jane, the young woman flung herself into Lucy's arms. Lucy prodded her, but Mary Jane was crying too convulsively to answer.

Leading Mary Jane to the bed, Lucy encouraged her to sit down. Then, lifting the hem of her long cotton gown, she sat down beside her. Speaking firmly, she said, "Honey, you got to stop cryin' so you can tell me what's wrong."

Striving to control her tears, Mary Jane said

between sobs, "Masta Alan's in my cabin. He said that I gotta be his bed wench!"

Again she fell into Lucy's arms, placing her head on the woman's shoulder. "I don't want 'im touchin' me! Oh Lucy, please help me! Masta John, he listen to you. Go ask 'm to tell Masta Alan to leave me alone!"

Suddenly Alan's voice sounded from the open doorway. "It won't do you any good to send Lucy running to Papa, 'cause I have his permission to do what I want with you!"

Lucy looked up quickly, meeting the angry man's hard gaze. Alan was only half-dressed. He had on his trousers, but was barefoot and his shirt was unbuttoned.

Standing, Lucy took a protective stance in front of Mary Jane. "Masta Alan, you leave this chile alone!" There was no fear in her voice.

Enraged, Alan thundered, "Why, you isolent black bitch! How dare you tell me what to do!" He stalked to her, drew back his arm and slapped her soundly across the cheek.

The powerful blow jerked her head to the side, and for a moment she tottered precariously. Then, righting herself, she turned her face back to his.

Mary Jane, panicking, begged, "Masta Alan, please don't hit her again! I'll do anything you say, but please don't hurt Lucy!"

"Hush, girl!" Lucy demanded with quiet authority. "He ain't gonna hit me again." She steadied her gaze on Alan. "If you bother Mary Jane, I'm gonna go straight to Masta John."

His anger boiling, Alan snapped, "Damn it! I already told you that I have Papa's permission! If you don't believe me, then go ahead and run to him! He'll tell you that Mary Jane's mine!"

"I ain't plannin' to talk to 'im about Mary Jane," she replied pointedly.

Confused, he stammered, "Wh—what are you getting at?"

"If I go to Masta John, I'm gonna talk to 'im 'bout Dottie and Sally."

Alan began to perspire. "What about Dottie and Sally?"

"I know you the one who got them girls pregnant."

Pretending innocence, Alan remarked, "Me? Hell, those gals are paired off with bucks."

"They wasn't paired off when they got pregnant. Both of them girls came to me when they realized they was knocked-up. They told me how you made them sleep with you. I was gettin' ready to tell Masta John what you done when it dawned on me that I shouldn't do it. But I knew those gals would soon start showin', and then Masta John would demand to know who'd knocked 'em up. So I went to the masta and brought it to his attention that Dottie and Sally were maturin' and needed to be coupled with a man of their own. He agreed, and told me pick out two unattached bucks. I chose Randy and Joe 'cause they light-skinned. That way, when the gals give birth, Masta John won't question their babies' parentage."

Astounded, Alan gasped, "I can't believe you'd do that for me! But I sure appreciate you protecting me."

Lucy wanted to laugh in his face. "I didn't do it for you," she replied, her expression unmoving. "I did it for Dottie and Sally. Those gals was born on this plantation, and I knew if Masta John learned they was carryin' your babies, he'd sell 'em away from Willow Hill. They knew it, too. That's why they came to me for help."

She raised her chin stubbornly and folded her arms beneath her breasts. "I think a lot of those two gals, but I think more of Mary Jane. If you insist on makin' her your bed wench, I'll go straight to Masta John and tell 'im everything. You know how he feels 'bout you pesterin' his wenches. When he sold Sabrina's maid, I heard 'im tell you that if you got another wench pregnant, he wasn't goin' to give you no money for your European tour. You's supposed to leave next spring, ain't you? You been looking' forward to it for a long time, too. It's a shame you's gonna miss it, but if you bother Mary Jane, you ain't never gonna see Europe."

Alan was enraged to the point of murder. "You goddamned bitch! I oughta kill you!"

Lucy knew that as long as John Delmar was alive, Alan's threat was hollow. Her expression remained set.

Perspiring heavily, Alan began to fidget uncomfortably. He wondered if Lucy was bluffing. Would she really go to his father and tell him the truth about Dottie and Sally? If she did, he didn't doubt that John Delmar would believe her. Going on an European tour meant a great deal to Alan, it was a trip every aristocratic young man was expected to make. He didn't want to be the only one among his peers to be denied the opportunity.

Afraid that Lucy was serious, he gave in. "All right, you God-damned slut! This time, you win!"

His eyes narrowed into angry slits. "Someday *I'll* be the master of Willow Hill. When that day comes, I'm going to kill you!"

"I take your threat kindly, Masta Alan. 'Cause when you become the masta, I'll be glad to die if that's the only way I can leave Willow Hill."

His face reddened with rage. "Damn you! God damn you!" Beaten, he whirled about awkwardly and left the room.

Lucy sat down beside Mary Jane and said soothingly, "You don't have to worry, honey. He ain't gonna bother you."

"Thank you, Lucy. But I'm afraid you done made a dangerous enemy . . . Masta Alan will try to get even with you."

Despite Lucy's courage, she found the possibility terrifying. She shuddered.

"Can I stay with you tonight?" Mary Jane asked, pleading. She was still frightened and didn't want to be alone.

"Of course you can stay," Lucy assured her. She helped Mary Jane into bed. Then, extinguishing the lamp, she lay down beside her.

Feeling safe next to Lucy, Mary Jane forgot her fear and her thoughts wandered to Daniel. Remembering the warm, special feeling that Daniel had evoked in her, she asked hesitantly, "Lucy? Can I talk to you 'bout somethin' important?"

"What's on you mind, chile?"

"Tonight, when I left the house to go to my cabin, Daniel was waitin' for me. We talked for a long time. He said that since he cain't buy you, he's gonna ask Masta John to sell me. He wants to take me to Texas and marry me."

Lucy wasn't surprised. She had sensed that her son was smitten with Mary Jane. "I'm happy for you and Daniel both. I think you'll make 'im a fine wife."

"Lucy, I ain't too sure I can be a good wife. I don't like it when a man pesters me. I told Daniel how I feel, and he said that pesterin' ain't like makin' love. Then he . . . he . . ."

"Go on," Lucy coaxed.

"He kissed me, and I felt all funny inside."

Lucy smiled. "Did you like it when he was kissin' you?"

"Yes!" she breathed.

"Honey, Daniel's right. You cain't judge love by what's happened to you in the past. Givin' yourself to the man you love is more beautiful than words can describe."

"Has you experienced that kind of love?"

Lucy was quiet for some time before replying pensively, "Yes, I know 'bout that kind of love."

"Lazarus?" Mary Jane prodded.

"I loved 'im with all my heart." She paused, then added firmly, "I'd rather not talk 'bout Lazarus. That was a long time ago."

"I think I understand," Mary Jane murmured.

"Go to sleep, Honey. You needs your rest."

Agreeing, Mary Jane rolled to her side and cuddled up with her pillow. Although she was soon slumbering, it was a long time before Lucy fell asleep; and when she did, she dreamt of Lazarus.

The next morning, as Alan entered the dining room, he found John sitting at the breakfast table alone.

Putting down his coffee cup, Delmar studied his son's sullen face. As Alan drew out his chair and sat down, he said, "You don't look very pert for a man who shared a bed with a beautiful wench."

At that moment, Lucy came into the room carrying a tray laden with ham and eggs. Giving the woman a surreptitious glare, Alan mumbled, "I didn't sleep with Mary Jane. I changed my mind about having her for a bed wench."

John was surprised. "I don't understand. Why did you change your mind?"

"I just did," he grumbled.

"But why?" Delmar insisted.

"Damn it! Can't I change my mind without getting the third degree?" Alan said, steaming.

Lucy, pretending to be busy, hovered about the table. This was one conversation she had no intention of missing.

Although John's curiosity was strongly aroused, he decided not to pressure his son. He was certain that something important had happened to alter Alan's decision to bed Mary Jane, but he had a feeling he would never learn what it was. "All right, son . . . I'll stop questioning you."

Young Delmar was too upset to eat, and pushing back his chair, he got abruptly to his feet. Without bothering to utter an excuse, he stormed out of the room.

John looked at Lucy. "Why do you suppose Alan changed his mind about Mary Jane? And why is he so angry?"

Heading back for the kitchen, Lucy replied with an inward smile, "I ain't got no idea, Masta John. No idea at all."

Chapter Twenty-One

Delmar was in his office, reading over his ledgers when a knock sounded at his closed door. "Come in," he grumbled. Although annoyed at the interruption, he was surprised to see Lucy's son.

Going to John's desk, Daniel didn't sit in the extra chair, but stood respectfully. "Excuse my intrusion, Mr. Delmar, but I need to talk to you about Mary Jane."

"Oh?" John questioned, curious. He wondered if Daniel had played a part in Alan's decision to discard Mary Jane.

"I'd like to buy her, sir."

"My, my," the planter drawled, leaning back in his chair and grinning. "That money you saved up to buy your mama must be burnin' a hole in your pocket. Boy, why don't you take that money back to Texas with you and buy up some cattle? Don't you realize that cattle are a better investment that a wench?"

Daniel strove to control his temper. The man's

attitude was irritating. "I'm a rancher, sir, and I'm well aware how much cattle are worth."

"Don't get uppity with me, boy!" Delmar spat. "I'll never understand why Kurt gave you an education and set you free. Sometimes I wonder if young Spencer isn't an abolitionist at heart." He cleared his throat and sat upright. "Well, that's beside the point. As for buying Mary Jane, she's not for sale."

"I'll give you fifteen hundred dollars."

John hid his interest. Fifteen hundred? If he accepted, he'd clear five hundred on the deal—Mary Jane had only cost him a thousand. He wondered how high Daniel was willing to go. "She's not for sale," he repeated flatly.

"Two thousand," Daniel offered.

Although it galled the planter to do business with a Negro, greed got the better of him. "How much money do you have, boy?"

"Three thousand," he lied. He wasn't about to admit that he had five thousand, for Delmar would probably hold out for the entire amount.

John watched him closely, trying to decide if he was telling the truth.

Daniel, reading the man's thoughts, put on his best poker face.

The deal was too lucrative to turn down. "All right, Daniel. You give me three thousand dollars, and the wench is yours."

"Thank you, sir," he replied, showing the planter the respect he demanded.

"You're as bad as Kurt," Delmar grumbled, "throwing your money away on wenches." He returned his attention to his ledgers, signifying that

Daniel was dismissed.

Leaving the office, Daniel hurried to the kitchen and was overjoyed to find that Mary Jane was there talking to Lucy.

Going to the table, he drew the young woman into his arms and hugged her eagerly. "Delmar agreed to sell you!" he exclaimed.

She was too ecstatic to talk, and as tears of joy rolled down her cheeks, she clung to Daniel as though she never intended to let him go.

Smiling happily, Lucy stepped to the couple, and they welcomed her into their embrace.

A few minutes later, Daniel left the kitchen and ran all the way to Abe's cabin.

As he swung open the door and darted inside, it dawned on him that he had forgotten to stop at the tool shed for a shovel—he'd need it to uncover his money. He made a half-turn to dash back outside when he was frozen by the sight that suddenly confronted him. Where his money was supposed to be safely buried there was a gaping, empty hole.

Daniel's strong frame tensed, and he unconsciously clenched his hands into tight fists. Who in the hell had stolen his money? Except for Mary Jane, no one knew where it was hidden: not even Abe.

Daniel stormed out of the cabin and hurried back to the kitchen.

Lucy knew something was wrong the moment she saw her son's face. "Daniel, what happened?" she asked.

"My money's been stolen." He turned to Mary Jane. "Except for you, no one knew where it was hidden."

"You don't think I took it, do you?" she cried.

"Of course not," he said sincerely. He went to her and took her tenderly into his arms. "I'm sorry if I gave you that impression."

"But I don't understand," Lucy began confusedly. "If no one knew where it was buried, then how come it's gone?"

"Masta Alan!" Mary Jane suddenly exclaimed. Looking at Daniel, she explained, "Last night when we was sittin' on the steps talkin', Masta Alan was in my cabin. When you was tellin' me where the money was buried, he probably heard every word."

"Why was he in your cabin?" Daniel demanded, his anger apparent.

Quickly Mary Jane told him everything that had happened with Alan, and the way Lucy had stopped him through blackmail.

"If my blackmail worked once, it'll work again," Lucy remarked. "I'll tell 'im if he don't give you back your money, I'll tell Masta John 'bout Dottie and Sally."

"It wouldn't do any good," Daniel replied heavily. "Delmar's punishment to withhold his finances is no longer a threat to Alan. He can pay for his trip to Europe with my money. Besides, he knows it's just his word against mine. Who do you think Delmar will believe?"

"If I talk to Masta John with you, maybe he'll listen," Lucy replied hopefully.

"I seriously doubt it, but it's worth a try."

Alan was closeted in the office with his father

when Lucy received permission to enter.

John was a little surprised to see that Daniel was with her. "What do you want, Lucy?" he asked mildly.

Alan was seated across from the desk, and taking a stance beside his chair, Lucy avoided looking at him as she said to his father, "Masta John, somebody stole Daniel's money. He had it buried in Abe's cabin, and when he went to get it, someone had dug it up."

John looked over at Daniel who was poised at the closed door. "Do you know who stole your money?"

Lucy answered for her son, "Yes, Masta, we know who took it."

When the woman said no more, Delmar questioned, "Well? Who's the thief?"

"Masta Alan," she replied.

"What?" Alan exclaimed angrily. "Why, you lying, black—"

Interrupting, John lashed out, "Be quiet, Alan! I'll handle this!" His eyes were smoldering as he returned his gaze to Lucy. "How dare you accuse my son! Apologize to your young master, then leave this room at once!"

Disobeying, Lucy's words raced, "Last night, Masta Alan overheard Daniel tellin' Mary Jane where his money was hidden. No one else knew where it was, that's why I know Masta Alan stole it."

"No, I didn't, Papa!" young Delmar claimed, sounding offended. Inwardly, he was gloating. Stealing Daniel's money had been as easy as taking candy from a baby. He wasn't even afraid of detection, for he had his stolen cash safely

313

stashed away.

John spoke to Daniel, "How much money was stolen?"

"Five thousand," he answered.

"Five thousand?" Delmar repeated archly. "Boy, this morning, you stood in my office and told me you only had three thousand! Did the extra two thousand materialize out of thin air? Or did you tell me a bare-faced lie?"

"I told you that I only had three thousand to pay for Mary Jane because I knew if you were aware of how much I really had, you'd have held out for the entire amount."

Delmar rose to his feet. His face reddening with rage, he began furiously, "Do you think I don't know what you're up to, boy? You never had five thousand dollars, or even three thousand! You had all this planned before you came here. You intended to offer me an outrageous price for Lucy, then when I agreed, you were going to come up with this cock-and-bull story about your money being stolen. You actually thought I'd feel responsible for your loss and let you have your mama for nothing! Then, when I refused to sell Lucy, you decided to try for Mary Jane!" A raging frown crossed his face. "I want you off this plantation immediately! If you ever set foot on my property again, I'll shoot you on sight!"

Delmar set his eyes upon Lucy. "As for you, if you don't leave this room at once, I'll have you whipped!" Despite his rage, he wasn't sure if he could actually carry out his threat. It was sickening just to think of punishing her.

"But, Masta John—" Lucy began desperately.

Daniel, afraid Delmar would order her whipped, went quickly to his mother, took her arm, and led her firmly from the room.

As they were leaving, John's voice rang out thunderously, "Remember what I said, Daniel! I want you off my land! Now!"

Rising from his chair, Alan's voice echoed his father's, "And don't come back unless you wanna be a dead nigger!"

Restless, Jolene paced back and forth across the spotless parlor. Kurt had told her to stay indoors, and in order to keep herself busy, she had cleaned the house from top to bottom. Now that her work was complete and there was nothing left to scrub or dust, boredom quickly set in. She hated being penned up and hoped Kurt didn't expect her to stay in the house indefinitely.

She knew Kurt felt he had a good reason for keeping her hidden. She was a woman staying alone, and the plantation was overflowing with unattached males. He was afraid she'd be too much of a temptation. However, Jolene believed Kurt was overreacting, and she had decided that she'd not stay hidden for days on end. If he didn't soon give her leave to go outside, she'd do so without his permission. She craved companionship and hoped to find some women slaves to visit.

Going to the parlor window and drawing back the lace curtain, Jolene looked toward the manor house. The sun was setting, and its fading rays slanted across the colonial mansion, casting a golden hue over the mammoth structure. Taking time to fully study the Spencer home, Jolene agreed with Kurt; it was too ostentatious to be in good taste. Evidently Kurt's grandfather had cared nothing of elegance but had simply wanted to flaunt his wealth. However, at first sight a visitor would find the manor house quite impressive. One had to look closely to see that it was a bit outlandish.

"Kurt's right; it is a monstrosity," she said aloud. "And a gaudy one at that."

She started to turn away from the window when she saw Richard coming toward the overseer's house. She wondered why he was calling. Did he have a message from Kurt?"

She opened the front door. Without waiting for an invitation, Richard brushed rudely past her and entered the house. Closing the door behind him, he raked her with his eyes.

"What do you want?" she asked curtly. His ogling was insulting to her.

"I just wondered how you were doing. I asked Kurt this morning if he planned to stay here with you, and he said he didn't. I know you colored gals are hot-blooded, so I thought you might be needing something." He grinned suggestively. "Is there anything I can give you?"

"Your absence," she replied tersely.

Annoyed, he spat, "Don't get smart with me, gal!"

"Will you please leave?"

He looked somewhat bewildered. "What happened to your slave dialect?"

She came close to telling him that she wasn't a

slave but was the mistress of Cedarbrook. But it'd merely be a waste of breath, for he wouldn't believe her.

He clutched her shoulders. "Answer me! Why aren't you talking like a slave?"

Twisting free, she uttered mockingly, "Can talk like a slave when I wants to, Masta, suh!"

"Why, you impertinent little piece of trash! You high-yellows are too insolent for your own good! I guess I'll just have to put you in your place!" Moving incredibly fast, he reached out and jerked her into his arms. "I thought about you last night sleeping out here all by yourself. I figured by now you'd be hungry for some company."

Pushing against his chest, she threatened, "If you don't let me go, I'll tell Kurt!"

Richard laughed hoarsely. "Do you think he'd care? Obviously he no longer wants to bed you, or else he'd be staying here."

He forced her closer, and holding her flush against him, he bent his head and kissed her wetly, passionately.

Struggling vainly, she tried to break away, but her strength was helpless against his.

Taking his lips from hers, he swooped her into his arms and carried her to the bedroom. Jolene fought desperately, but to no avail. Richard was determined to have her, and her squirms merely whetted his desire.

As he dropped her onto the bed, his frame fell forcefully upon hers. He was about to kiss her, but before he could, she turned her head to one side, opened her mouth, and screamed loudly.

317

"Be quiet, you little bitch, or I'll knock the hell out of you!" he threatened, meaning it.

Jolene, refusing to submit, continued her struggles. Then, suddenly, Richard was pulled up and away from her.

Kurt was just entering the house when he'd heard Jolene's scream. He'd rushed into the bedroom expecting to find a stranger or one of his father's male slaves. Richard was the last person he had expected to see.

Enraged that the attacker was his own brother, Kurt's fist slammed powerfully against Richard's jaw, the solid blow knocking the man to the floor.

"Get up, you scum!" Kurt bellowed.

Dazed, Richard got up awkwardly, and the moment he was back on his feet, he was struck again. This time Kurt's knuckles plowed across his mouth, laying open his lip. The blood from the fresh cut spurted onto Richard's white shirt.

Kurt's rage was blinding, and he delivered a painful punch to his victim's stomach. Then, as Richard was bent over, Kurt was about to send another jab across the man's chin, but Jolene's sudden hold on his arm deterred him.

"Kurt, that's enough!" she cried.

Her cry got through to Kurt, and stepping back from Richard, he dropped onto the edge of the bed. Leaning over, he rested his arms on his knees, bowed his head, and breathed in deeply.

Richard, holding his hand over his bleeding mouth, stumbled out of the room. Leaving, he headed straight for the manor house.

Meanwhile, sitting beside Kurt, Jolene said worriedly, "Your parents will side with Richard, won't they?"

"Katherine will, but I don't know about my father."

"I wish you hadn't reacted so violently," she moaned.

"I was mad enough to kill him!" Turning to Jolene, he grabbed her arms so tightly that his grip was painful. His gaze pierced hers. "You belong to me, and I'll kill any man who dares to harm what is mine!"

His temper still boiling, Kurt got brusquely to his feet and left the room. As he headed for the front door, his head spun. He had always prided himself on being his own man, the master of his emotions— but he was no longer in control. Jolene dominated his mind and ruled his heart. She was in his thoughts constantly and haunted his dreams. How had such a snip of a girl gained so much power over him? Expecially one who had lied to him over and over again!

Realizing he could've killed his own brother over a woman who constantly played him for a fool, Kurt opened the door so angrily that it was jerked off the hinges.

As the door fell forward, Kurt shoved it to the side, and as it hit the floor, he kicked it out of his way.

The racket carried into the bedroom, and hurrying to investigate, Jolene was shocked to find the fallen door.

Hurrying out to the porch, she watched wide-eyed as Kurt strode swiftly to his parents' home. She had never dreamed that he could be capable of such violence, and as her knees weakened, she sat down on the top step.

Tears made her eyes smart. She sympathized with Kurt and understood his anger. He had fought with his own brother and hurt him badly. She had a feeling this incident was only the tip of the iceberg. Her presence was certain to cause more trouble between Kurt and his family. From the first moment she had laid eyes on Kurt's stepmother, she had felt the woman's animosity. This fight between Richard and Kurt would certainly make Katherine hate her even more. She didn't doubt that the woman would place the blame on her. Furthermore, Jolene had an uneasy feeling that Katherine wouldn't let the incident rest but would find a way to make her pay for what had happened.

I must leave here, she suddenly decided. For my own sake, as well as Kurt's. But how? How can I run away without being caught?

She groaned defeatedly. Escape was impossible. John Delmar had taught her that lesson the hard way.

A cold chill ran up her spine. Unless she could convince Kurt to set her free without further delay, she had no choice but to wait like a sitting duck for Katherine to carry out her vengeance.

Chapter Twenty-Two

As Kurt entered the house, he could hear Katherine carrying on as though Richard was on the brink of death, and hurrying up the marble stairway, he went down the hall and to Richard's room.

Katherine, fussing fretfully, sat on the edge of Richard's bed. She was gently pressing a wet cloth to her son's bruised lip.

Edward was also in the room. Hearing Kurt enter, both his parents turned and eyed him accusingly.

Sharply, Katherine demanded, "How could you fight with your own brother over . . . over a slave woman?"

Walking farther into the room, Kurt ignored her anger, went to the foot of the bed, and asked Richard, "How badly are you hurt?"

"I'll live," he replied dryly.

Katherine, refusing to be ignored, raved shrilly, "Kurt, answer me! Why did you do this to Richard?"

Kurt responded calmly, "Mother, this is between Richard and me."

"You almost kill your brother, then you have the

gall to tell me that what happened is none of my concern?" Katherine was working herself into a frenzy.

Seeing this, Richard intervened quickly, "Kurt's right, Mother. There's no reason for you to get so upset." Because of his sore lip he smiled carefully. "Besides, I'm not hurt very badly." He looked levelly at Kurt. "I'm willing to forget this if you are." He was sincere, for he preferred not to have hard feelings between himself and his brother.

"Of course I'm willing to forget," Kurt answered without delay. "And I'm sorry that I lost my temper."

"You should've told me that you didn't want to share the wench. I'd have respected your property."

Kurt cringed inside. He hated hearing Jolene referred to as his property.

Richard continued, "You'll still be my best man, won't you?"

"Just try and stop me," Kurt said with a wry grin.

Placing a hand carefully to his swollen lip, Richard replied lightly, "Oh no! I'm not going to tangle with you again. I'm looking forward to my wedding night, and I don't intend to be too disabled to perform."

"Richard!" Katherine chastised. "Is that any way to talk in front of your mother?"

"Sorry," he apologized lamely.

As Kurt and Richard dismissed their fight and began kidding in a brotherly fashion, Katherine left the bed and stepped to the window. She gazed outside, and from this vantage point, she could see part of the overseer's house. From the moment she had set eyes on Kurt's wench, she had known the

322

young woman was trouble. Quadroons as beautiful as Jolene were dangerous. Men found them too tempting.

Turning away from the window, Katherine studied her husband who was joking frivolously with his sons. Would Edward be Jolene's next conquest? Why not? He was still a handsome, virile man. She groaned inwardly, imagining the violent scene that would erupt if Kurt were to catch his father in Jolene's bed.

Her musing focused on Kurt. Apparently the wench had her stepson hopelessly enamored. What if he were to marry her and take her back to Texas with him? If the marriage became public knowledge, she, Edward, and Richard would be ruined! Katherine shuddered at the possibility. Well, she'd not stand idly by and let a quadroon destroy her family. She'd find a way to extricate the wench from Kurt's life . . . permanently!

Edward and Kurt, deciding to let Richard rest before dinner, excused themselves and left the room. As they headed down the stairs, Edward said firmly, "Son, last night when I tried to talk to you about Jolene, you managed quite well to avoid my questions. Now, considering what took place between you and Richard, I insist you tell me exactly how you feel about this quadroon."

"I'm not sure she's a quadroon."

Edward paused, his feet planted on one step. "What do you mean?"

"I think she might be white."

His father was shocked speechless.

Kurt explained, "Jolene claims to be the mistress of Cedarbook, a plantation outside of Natchez."

"Yes, I'm familiar with Cedarbrook, and I read about Sam Warrington's and his son's murders in the newspaper. In fact, about five or six years ago on one of my trips to New Orleans, I met Sam Warrington. I remember his mentioning that he had two children, a son and a daughter."

"He didn't say he had twin daughters?"

Edward thought for a moment. "No, I'm sure he mentioned only one."

"Jolene says that she has a sister, and that they were raised as twins until Sam Warrington's will revealed that one of them is a quadroon slave."

"Does she claim that her sister is the real slave?"

"Yes. She told me that her lawyer and sister committed fraud."

"Do you believe her?"

"I don't know, but after Richard's wedding I plan to visit Cedarbrook and find out for myself."

"Let's go to my study and talk more about this over some brandy."

Kurt agreed, then suddenly remembering a more pressing matter, he said, "First you need to send someone to the overseer's house and have the front door put back on its hinges."

Edward gaped, incredulous. "You didn't knock Richard through the door, did you?"

"No," Kurt replied, his grin somewhat contrite. "I tore down the door on my way out of the house."

The older man laughed. "Even as a boy you had a hair-trigger temper and never knew your own strength."

*   *   *

Following dinner Edward asked Kurt to walk out onto the front porch with him, and as they left the house, Edward explained, "I want to talk to you privately."

"What's on your mind, Dad?"

He handed Kurt a cigar, took one for himself, lit up their smokes, then answered, "Jolene's a very attractive woman, and I'm not sure that it's safe for her to stay alone, especially at night. I want you to start sleeping in the overseer's house."

Kurt sighed audibly.

"What's wrong?" Edward questioned.

Deciding to be completely honest, Kurt replied, "If I stay with Jolene, I'm going to fall even more in love with her."

Edward understood, for during their discussion in the study, Kurt had explained his relationship with Jolene in detail. "Son, take some advice from someone who's a lot older and wiser. Don't fight your love for Jolene. True love is hard to find, and for some of us, it only comes around once in a lifetime. When you're lucky enough to find it, grab on and enjoy it to the fullest. Live each day for all it's worth, for there are no guarantees. You can be ecstatically happy one day, and the next totally devastated."

"You're thinking about my mother, aren't you?"

"Yes, I am. I loved her very deeply."

"And Katherine?"

It was a long moment before Edward answered, "I'm very fond of her, but I don't love her the way I loved your mother."

Tentatively, Kurt asked, "What if I learn that

Jolene has lied and is truly a quadroon? Would you still advise me to hold onto her?"

"Yes, if you loved her and still wanted her."

Kurt started to say more, but making out a rider approaching, he tried to distinguish the visitor. The darkness of night concealed the horseman, but as he drew closer, Kurt realized who it was. "Daniel!" he exclaimed. "He was supposed to wait and come with the Delmars. Something must have happened."

The two men went down the porch steps, and as Daniel pulled up and dismounted, Kurt asked anxiously, "What went wrong?"

Daniel cast a cautious glance at Edward. He knew that Kurt's father and John Delmar were good friends. Deciding to play it safe and not say anything disrespectful about the Delmars, he said to Kurt, "I had a slight falling-out with Delmar and his son. I'll tell you about it later."

Kurt knew Daniel was underreacting, but guessing his reason for doing so, he was quick to agree. "There's no hurry. You can tell me what happened some other time."

Admiring Daniel, Edward remarked amicably, "Texas must have agreed with you. You've grown into a fine-looking man. I suppose Lucy was happy to see you."

"Yes, sir," Daniel replied.

Edward was aware of the tension in Daniel and suspected that the falling out between him and John hadn't been a slight one. However, deciding it was none of his concern, he set his mind to finding a place for Daniel to stay. "There's an empty room off the main stable. It's small but has a bed and a chest

326

of drawers. You're welcome to use it. My head stableman used to sleep there, but last week he moved in with one of the field wenches, so he doesn't need the room anymore."

"Thank you," Daniel answered.

Sensing that the two men were eager to talk alone, Edward reminded Kurt about staying with Jolene, then went back into the house.

"I'll go to the stable with you," Kurt said to Daniel. "And while you bed down your horse, you can tell me why you left Willow Hill."

Daniel was eager to comply.

It had taken several kettles of heated water to fill the large tub, and as Jolene emptied the last one, she was relieved to find the chore completed. Eagerly anticipating a long, relaxing bath, she undressed with haste.

Stepping to the stove, she poured herself a cup of coffee, and taking the beverage with her, she climbed into the roomy tub. Leaning back and immersing herself in the warm water, she sighed contentedly.

For a moment she drifted into a dreamlike state. Then, all at once, she sat upright and frowned testily as she remembered she'd forgotten to lock the front door.

She started to get out of the tub, but the sudden sound of heavy footsteps crossing the parlor toward the kitchen rendered her immobile. She stared apprehensively at the closed door separating the two rooms.

It swung open, and as Kurt barged inside Jolene

gasped. Her fear was quickly supplanted by a feeling of petulance. "Don't you know how to knock?" she spat.

"Don't you know how to lock the front door?" he retorted gruffly.

Her saucy smile was unexpected. "Somehow I imagine it'd take more than a locked door to keep you out."

"I wasn't thinking about myself. In case you haven't noticed, this plantation is overrun with male slaves."

She glanced at him archly. "It's not the slaves who pose a danger, but your brother."

"He won't bother you again," Kurt said assuredly. "Speaking of brothers, why haven't you mentioned yours? Did he slip your mind?"

"My brother is dead," she answered. "He and Papa were killed by a gang of runaway slaves." She was bewildered. "How did you know I had a brother?"

"I told my father about you, and he said he once met Sam Warrington. Your father told him he had a son and a daughter. He never mentioned twin daughters."

"Papa had a way of ignoring Johanna. He usually treated her as though she didn't exist."

As Kurt moved toward the tub, he studied her closely. Her shiny black hair was pinned on top of her head, baring her long, slender neck. He was mesmerized by her beauty, and as he drew closer, she unconsciously submerged herself farther under the water.

Wearing a devilish grin he reached over and took

the cup of coffee out of her hand and placed it on the table. He began to unbutton his shirt.

"What are you doing?" she demanded.

"I'm going to take a bath," he answered flatly.

"If you don't mind, I'd rather bathe alone."

"But I do mind," he replied, removing his shirt.

His arrogance was annoying. "Kurt Spencer, you're the most infuriating man I've ever met! If you want a bath, return to the manor house and bathe in your own room!"

"I no longer have a room at the manor house. I'm moving in here with you." He continued disrobing.

Jolene could not control the joy that filled her heart. Kurt was planning to stay with her! She hoped desperately that his reason for moving in was governed by love and not lust. Had the separation been more than he could bear?

She tried to sound nonchalant. "Oh? Why did you decide to stay here?" Hoping he was about to declare his love, she waited breathlessly.

He pulled out a kitchen chair, sat down, and began taking off his boots. "Considering what took place today between you and Richard, my father things my presence here will stop anything like that from happening again."

Jolene's hopes plunged. How could she have been so foolish as to think he was falling in love? He was moving in because he had been ordered to do so, not because he was in love! Oh, she had been right about him all along! He was an unfeeling cad, and all he wanted from her was a tumble in bed! Furthermore, he probably had no intention of setting her free until he was ready to return to Texas, or else marry

Sabrina Delmar; and in the meantime, he planned to use her!

Kurt was getting ready to remove his trousers when Jolene unexpectedly sprang to her feet. He grabbed ahold of her arm before she could climb out of the tub.

"Let go of me!" she cried. "I refuse to share this tub with you! I'd rather bathe with a skunk!"

Her unexplained wrath had Kurt at a loss. "Why the hell are you so mad?"

Trying vainly to break his grip, she screamed, "Turn me loose, you contemptible, sorry excuse of a man!"

Her anger combined with her bared loveliness was provocative. Kurt lifted her out of the tub, and holding her wet, nude body flush to his chest, he turned and carried her from the kitchen.

As he made a beeline for the bedroom, Jolene raged, "I hate you, Kurt Spencer, and if you try to make love to me, I'll fight you all the way!"

"We might fight more than we should," he murmured, carrying her into the room. "But haven't you ever noticed that we never fight in bed?"

She wanted to deny his words, but his lips were suddenly on hers, halting further protest.

Without disrupting their kiss, Kurt knelt on the bed, laid her down gently, and placed his frame over hers.

Jolene, her defenses crumbling, made a futile effort to push him aside. Her struggles, however, only made it easier for Kurt to lie between her parted legs. His trousers couldn't prevent her from feeling his exciting hardness.

As his lips continued to ravish hers, Jolene's resistance melted, and her arms went about his neck with a will of their own. She returned his kiss ardently, demandingly; then, with complete surrender, she arched her thighs, thrusting upward against his hard erection.

"Oh, Kurt," she moaned, "I wanted to fight you, but I can't."

"I know, darlin'," he whispered. "God, I've never desired a woman as much as I desire you!"

Taking the initiative, she put her hand on the nape of his neck and urged his lips down to hers. She kissed him daringly, her tongue darting to taste the recesses of his mouth.

Kurt, his passion on fire, left her side long enough to discard the rest of his clothing, then stretching out his long frame next to her, he drew her back into his arms.

She turned toward him as his hand caressed her smooth back before moving downward to her rounded buttocks. He pressed her up and against his throbbing arousal, lifted her leg, and placed it over his hip. She was now open to receive him, and he slid into her moist depths.

His entry was thrilling, causing Jolene to cry aloud with breathtaking ecstasy. Entwining her arms about his strong shoulders, she matched his rhythmic strokes, reveling in the feel of his manhood gliding deep within her.

His passion soaring, Kurt leaned over her, wrapped his arm about her waist, and lifted her thighs snugly to his. Responding, Jolene's legs went about his back, allowing even deeper penetration.

331

Their problems no longer existed as they became wonderfully engulfed in each other and the sensations that were now all-consuming. Driven onward by their unbridled passion, they reached love's ultimate victory, achieving total, breathless release.

Remaining on top of her, Kurt kissed her soundly, then suggested with a playful smile, "Shall we take that bath?"

"By now the water is probably cool."

"That's all right. We can keep each other warm."

"There's a kettle of water simmering on the stove. We can pour it in the tub."

Standing, he reached down, took her hand, and drew her to her feet. Ushering her from the bedroom and into the kitchen, Kurt took the kettle off the stove and poured the hot water into their bath. He then lifted Jolene and placed her in the tub. Sitting at one end, she made room for him.

Joining her, he rested comfortably against the high back of the tub, then told her of Daniel's arrival. As he washed he explained why Delmar had ordered Daniel to leave Willow Hill.

Jolene was troubled. "I feel so sorry for Lucy and Mary Jane. It must have been terrible for Lucy, and Mary Jane's probably heartbroken." A frown crossed her face. "Alan Delmar is despicable!"

"I offered to give Daniel enough money to buy Mary Jane. I don't have that much with me." He arched a brow. "You cost me quite a sum, you passionate little vixen. However, I told Daniel that I'd borrow the money from my father. But Daniel turned me down. He's bound and determined to get his five thousand back from Alan."

Alarmed, she cried, "If he even tries, he'll be killed!"

Kurt sighed gravely. "I hope I can talk him out of trying something so drastic."

"Do you think you can?"

"I don't know . . . Daniel's stubborn." Although Kurt was extremely worried about his friend, he decided for now to set his worry aside.

Sitting upright, he rubbed the bar of soap over the washcloth, then pulling Jolene closer, he began to wash her. He tended to her breasts, washing them gently, lingering at the nipples before moving the cloth up to her shoulders and down her arms, going so far as to wash her hands.

She shuddered exquisitely as he tenderly spread her legs, running the cloth carefully over her flesh and down to her ankles. Slowly, temptingly, he turned his ministrations to her most sensitive area.

With an ardent sigh, she leaned back against the tub, and parting her legs even wider, she let him have his way with her. Discarding the cloth, Kurt caressed her intimately. Then, as his passion became fully aroused, he grabbed her waist, brought her up to her knees, and kissed her delectable womanhood.

"Oh, darling!" she cried ecstatically, lacing her fingers in his hair.

Inspired, Kurt ravished her thoroughly, his warm lips and probing tongue driving Jolene to wildly rapturous heights.

Needing to take her completely, Kurt eased her down onto his lap, and as his hardness impaled her, she purred seductively, "You feel so wonderful."

"Jolene," he murmured huskily, welcoming her

unrestrained passion. Tightening his hold on her waist, he encouraged her to move up and down. He watched as his manhood rode in and out of her.

Moments later, Jolene's body was racked with tremors as she gained sweet completion. Surrendering to his own fulfillment, Kurt then released his seed deep within her enfolding heat.

Wonderfully fatigued, she fell atop him, and hugging her close, he kissed her cheek.

They were content to stay that way until the water grew cold. Then, taking her from the tub, Kurt dried her off, carried her to bed, and lay beside her until she was asleep. Wanting to have a smoke, he slipped on his trousers, went to the kitchen, and took a cheroot and matches from his shirt pocket. He went out to the front porch and sat on the top step.

As his thoughts centered on Daniel, he heaved a worried sigh: he feared for his friend's life. If Daniel returned to Willow Hill, Delmar would kill him!

Lucy, wearing her cotton nightgown, was about to retire when the door opened and John barged into her bedroom. Shortly after dinner he had gone to the kitchen and told Lucy that tonight she was to come to his bed, and he had been waiting restlessly for her arrival. Finally, losing patience, he had decided to find out what was keeping her.

Now, seeing that she had deliberately disobeyed, he raged, "How dare you disregard a direct order!" He went to her and clutched her wrist painfully. "God damn you, Lucy! Are you trying to see just how far you can push me?"

Taking him by surprise, she pulled away from his tight hold.

"It's Daniel, isn't it?" he questioned angrily. "You're going to pout and be insolent because I sent him away! I should have you strung up and whipped!"

"Go right ahead, masta," she replied calmly. "You done broke my heart, you might as well break my body."

He threw up his hands in despair. "Ordering Daniel off my property didn't break your heart!"

"Ain't talkin' 'bout that."

"Then what the hell are you talking about?" he demanded irritably.

"You broke my heart years ago, Masta John . . . when you sold Lazarus, and again when you sold my son."

"Selling Daniel was the best thing I could've done for him. He's free, isn't he? If he'd remained at Willow Hill, he'd still be a slave."

"You didn't know that when you sold 'im."

He ignored her point. "As for Lazarus, he tried to run away and took you with him. He was a damned runner, and I was glad to be rid of him. Furthermore, you were only sixteen. How could losing Lazarus break your heart?"

"I loved 'im," she answered simply.

His eyes took on a weird gleam. "I've always known that Lazarus is Daniel's father."

Lucy was too astounded to respond.

John's words were filled with bitterness. "I knew it was Lazarus who got you pregnant and not my overseer."

"How can Lazarus be Daniel's pappy? You can tell by lookin' at Daniel that he's got white blood."

"Lazarus's father was an Arab, and his mother was a mulatto. That's why Lazarus is as light-skinned as some white men. Obviously Daniel gets his light coloring from his Arab ancestors and his mulatto grandmother."

Numb, Lucy sat on the edge of the bed, and as her thoughts came together, everything fell into place. When she finally spoke, her tone was cold. "Now I know your true reason for sellin' Daniel. You was jealous of 'im 'cause you thought Lazarus was his pappy. You didn't want my son on this plantation 'cause he was a constant reminder that I loved Lazarus." When John made no reply, she insisted, "I'm right, ain't I?"

"Yes!" he admitted.

Standing, Lucy began to laugh. It was a strange, hollow sound.

"What the hell's so funny?" John demanded.

Her laughter stopped as suddenly as it had begun, and meeting her master's questioning gaze, she said dispassionately, "Lazarus ain't Daniel's pappy. You are."

Chapter Twenty-Three

John was too overwhelmed to respond, and silence hung heavily in the small room. Then, with a semblance of calm, he said quietly, "I don't believe you. You're lying to me."

Lucy sat on the edge of the bed, gave her master an unwavering gaze, and replied, "I ain't lyin'. Daniel's your son."

His composure deteriorated. "Why the hell are you trying to make me believe such a thing? Are you hoping I won't kill Daniel if I think he's my son? Well, it won't work! If I see Daniel on my property, I'll shoot him on sight!"

"Masta," she began tolerantly, "I know you bein' Daniel's pappy wouldn't stop you from killin' 'im."

"Then why are you trying to make me believe that . . . that he's mine?"

"'Cause it's the truth," she answered candidly. She gestured toward the hard-backed chair placed beside the bed. "Sit down, Masta John, and I'll tell you everything."

337

He went to the chair on unsteady legs, sat down, and waited for her to continue.

"A couple of weeks after you sold Lazarus, you went into Mobile, and when you came home, you was drunk. Do you remember?"

Nodding, he guiltily lowered his gaze.

"Hattie was the cook and I was her helper. We was sharin' this bedroom. That night when you was drunk, you came here and told Hattie to sleep in the kitchen. You got into bed with me and made me submit to you."

John interrupted, "Lucy, I'd wanted you from the first moment I set eyes on you. But I was against sleeping with my wenches. If I hadn't been drunk . . ." His voice faded. Why should he excuse his behavior to a slave? Besides, it had happened over thirty years ago!

"A few days later you took a trip to St. Louis. While you was gone, I found out that I was pregnant. I knew the baby wasn't Lazarus', for on the day you sold 'im away from Willow Hill, I was havin' my time of the month. There hadn't been nobody except you and Lazarus, so I knew you was the one who got me pregnant. I was afraid that when my baby was born, it's be light-skinned and you'd realize it was yours. I'd heard how after your pappy died, you sold every child you'd sired, so I was scared you'd sell my baby. I went to your wife and told her I was pregnant 'cause the overseer raped me. The mistress was a good woman, and I was sure she'd fire the overseer. I wanted the man gone 'fore you came back from St. Louis.

"I was afraid he'd convince you that I was lyin'. I

338

didn't feel bad 'bout havin' the man dismissed. Although he never touched me, he was forcin' hisself on the field wenches. He deserved to be fired. When you returned, the mistress told you that the overseer got me pregnant. Until today I thought you believed her. I never imagined you thought Lazarus really was Daniel's pappy."

John's voice was strained. "After that night when I forced myself on you, I swore I'd never touch you again—not because I didn't desire you, but because I was afraid of getting you pregnant." He looked at her desperately. "Lucy, you had to know how fond I was of you! When you were in labor and the midwife told me you might die, didn't I send for a white doctor? I had to pay him very well indeed to tend to a wench." Delmar hesitated, then said with a sigh, "When the doctor informed me that you'd never conceive again, I was overjoyed."

"'Course you was, Masta John," she said bitterly. "You knew you could have me for a bed wench and never have to worry 'bout knockin' me up. You could have your cake and eat it, too."

His eyes glared. "Don't use that surly tone with me! How can you sound so ungrateful when I've been good to you for over thirty years?"

"Remember that hound dog you was so fond of? She died 'bout five years ago. You was good to her, too."

John bounded to his feet. "I'll not tolerate any more of your insolence! Lucy, you'd better keep your place!" He whirled about and began pacing the small room. "Does Daniel know the truth?"

"No, suh. He thinks the overseer's his pappy."

339

Perspiration beaded Delmar's brow, and his stomach was tied into knots. "I forbid you to tell him or anyone else that he's mine."

"Masta, why does it bother you so much to father a slave child?"

"Delmar blood is superior, and it should never be mixed with an inferior race."

"Inferior?" Lucy smirked. "Daniel's more of a man than Alan will ever be!"

Enraged, John stepped swiftly to Lucy, grasped her shoulders, and jerked her to her feet. Shaking her, he threatened furiously, "If you defy me one more time, I'll have you lashed within an inch of your life!" He released her brusquely, and she sank back down onto the bed.

He stalked to the door, opened it, then turned back and faced her. "Why, after all these years, did you decide to tell me about Daniel?"

"Retribution, I reckon," she answered softly.

"I don't understand!" he said, his tone pleading. "Why do you seek retribution from me!"

Lucy smiled vacuously. "You sold the man I loved, then you sold my son, and you ask why I want revenge?"

"You ungrateful wench!" he grumbled. "Apparently you've never once appreciated the way I've pampered and coddled you! You can't think any further than Lazarus and Daniel! Well, if it's retribution you're wanting, you've got it! I can't stand the thought of Daniel possessing Delmar blood!"

"Good," she replied placidly. "Now I can die knowin' I got a taste of revenge. That's 'bout all a slave can hope for."

"I forbid you to talk about dying! You're still a relatively young woman, and a healthy one."

"Masta, you got a lot of power, but the good Lord's got more. When He calls me to the promise land, there won't be nothin' you can do 'bout it."

John couldn't imagine life without Lucy. She was the mainstay of his existence. As he studied the beautiful, statuesque woman, he changed his mind about leaving. Closing the door, he stepped to the bed.

He made love to Lucy tenderly but fervently, and for the first time in thirty-odd years, he slept with her for the entire night. Throughout the evening and into the morning, he held onto her possessively as if he did indeed have more power than God. She belonged to him, and not even God had the right to take away John Delmar's property.

The morning sun shone brightly upon Cedarbrook. It was a cloudless day, but the pleasant breeze drifting from the north kept the summer temperature bearable.

Johanna paced anxiously across the parlor. She was grateful for the clear day, but the weather was not the main thing on her mind.

Stepping to the table where she kept her liquor, she picked up a decanter and poured herself a liberal amount of sherry. She drank it in three gulping swallows. Her hand shook as she put down the empty glass.

Restless, she walked to the front window, drew the heavy drapes, and peered out. Her gaze became glued to the driveway as she mentally willed Marshall Walker to materialize.

Oh, what if he didn't come? If he failed to show up, all her plans would be ruined! The possibility was depressing, so she quickly thrust it from her thoughts.

Johanna had plotted a deceitful scheme to destroy Marshall's relationship with Amanda Mitchell, and if it worked, Amanda would break their engagement. Johanna smiled smugly. Marshall would be heartbroken, of course, but she'd ease his pain, and in a relatively short time he'd be in love with her.

Johanna's thoughts floated back to Marshall's engagement party. Discarding her mourning clothes, Johanna had attended the festivities. As Marshall had speculated, a few of his guests had disapproved of her socializing so soon after her father's and brother's deaths. They believed she should remain in mourning for the traditional year. Johanna couldn't have cared less what they thought. She was only interested in seeing Amanda Mitchell so she could evaluate her rival. She had been pleased to note that Amanda was not pretty; in fact, she was quite plain. The young woman's lack of beauty had given Johanna confidence. She was then certain she could lure Marshall with her own voluptuous charms. But as the evening wore on, Johanna became painfully aware that Marshall adored Amanda. Her self-confidence died. Evidently, in Marshall's eyes, Amanda was beautiful. It was apparent even to a casual observer that the couple were very much in love.

However, Johanna was not about to be deterred

by true love. Setting her wicked mind to work, she came up with a ploy that, if successful, would demolish any possibility of marriage between Marshall and Amanda.

Before returning to Cedarbrook, Johanna had gone to Amanda and asked to speak to her alone. Privately she had given the young woman her best wishes, even adding how fortunate she was to marry a fine man like Marshall Walker. Then, pretending that she wanted them to become good friends, she invited Amanda to Cedarbrook for lunch the following Thursday. Amanda sincerely wanted them to be friends and readily accepted. Johanna knew she'd need a biased witness to her prospective ploy, so she insisted Amanda bring her brother James. Thinking Johanna was infatuated with James, Amanda assured her they would both come for lunch.

The first part of Johanna's plan was put successfully into motion. The second part wasn't initiated until this morning, for this was the day she expected Amanda and her brother.

Shortly after dawn Johanna had written a message to Marshall, telling him there was serious trouble at Cedarbrook and asking him to come immediately. Giving the note to Lazarus, she told him to deliver it to Marshall as quickly as possible.

Now, remaining at the window, she waited anxiously for Marshall. For her plan to work, timing was of the essence.

Suddenly, spotting two horsemen coming down the long lane, she was happy to see that the riders were Marshall and Lazarus.

Moving away from the window, she hurried to a gold-framed mirror which hung behind the sofa. Pausing, she appraised her reflection. Her golden-brown hair fell past her shoulders in lustrous, soft curls, and the rouge she had dabbed sparingly on her cheeks and lips gave her face just the right amount of color. Her dress of white organdy, trimmed with black aplaca braid, was worn off the shoulders. She knew she was a fetching sight, and she hoped Marshall wouldn't be too blinded by his love for Amanda to see her beauty.

Hearing the front door opening, Johanna stepped quickly to the center of the parlor and waited for Marshall.

Barging into the room, he said anxiously, "I got here as soon as I could! What's wrong? I asked Lazarus but he said he didn't know anything."

Johanna, pretending embarrassment, dropped her gaze. Then, looking up at him through lowered lashes, she recited the crisis she had fabricated. "Oh, Marshall, I'm so ashamed! I'm afraid I acted foolishly and irrationally. I woke early this morning, and because I couldn't fall back asleep, I got up and came down to the kitchen for a cup of coffee. While it was brewing, I stepped out to the back porch. I looked toward the overseer's house and I was alarmed to see five of my Negro men leaving Mr. Sullivan's home. They seemed to be sneaking around. I was afraid they'd killed my overseer and were planning an uprising. I hurried back into the house, wrote a note to you, roused Lazarus, and sent him on his way. I was so frightened that I didn't even take time to tell Lazarus what I suspected. Well, shortly after Lazarus left, I saw Mr. Sullivan walk out of his home."

Now feigning total shame, she covered her face with her hands, drew an apprehensive breath, then continued reciting her made-up story. "It seems Mr. Sullivan sent for the slaves because he needed to talk to them about today's work. Marshall, I'm so sorry that I panicked! But sometimes I get so scared living here alone!"

Marshall was perturbed, for she had taken him away from his busy schedule, but he didn't have the heart to chastise Johanna. Going to her and drawing her gently into his arms, he murmured soothingly, "It's all right. I understand."

She asked beseechingly, "You aren't angry with me?"

"Of course not."

Pleased that he had fallen for her ploy, she smiled secretly. Then, gazing up at him, she batted her long lashes and said, "To make amends, I had Dixie pack up a lunch basket. Since it's such a pretty day, I thought maybe we could have a picnic."

Marshall was unconvinced. "I really should get back home."

"Nonsense," she rebuked, her tone sugar-coated. "You must have something to eat before you leave, anyway." As she anxiously awaited his consent, she admired him without being too obvious. He was handsome indeed! His tan trousers fit him like a glove, and his beige shirt was stretched tightly across the strong width of his shoulders. His golden hair, mussed, fell attractively across his brow in blondish disarray.

Marshall seemed confused. "But aren't Amanda and James coming here for lunch?" His fiancée had mentioned the luncheon date.

Johanna lied without hesitation. "They're supposed to come for lunch next Thursday, not today."

"I guess I was mistaken," he replied.

She smiled irresistibly. "Please say we can have a picnic!"

Marshall could see how much it meant to her, so he agreed. Besides, he felt a little guilty about the way he'd been neglecting her. He owed it to Sam Warrington to take more interest in Johanna. From now on, he'd make an effort to visit more often.

As Johanna spread the blanket upon a patch of soft grass, Marshall, looking about, asked, "Don't you think we're a little too close to the road? I thought picnics were supposed to be more secluded."

Johanna smiled. "No one ever uses this road unless they're visiting Cedarbrook, and I'm not expecting any company." She lowered her gaze. Oh, there would be company all right! Within the hour Amanda and James would be coming down that road, and when they did . . . !

Returning her gaze to Marshall's, Johanna gestured toward their parked buggy. "Get the basket, will you?"

Soon they were enjoying the lunch Dixie had prepared. The fried chicken, crisp on the outside, was tender and juicy. The potato salad, biscuits and honey were delicious, and a bottle of wine Johanna had remembered to pack complimented the meal.

Satisfied, Marshall lay back and folded his arms under his head. He felt a little woozy, for Johanna had kept refilling his glass, and he had had too much wine. They were sitting beneath a tall elm, and gazing upward through the canopy of branches, Marshall said contentedly, "I'm so stuffed I can't eat another bite. I'm also slightly inebriated."

Johanna was pleased. So far everything was going well. "I hope we didn't eat too early. When do you usually have lunch?" She cast an anxious glance toward the road. Amanda and James would be arriving soon. For her plan to succeed, she must hurry and find a way to compromise Marshall.

"We didn't eat too early," Walker was saying. "Since I skipped breakfast, I was hungry."

Johanna pouted prettily. "It was my fault that you didn't have breakfast. I can't believe that I reacted so foolishly." She looked as though she were about to cry.

Her distress touched him, and sitting upright, he reached for her. Holding her tenderly, he murmured, "Johanna, don't feel bad about what happened."

Moving subtly, she managed to snuggle within the circle of his embrace. She laced her arms carefully about his neck, lifted her face to his, and whispered brokenly, "Marshall, I'm so lonely! Please hold me close!"

He was reluctant.

His hesitancy was exasperating, but concealing her impatience, she continued as though heartbroken, "I miss Jolene so desperately, and I still cry

347

all the time for my brother and Papa!"

He was immediately sympathetic and drew her closer, but before he knew what was happening, her lips were pressed against his.

Marshall came close to ending their kiss, but when Johanna's tongue entered his mouth as her hand simutaneously dipped downward to caress his manhood, his defenses crumbled.

Marshall never slept with his female slaves, and his sexual desires went unfulfilled except when he was in Natchez and could visit a house of ill repute.

It had been a long time since he'd had a woman, and this abstinence, coupled with the wine he had consumed, made it easier for Johanna to seduce him.

As Marshall eased her down onto the blanket, a voice suddenly nagged at him, telling him to stop before it was too late. He loved Amanda Mitchell, and what he was doing was terribly wrong. He was being unfair not only to his fiancée, but also to Johanna.

His better judgment was almost victorious, but Johanna, sensing this, planted another passionate kiss on his mouth. Taking his hand, she slipped it under the bodice of her dress.

The feel of her soft, voluptuous breasts aroused Marshall's passion to its zenith, and wiping all thoughts from his mind, he returned her kiss fiercely.

Johanna was in heaven, for she had dreamt of this moment. The touch of Marshall's lips and his hand caressing her breasts sent a wonderful tingling sensation coursing between her thighs. She wished she could give their union her undivided attention, but she knew that it was vitally important for her to keep her ear tuned for sounds from the road. Any moment now she should detect the sound of carriage wheels.

Knowing time was of the essence, Johanna stood up, and as Marshall looked on, she boldly removed her dress. Beneath, she wore only a chemise and a pair of lace panties.

Walker's conscience was now forgotten, and he gasped at the sight of her partial nudity. He had never encountered a woman so seductive.

Returning to his embrace, Johanna's lips descended to his, and as his hand slipped under her panties, she moaned throatily. His finger probed intimately, and she arched her hips, encouraging his passionate fondling.

Now, fully involved in their lovemaking, Johanna forgot to listen for Amanda and James, causing her and Marshall to hear them at the same time.

At the sound of carriage wheels, Marshall released Johanna abruptly and leapt to his feet. Turning toward the road, he was shocked to see Amanda and James.

Bringing the buggy to a stop, James's eyes pierced Marshall's before he looked disdainfully at Johanna.

Meanwhile, crying heavily, Amanda covered her face with her hands and her shoulders shook with sobs.

With an inward smile, Johanna got to her feet and slipped calmy into her dress.

Telling his sister to stay seated, James jumped

down to the ground and went over to Marshal. His face red with rage, he shouted, "You sorry son of a bitch!" His hands were doubled into fists, and he was itching to send them plunging into his adversary's face.

Johanna knew she had to act surprised, for if Marshall were to learn that she had plotted this scene, he'd despise her forever. Sounding confused, she asked James, "What are you doing here?"

Glaring, he snapped, "You invited us to lunch, remember?"

"Yes, but you were supposed to come next Thursday," she lied convincingly.

He laughed coldly. "Well, it's a good thing we were mistaken and came a week early, or else we'd have missed the show!"

Marshall wanted to go to Amanda and beg her to forgive him. But what could he say to make amends? How could he expect such a delicate lady to understand that a man's sexual drive often led him astray? What had almost happened between him and Johanna had nothing to do with love. It was passion—primitive lust! Tears came to Marshall's eyes as he continued to gaze at his fiancée. He'd never wanted to hurt her . . . he loved her! Marshall was heartbroken.

Johanna, gloating, took a stance beside Marshall. Then she secretly bestowed a catty glance upon the distraught Amanda.

Without warning, James reached under his coat jacket, drew out a pistol, and aimed it at Walker. "I should blow you to hell!" he sneered.

Marshall wasn't alarmed . . . James Mitchell had

a temper to match his red hair, and it was common knowledge that when angered, he'd often threaten to shoot someone. His threats were harmless.

Johanna, however, didn't kinow this about James, and she was terrified. Believing young Mitchell was about to shoot Marshall, she lunged forward and grabbed for the pistol.

James was taken totally unaware, and as Johanna's hand struck his arm, the gun accidentally discharged.

The fired bullet lodged deep in Walker's chest, the forceful impact throwing him to the ground.

Screaming, Johanna dropped to her knees beside Marshall. The front of his shirt was soaked with blood.

Joining her, Mitchell stared down into Marshall's open, sightless eyes. "God, he's dead!" James cried, his voice quivering. He glanced over his shoulder to check on his sister, and seeing that she was heading toward them, he jumped up and met her halfway. Drawing her forcefully into his arms, he kept her from going to her dead fiancé. He wanted to spare her the tragic sight.

Johanna's screams continued until her throat was too dry to expel the shrill sound. Then, sobbing convulsively, she fell across Marshall's body and cried hysterically.

The mansion was not very far away, and Johanna's piercing screams had carried to the house.

Lazarus, having heard his mistress's distress, had run headlong down the lane and to the road. Now, coming upon the scene, he went to Johanna,

351

grasped her shoulders, and drew her away from Marshall's body.

As she looked up at the servant, her eyes rolled back in her head, her face ashen, her legs buckled and she fainted into Lazarus's arms. Lifting her, he carried her to the buggy that she and Marshall had used. Gently he laid her on the seat.

Lazarus couldn't be sure what had happened. But since he was familiar with his mistress's deceitful tactics, he was able to make an accurate guess. He turned and looked at Walker's body and tears came to his eyes. He had always liked and respected young Walker.

Then, taking control of the situation, Lazarus said to James, "Masta, you best go to town and get the constable. I'll take Miz Johanna home, then come back and cover Masta Walker's body. I reckon we'd better leave everything as it is till the constable gets here."

James agreed, and he quickly helped his sister into the carriage, turned the conveyance about, and headed back for town.

Lazarus watched their hasty retreat. The horses' pounding hooves stirred up loose dirt and the carriage was soon obscured by a cloud of swirling dust.

Lazarus leaned against the buggy and heaved a deep, lamenting sigh. It seemed ironic that the surrounding tableau should remain undisturbed when a man as kind as Marshall Walker had just died.

Chapter Twenty-Four

The Delmars were the first guests to arrive for Richard's wedding. Within the week more families would be arriving, for the ones who lived a good distance away would stay at Heritage Manor. Southern hospitality dictated that the Spencers open their house to their guests and display unlimited cordiality.

The parents of the bride lived in the city, and because their home was small compared to their future son-in-law's, the wedding would be held at Heritage Manor.

A plantation wedding was a social event which people looked forward to from the day they received their invitations. The days leading up to the ceremony would be filled with barbeques, lawn games, hunting sports for the men, and other activities. Each evening a five-course dinner would be served, and the night before the wedding, a formal ball was planned.

Taking their rich and pampered lifestyle for

granted, the Spencers and their guests would thoroughly enjoy the festivities. They were above common labor, so naturally all the work fell to their slaves. The upcoming wedding represented fun and games to the Spencers and their guests, but to the slaves at Heritage Manor, it simply meant more hard work.

Although the Delmars arrived at dinnertime, their untimely interruption caused no inconvenience. Meals at Heritage Manor were always plentiful in case unexpected company should drop by. Richard was having dinner at his fiancée's house, and as the Delmars were seated at the table, Alan was given the chair that Richard always occupied. John sat next to his son, and Kurt and Sabrina were across from them, and the host and hostess were seated at each end.

The formal dining room at Heritage Manor was imposing, and the room's distinctive decor represented its owners' prestige. In one corner stood a walnut cupboard filled with delicate china and sparkling crystal. The finely scrolled cupboard was early nineteenth-century. Edward had ordered the piece from Natchez, and its extensive inlay marked it as extravagantly expensive. The walnut dining table could easily accommodate thirty people. Three chandeliers graced the large room, and a tall clock occupied one corner. The walls, papered in a bright flowery pattern, were adorned with several gilt-framed oil paintings. An impressive oaken sideboard dominated one side of the room.

Sabrina, picking absently at her dessert, regarded her elaborate surroundings. The room and its decor met with her approval as she envisioned herself the mistress of such grandeur. If she were to marry Kurt, Heritage Manor would someday be hers. She found the prospect delightful. First, of course, she must persuade Kurt to give up his ranch. Imagining the work connected with ranching, not to mention the threat of wild indians, caused Sabrina to shudder. She wouldn't move to Texas under any condition!

As Sabrina brought herself out of her reverie, the conversation at the table turned to the prospect of Alabama withdrawing from the Union.

"If the Republican Party doesn't keep its nose out of our business," John Delmar was saying, "then it's going to force us to secede. The damned Republicans want to abolish slavery in all territories and end the interstate slave trade."

Edward agreed. "The government is becoming worthless, impotent, and a nuisance. Furthermore, it no longer protects the interest of the people of Alabama."

"I hope we go to war with the damned Northerners!" Alan said excitedly. "I'd love to blow those nigger-lovin' bastards to hell!"

"Son, watch your language," John reminded him. "There are ladies present."

Lamely Alan apologized to his sister and Katherine.

Kurt, leaning back in his chair, looked at young Delmar. "Don't you think before war is declared, it might be wise for Alabama and the other southern states to establish an arsenal, a firearms factory, and a powder mill? Otherwise, if the war were to drag on, how will the South replenish its weapons?"

Alan frowned testily. "If there is a war, it won't last very long. Within a couple of months, we'll have those Yankees turning tail and running back to their mamas."

Kurt smiled. "I think you're underestimating your enemy."

Young Delmar was agitated, but before he could spout a retort, Katherine interjected, "Gentlemen, if you're going to talk war and politics, Sabrina and I will leave you to your discussion, brandy, and cigars." She smiled at the other woman. "Shall we go into the parlor?"

Sabrina was more than willing to leave, for she had no interest in politics. Her beliefs, however, coincided with Alan's. If war erupted, the South would be victorious within no time. Furthermore, the distasteful, violent conflicts would take place at some distant place and couldn't possibly disrupt her pleasant life.

The ladies went into the parlor. Katherine sat in her favorite chair, and Sabrina began pacing.

Katherine was puzzled by her guest's apparent restlessness. Kurt's stepmother liked Sabrina, for the young woman reminded her of herself. She was well bred and a true lady. Yet beneath her refined exterior lurked a strong nature, and like Katherine Spencer, Sabrina Delmar got what she wanted.

The Delmars had arrived too late for Sabrina to change, and she was still wearing her traveling gown. But the garment was flattering. The dress, made of purple silk, was edged with white fluted ruffles and trimmed with black velvet. The long skirt whipped gracefully about Sabrina's feet as she continued to pace.

Kathering always dressed meticulously for dinner, and she was wearing a white silk gown. The box-pleated skirt was adorned with blue ribbons and had a blue sash at the waist.

The two women's wardrobes were a reflection of their rich life, which they took for granted. Furthermore, they accepted their wealth as their due, never once having a charitable thought for those less fortunate.

"Sabrina, why are you so restless?" Katherine asked. She gestured to the sofa. "Sit down, Dear, and tell me what's bothering you."

Sabrina did as she requested. "I'm anxious for the men to stop talking politics and come join us."

"Oh?" the older woman asked. She smiled speculatively. "I can't believe you're impatient to see Edward, your father, or Alan, so you must be waiting for Kurt."

Sabrina blushed becomingly. "I'm quite taken with your son. Do you object?"

"Heavens, no!" she exclaimed. "I think you're perfect for Kurt." Katherine spoke the truth, for she wholeheartedly approved of a marriage between Kurt and John Delmar's daughter.

Learning that Katherine was her ally pleased Sabrina. However, she suspected the woman wouldn't be quite so supportive if she told her she didn't plan to return to Texas with Kurt, but intended to persuade him to stay at Heritage Manor. Sabrina guessed correctly that Katherine wanted Richard to inherit full control of the plantation. After all, he was her natural son, whereas Kurt was

357

merely her stepson. Sabrina decided at present to keep her future plans for herself and Kurt a secret from Katherine.

"Is Kurt smitten with you?" Katherine asked.

Sabrina emitted a sigh. "I'm not sure. He hasn't said or done anything to make me think so. I was hoping he'd ask Papa permission to pay court."

"He hasn't?"

"No," she answered despondently. "I don't understand why."

Suddenly Katherine frowned. "I think I know why . . . it's because of that . . . that quadroon slut!"

"Jolene?" Sabrina asked.

"Yes! He's infatuated with her!"

"I can't believe I have a colored wench as a rival!"

"Well, you'd better start believing it! She has Kurt so bewitched that he's actually living with her in the overseer's house."

Edward and Kurt had decided not to tell Katherine that Jolene might be the true mistress of Cedarbrook, for they knew she was the biggest gossip in the county, and within days Jolene's plight would be the topic of conversation for miles around.

Sabrina gasped. "He's actually living with her?"

Katherine nodded. "Yes, and he even has Edward's approval! Can you imagine?"

"My goodness!" Sabrina declared. "How can your husband and son expose you to something so distasteful?"

"Well, I can tell you, I intend to put a permanent stop to Kurt's infatuation!" She placed her hand over her heart, inhaling deeply. "What if he were to marry her? How could we live with such shame?

Edward, Richard, and I would become outcasts!" She moved to the very edges of her chair. "Sabrina, Darling, you must help me save Kurt from that . . . that quadroon witch!"

"Of course!" she agreed. "But how?"

"We must find a way to get rid of her. As long as Jolene is around Kurt will be too interested in her to notice you and to realize that you'd make him the ideal wife."

Sabrina concurred. "Do you have a plan?"

"For some reason which Edward refuses to explain, Kurt has decided not to return to Texas immediately following Richard's wedding. Edward told me that Kurt plans to take a short trip and will be gone a few weeks. He intends to leave Jolene here."

"Where is he going?"

"I have no idea—Edward wouldn't tell me. But that's beside the point." She commenced to explain her plan. "Kurt is leaving on his mysterious trip the day after Richard's wedding. You must convince your father not to leave for home until Kurt has left. Then you'll invite me to return to Willow Hill with you for a short visit and I'll accept."

Rising from her chair, Katherine stepped to the fireplace, turned, and faced her avid listener. Katherine was somewhat flustered. "We must find a way to persuade Edward to allow Jolene to accompany us to Willow Hill, for it'll be easier for us to get rid of her if she's not under Edward's watchful eye."

Sabrina's face lit up. "That doesn't pose a problem. Before we left home, Lucy was feeling poorly. In fact, Papa almost didn't come." Her brow furrowed. "Honestly, the way Papa pampers Lucy is exasperating!" She returned to the matter at hand. "When Jolene hears that Lucy isn't well, she'll want to return with us. She's quite fond of Lucy."

"Good!" Katherine remarked. "If Jolene is willing to accompany us, then Edward won't object. You must make sure Jolene hears of Lucy's poor health."

Sabrina had brought Mary Jane with her. "My maid will tell Jolene."

"When we reach Willow Hill, we'll find a way to be rid of her permanently."

"But how?"

Katherine shrugged. "I'm not sure."

"I have a suggestion," a male voice suddenly sounded from the open doorway. Grinning expansively, Alan entered the room.

"How long have you been eavesdropping?" Sabrina demanded.

"Long enough," he answered, his tone light.

"You should've made your presence known," his sister spat.

'Don't get upset," he replied. "I happen to be on your side." He smiled warmly at Katherine, bowed from the waist, and said gallantly, "I offer you my services, Mrs. Spencer. I agree that the wench should be disposed of, and I know how to do it."

"How?" Katherine pressed, grateful for his help.

"I'm acquainted with a group of slave patrols who, shall we say, are not above reproach? If I ask them to steal an insolent wench and sell her in their own way, they'll be glad to oblige. And once a slave is sold in that market, the slave is never heard from again. Kurt will never find her."

"But aren't most slaves sold illegally sent to cane plantations?" Katherine asked.

Nodding, Alan grinned malevolently. "The uppity little wench will be dead within the year. She's too fragile to last very long on a cane plantation."

"Your plan is delightful!" Katherine declared.

"We need to make it look as though Jolene ran away, which shouldn't be too difficult since she's already tried to run.

Katherine exclaimed, "Oh Alan, you are indeed cunning!"

Sabrina, suspicious of her brother's motives, asked carefully, "Alan, what's in this for you?"

"Satisfaction," he answered flatly. "The wench is impertinent."

His sister smiled knowingly. "You mean she turned down your favors, don't you?"

Katherine intervened. "Alan's reason for helping us is unimportant."

At that moment Edward's deep voice carried into the room, and they knew that the men were leaving the dining table.

The conspiracy inside the parlor ended abruptly. Taking a seat on the sofa beside his sister, Alan smiled inwardly with anticipation. Before he handed Jolene over to the slave patrol, he'd make good use of her!

When John and Edward came into the room, Sabrina was disappointed to see that Kurt wasn't with them. "Where's Kurt?" she asked.

Edward answered, "He went to the overseer's house, but he asked me to bid you and his mother a pleasant goodnight."

"The overseer's house," Katherine repeated point-edlyy, her eyes meeting Sabrina's, then Alan's. Secretly their gazes confirmed the urgency in carrying out their conspiracy.

As Jolene's fate was being discussed in the Spencer parlor, Jolene was standing on the front porch watching Daniel walk away. When he disappeared into the darkness of night, she sat down on the top step, cupped her chin in her hands, and sighed disappointedly.

Daniel had come to the overseer's house, and along with Jolene, he had hoped that Mary Jane would show up. They had waited for over two hours before deciding that she had apparently been ordered to stay in her mistress's room.

Hopeful that he'd see Mary Jane tomorrow, Daniel had left to return to his room at the back of the stables.

Now Jolene wondered if she should stay on the porch and wait for Kurt, or go into the house and get ready for bed. Would Kurt leave directly after dinner, or would he linger at the manor house so that he could be with Sabrina?

A frown crossed her pretty face. If Sabrina Delmar had her way, Kurt certainly wouldn't be returning anytime soon!

She spotted a tall figure approaching, but because of the darkness, she couldn't make him out. Thinking it must be Kurt, Jolene's frown disap-peared quickly. But as the man became distinguishable, her spirits tumbled. It wasn't Kurt, but the slave Samson.

Pausing at the bottom of the steps, the slave smiled affably. "How's you doin', Jolene?"

"Fine, thank you," she replied warmly. "I didn't know you were at Heritage Manor."

"I drove the buggy for Miz Sabrina."

Pointing to the bottom step, Jolene asked him to sit down. "How's everything at Willow Hill?"

Samson wasn't aware of Lucy's ailing health. "Everything's fine, I reckon." He began to fidget nervously.

"What's wrong?" she asked.

"What makes you think something's wrong?"

"You seem jittery."

Samson began hesitantly, "Remember that day when you ran away and George and me caught up to you 'fore the masta got there?"

"Of course I remember."

"I told you 'bout that northern abolitionist who's gonna help me and George escape. Well, he got in touch with us, and we're gonna be runnin' 'fore too much longer. We gots five more of Masta John's slaves to run with us—three children and two wenches. The most dangerous part of our escape is gettin' away from Willow Hill. We got 'bout twenty miles of open road 'fore we reach the farmhouse where this abolitionist is supposed to meet us. We gonna need a written pass in case we run across any slave patrols. But none of us can write, and you's the only slave I know who can. I needs to ask you to write a pass for us. All you needs to say is that these five slaves has your permission to travel."

He reached into his shirt pocket and withdrew a sheet of paper. "I stole this from Masta John's stationary. All you gots to do is get a pen and some ink and write out a pass."

He held out the paper to her, but she made no move to accept it. "Samson, I don't think I should be an accomplice. Believe me, I wish you and the others well, but I don't want to be part of this."

"Please! You gots to help us!"

She shook her head. "I just can't!"

"I's beggin' you!" he pleaded. "If you was still at Willow Hill, I'd ask you to come with us."

She was weakening. "Oh, Samson, I'm *afraid* to help you!"

Samson's huge frame slumped, and bowing his head, he groaned, "I don't wants to be a slave for the rest of my life! Neither do them wenches and kids who's plannin' to run with us!"

Jolene understood their sorrow only too well. "Samson, can you give me your word that no one will be hurt?"

"Yes, sure I can," he was quick to answer. "Me and George, we don't aim to hurt nobody. And the women and kids, they's harmless."

Believing everything he'd told her, she reached down and took the paper from his hand. "Stay here," she said, getting to her feet. "There's a pen and ink in the house. I'll write a pass for you."

Subduing his elation, he replied calmly, "You best sign it Sabrina Delmar, 'cause if we're stopped by the patrols, they's gonna know the handwritin' ain't Masta John's."

She agreed, and Samson watched as she hurried

into the house. The moment the door closed behind her, a grin spread across his face. He had made out Jolene correctly; she had a sympathetic heart. He had lied about the three children and the two women. Five young, strong and rebellious men were planning to escape with him and George. But Samson had thought the lie necessary, for if he had told Jolene the truth, she'd have sensed violence and withheld her help.

Samson didn't want to cause Jolene any trouble, for he not only found her exceptionally pretty, he also liked her. However, he was confident that she'd suffer no harm, for he didn't plan for any of them to be caught. No one would know Jolene had helped them.

Samson was still determined to kill the Delmars, including Sabrina. First, though, he'd murder their white overseer. He hated the overbearing man almost as much as he hated the Delmars.

His strong hands knotted into fists as he imagined wrapping them about John Delmar's throat. When he finished with the "masta", he'd tend to Alan and make damned sure that the man died mercilessly. Then it'd be Miz Sabrina's turn!

Oh yes, he'd kill them all, and take great pleasure in doing it!

Chapter Twenty-Five

Leaving his parent's home, Kurt walked swiftly toward the overseer's house. Mulling over the conversation at dinner, he recalled Alan's saying that if war erupted, the South would win within two months. Unfortunately, the majority of southerners would agree with Alan. Kurt experienced a pang of dread. He believed war was inevitable, for the southern delegates and politicians would continue to insist that slavery be extended into the territories. Furthermore, in the new political and economic world the South's leaders would be in the minority. He could foresee the southern states seceding, which in itself would be a declaration of war. However, southerners like Alan Delmar would be in for a rude awakening, for the conflict between the North and South would most assuredly drag on for years.

Several times Kurt had asked himself what he'd do if the North and South were to declare war. Would he leave his ranch, return to the South, and fight for his homeland? But a man had to fight for what he believed in, and Kurt didn't believe in slavery, nor did he believe in secession. For this country to remain impregnable, it must stay united. The prospect of war, which Kurt deemed inevitable, divided his loyalties. His convictions lay with the North, but he had an innate love for the South.

Nearing the overseer's house, Kurt cleared his mind. He'd make his decision when and if war was declared.

The darkness prevented Kurt from recognizing the man on the porch with Jolene, but as he approached, he saw it was Delmar's slave, Samson. Pausing, Kurt wondered why he'd be visiting Jolene. Then, remembering the day Jolene had run away, he recalled that she'd been in Samson's arms when he and the others had arrived. Kurt's eyes narrowed angrily as he remembered that later she'd insisted on riding with Samson. He'd sensed there was some kind of involvement between them, and now, as he watched Samson hurrying away from the house and heading toward the slave cabins, he was sure he'd been right. There was something going on between those two, but Kurt had no inkling what it could be.

Kurt's strides continued, and when he reached the house, Jolene had already gone inside. Crossing the porch, he let himself in.

Jolene was in the parlor, sitting in the pine rocker, but at Kurt's sudden entrance she sprang to her feet. She was surprised to see him so soon, for she'd been certain that he'd linger at the manor house and visit with Sabrina.

"Kurt," she said, smiling. "How was dinner?"

"Fine," he answered. His eyes traveled intensely

367

over her slender frame. God, she was beautiful! Her hair, black as a raven, draped lustrously past her shoulders, and her large blue eyes enhanced her rare beauty. She was wearing the dress Delmar had bought for her, but the plain, shapeless garment failed to conceal her firm breasts, tiny waist, and delicate hips.

Kurt, mesmerized by her beauty, fought back the urge to sweep her into his arms and carry her to the bedroom.

Meanwhile, Jolene found his manner perplexing. "Kurt, is something wrong?"

"No," he answered, mustering control over his need to ravish her. "How was your evening?" He watched her closely. Would she tell the truth?

"Daniel stopped by. He was hoping to see Mary Jane, but she never showed up. Apparently Sabrina gave her orders not to leave the house. Otherwise she'd have been here."

Walking into the parlor, Kurt went to the liquor cabinet. It was well stocked, and he poured himself a glass of brandy. He took a large swallow, then wheeling about and facing Jolene, asked, "What else did you do this evening besides wait with Daniel?"

"Nothing," she replied. She couldn't possibly tell him about Samson's visit. If Kurt knew Samson and the others were planning to run away, he might consider it his duty to inform John Delmar. Also, Kurt would be furious to learn that she had become an accomplice by forging a pass.

Kurt took another liberal drink. Evidently she didn't plan to tell him about Samson's visit! Damn it! Just when he'd begun to trust her, she did this to him—he'd been a fool to think her lies had ceased! The deceitful little minx didn't know how to do anything else!

His face implacable, Kurt questioned, "Did Samson's visit slip your mind?"

Jolene paled. "How . . . how did you know he was here?"

"I saw him leaving."

Placing her hands on her hips, she accused him angrily, "Have you been spying on me?"

"Spying?" he repeated, rage creeping into his voice. "I couldn't very well miss seeing him, since he was leaving as I was arriving!"

He waited for her to say something, but when no reply was forthcoming, he demanded, "Well? What did he want?"

"He stopped by to pay his respects," she said evasively.

Kurt laughed harshly. "Oh, Jolene! You can do better than that! You're an experienced liar; yet you sound like an amateur!"

Resenting his cutting remarks, she snapped, "Kurt Spencer, you can go straight to the devil! You arrogant cad! I don't owe you any explanations!"

"Is that any way for a slave to talk to her master?" he retorted.

"I'm not your slave!"

"No?" he asked. "Well, I have a piece of paper that says you are indeed my slave."

"That piece of paper is just as worthless as you are!"

"Worthless, am I? You know, Jolene, you have a hell of a way of showing your gratitude. Aren't you the least bit grateful to me for saving you from John Delmar? If I remember correctly, he was about to have you strung up and given twenty lashes of the whip."

"If it's gratitude you want, then set me free!"

"I'll set you free when I'm ready."

"Kurt, you must let me go immediately! It's not safe for me to stay here at Heritage Manor."

He was dumbfounded. "God!" he groaned. "What outrageous lie are you now about to fabricate?"

Exasperated, she spat, "Don't you realize that Katherine will make me pay for what happened between you and Richard?"

"That's ridiculous," he said impatiently. "There are no hard feelings between Richard and me. Katherine is aware of this, so there's no reason for her to harbor hard feelings toward you. Besides, she's too wrapped up in Richard's wedding to think about anything else."

"Must you be so blind? Don't you realize that a woman like Katherine is vindictive?"

"That's quite an observation, considering you only met her once."

"Once was enough!" she asserted. "I know her kind! My sister is just like her!"

He arched a brow. "Jolene, it's not going to work."

"What isn't going to work?" she asked, confused.

"Your ploy to direct our discussion away from Samson and onto my mother. Now I'm going to ask you again, and this time I expect a truthful answer. Why was he here?"

Determined to protect Samson and the others, she

raised her chin defiantly. "I told you. He stopped by to pay his respects!"

Furious with her, Kurt downed his drink, then threw the glass across the room. It smashed against the fireplace and shattered into tiny fragments.

"Damn you and your lies!" he raged. "You've never once been honest with me, have you?"

Jolene's nerve didn't falter. "I refuse to defend myself to you! It's be a waste of breath! You wouldn't believe a word I said!"

His lips twisted into a bitter grin. "A moot point, my love."

Through arguing with him, she started out of the parlor. "You're being totally unreasonable," she said icily. "This discussion is closed! There's an extra bedroom in this house, and I hope you'll be a gentleman and use it!"

As she brushed past him, he grabbed her about the waist and lifted her into his arms. His dark eyes probed hers, their expression coldly dangerous. "I've always prided myself on being a gentleman, so I'll abide by your wish."

"Then put me down!" she commanded.

"Not on your life, my lying beauty! If I must sleep in the other bedroom, then you'll be sleeping there, too!" Moving decisively, he carried her from the parlor.

"Kurt!" she spat angrily. "I swear this time I'll fight you to the bitter end!"

"Good!" was his riposte. "I like a woman with spirit!"

Taking her into the room., he carried her to the bed and dropped her roughly onto the mattress. As she made a desperate move to get up, he uttered threateningly, "Don't try it, Jolene! I can catch you before you're halfway across the room."

"You beast!" she remarked heatedly. "Do you plan to add rape to all your other vices?"

He lit the bedside lamp, then removing his shirt with an air of calmness, he questioned, "Other vices?"

"Yes! Do you want me to list them?"

"I'd rather be spared your biased opinion of me."

His shirt was now removed, and as he sat on a chair to take off his shoes, Jolene tried not to notice the way his muscles rippled, or the obvious strength of his chest. If only she could look at him with indifference!

Entranced, she continued to look on as Kurt shed his shoes, then, standing, he slipped off the rest of his clothing. The saffron lamplight fell across his splendid form, and as Jolene's vision traveled the full length of him, desire coiled within her. Her heart began to beat wildly as her eyes lingered over his build. She admired every inch of his body before her gaze came to rest on his face.

His expression reflected his determination to make love to her, and although Jolene wished for the willpower to spurn his advances, she knew she was helpless against him. The sight of his naked body had already weakened her defenses, and she knew that the moment he took her into his arms she'd surrender completely—even fervently!

I can't refuse him! she cried to herself. I love him too much! She wished she knew what was in his heart. Did he love her at all? Or were his feelings governed only by passion?

He stepped to the bed, caught her wrist, and drew her to her feet. Turning her about, he began unfastening the buttons at the back of her dress. Calling upon her last shred of will-power, Jolene tried to escape, but his strong arm went about her waist. As he imprisoned her in his powerful grip, she fought wildly, and losing his patience, Kurt grasped her gown and ripped it free. Pitching the tattered garment to the floor, he swung her around and brought her frame flush to his. Holding the struggling beauty close, Kurt kissed her fiercely, his lips branding hers with fiery passion.

His demanding ardor melted her flimsy defenses, and as her knees weakened, she leaned helplessly into his firm embrace. Entwining her arms about his neck, she responded zealously to his heart-stopping kiss.

Kurt held her so possessively that she felt as though she were an inseparable part of him. Raining soft kisses over her face and down to her slender neck, Kurt whispered huskily, "You seductive little vixen, you've totally bewitched me!"

Jolene started to tell him that she'd never tried to bewitch him; she'd only wanted to love him—but Kurt's lips were suddenly on hers, smothering her words.

Anxious to make love to this enticing minx, Kurt removed the rest of her clothing, then lifted her onto the bed. Hungrily, his eyes devoured her supple curves, his gaze piercing her firm breasts, dainty waist, and the dark triangle between her ivory thighs. As he lay beside her, she turned to him willingly, pressing her body intimately to his.

Jolene's hands roamed anxiously over Kurt's muscular shoulders, then down his back before, daringly, she caressed his tight-muscled buttocks. As her fingers traveled between them, he moved so that she could grasp him fully. Her touch was dangerously stimulating, and needing to consummate their joining, Kurt eased his frame over hers.

Wrapping her arms about him, Jolene awaited his breathtaking entry. With one quick thrust, his hardness slipped deeply inside her.

His maleness filled her with ecstasy. His strokes were demanding, and loving his aggressiveness, she lifted her hips in perfect rhythm.

Kurt, realizing how much he loved her, moaned hoarsely, "I'll never let you go! Never!"

Jolene misconstrued his declaration and assumed erroneously that he intended to keep her enslaved. Was she nothing more to him than a bed wench?

Valuing her pride, she almost mustered the strength to push him away, but before she could, Kurt lifted her legs about his back. He plunged into her deeply, rapturously, and his stimulating invasion conquered her pride.

Now, oblivious to everything except their fiery union, Jolene writhed beneath Kurt as, increasing the tempo, his hips pounded roughly against her. Clinging, she equaled his driving passion until, ecstatically, they climbed to love's supreme culmination.

As Kurt kissed her softly, Jolene drifted slowly back to earth. He lay beside her, but as he attempted to draw her closer, she pushed away.

Her passion sated, she was now able to think rationally. Regardless of how much she loved Kurt, she'd not be his slave! Recalling his declaration never to let her go sent anger surging through Jolene.

Kurt, mystified by her sudden coldness, asked, "What's wrong?"

"Need you ask?" she retorted tartly.

Immediately irritated, he grumbled, "What kind of game are you now playing?"

"You're the one who plays games!" she snapped.

Kurt drew into a smoldering silence. The exasperating chit could drive a preacher to drink! Her moods constantly switched from hot to cold without warning or provocation! Furthermore, she was totally untrustworthy! Kurt groaned regretfully. If only he didn't love her, then he could simply set her free and send her on her way. But, damn it, he was so hopelessly in love with the lying little vixen that he'd rather die than lose her! God, what was he going to do? He knew what he wanted to do—he wanted to marry her and take her back to Texas with him— although he seriously doubted that she'd accept his proposal. However, he should keep his thoughts in perspective. First he must go to Cedarbrook. If by some small margin Jolene had told the truth, then her sister and lawyer should be exposed. For a moment he considered telling Jolene that he planned to go to Cedarbrook and carry out his own investigation, but he quickly decided against it—he had his pride, regardless of how deeply he loved her. If she had fabricated the story about her sister and her lawyer, then he didn't want her to know that he'd been fool enough to give her the benefit of the doubt, even going so far as to travel to Cedarbrook. Kurt knew his refusal to confide in Jolene was based on male pride, but nonetheless he held onto it stubbornly. She'd tricked him too many times, and his vanity was seriously wounded.

Now, as Jolene tried to leave the bed, Kurt's hand snaked out and captured her wrist. "Where are you going?"

"To my own bedroom," she answered sharply.

"You're sleeping right here." His tone brooked no argument.

"Kurt Spencer, you're impossible! Don't you realize I'd rather sleep with a skunk?"

He replied calmly, "I'm beginning to find your constant name-calling tedious." His temper hanging by a thread, he jerked her forcefully to his side. Holding her extremely close, he mumbled, "Be quiet and go to sleep."

She made a futile attempt to free herself. Then, realizing it was hopeless, she gave up and said threateningly, "If you don't soon give me my manumission papers, I'll run away!"

Kurt cringed. "Don't talk like a silly fool. Don't you understand how dangerous it'd be for you to run away?" Kurt was referring to all the frightening possibilities that could befall a beautiful woman on the run.

Jolene, however, took for granted that his warning referred to himself as the danger. Was he telling her that he'd hunt her down, perhaps even have her whipped? Oh, the insufferable, overbearing cad! If only she could hate the arrogant scoundrel!

For her own sake, she must find a way to stop loving him!

Determined to leave his bed and take her heart with her, she insisted harshly, "Kurt, let me up! I don't want to sleep with you—not tonight, nor ever again!"

His fury igniting, he demanded, "How can you make love to me so willingly, yet find sleeping with me so distasteful?"

Jolene sensed Kurt wouldn't give her permission to leave unless she could find the right words to change his mind. Preferring to avoid a lie, she came close to surrendering, but her pride was as strong as his. If he wanted a humble bed wench, he could look elsewhere! She'd destroy his arrogance, and in doing so, secure her permanent absence from his bed. Surely if he thought she loved another man, his male pride would demand that he give her her manumission papers! Then, freed, she'd return to Cedarbrook and regain her rightful place! Once that was taken care of, it'd only be a matter of time before she'd get over Kurt Spencer!

Growing impatient, Kurt suddenly moved her so that she was sitting upright. Staring into her eyes, he repeated, "How can you find sleeping with me so distasteful?"

Jolene, determined to end this once and for all, lied convincingly. "Kurt, I admit that I enjoy making love to you. I suppose, by nature, I'm a very passionate woman. I've often heard that some woman have a man's sexual drive, and I guess that's why I respond to you so willingly. However, my response is lust, not love." She swallowed nervously.

"I prefer not to sleep with you because I'm in love with someone else. When I'm sleeping at your side, I still dream about him."

Silence followed Jolene's dishonest confession. A little frightened, she'd looked away from Kurt the moment she'd finished her declaration. Now, cautiously, she dared to meet his eyes. The expression in them was inscrutable.

"Who do you love?" he asked, his tone strangely quiet.

Refusing to involve an innocent party, she answered emphatically, "His name is none of your business. You might own my body, but my heart is my own!" Successfully holding back tears, she wished her heart was truly hers! But, God help her, it belonged to Kurt!

Jolene, expecting a violent outburst, caught her breath apprehensively. Then, to her amazement, Kurt left the bed, picked up her discarded clothes, and handed them to her. His mild manner belying his inner rage, he said, "You needn't worry—I'll never touch you again. The day after Richard's wedding, I'll go to New Orleans and have manumission papers drawn up."

Leaving the bed by the far side, Jolene slipped into her torn dress. "Why New Orleans? It'd be much faster if you went to Mobile."

"New Orleans offers a much more exciting night life, and before returning to Texas, I intend to thoroughly enjoy myself." Kurt was astounded by his own composure. He could hardly believe that he was reacting so calmly when Jolene had just rejected him! Perhaps a few nights in New Orleans would help erase her from his mind as well as his heart. Continuing his unruffled manner, he said, "From now on, I'll use this room and you can sleep in your own bed undisturbed."

Jolene wondered why she fèlt so sad. Her lie had been successful, and Kurt had agreed to give her her freedom. She should be ecstatic! Sudden tears flooded her eyes. So that Kurt wouldn't see them, she ran from the room.

As the door closed behind her, Kurt stepped to the window and gazed out into the darkness. His strong hands were clenched into fists as he tried to keep a rein on his temper. Losing control would gain him nothing. Despite his sizzling rage, a small warning at the back of his mind interjected a thought. Jolene had lied to him before—why was he so damned sure she hadn't lied this time? Before his better sense could rule his thoughts, the memory of Jolene in Samson's arms flashed in front of him. He shook his head as though the image was misleading. He couldn't quite fathom Jolene falling in love with Samson.

Then why did Samson come to see her? And why did she try to avoid telling him of Samson's visit? Well, if she was in love with Samson, she certainly wasn't the mistress of Cedarbrook. His brow furrowed. Could Jolene possibly be in love with someone she'd known when she lived at Cedarbrook? A wealthy planter, perhaps? He shrugged. What difference did it make? To hell with her and her lover!

Suddenly a frown crossed his face. Damn, it was time to admit the truth to himself: Jolene had lied from the very beginning. She was a quadroon slave. And to think that he had actually planned to go to Cedarbrook! He had let the woman make a complete fool of him! To hell with Cedarbrook, and to hell with Jolene! After the wedding, he'd take a trip to New Orleans, gamble, enjoy a few whores, then come back to Heritage Manor, give Jolene her manumission papers, and return to his ranch!

Bolstered by his resolutions, he went back to bed, but his inner torment kept him awake for hours.

Meanwhile, with only a wall separating their rooms, Jolene lay alone in her bed longing for Kurt. More than once she was tempted to go to him and tell him the truth. There *was* no other man in her life, and she loved him with all her heart and soul! But what would her confession gain? It'd merely feed his arrogance, and he'd continue to use her as a bed wench, refusing to set her free until he tired of her. Furthermore, he wasn't worthy of her love. She had tried being honest with him and had told him about Johanna and Robert. Had he believed her? No, of course not!

Finally, after several hours of restlessness, she was able to sleep. But not even in repose could she obtain peace, for she dreamt only of Kurt.

Chapter Twenty-Six

As the constable from Natchez waited for Johanna to come downstairs, he paced the parlor restlessly. The law officer had liked Marshall Walker, and he was saddened by the man's death. Damn James Mitchell and his explosive temper! If the young man had kept his pistol holstered, Walker would still be alive.

The constable stopped pacing and poured himself a shot of bourbon. He quaffed it down neatly, then heaved a deep sigh. Accidents happened, and apparently James hadn't meant to kill anyone.

The officer had questioned James and Amanda shortly after the shooting and had gotten their side of the story. He had believed them, for in Natchez the Mitchells were thought to be above reproach. After questioning the pair, the constable had been eager to talk to Johanna so he could close his investigation and hand the case over to the courts.

The officer continued his pacing. Marshall had now been dead for a week, and the constable still hadn't received permission to question Miss Warrington. Her lawyer had informed him that she was too emotionally upset to undergo an interrogation, and Dr. Elliot had confirmed this.

Early this morning Hawkins had come to the constable's office to tell him Johanna was now able to answer his questions. He'd ridden with the lawyer out to Cedarbrook and was waiting for Robert to bring Johanna into the parlor.

Now, as the couple entered the room, the officer was taken aback by Johanna's pallor. She leaned against the attorney as though she were too weak to stand without support. The constable was immediately sympathetic.

Assisting Johanna to the sofa, Robert then turned to the lawman and said, "I hope your questions won't take too long. As you can see, my client is not completely recovered."

The constable, a middle-aged, compassionate man, assured Robert that he'd finish as quickly as possible. Sitting in the wing chair across from the sofa, the officer favored Johanna with a warm, encouraging smile. Despite her delicate health, she was beautiful. Her golden-brown hair fell softly across her shoulders, and her sea-green dress matched her eyes. The constable was impressed . . . Johanna Warrington was indeed a lovely young lady. As his mind went over everything James and Amanda had told him, he couldn't blame Walker for falling prey to Johanna's charms.

"Miss Warrington," he began gently, "just tell me in your own words what happened the day Mr. Walker was shot."

Johanna's face was impassive, but her heart was filled with malice. She hated James Mitchell and intended to see that he paid for Marshall's life with his own. She knew he and Amanda were claiming that the shooting was accidental. Accidental, ha! If James had never drawn his pistol, Marshall wouldn't be dead, and she'd be damned if young Mitchell would get off scot-free!

Meeting the constable's eyes, she proceeded to tell him the same story she'd told Robert. "That morning I had reason to suspect some of my slaves had murdered my overseer and were planning an uprising. I was frightened, so I wrote a note to Marshall, asking him to come immediately. I sent Lazarus with the message. My suspicions were unfounded—there was no uprising. Since Marshall had ridden all the way over here, I asked him to stay for lunch. I was expecting Amanda and her brother, and Marshall and I decided to surprise them with a picnic. We set it up close to the road, so we'd be sure and see them."

At this point in her story, Johanna paused and forced tears to her eyes. Then, appearing heart-broken, she continued, "As we were waiting for Amanda and Robert, our conversation turned to Papa and my brother. I'm still grieving terribly over their deaths, and as we were discussing them, I broke down and started to cry. Marshall drew me into his arms to console me, and because I was weeping so heavily, we didn't hear James and Amanda until their buggy was almost upon us."

Johanna had a handkerchief wadded in her hands, and she dabbed at her tears. "James and

Amanda thought we were sharing a lover's embrace. Marshall and I tried to convince James of the truth, but he didn't believe us. He was furious because he believed Marshall and I had maliciously planned for Amanda to see us in each other's arms. Before we knew what was happening, James drew his pistol."

Johanna sobbed chokingly. "He told Marshall he was going to blow him to hell, and then he pulled the trigger."

The constable, leaning back in his chair, studied Johanna intently. It was a long moment before he spoke. "Your version of what happened is very different from James's and Amanda's."

"Then apparently they are lying."

"James and his sister claim that when they arrived, you and Marshall were lying on the blanket. They also say that you were partly undressed."

Johanna leapt to her feet. "That isn't true!"

"James admits he drew his pistol, but he says he had no intention of shooting Walker—he merely wanted to scare him. He said you lurched for the gun, and in the process, the pistol accidentally fired. His sister confirms his account."

"She's lying to protect James. She doesn't want to see her brother go to the gallows! I tell you, it was cold-blooded murder!"

The constable cautioned, "It's your word against theirs. A jury will have to decide who's telling the truth." He got to his feet. "Your note, which was found on Walker's body, verifies the first part of your story. You did send him an urgent message."

Robert spoke up. "James's and Amanda's account of what happened is absurd. Why would a man as kind as Walker want his fiancée to find him in another woman's arms? Such maliciousness isn't consistent with Walker's nature! There's not a jury in the county who'll believe James and his sister. Marshall Walker's integrity was well known."

"You don't have to convince me, Mr. Hawkins. I'm not the jury." The constable looked at Johanna. "If you'll come to my office this afternoon, we'll take your story down on paper. Then, after you sign it, I'll have James Mitchell arrested for murder."

"I'll be there," she assured him. "And my lawyer will accompany me."

"Is three o'clock all right?"

She agreed, and Robert showed the officer to the door. Returning to the parlor, he fixed himself a tall glass of bourbon. He took a long drink, then turning to Johanna, asked somewhat suspiciously, "You *are* telling the truth, aren't you?"

"Honestly, Robert!" she complained. "You've asked me that at least a dozen times! Of course I'm telling the truth! Why else would Marshall and I have been in each other's arms? He was devoted to Amanda, and I'm very much in love with you."

"It's hard for me to believe that you were crying over Sam and Carl."

"I sincerely loved Papa and my brother. It wasn't my fault that my love wasn't returned." She gave the impression that she was about to cry. "You and Mama are the only people who have ever cared about me."

Touched, Robert put down his drink, went to Johanna, and took her warmly into his arms. "I'm sorry, Darling. I had no right to accuse you."

385

She leaned into his embrace, and as her thoughts turned to Marshall, real tears came to her eyes. Why was she always denied love by those whom she could love in return? She felt terribly sorry for herself.

"Mistress, ma'am?" Lazarus' voice suddenly broke their embrace.

"What do you want?" Johanna asked sharply.

"Masta Thomas is here," he answered.

"Who?" she questioned, unable to place the caller.

Lazarus' spirits were soaring, for he had reason to hope that the caller would expose Johanna. However, concealing his elation, he replied, "It's Masta Thomas Warrington, ma'am. He's your uncle from England. He asked for Miz Jolene. When I told 'im she wasn't here, he asked to see you."

Turning anxious eyes to Robert, Johanna exclaimed, "God, I hope he doesn't know the truth!" Then, realizing she shouldn't say more in Lazarus's presence, she told the butler to show her uncle into the parlor.

The moment Lazarus stepped out of the room, Robert clutched Johanna's wrist, drawing her close. "Remember that document we burned?"

"Of course I remember it," she spat.

"If your father sent a copy of it to your uncle, then we're ruined! I'll go to prison, and you . . . you'll be a slave."

Johanna's heart was pounding fearfully. "Why, after all these years, has Thomas returned?"

Robert groaned. "I don't know, but we're about to find out."

The tall, well-dressed man entering the parlor resembled Sam Warrington. His stylish beard and

386

black hair were streaked with gray, and his lissome, youthful frame belied his fifty-odd years. As his gaze fell across Johanna, a warm twinkle shone in his brilliant blue eyes.

Going to her and embracing her fondly, he said, "Johanna, you're such a beautiful young lady."

"Thank you," she murmured, stepping out of his arms and watching him guardedly. Did he know the truth? Was his affection merely a pretext?

Johanna was seeing her uncle for the first time. Twenty years ago, he had left Cedarbrook to tour Europe, and while in England, he'd met and married an Englishwoman. During that time he had never returned stateside.

"I suppose you're quite surprised by my visit. I know I should've let you and Jolene know I was coming, but I'm not one for writing letters. Besides, I made this trip on the spur of the moment." He cast Robert an inquisitive gaze.

Quickly Johanna made perfunctory introductions.

As Robert fixed himself and Thomas a drink, Johanna sat on the sofa beside her uncle.

Thomas took time to admire his niece. His perusal didn't disturb Johanna—she was perfectly aware that he was finding her attractive. She began to feel more at ease. Obviously he didn't know the truth and believed that she and Jolene were twins. Knowing she'd have to tell him about Jolene made her feel apprehensive: would he believe her? Her self-confidence surged. Of course he'd believe her! He was a man, wasn't he? She could make a man believe anything!

As Johanna's confidence was building, Thomas, deep in thought, was remembering the day he had received Sam's document that revealed Johanna's true bloodline. His brother had also notified him that Johanna's heritage would be exposed in his last will and testament. Now, as he continued to regard the young woman, his admiration for her grew. She was holding up very courageously. If he'd been raised to believe that he was white, and then found out that he was a quadroon, he knew he wouldn't be accepting it with Johanna's good grace. He was sure that part of the credit belonged to Jolene: evidently she loved her sister and was being supportive of her.

Robert brought Thomas a glass of bourbon, then sat in a wing chair facing the sofa.

"I suppose I should explain why I'm here," Warrington began. "My wife passed away recently. In fact, I was notified of Sam's and Carl's murders shortly after her death. We never had any children, so we were completed devoted to one another. Losing her devastated me. When she and I married, I bought into my father-in-law's business. After I lost her, I thought I could remain in England and run the business. But England held too many painful memories, so I sold my interest in the business to my wife's brother and decided to come back to the states."

"Are you planning to live at Cedarbrook?" Johanna asked. Oh, how she'd resent his presence!

He reached over and patted her hands fondly. He thought no less of her because she was a quadroon. She was family, and he hoped to build a loving relationship with both of his nieces.

"No, my dear," he assured her. "I don't plan to stay here permanently. I wouldn't dream of intruding on you and Jolene. Besides, I hope to buy my own business."

Johanna sighed with relief. Thank goodness, he didn't want to remain at Cedarbrook! She certainly didn't need a nosy uncle underfoot!

Smiling sweetly, Johanna was quick to say, "But Uncle Thomas, you're more than welcome to stay for as long as you want . . . even indefinitely."

"Thank you, Hon, but I don't want to impose." His voice, however, lacked conviction.

Johanna, detecting his uncertainty, didn't insist that he'd be no imposition.

"Where's Jolene?" Thomas asked.

Robert tensed, took a large drink of bourbon, and waited nervously for Johanna's reply.

Johanna, appearing heartbroken, began to tell her uncle how Sam's will had revealed Jolene's true heritage. With tears in her eyes, she let him know that Jolene had decided to go north.

Throughout her explanation, Thomas had managed to keep his expression merely one of concern. His face never once revealed that he knew she and Hawkins had falsified Sam's will.

Wiping at her trickling tears, Johanna finished by saying, "Jolene promised she'd write, but I haven't heard one word from her. I think she decided to leave her past behind. I have a heartsick feeling she'll never contact me."

"I'm shocked!" Thomas exclaimed, deciding prudently to play along. He knew there was nothing he could do now, but he had every intention of finding

Jolene and reinstating her in her rightful position. His gaze swept fleetingly over Robert. The man's nervousness was visible. Thomas surmised that the young lawyer would break under interrogation.

Thomas, continuing to act as though he believed everything she'd said, asked the appropriate questions and made all the right comments. Upon his arrival, he'd seen the constable leaving, and from the moment he'd entered the house, he'd wanted to ask Johanna about the lawman's visit. But politeness had kept him from doing so. Now, though, learning of Johanna's and Robert's crime, his curiosity about the constable deepened.

Waiting until he was confident that they had discussed Jolene sufficiently, he mentioned as though mildly curious, "By the way, when I was arriving, I saw the constable leaving. We exchanged greetings, but he didn't tell me why he was here." Looking at Johanna, he arched a brow. "Nothing's wrong, I hope."

Johanna was growing more and more annoyed with her uncle's untimely visit. Why hadn't the man stayed in England?

Drawing a deep breath, she proceeded to tell him about Marshall's death, reciting the same story she'd given the constable.

Thomas, now understandably suspicious of his niece, gave the impression that he accepted her explanation, going so far as to express his sympathy. Then, anxious to question Lazarus, he asked that the servant show him to his room.

Johanna saw to his request and had Lazarus take Thomas upstairs to the guest room that was always kept ready for unexpected company.

Alone with Robert, Johanna went into his arms, smiled complacently, and remarked, "Uncle Thomas is no threat. Papa never told him about me."

The lawyer sighed happily. "Apparently we no longer have to worry about being caught. If Sam told anyone about you, it'd have been his brother." He hugged her eagerly. "Darling, don't you think it's about time for us to announce our engagement?"

Johanna didn't want to marry Robert. She was finding him less and less attractive. She hoped to remain free so she could date a variety of men. Maybe in time she could find one who would measure up to Marshall. But for now she had no choice but to pacify Robert. Damn, she must find a way to get rid of him! But how? *How?*

"Darling?" he pressed. "Let's announce our engagement."

She placed her head on his shoulder and snuggled close. "I think we should wait until after the trial, don't you?"

"I guess you're right. Marshall's murder is causing quite a scandal, and this isn't the best time for us to become engaged. But as soon as the trial is over, we'll make our wedding plans public."

He kissed her, and she pretended to respond.

"Lazarus," Thomas remarked.

"Yes, masta?" The servant had been about to leave the guest room.

Warrington pointed to a chair. "Sit down. I want

391

to talk to you."

Doing as he was told, Lazarus asked, "Is somethin' wrong, masta, suh?"

Thomas regarded him silently as he wondered how much he knew about Johanna and Robert.

The man's intense scrutiny didn't intimidate Lazarus. He'd been a servant at Cedarbrook for over thirty years and had known Thomas before he left for Europe. Lazarus had seen a compassion in Thomas that had been sorely lacking in Sam. He had often wished that Thomas was the older brother and the master of Cedarbrook.

Thomas, remaining standing, looked directly into Lazarus's eyes and remarked, "I want you to tell me everything you know."

Lazarus was dubious. "'Bout what, masta?"

"About Johanna and Mr. Hawkins."

The servant's hopes soared. Lord, did Masta Thomas know the truth about Miz Johanna? Was justice about to prevail?

Thomas decided to be perfectly candid. "I know it's Johanna, and not Jolene, who's the quadroon." Quickly he told Lazarus about the document that Sam had sent.

Lazarus, in turn, told Thomas that Jolene hadn't gone north as Johanna claimed. He explained about ther night he had seen the slave trader carry Jolene out of the house, adding that he was quite sure Jolene had been sedated.

Warrington was shocked, and he stepped weakly to the bed and sat down. "My God!" he moaned, finding Johanna's wickedness almost beyond belief. "You mean Johanna actually sold her sister into slavery?"

"Yes, suh."

It was a moment before Thomas could compose himself. "Do you know the trader's name?"

"Cal Atkins," Lazarus answered.

"Where do you suppose he took her?"

"New Orleans, probably."

Rubbing a hand over his perspiring brow, Thomas shuddered, imagining the degradation Jolene must had suffered.

Lazarus was unable to suppress his anxiety. "What you gonna do, masta?"

"First I'm going to find Jolene. Exposing Johanna and Hawkins can wait."

"Is you plannin' to go to New Orleans?"

"Yes," he replied. "If she was sold on the vendue block, there should be a record of the sale. I'll find out who bought her." He cringed as he thought about his young niece standing helplessly on the auction block while prospective buyers bidded for her.

"Can I go to New Orleans with you, Masta Thomas?" Lazarus asked excitedly. "I's awful anxious to help you find Miz Jolene."

The man thought for a moment. "I don't see why not. I'll tell Johanna I have business in New Orleans and ask her to let you accompany me as my valet."

"When we gonna leave?"

"I think I should visit for a couple of days before departing. It might look peculiar if I were to arrive one day and leave the next. I don't want to do anything to arouse Johanna's suspicions."

"I sure hope it don't take us too long to find Miz Jolene!"

"So do I," Thomas agreed, then added with a sigh,

"I pray she hasn't been mistreated."

Silence ensued. Then, bringing himself out of his somber thoughts, Thomas said briskly, "Tell me what kind of mistress Johanna has been. I also want to know more about Marshall Walker's death. I've a feeling that it didn't happen the way Johanna claims."

"I don't know much 'bout the way Masta Walker died, but I got an idea what really happened."

"You can tell me your idea later. Now, tell me if Johanna has been a fair mistress."

Lazarus laughed dryly. "Fair? That woman don't know the meanin' of the word." The servant was more than willing to discuss Johanna's cruelty.

Later, after they had finished discussing both Johanna and the overseer, Thomas remarked strongly, "Johanna's and Mr. Sullivan's reign will soon come to an end. However, Jolene's welfare must take priority."

"I understand, masta."

Intensely, Thomas murmured, "God, I hope she's still alive!"

Chapter Twenty-Seven

The elaborate wedding and reception were now history. The bride and groom had left on their honeymoon, and upon their return, they would make their home at Heritage Manor. All the guests except the Delmars had departed.

Mary Jane, in her cramped bedroom adjacent to Sabrina's, waited anxiously for her mistress to fall asleep. The hour was late before Mary Jane decided to venture from her room. Surely by now Sabrina was sleeping soundly.

To reach the hall the young woman had to cross her mistress's quarters. Moving furtively, she crept past the canopied bed where Sabrina lay deep in slumber, opened the door cautiously, and slipped into the hall. Using the servants' stairway, she hurried through the back of the house and outdoors.

Her heart hammered as she fled stealthily toward the stables. Tomorrow the Delmars planned to return to Willow Hill, and Mary Jane knew tonight was her last chance to be alone with Daniel. Since her arrival, Sabrina had kept her so busy that she had seen very little of him. Reaching the stables, she darted inside, and going to the room at the back, she knocked softly as she called Daniel's name.

Daniel wasn't expecting her clandestine visit and was surprised to hear her voice. Getting out of bed, he slipped quickly into his trousers. Hoping nothing was wrong, he opened the door and asked urgently, "Are you all right?"

"Yes, I'm fine," she answered, brushing past him and entering the dark room.

Daniel secured the door, then lit a small kerosene lamp. He was worried. "It's risky for you to be here. If Sabrina were to find out—"

Interrupting him, Mary Jane cried, "Daniel, I had to come! After tonight, we may never see each other again!" Tears glistened in her large eyes.

Mary Jane was lovely in the amber lamplight, the golden rays reflecting the shiny streaks in her long black hair. Entranced, Daniel looked at her slowly, admiring her pretty face and her curvaceous form. Her nondescript dress, one size too small, hugged her voluptuous curves.

His desire to make love to Mary Jane hit him so acutely that he groaned aloud.

"Is somethin' wrong?" she asked, concerned.

He smiled wanly. "I want you so badly that . . . that not having you is torture."

"I know," she answered shyly, "I feel the same way—that's why I'm here."

Daniel remained nonplussed. He knew Mary Jane's feelings about such intimacy. Thanks to her white masters, she knew nothing of love, only degradation. "Are you sure?" he insisted, almost afraid to hope.

She smiled reassuringly. "I love you, Daniel. I doubt if I'll ever see you again. But 'fore I lose you for good, I want you to show me how beautiful love can really be. I got to know if it's like you and Lucy say."

In one sweep Daniel had her in his arms, and bending his head, he pressed a fiery kiss to her lips.

Desire flamed within Mary Jane as she returned his ardor, her tongue joining his in sensual foreplay.

Lowering her pliable form onto the bed, Daniel lay beside her, and as his hands moved anxiously along her body, she gave in to the wonderful sensations he was awakening in her.

Eager to see her unclothed, Daniel helped her remove her dress and petticoat. Then he slipped off her cotton pantalets, revealing all her seductive beauty to his loving scrutiny.

Daniel was well practiced in the art of making love, and his expertise spiraled Mary Jane upward to ecstatic heights as, reaching for wonderful torment, her body cried out for complete fulfillment.

Daniel, impatient now to make them as one, quickly removed his trousers. His mouth crushed against her as simultaneously he drove deeply into her warm depths.

Trembling with passion, Mary Jane whispered, "Oh, Daniel, with you love is beautiful!" Grasping his strong shoulders, she arched beneath him, taking in the full length of his hardness.

Placing his hands under her hips, he molded her

thighs to his, and thrusting powerfully, entered her as deeply as possible.

Drifting serenely into love's hypnotic bliss, Mary Jane became totally enveloped in the sensuous pleasure Daniel was giving her.

Closing their minds to the real world, the couple lost themselves in their euphoria. There were no yesterdays, no tomorrows. Nothing existed but this blissful moment in time.

Engulfed in paradise, their bodies entangled, the lovers felt their emotions soar gloriously upward, and they soon found and achieved passion's ultimate pinnacle.

Moving to lie at her side, Daniel drew her close. "Mary Jane," he murmured huskily, "somehow I'll find a way for us to be together."

Mary Jane was still basking in the afterglow of their love, but Daniel's words brought her back to reality. Sitting up and retrieving her clothes, she said depressingly, "There ain't no way for us to be together. You know that, and so do I."

Daniel, leaving the bed to slip on his trousers, answered, "I intend to return to Willow Hill and make Alan give me back my money. Then I'll buy you from Delmar."

Mary Jane gaped at him. "Daniel, is you crazy? You cain't come back to Willow Hill! And how in God's name do you plan to make Masta Alan give you your money? For an educated man, you talkin' awful foolish!"

Daniel sat on the edge of the bed. "I'm not going to let Alan steal five thousand dollars from me and do nothing about it. It's my money, and I'm getting

398

it back!"

A cold chill ran up Mary Jane's spine. She finished dressing quickly, then going to Daniel and kneeling at his feet, she gazed imploringly into his eyes. "I's scared! If you comes to Willow Hill, I just know Masta John's gonna kill you! Daniel, if not for my sake, then for your mama's, don't try somethin' so crazy!" Mary Jane was tempted to let him know that he shouldn't do anything to upset Lucy. But the woman had made her promise not to tell Daniel or Kurt that she was ailing.

Standing, Daniel drew her to her feet and into his arms. Holding her close, he said determinedly, "It's my money, and I'm going to get it back or die trying!"

With a half-sob, Mary Jane cried, "Then you're gonna die! In Alabama, they kills nigras who stand up for their rights!" Clinging, she begged pathetically, "Daniel, please don't do it! If you was to die, I'd die too! And what about Lucy? You cain't bring such sorrow upon her! Ain't she suffered enough in her lifetime? Your money ain't worth it! Neither is your pride! If you come to Willow Hill, it's 'cause you love your money more than you love me and Lucy!"

"You know that isn't true," he insisted.

"Then prove it and don't try to get Masta Alan to return your five thousand dollars!"

Daniel was defeated. Furthermore, Mary Jane was right. His money wasn't worth his bringing sorrow upon Lucy and Mary Jane. "All right," he relented reasonably. "I won't come to Willow Hill."

"You'll go back to Texas?" she asked hopefully.

"Yes, I will. Then I'll get a loan on my ranch, come back, and buy you from Delmar."

She smiled radiantly. "Now you talkin' sensibly."

He returned her smile. "You will marry me, won't you?"

"Oh, yes . . . yes!" she cried happily, leaning into his embrace to hug him tightly.

The next morning Jolene awoke early, and went to the kitchen to fix a pot of coffee. She knew Kurt was up, for she could hear sounds coming from his room. Last night he'd informed her that he planned to get up early and leave for New Orleans. When he returned, he'd have her manumission papers.

As the coffee brewed, Jolene sat at the table. Since the day Kurt had bought her from Delmar, she had longed for him to set her free, and now he had promised to do so. She should be elated. Why, then, did she feel so gloomy?

Her thoughts drifted back over the past few days. Kurt, believing she was in love with another man, had avoided her like the plague. He still slept in the overseer's house, but he had made a point of arriving late and leaving early. She was always in bed when he came to the house and was still abed when he left the next morning. Last night when he'd knocked on her door, she'd sensed he was about to let her know he was departing for New Orleans. He had delivered the message tersely, then without further comment had gone to his own room and closed the door.

Clearing Kurt from her mind, she turned her thoughts to Lucy. Mary Jane had told her the woman wasn't well, and she was gravely worried. She wished she could go to Willow Hill and see Lucy, but she figured that was unlikely.

Jolene was so involved with her thoughts that she didn't hear Kurt enter the kitchen. Pausing in the doorway, he studied her intently. He wondered why she seemed so somber. She looked awfully forlorn for a slave who was about to be set free. Damn, if only he could read her mind—but his Sleeping Beauty had always been a mystery. He never knew where her thoughts were or what was in her heart. He sighed. Of course he didn't really know her; it was impossible to know a woman who constantly lied!

He told himself he'd be glad to be free of her once and for all. Then, going to the stove, he poured a cup of coffee.

As he sipped the hot brew, Jolene watched him uneasily. As always, his presence stirred her senses. She allowed her eyes to roam over his handsome physique. He was wearing a partially unbuttoned light blue shirt, and it revealed the dark curly hairs that grew thickly across his chest. His snug brown trousers revealed his muscular thighs, and tapered downward to his western boots. Slowly she looked upward into his face: he was watching her, and she tried to discern the expression in his dark eyes, but they were inscrutable. A sandy-colored curl fell haphazardly across his brow, and as he absently brushed it into place, the corners of his moustache lifted with a wry grin.

"Would you like a cup of coffee?" he asked. His smile was so cold that it chilled her to the bone.

Glancing away from his icy scrutiny, she answered

softly, "Yes, thank you."

He placed the filled cup on the table, then said in an unemotional tone, "During my absence, my father has promised to take care of you. If you need anything, let him know." He paused, then continued somewhat hesitantly, "It'll take about five days to reach New Orleans. I plan to stay for a couple of days, so it'll be close to two weeks before I get back."

Holding dearly to her pride, Jolene replied quietly, "Good-bye, Kurt."

Turning on his heel, Kurt left the room, and the moment she heard the front door close, Jolene hurried into the parlor. Going to the window, she watched him stride swiftly to his parents' home. She fought back the urge to run after him, throw herself into his arms, and beg him to love her! But her pride held firm—she'd be no man's bed wench! If she couldn't have his love and respect, she'd rather not have him at all. She'd be damned if she'd share his bed until he returned to Texas, or else married Sabrina Delmar! Her self-esteem was strong, and it demanded that she hold tenaciously to her dignity.

Returning to the kitchen, Jolene got her coffee, and taking it back to the parlor, she drew a chair to the window. She waited for Kurt to ride away from Heritage Manor. From this vantage point she could see the long lane that led to the mansion.

Kurt was eager to be on his way, and Jolene didn't have long to wait. Quickly he made his good-byes to his parents and the Delmars. Then, hurrying to the stables, he advised Daniel to stay at Heritage Manor. Putting Kurt's mind at rest, Daniel told him that he had no intention of leaving and would be here upon his return.

Kurt mounted his horse and galloped down the lane. He was unaware Jolene was watching his departure through a teary haze.

Jolene remained seated a long time after he'd ridden out of sight. She had never felt so alone—Kurt was gone, and soon Mary Jane would be leaving. She was grateful that she'd at least have Daniel's company.

Jolene glanced back out the window, and the unexpected sight of Katherine waking toward the overseer's house sent her bounding to her feet: why was the woman coming here? What did she want? Jolene was apprehensive. She didn't trust Kurt's stepmother, and she knew she must be on her guard.

Jolene stepped outside and waited for Katherine to reach the porch steps before saying respectfully, "What can I do for you, Mrs. Spencer?"

Jolene's voice astounded the woman. The wench not only spoke in a refined manner but addressed her as Mrs. Spencer. Inwardly Katherine was furious with the slave's insolence, but concealing her anger, she began her ploy to inveigle Jolene away from Edward's protection. "I've been invited to Willow Hill for a few days. I'll be back before Kurt returns. However, my personal maid isn't feeling well, and I need a servant to accompany me. Sabrina informed me that you're adequately trained as a lady's maid. You aren't my slave, so I can't order you to come with me, but I think you'll agree to take my maid's place."

Jolene eyed her suspiciously. "Oh? Why do you think that?"

"Sabrina said you and Mary Jane are good friends, so I imagine you'd enjoy spending more time with her. Sabrina also mentioned that you're very close to the Delmars' cook. I understand the woman is not feeling well. I was sure you'd jump at the opportunity to visit her."

Jolene was tempted—it was a chance to see Lucy—but her suspicions held her at bay. Was Katherine using Lucy's illness as bait? Was the woman setting a malicious trap, one she'd fall into if she accompanied her to Willow Hill?

Seeing Jolene's uncertainty, Katherine decided prudently to use it to her advantage. Shrugging as though mildly disappointed, she said tediously, "Very well, I'll take one of my cleaning maids with me." She whirled about and had taken only a single step when, as she'd suspected, Jolene called out.

"Wait, Mrs. Spencer. I'll work as your maid. But I expect to be treated decently."

Katherine turned to look at her. "Don't be impertinent, girl. If you do your job satisfactorily, I'll treat you fairly. Regardless of what you might think, I'm not a tyrant."

Jolene believed she *was* a tyrant, but that was beside the point. She wanted to see Lucy so badly that she was willing to take her chances. Besides, she could be mistaken. Maybe the woman wasn't harboring malevolent feelings.

Kurt's stepmother continued, "We'll be leaving within the hour, so pack your things and come to the house." With that she walked away.

Jolene went back into the house. Her emotions were in a turmoil. She didn't trust Katherine's motives, but her need to see Lucy was pressing.

Praying she had made a wise decision, she hurried into the bedroom to pack her meager belongings.

Katherine shared Sabrina's carriage, for Edward planned to come to Willow Hill in their own brougham and escort his wife home. Mary Jane and Jolene were told to ride on the perch seat with Samson. John Delmar and his son would ride horseback. The ladies' luggage was attached firmly to the rear of the conveyance.

Now, as they prepared to leave, Edward went to the front of the buggy and glanced up at Jolene. She was sitting between Samson and Mary Jane. "Kurt left you in my care, and I'm not sure if he'd want you going to Willow Hill."

"Mr. Spencer, I can't wait to see Lucy, and it's not as though I won't be back before your son returns."

Although Edward had reservations, he could find no logical reason for refusing to let Jolene accompany his wife. "All right," he agreed. "You take care, and I'll see you in a few days."

Meanwhile, John, eager to get home and check on Lucy, said cordially to Edward, "Thanks for your hospitality." He spurred his horse into a trot.

As Samson slapped the reins, Katherine and Sabrina waved farewell to the master of Heritage Manor.

Alan, bringing up the rear, caught sight of Daniel in front of the stables. With an inward, spiteful smile, he rode over to him. Pulling up, young Delmar said with malicious intent, "Your mama's sick."

Daniel tensed. "What the hell do you mean?" Alan

had to be lying! If Lucy was ill, Mary Jane would have told him.

"I mean exactly what I said. Your mama's health is failing. If you don't believe me, ask Mary Jane." He nodded toward the slow-moving buggy.

Breaking into a run, Daniel chased after the carriage, yelling, "Wait up!"

Samson drew back on the reins. Running to the side of the buggy, Daniel asked breathlessly, "Mary Jane, is Mama sick?"

She didn't answer, but the look on her face confirmed his fear. "Why didn't you *tell* me?" he pleaded.

"She made me promise not to say nothin'." Mary Jane's voice quivered. "She was afraid you'd try to come see her."

Looking on, Alan was complacent. Daniel's concern for his mother would compel him to take his chances and sneak back to Willow Hill. Alan planned to lie in wait for him, but he wouldn't shoot the uppity buck. He'd take Daniel prisoner, then sell him along with Jolene. The backbreaking work on a cane plantation would not only cure their insolence, but in time, it might also kill them.

Mary Jane, afraid Daniel would come to Willow Hill, implored, "Please don't try to see your mama! Jolene will be back in a few days, and she'll let you know how Lucy's feelin'."

John, riding back to the buggy, demanded impatiently, "Samson, why did you stop?" Without giving the driver time to answer, Delmar set his heated glare upon Daniel. "Boy, get the hell away from here!"

"Has my mother been seen by a doctor?" Daniel's tone was intimidating.

Enraged, John bellowed, "I should take a buggy whip to you!"

Edward had seen Daniel stop the buggy, and now as he arrived, he overheard Delmar's threat. In an attempt to restore peace, he interjected quickly, "I don't know what's happening here, but there'll be no fighting." He looked firmly at Daniel. "I think you'd better go on back to the stables."

Daniel didn't want any trouble with Kurt's father, and he complied. But before he left, he returned John's heated gaze.

Fuming, Delmar kept his eyes on Daniel as he walked away with long, determined strides. The insolent buck! That's what came of mixing white blood with colored! That it was his own blood flowing through Daniel's veins didn't even touch his cold heart.

As Edward was offering his good friend an apology for this unfortunate incident, Mary Jane grasped Jolene's hand, saying desperately, "I just know Daniel will come to Willow Hill! If he does, Masta John will kill 'im!"

Jolene wished she could say something to alleviate Mary Jane's fear, but what? She knew that regardless of the danger involved, Daniel would come to Willow Hill.

Chapter Twenty-Eight

The small campfire flickered brightly in the dark night. The chirping of crickets and the constant croaking of tree-frogs surrounded the woods. The two travelers had set up camp close to the rural road that stretched from New Orleans to Willow Hill.

The men had finished their evening repast, but a second pot of coffee was brewing.

Lazarus, leaning back against a large cedar, stared thoughfully into the darting flames.

As the servant remained lost in thought, Thomas watched him curiously. They'd left New Orleans two days ago, and since then Lazarus had been acting strangely withdrawn. Thomas wanted to question his companion, but he had a feeling that whatever bothered Lazarus was personal, and he didn't feel free to intrude. Unlike most of his southern kinsmen, Thomas believed slaves had rights. From the time he was a boy, he'd had mixed emotions concerning slavery. Now, as a man, he thought the system was wrong. He understood, however, that in the south it was a way of life and couldn't be changed overnight.

Pouring a cup of coffee, Thomas stopped thinking about Lazarus as he reflected on their short stay in New Orleans. They'd arrived late at night, and it wasn't until the next morning that Thomas was able to visit the slave jail. If Jolene had been sold at auction, he knew a record of her sale would be on file. The slavekeep was very informative, for he remembered Jolene quite distinctly. She had not only escaped his jail but had also given him a slight concussion! More than willing to discuss the rebellious wench, the man let Thomas know she'd been purchased by John Delmar of Willow Hill.

Returning to his hotel Warrington questioned a few of the patrons until he found one who could give him directions to Willow Hill. Learning that the plantation was close to a week's ride, he and Lazarus replenished their supplies and left at dawn.

Now, as Lazarus moved listlessly to the fire and poured himself a cup of coffee, Thomas noticed that the man's hands trembled. Something was bothering him. Hoping he could help, Thomas decided to pry.

"Lazarus, you've been acting strangely since we left New Orleans, and I know something's wrong. Would you like to talk about it?"

Taking a shaky drink of his coffee, Lazarus's eyes met Thomas's over the rim of the cup. Then, looking away, Lazarus lowered the cup and sank deeply into his own thoughts. It was a long time before he responded.

"Masta Thomas, I been in some kind of trance ever since you told me that Miz Jolene was sold to

John Delmar."

"Do you know Delmar?"

"Yes, suh. I belonged to 'im 'fore I came to Cedarbrook. I was born at Willow Hill."

"I didn't know!" Thomas exclaimed. "Do you think you might still have kin there?"

"I ain't got no kin that I know of. My mama was pregnant with me when she was sold to Willow Hill. I understand that my pappy was an Arab. I don't know nothin' more 'bout 'im. Mama died when I was still a baby. When I was fifteen, I was took into the big house and trained as a butler."

"Why did Delmar sell you?"

"Your pappy was at Willow Hill, and he took a likin' to me. He offered Delmar a good price, and 'fore I knew what was happenin', I was 'bout to be sold." Lazarus paused, then continued gravely, "I ran away, but was caught and given thirty lashes of the whip."

"But why did you run?"

"I was in love, and I knew if I was sent to Cedarbrook, I'd never see her again. I convinced her to run with me."

"Was she whipped too?"

"No, suh."

"Do you think she might still be at Willow Hill?"

"I reckon she could be. But that was over thirty years ago. By now she could be most anywhere."

"You must have loved her very much."

"Why do you think that, Masta Thomas?"

"Over thirty years has passed since you last saw her, yet the possibility that you might see her again causes your hands to tremble. She must've been a

410

remarkable girl."

"I ain't never told nobody 'bout Lucy. But I reckon I'd like to tell you. Lucy was 'bout fifteen when Masta John bought her at a slave auction in New Orleans. Lucy and her parents belonged to a storekeeper and his missus. When the masta died he left a lot of debts, and his wife had to sell their three slaves. Lucy had never been away from her mama and pappy, but at the auction they was sold separately. Her mama and pappy was bought as a couple, and Lucy was bought by Masta John. When the masta brought Lucy to Willow Hill, she was grievin' for her folks. She was also scared, timid. . . ." Here Lazarus paused dreamily. ". . . And she was the most beautiful woman I ever set eyes on. I loved her at first sight. She was bought to be the cook's assistant, so Lucy and I saw a lot of each other. She had lived a sheltered life, so I kinda looked out for her. I had a feelin' Masta John was thinkin' 'bout makin' her his bed wench. The masta, he'd always been against sleepin' with his wenches, but I suspected he wanted Lucy somethin' powerful."

Lazarus finished his coffee, placed the cup on the ground, and continued, "It took a long time for me to win Lucy's love, but when I finally realized she shared my feelins', I was the happiest man on earth. I ain't never loved no woman except Lucy. After I lost her I closed my heart to emotion. Losin' her almost destroyed me, and I made damned sure that I never went through that kind of pain again."

It was a moment before Thomas asked, "Are you hoping Lucy's still at Willow Hill?"

411

"I ain't for sure. In a way, I wants to see her again. Then, in another way, I wish everything could just stay in the past."

Thomas understood Lazarus's turmoil. The past had wrapped his and Lucy's love into a protective cocoon where it had remained untouched by time. Now, if it were to emerge, would it be as a beautiful butterfly, destined to fly only briefly?

Kurt, traveling to New Orleans, had passed a popular roadside inn and was a good distance from the public house before he turned his horse about.

Backtracking, he decided when he reached the inn, he'd stay ther for the night, rise early, and return to Heritage Manor.

Kurt's decision to go back to the plantation wasn't made on the spur of the moment. He'd been debating the issue all day and into the night.

Spencer spurred his horse into a faster gait. He should've know he couldn't simply set Jolene free and then just send her on her way. He'd reacted out of anger, and now that his temper had cooled, he knew he had to help Jolene, regardless of their differences.

He'd take Jolene to New Orleans, and if she wanted manumission papers, he'd get them for her. Afterward, if she was still determined to return to Cedarbrook, he'd accompany her. If her allegations concerning Johanna and Robert were true, then a close examination of Warrington's will should clear up the matter once and for all. Taking Jolene to Cedarbrook was what he should have done in the first place, instead of letting his pride get in the way.

If Johanna and Robert could prove their innocence, and Jolene *had* merely fabricated the crime, then Kurt no longer cared that once again she'd made him feel like a fool. Regardless of the outcome, at least this way he could return to Texas with his conscience at ease, knowing he'd done everything he could to help her.

That he was in love with Jolene was something he buried. She had been dishonest with him from the beginning, and now she'd rejected him for another man. He had to learn to get over her, and he might as well start now.

Reaching the inn, he dismounted, flung the reins over the hitching post, and went in. His gaze swept fleetingly over the interior, and he was pleased to note that it was cleaner than most rural establishments.

A large, bearded man greeted him at the door, and motioning him to the front desk, asked heartily, "Do you need a room for the night?"

Kurt said he did, and he signed his name in the registry, then made arrangements for his horse to be fed and stabled. Glancing into the small dining room in the lobby, Kurt asked, "Am I too late for supper?"

"No, you ain't too late," the innkeeper assured him. Escorting his patron into the dining room, the man yelled in the direction of the kitchen, "Lillian, we got another customer."

There was only one other patron in the room, and as Kurt went to a table and sat down, he paid the man scant attention. It wasn't until Lillian, a small black woman, had taken his order that Kurt recognized the man.

413

Pushing back his chair, Kurt stepped to the man's table. "Do you mind if I join you?"

The man, his mouth full of food, glanced up at Kurt. He swallowed, then took a big drink of ale before saying, "Suh, you look familiar. Have we met before?"

Without waiting to be invited, Kurt drew out a chair and sat down. "Yes, we've met before, Mr. Atkins. I took one of your slaves to Dr. Mayfield's house."

Cal gulped in recognition. How did the man learn Jolene wasn't his wife? He hoped the man harbored no hard feelings. The man gave Kurt's strong build a quick appraisal. If the man wanted to fight, Cal knew he'd have no chance against him.

Atkins searched his memory for the man's name, then recalling it, began nervously, "Mista Spencer, I apologize for tellin' you that the wench was my wife, but I was afraid if you knew the truth, you'd have refused to take her to the doctor."

Kurt smiled easily. "An apology isn't necessary, Mr. Atkins—I understand. In your place I might have done the same thing. The wench was too valuable to take a chance on losing." Spencer's urbanity was merely a ploy. Through Atkins he hoped to learn the truth about Jolene.

Relieved, Cal replied, "I'm glad you understand, Mista Spencer."

"Call me Kurt."

"Why, that's mighty friendly of you. My name's Cal."

Lillian brought Kurt his dinner of ham, fried potatoes, and eggs.

Drawing Cal into small talk, Kurt kept up his

414

affable pretense. He had a lot of questions to ask the trader, but in order to receive answers, he knew he had to put Atkins at ease. Kurt ordered another round of ale, for liquor could loosen a man's tongue.

Following three more rounds of shared camaraderie, Kurt subtly turned their conversation to Jolene. "I suppose you're wondering how I knew that wench wasn't your wife."

Cal was thoroughly enjoying himself. Sharing ale and friendly conversation with an aristocrat was quite a novelty. Feeling the effects of his drink, his words began to slur. "As a matter of fact, I am kinda curious."

"While I was in New Orleans, I stopped at the slave jail to look over the merchandise. I saw the little gal and recognized her." He took a sip of his ale, waited for his lie to sink in, then asked casually, "By the way, what ever happened to her?"

"John Delmar of Willow Hill bought her."

"Delmar? Why, he's a good friend of my father's." Kurt paused, watched Cal stealthily, then set his trap. "Did you tell John the wench had amnesia?"

Perspiration suddenly beaded Cal's brow. He'd sold Jolene as a healthy wench. If Delmar were to learn that he had sold her under false pretenses, the planter could bring serious charges against him.

Stuttering, Atkins replied lamely, "I . . . I don't know what you're talkin' about. There weren't nothin' wrong with the wench."

"That isn't what Dr. Mayfield said," Kurt remarked, casting out his bait and hoping Atkins would grab it. "After leaving New Orleans, my travels took me back by his house. I decided to pay him a visit. He told me that Mrs. Atkins' fall had caused amnesia."

"Oh, that!" Cal said, dismissing the matter with a wave of his hand. "Yeah, the gal had amnesia, but it was only temporary. She was over it by the time we reached New Orleans."

Kurt's expression didn't change, but his thoughts were churning. So Jolene hadn't lied about having amnesia! He chastised himself for not believing her. Kurt, reading Cal like an open book, knew that the man's claim was untrue. Jolene had still had amnesia when she was sold to Delmar.

Meanwhile, Atkins continued, "I got a reputation to uphold. I wouldn't sell a wench who was addle-headed. No, suh! When we reached New Orleans, that gal had her memory back."

Kurt quickly ordered another ale for the trader. "I believe you, Cal. I've heard your reputation is above reproach."

Atkins was flattered. "Is that right?"

The proprietor brought Cal his fresh ale.

Sounding mildly interested, Kurt asked, "Where did you find such a beautiful wench?"

"I got her from a plantation called Cedarbrook." Lifting his heavy mug, Cal quaffed half of it. He was now thoroughly drunk and beyond reason. He belched loudly, then drank the remainder.

Kurt motioned for the innkeeper to bring Cal another.

Atkins, holding his mug in his hands, leaned back in his chair. He looked across the table at his companion, tried to bring him into focus, then gave up. Reflecting drunkenly, he slurred, "Yeah, I got the little gal from Cedarbrook. When I went there that day, I sure didn't think I'd end up with such a

416

prize. It was Johanna Warrington who came out to greet me. I got the feelin' she was about to dismiss me, then all at once she wanted to talk to me alone. When we'd walked a distance from the house, she told me her sister Jolene had been raised to be white, but that Sam Warrington's will revealed she was a quadroon slave. For some reason I got the feelin' the woman was lyin'. She went on about Jolene, tellin' me that she was stirrin' up her slaves. Miz Warrington claimed she was scared Jolene would murder her in her bed."

Cal leaned forward, helped himself to a gulping drink, wiped the ale from his mouth, and continued, "You know what Miz Warrington wanted me to do?"

"No, what?"

"She wanted me to sneak Jolene away from Cedarbrook, kill her, and bury her body where it'd never be found."

Kurt's heart hammered. Evidently Johanna Warrington was as wicked as Jolene had tried to make him believe.

Atkins went on, "But hell, I wasn't about to kill a wench as valuable as Jolene. So I took her to New Orleans and sold her at a hundred percent profit."

"I don't blame you," Kurt was quick to comment. "Did you have any trouble getting the wench away from Cedarbrook?"

"Naw, it was easy as pie. Miz Warrington slipped her a sleeping powder."

Kurt groaned inwardly. My God, Jolene had tried to tell him that her sister had sedated her. His attention reverted back to Atkins. "You mentioned that at first you thought Miss Warrington was lying.

There must've been a reason for you to feel that way."

Cal shrugged. "It was just a feelin' I had. There seemed to be somethin' about the woman that just wasn't right. Like she was too desperate . . . you know what I mean?"

"I think so. What made you change your mind about her?"

"Well, I kinda suspected she was the real quadroon—till I saw her sister, anyways. That black hair of Jolene's was a dead giveaway."

"When the wench awoke to find herself a part of your coffle, what did she have to say for herself."

"She tried to convince me that her sister and her lawyer changed Sam Warrington's will. But Miz Warrington had already warned me that Jolene would come up with some cock-and-bull story like that."

Atkins sloppily downed the rest of his ale. "I put that uppity wench in her place real quick-like. After I hit her across her insolent mouth, she learned to stay in her place."

"When she fell and hit her head, was she trying to run away?"

Cal laughed gleefully. "The smart aleck wench got what she deserved. I was tryin' to be real nice to her, was gonna pleasure her, but the damned bitch pushed me away and took off runnin'. Served her right."

Kurt got to his feet. He'd heard enough.

"You ain't leavin', are you?" Cal asked. "Let's have another drink."

Stepping to Atkins, Spencer grasped the man's shirt collar and drew him to his feet. He waited until

418

the trader got his full balance before releasing him.

Kurt smiled vindictively. "When you hit Jolene across the mouth, didn't you realize that it'd hurt? With your permission, I'll demonstrate what I mean."

Spencer's fist plowed into Cal's face, a tremendous blow propelling the man off his feet before he fell heavily to the floor. He didn't get up.

Rushing over, the innkeeper said urgently, "Mr. Spencer, if this man did anything to offend you, I'll throw him out on his butt!" The proprietor wasn't about to take sides with a slave trader against an aristocrat.

"No, let him stay. Maybe he can't help being what he is. When he comes to, give him another ale on me." Kurt took a step, then turning back to the innkeeper, asked, "Can you wake me early?"

"Sure, Mr. Spencer."

Kurt said he wanted to be awakened at four in the morning.

"That's kinda early, ain't it?"

"I'm eager to get home—I owe a certain lady an apology." As he ambled out of the dining room, Kurt wondered if Jolene could possibly forgive him. He wouldn't blame her if she told him to go straight to hell.

The innkeeper called after him, "I hope your missus accepts your apology."

Kurt paused, looked back at the man and replied, "I'm not married. I owe my apology to the mistress of Cedarbrook."

Chapter Twenty-Nine

Jolene's face was etched with worry as she sat beside Lucy's bed. The woman's condition seemed to be growing worse, for her breathing was labored and she complained of a tightening in her chest.

During the two days that Jolene had been back at Willow Hill, she'd sorely neglected her duties as Katherine's maid in order to tend to Lucy. Although her new mistress resented her negligence, she didn't make an ugly scene. Inwardly Katherine was satisfied. After all, she'd brought Jolene to Willow Hill so Alan could get rid of her. She was managing quite well without Jolene's services, for Sabrina had ordered Mary Jane to take care of them both.

Mary Jane was willing to accept her extra work. She was gravely worried about Lucy and wanted Jolene to stay with her.

Now, as Jolene placed a cool cloth on Lucy's fevered brow, the bedroom door opened and John Delmar strode inside.

"How is she?" he asked.

"I think she's worse," Jolene answered him.

He sat down on the edge of the bed and placed a hand over Lucy's. She looked up at him through fever-glazed eyes. "How do you feel?" he asked softly.

"I'll be all right, Masta John," she answered, her voice terribly weak. Suddenly her body was racked with such a violent coughing bout that she couldn't catch her breath. When the spasm passed, John leapt to his feet, his face deathly pale.

"I'm going to ride into Mobile and get Dr. Evans!"

"But, masta," Lucy began, her chest heaving as she labored for each breath. "Doctah Evans is a white man. He won't ride all the way out here for a wench."

"He will if I tell him to!" John said with certainty. He looked across the bed at Jolene. "You're to stay here with her until I get back with the doctor. Do you hear me, gal?"

Jolene bristled. "There's nothing wrong with my hearing, Mr. Delmar."

He eyed her severely. "You impertinent bitch! I should have you whipped!"

"I'm no longer your property, Mr. Delmar. I belong to Kurt, and I don't think he'd take kindly to your abuse."

Heading for the door, he grumbled, "I'll take care of you later—with or without Kurt's permission!"

As Delmar stormed out of the room, Lucy groaned, "Honey, you gots to stop angerin' Masta John."

"I'm not scared of him," Jolene said with a confidence she wasn't sure she felt.

Meanwhile, as John rushed outside, Alan was leaving the stables and they met halfway.

"Where are you going, Papa?" Alan asked.

"To Mobile to get Dr. Evans. Lucy's worse."

"You can't be serious!" Young Delmar was incredulous. "Damn, Papa, you can't ask a fine doctor like Evans to tend to a slave!"

"I can and I will!" John insisted, brushing past his son and continuing onward.

Alan, knowing it'd be futile to try and stop his father from acting like a crazed fool, went into the house and to the parlor. He was pleased to find Sabrina and Katherine. Grinning delightedly, he told them, "Everything has been arranged. I contacted the patrol, and they're camped a couple of miles from here. Later I'll sneak Jolene away from the house and deliver her to these men. No one will ever see or hear of her again."

"Wonderful!" Katherine exclaimed.

Pouring a glass of brandy, Alan asked, "Did you two know that Papa is on his way to Mobile?"

They said that they didn't.

"He's gone to fetch Dr. Evans."

"For Lucy?" Sabrina demanded, astonished.

"You guessed correctly, little sister." Alan's tone reflected his annoyance.

"How embarrassing!" Sabrina moaned. "The whole town will learn that Papa is acting like a fool. How can he bring such shame on his family?"

"You poor dears," Katherine sympathized.

Alan shrugged. "Well, we can always hope that Lucy will die."

*   *   *

It was close to midnight and the house was quiet. Alan sat alone in his father's office. He was supposed to deliver Jolene to the patrol within the hour, which still gave him a little time before he had to seize the wench and sneak her away. When he got her to the patrol camp, he'd make good use of her. Then, when he was finished, the others could have her.

Although Alan was looking forward to raping Jolene, he was in an ill temper. He'd been so certain Lucy's illness would bring Daniel sneaking back to Willow Hill! Periodically he kept barging into Lucy's room, hoping to find Daniel at his mother's bedside. Well, if the uppity buck didn't show up soon, then to hell with him! He'd find some other way to cut the man down to size. Still angry over Lucy's blackmail, Alan was determined to get even with her through Daniel. Somehow he'd get his revenge!

But as Alan remained seated at Delmar's desk, he was completely unaware of the danger lurking outside.

Contrary to most northerners' popular belief, slave uprisings were actually uncommon. When a rebellion did take place, the slaves were apprehended and horribly punished. Their bodies were usually left hanging where their kinsmen were sure to see them. The executions were a frightening warning to the others, and any slave who might have been contemplating an uprising was quickly disabused of such notions.

Samson, his brother, and the five men running with them were perfectly aware of the consequences of getting caught. But they were confident they'd escape unharmed. Enticed by the thought of freedom, and compelled by their hate for their white owners, the murder-lusting slaves crept stealthily across the dark yard to the big house.

Motioning for the others to stand back, Samson edged his way to the side entrance of Delmar's office. The glass panes in the double doors were covered by curtains, but through a small slit Samson could see inside. Alan still sat at Delmar's desk. Samson, breathing rapidly, was hungry for blood . . . he'd already murdered the overseer and was now anxious to kill the Delmars.

Knocking, the slave called, "Masta! Masta, it's Samson! I gots to talk to you!"

Alan's hopes soared. Had Samson found Daniel sneaking around the plantation? He'd ordered Samson and George to keep an eye out for him. Quickly he crossed the room and opened the door.

Samson, flanked by his comrades, barged inside. "What's the meaning of this?" Alan demanded.

"Where's Masta John?" Samson asked harshly. Murder was in his eyes.

Alan's fear didn't hit him all at once. It came to him slowly, spreading through his body with an icy chill. His knees grew weak and his heart began pounding irregularly.

Striking with the swiftness of a snake, Samson grasped Alan about the throat. "Answer me! Where's Masta John?"

"He . . . he went into town," young Delmar croaked.

"Damn!" the angry slave bellowed. He was furious. Of the three Delmars, John had been the one he'd most relished killing.

George, speaking to the others, commanded hastily, "We needs to check the house!"

Samson called after them, "When you finds Miz Sabrina, bring her here. I wants the pleasure of killin' her!"

One of the slaves asked urgently, "Ain't we gonna get to rape her?"

"If you stick your rod in that cold bitch, it'll drop off from frostbite," Samson spat, his hand still wrapped about Alan's throat.

"You's probably right," the slave agreed. "But I's willin' to take my chances." He quickly followed the others from the office.

Samson's brutal grip was cutting off Alan's breath, and his face was turning a sickening blue. The slave loosened his hold only long enough to say with deadly intent, "I's gonna strangle you, Masta Alan. But I's gonna do it real slow, so's it'll take you a *long* time to die. When I finish, your eyes is gonna be burstin' out of your head, and your tongue's gonna be hangin' down the front of your shirt like a red tie."

Vainly Alan tried to plead for his life, but Samson's strong fingers tightened, cutting off his victim's air. He didn't stop squeezing until Alan Delmar was dead.

Lucy was asleep, and Jolene turned down the lamp. A dim glow lit her way as she went to an overstuffed chair in the corner and curled up in its soft contours. She was sleepy, but afraid Lucy might wake and need her, she didn't dare doze off.

She tried to keep Kurt from her thoughts, but the effort was futile. She now regretted telling him she loved someone else, but at the time it had seemed the only real solution. Otherwise he'd continue to selfishly use her, then when he was ready to return to Texas, he'd callously cast her out of his life. She was nothing more to him than his chattel! When she saw him again, she must remain strong and hold dearly to her pride. She mustn't let her love for Kurt weaken her defenses!

The door swung open, interrupting Jolene's reverie. She was surprised to see George.

"Come with me," he said, motioning to her to join him.

"I don't want to leave Lucy." She got to her feet. Keeping her voice low, she asked, "George, what are you doing here? Is something wrong?"

He stepped up to her, grasped her wrist, and insisted, *"Come on!"*

Jolene was shaken. She tried to break his firm hold, but it was useless. Not wanting to disturb Lucy's sleep, she said quietly, "George, turn me loose. What's wrong with you?"

Pulling her to the open door, he mumbled, "You gots to come with me. Don't worry, you ain't gonna be hurt."

As George ushered her through the kitchen, she tried to grasp what was happening. Were Samson and George running? But if they were, then why was George in the house? And where were the others? Where were Samson, the women, and the children?

All at once she was struck with a cold foreboding. Samson had lied to her! He and his brother weren't

426

simply running away . . . they were leading an uprising! She knew, suddenly, that there were no women and children escaping with George and Samson. She felt sick, and her stomach coiled into knots.

Now, furious, she fought against George's grip, her struggles forcing him to practically drag her all the way to Delmar's office. The door was open, and the slave slung her across the threshold.

As Jolene stumbled to her knees, Samson shouted angrily, "Why is you treatin' her so rough?"

"She kept fightin' me," George explained.

Samson stepped over to Jolene and helped her to her feet. "Don't be scared. Ain't nothin' gonna happen to you."

His hand was on her arm, and jerking away as though she found his touch repulsive, she cried desperately, "Samson, why are you doing this? Have you gone mad?" Then, seeing Alan's body, she gasped. "Oh, God, no!"

Jolene was worn out from nursing Lucy, and as the little strength she had left ebbed, her knees buckled. The room began to blacken, and there was a deafening roar in her ears. She fainted into Samson's waiting arms.

Lifting her, he carried her to the couch and laid her down gently.

Jolene found peace in oblivion, but it was short-lived. She had only been unconscious for a few minutes when Sabrina's shrill screams brought her back to consciousness.

Jolene sat bolt upright. Her head was swimming, and for a moment she thought she was going to faint again. As the strength slowly flowed back into her limbs, she looked about the room. The five slaves accompanying Samson and George had returned, bringing all the house servants, Sabrina, and Katherine into the office. Except for Lucy and Mary Jane, every member of the household was present. Jolene wondered why Mary Jane wasn't here, then decided she was probably asleep in her cabin and had no inkling of what was taking place. Glancing about the room, Jolene bristled: the men had broken into Delmar's gun cabinet. A couple of the slaves held rifles, and the rest of the weapons were stacked on the desk.

Sabrina was kneeling beside her brother's body and was still screaming hysterically. Katherine stood amidst the servants, her face white as a ghost, her eyes glazed with fear. The household servants, too terrified to move, stood as though frozen.

Roughly Samson clutched Sabrina's shoulders and jerked her upright. Jolene, frightened that Samson might take Sabrina's life, bounded from the couch. She must find a way to stop him!

Leering down into his mistress' ashen face, Samson was saying with cold rage, "I's gonna kill you, but first I's gonna let my men pleasure you."

"No!" Jolene cried, grabbing at the slave's arm and trying vainly to jerk him away from Sabrina.

Samson pushed Jolene aside gently. "Stay out of this—it ain't none of your business."

"For God's sake, Samson, stop this violence!" she pleaded. "Why did you kill Alan, and why do you want to kill Sabrina? How can you commit cold-blooded murder?"

"Cold-blooded murder?" he asked mockingly. "I only wish I could kill them more than once!"

"Why do you hate them so?"

"Masta John sold my mama's firstborn 'cause it was his. She never recovered from losin' her chile, then Masta John sold Sabrina's maid, 'cause she was pregnant with Masta Alan's baby. Her maid was my little sister, and losin' a second chile killed my mama. She died of a broken heart." Samson paused and drew a gasp so filled with hate that it shook his body. "I could tell you a hundred reasons why I wants to kill 'em, but I ain't got time."

"Samson, please don't do this! I'm *begging* you!"

Releasing his grip on Sabrina's throat, he gazed down into Jolene's enchanting eyes and was suddenly overwhelmed by her beauty. He had desired her from the first moment he'd set eyes on her. What he wouldn't give to have her as his own! He wondered how far she'd go to save Sabrina's life.

A smile crossed his face. "If you'll agree to run with me, then I'll let Miz Sabrina live."

Jolene gasped. "Run with you?"

He nodded. "But you gots to promise to be my woman. I knows how to pleasure a woman *real* good. After you get a taste of me, you won't want no other man."

Jolene was dumbstruck. Oh God, this must be a nightmare! Surely she'd soon awaken!

Samson, eager to prove how much he desired her, placed his hands on her shoulders and drew her flush against him. He was about to kiss her, but before he could, the smell of smoke drifted into the room. Turning Jolene loose, he whirled about. "Who done

429

set fire to the house?" he bellowed.

"I did," one of his comrades answered, obviously proud of himself.

"You fool!" Samson yelled. "This house will make a fire so big that every slave patrol for miles 'round will spot it! We gots to get out of here, and we gots to go now!" He reached out and once again grabbed Sabrina's throat.

. Terrified, Sabrina felt her body grow limp. Only Samson's death-hold kept her on her feet.

His long fingers easily tightened about her slender neck. "'Fore I leaves, I's gonna finish you!" He glanced at the man who had started the fire. "You kill that other white bitch!"

The slave was glad to oblige and stepped quickly to Katherine. He'd gotten a knife from the kitchen, and now he pulled it out of his waistband.

"No!" Katherine screamed. *"Please don't kill me . . . Please!"* She dropped to her knees, begging.

"Stop it!" Jolene screamed so loud that all motion ceased. "Samson, if you'll spare Sabrina and Katherine, I'll go with you!"

"You'll be my woman?" he pressed, eying her emphatically.

"Yes!" she agreed. Her heart was pounding and once again she felt faint. The thought of being this murderer's woman was revolting, but she couldn't let him kill Sabrina and Katherine. She had no choice.

Finally satisfied, Samson turned Sabrina loose and grabbed a rifle. Stepping up to Jolene, he took her arm and ushered her to the door.

Looking back at the women and the servants,

Jolene said desperately, "Put the fire out before the whole house burns down with Lucy in it!"

Fully armed, the escaping slaves followed Jolene and Samson across the yard toward the stables. Jolene dared to glance over her shoulder to see how much of the house was actually burning. She was relieved to see that the fire hadn't yet gotten out of control.

Horses had been saddled. Moving swiftly, Samson lifted Jolene onto his mount and swung up behind her. Losing no time, the runaways galloped out of the stables and headed at breakneck speed for the road.

Daniel had ridden onto Delmar property and was approaching the lane leading to the house when he decided to dismount and go the rest of the way on foot. But as he spotted riders thundering in his direction, he guided his horse off the road and into the thicket.

As the group thundered past his place of concealment, Daniel was astounded to catch sight of Jolene on the lead horse with Samson. He had seen that the riders were armed, and ascertaining what had taken place, he was torn between following Jolene and going to the house to check on Lucy and Mary Jane. Knowing the runaways had no reason to hurt his mother and Mary Jane, he decided to pursue Jolene. He was quite certain she hadn't left with the slaves of her own accord. Maybe they had taken her hostage . . . but somehow, that didn't quite add up. Sabrina would have made a much

431

better hostage. Why *Jolene* was traveling with the runaways had Daniel totally baffled. But he wasn't overly alarmed. He didn't think she was in grave danger, for Samson and the others thought of her as a slave.

If Daniel had known about the slave patrol who was waiting to rendezvous with Alan, he'd have known Jolene was in serious danger indeed. However, Daniel had approached Willow Hill from the west, and these patrols were camped to the east, the same direction in which the runaways fled.

Samson and his comrades kept their horses running at a steady speed, unaware that their course would soon lead them and Jolene into a deadly ambush.

Chapter Thirty

As Adam Coffer spat a stream of tobacco juice into the campfire, part of the brownish liquid clung to his unkempt beard. Wiping his mouth with the back of his hand, he grumbled, "What the hell's keepin' Joe and Henry? They should be back by now."

There were six men seated about the fire with Coffer, but none bothered to make a guess as to why Joe and Henry hadn't returned. But Coffer had expected no reply. He spit another stream into the flames.

Adam Coffer and his companions were the patrol Alan had hired to steal Jolene. Young Delmar had told them he'd deliver the wench an hour after midnight. When the designated time came and went and Alan hadn't appeared, Coffer sent Joe and Henry to Willow Hill to find out what was keeping him.

Coffer continued to chew his tobacco, letting bits of it dribble down onto his hairy chin. As his two men suddenly rode into camp, he got to his feet, spat the entire wad onto the ground, and asked, "Did you see Delmar?"

Dismounting, Henry answered hurriedly, "We was almost to the house when we spotted smoke and a gang of niggers headed this way."

"Shit!" Coffer cussed. "Looks like we got an uprisin' on our hands. How many niggers are runnin'?"

"We didn't have time to count 'em," Henry answered. "But I'd guess 'bout seven or eight."

"How far back are they?"

"Two, maybe three minutes," he replied.

"Good! That gives us time to set up an ambush." His orders quick and crisp, Coffer told five of his men to go down the road a piece and hide in the bordering shrubbery. Meanwhile, he and the others would remain and take cover where they were.

"When those niggers try to pass, we'll have 'em trapped between us," Coffer remarked. "We'll open fire from both ends."

The men in the patrol were good marksmen, and Samson and his party wouldn't have a chance. Although Samson and George were experienced with rifles, the five slaves running with them were unskilled.

Coffer's men mounted their horses, raced a short way down the road, then headed into the dense shrubbery. Tethering their horses, they took cover behind a cluster of thick bushes. In the meantime Coffer kicked dirt over the small campfire, smothering the flames. Then he and the others prepared for the ambush.

* * *

The runaways, eager to put distance between themselves and Willow Hill, kept their horses running at an exhausting pace. The stallion Samson and Jolene were riding had a powerful, jolting gait, and Jolene had to hang on for dear life. The wind whipped at her hair, blowing the long tresses about her face and into her eyes. Her cotton dress had worked up her legs and the leather flap was chafing at her bare thighs.

She was about to ask Samson to slow down when all at once a barrage of bullets exploded nearby. Samson drew back on the reins and turned his horse about so brusquely that Jolene reeled and nearly fell.

Samson jabbed his feet into the steed's sides, and the skittish animal took off with a bolt. Jolene saw two of the slaves drop from their mounts and fall to the ground before she and Samson were able to flee. However, their horse had taken only a few strides when, unexpectedly, they were met by more gunfire. Forcefully Samson jerked back on the reins, but the sudden stop caused his horse to balk. As it reared up on its hind legs, Jolene could no longer hold on. She slipped out of the saddle and fell to the ground.

The impact knocked the air from her lungs. It was a moment before she could catch her breath. Samson's horse was dangerously close, and more than once its deadly hoofs barely missed her head.

Samson and the others were now caught in the crossfire from the patrol, and as the slaves tried in vain to defend themselves, Jolene crawled away from the midst of the action. Remaining on her hands and knees, she made a frantic dash for the bordering shrubbery. She spotted a full bush and decided to hide beneath it, but the ground around

435

the foliage was uneven, and losing her balance, she began tumbling down the rough incline.

Suddenly a pair of strong arms reached out, caught her about the waist, and broke her fall. She started to scream but the sound died in her throat when she saw that it was not a member of the patrol who had hold of her . . . but *Daniel.*

Over the deafening gunshots, Daniel yelled, "My horse is close by. Let's get out of here!"

Shifting his rifle to one hand, he grasped her arm and they fled farther into the woods. Although their flight was short, by the time they reached Daniel's horse, the gunfire from the road had ceased. The sudden quiet was eerie.

"Do you suppose Samson and the others are dead?" Jolene gasped.

"Either that, or they surrendered," Daniel replied, lifting her and placing her in the saddle. "Are Mama and Mary Jane all right?"

"Yes, I think so. But what are *you* doing here?"

"I was on my way to Willow Hill when I saw what was happening. I suspected you weren't with Samson voluntarily, so I decided to follow."

Daniel was about to swing up in the saddle, but a gruff voice coming from the surrounding darkness caused him to pause.

"Make one move, nigger, and you're dead meat! Drop your gun, then kick it over this way."

As two of the patrollers stepped out of the dark shadows and into the moonlight, Jolene's heart sank . . . *they held their rifles aimed at Daniel.*

Cautiously, Daniel turned to face them. He placed his Winchester on the ground, and using the toe of his boot, he shoved it away. "I know what you're thinking," he began, "but I'm not a runaway slave."

The two men glanced at each other, their expressions hard, merciless.

"Well, well," one of them drawled. "For a nigger, this buck sure talks highfalutin'."

"Please!" Jolene entreated. "You must believe him!"

The patrollers looked her over carefully. Then the one who'd done all the talking commented, "I bet you're the quadroon wench Alan Delmar was bringin' us. You fit the description. Reckon your name is Jolene."

She didn't answer, but her silence confirmed his suspicions.

"What are we gonna do with these two?" the other man asked.

"I guess we'll let Coffer decide. He'll probably want to take 'em back to Willow Hill." The brawny patroller eyed Daniel and Jolene before saying threateningly, "If any white folks was killed, you two niggers is gonna hang by your necks till you're dead!"

When Coffer and his party entered the lane leading up to the Delmar home, they had one other captive besides Jolene and Daniel. Of the runaway slaves, Samson was the only survivor.

As they drew closer to the elegant mansion, Jolene was relieved to see that the fire was out. The damage had been slight. Jolene was eager to see Lucy and hoped it wouldn't take too long for Sabrina to inform the patrol that she and Daniel hadn't been involved in the uprising.

The riders were spotted by a young slave who hastened into the house to tell his mistress of their arrival. Sabrina and then Katherine walked out onto the porch to greet the visitors.

Coffer led the procession, and his captives were on horseback, surrounded by his men. Reining in, the head patroller acknowledged the ladies by tipping his hat. He inquired, "Did these damn niggers hurt anybody?"

Sabrina answered in a trembling voice, "My brother was killed, and so was our overseer." She glared at Samson and pointed an accusing finger. "That's the one who murdered Alan!"

"How did you men get here so soon?" Katherine exclaimed. "And how did you manage to capture that murderer?"

"We were camped a couple of miles down the road. Two of my men spotted the fire and the niggers fleeing. We set up an ambush. Except for these three, all the niggers were killed."

Both women looked at Jolene, but neither bothered to mention her innocence.

Coffer continued, "Where's Mista Delmar?"

"He went into Mobile before the uprising," Sabrina answered. "He should be home any time now." She sobbed brokenly. "Oh, God, Alan's death will almost destroy him!"

Immediately sympathetic, Coffer said soothingly, "Well, ma'am, at least he'll have the satisfaction of watchin' his son's murderers swing from a rope."

"Murderers!" Jolene intervened. "Daniel and I had nothing to do with what happened!"

Coffer watched the young mistress of Willow Hill,

438

waiting for her to deny or confirm the wench's declaration.

Meanwhile, Sabrina was staring at Jolene with contempt. Wanting Jolene out of Kurt's life, Sabrina decided that the woman would hang alongside Samson. Furthermore, when Kurt was told that his bed wench had instigated a violent uprising, he certainly wouldn't mourn her death. That Jolene had saved her life didn't matter to Sabrina.

"This wench," Sabrina began harshly, gesturing toward Jolene, "led the uprising!"

"What!" Jolene cried incredulously. "Why, you lying. . . ."

One of the patrollers edged his rifle cautiously in Jolene's back, halting her outburst.

Sabrina solicited Katherine's support. "That wench led the uprising, didn't she?"

Katherine understood why Sabrina was lying, but grudgingly, she was grateful to Jolene for saving her life. Although she backed up Sabrina's accusation, she did so tentatively. "Yes, Jolene led it."

Jolene's anger erupted. "So this is the thanks I get for saving your worthless lives! Oh, I wish I had it to do all over again! I'd let Samson kill you both!"

Coffer spoke to the man mounted behind Jolene. "Teach that bitch some manners!"

The patroller struck the barrel of his rifle in Jolene's back, the solid blow almost knocking her from her horse. The jab was so painful that she cried out in anguish.

Daniel's fist shot out without warning, ramming hard against the man's jaw. The powerful impact

439

knocked the patroller completely out of his saddle and to the ground.

"Restrain that nigger!" Coffer yelled to his men.

Daniel's hands were quickly bound and tied behind him.

Coffer was enraged. How dare a nigger strike one of his men! "Miz Delmar, that buck claims he's free and wasn't involved with your runaways."

"That's true," Sabrina answered. "However, my father warned him to stay away from Willow Hill. Papa said if he ever caught him on his property, he'd shoot him on sight."

"Well in that case, I reckon we'd better keep 'im and let your father decide what to do with 'im. Where should we chain these niggers 'til Mista Delmar returns?"

"Take them to the barn. There are manacles there."

As Coffer and his men took the prisoners to their temporary jail, Sabrina watched with smug satisfaction. Smiling at Katherine, she remarked, "You don't have to worry about Kurt marrying Jolene. By the time he returns home, she'll already be dead and buried."

Katherine, to Sabrina's dismay, was still having second thoughts. Uncertainly, she stammered, "But . . . but Jolene *did* save our lives. Maybe having her killed is . . . is going a little too far. Couldn't we just ask the patrol to take her away and sell her? I'm sure they're the same men Alan was dealing with."

Placing her hands on her hips, Sabrina declared, "Katherine, don't get soft-hearted on me! After all, it's not as though we're having a white woman killed. She's nothing but a quadroon slave, and an impertinent one at that!"

Kurt's stepmother conceded. "You're right, of course. She's only a colored wench."

The prisoners had been manacled in the barn for a little over an hour when John Delmar appeared. The door was open, and the master of Willow Hill paused in the entryway as his eyes roamed murderously over the three captives.

Jolene was chained between Daniel and Samson. Appalled by the glare in Delmar's gaze, she unconsciously inched closer to Daniel, as though his presence could afford a degree of protection.

Delmar held a lantern in one hand, its glow illuminating the violent anger on his face. Jolene knew he wouldn't show her and Daniel any mercy. His son had been killed, and he was out for blood!

Despite Delmar's fury, his aristocratic manners were impeccable, and he spoke politely to Coffer and his men before walking over to the manacled prisoners.

They were seated, and because John remained standing, they had to look up to see into his face.

Samson was Delmar's first target. Drawing back his foot, he kicked the slave, the toe of his boot smashing into the man's groin. As Samson groaned in pain, Delmar bellowed thunderously, "You goddamned son of a bitch! I took you and your brother out of the fields, made you my personal guards, and what do I get in return? You two ungrateful bastards kill my son! I'd hang you, but hanging is too good for you! You're going to die from the whip, boy!"

Delmar turned to Daniel. "As for you, you

educated nigger . . . don't think for one minute that I don't know you were the brains behind this operation. You talked my slaves into running! And you told them to kill Alan, didn't you?"

"No," Daniel answered, striving to remain calm. "I had nothing to do with the uprising. Neither did Jolene."

Delmar, believing his own accusations, argued, "Samson and the others were too damned stupid to plan an uprising by themselves. They had to have outside influence! Someone with a measure of intelligence—like you and Jolene!"

"No, suh!" Samson spoke up. The slave knew his fate was sealed. There was nothing he could say or do to stop his own execution. But he made a stab at saving Jolene's and Daniel's lives. "Masta John, they had nothin' to do with it."

"Bullshit!" John retorted.

"He's telling the truth!" Jolene cried desperately. "Daniel came to Willow Hill to see Lucy, and I knew nothing about an uprising!"

His eyes bulging, Delmar raged, "I rue the day that I bought you! I should have known an educated high-yellow would incite my slaves! Did you tempt Samson with your body? Did you get the poor, ignorant bastard to do your bidding by taking him to your bed?"

John glanced at Samson. "I almost feel sorry for you, you dumb savage! You think with your pecker instead of your brain, but I suppose that's because your pecker is a lot bigger!"

Intruding, Coffer walked up to Delmar and handed him a piece of paper. "By the way, Mista Delmar, I found this in Samson's pocket . . . it's

442

a written pass. Whoever wrote it forged your daughter's name."

Quickly John scanned the pass. Then, leaning over and holding the paper in front of Samson's face, he demanded, "Who wrote this?"

The slave didn't want Jolene to become more involved. "I . . . I cain't tell you, Masta John."

"The hell you can't!" he yelled. "There's ways to make you talk!"

"You can torture me all you wants, masta, but I won't tell." He was determined to protect Jolene at any cost.

John, grinning coldly, spoke to Coffer. "Would one of your men like to cut this buck into little pieces?"

"Hell, I'll do it," Coffer volunteered. He motioned for a couple of his companions to unchain Samson. Coffer intended to take him outside so blood wouldn't be spilled in the barn.

"Wait!" Jolene cried. She couldn't let Samson go through such torture to protect her. "I wrote the pass, but I didn't know about the uprising."

Daniel groaned to himself—forging a pass was a very serious offense. If Delmar had planned to hand her back over to Kurt, he certainly wouldn't do so now.

Kneeling, John grasped a handful of her hair, jerking her head backward and tilting her face up to his. "Because you belong to Kurt, I had intended to leave your punishment up to him. But now, you sneaky little bitch, you're going to hang!" He released her brusquely, stood upright, and announced, "They'll all three die at sunrise—Samson by the whip, and these other two will swing at the

443

end of a rope!"

With that, he invited Coffer and his men inside the house for a drink. Accepting, they followed the master of Willow Hill out of the barn.

Displaying his thanks, Delmar poured a round of expensive port for the patrollers, then leaving them with their drinks, he went to check on Lucy.

Dr. Evans, with Mary Jane's assistance, had just finished his examination when John entered the room. Lucy had fallen asleep, and after the two men had discussed her condition, Delmar gave the doctor a full account of what had taken place in the barn.

The men were too deep in conversation to notice that Mary Jane had slipped quietly from the room. She hurried through the kitchen and outside. Mary Jane could hardly believe Daniel and Jolene had actually been sentenced to hang. Although she'd been asleep in her cabin during the uprising, she knew beyond any doubt that Jolene hadn't participated. She was also certain that Daniel wasn't remotely involved.

As Mary Jane neared the barn, she was disheartened to see Delmar had ordered two of his slaves to stand guard. She wasn't well acquainted with the two, but the few times she'd spoken to them, they'd seemed quite nice. She hoped she could convince them to let her see the prisoners.

The guards, fearing their master's wrath, were reluctant. But finally, they weakened under her pathetic pleas and gave their permission. They made her promise to stay only a few minutes.

One of the slaves opened the barn door, and Mary

Jane darted inside. A lantern had been left burning, and she could see the threesome. The men's legs and arms were manacled, but although Jolene's ankles were chained, her arms were unbound.

Rushing to the prisoners, Mary Jane dropped to her knees, grasped Jolene's hands, squeezed them tight, and placed a hasty kiss on her cheek. Then, turning to Daniel, she threw her arms about his chest and hugged him hard.

"Mary Jane," Daniel murmured, wishing his arms were free so he could hold her close.

She pressed her lips to his, kissing him desperately. Her heart breaking, she leaned her head against his chest and began to cry copiously.

He tried to soothe her sorrow with whispered endearments, but when they failed to elicit any response, he asked, "How's Mama?"

Mary Jane was sobbing too hard to answer.

Firmly, Daniel insisted, "Is Mama all right?"

It was a moment before Mary Jane could control her sobs. Moving to sit at his side, she answered, "The doctah, he says Lucy's got pneumonia."

"God!" Daniel groaned.

"What else did he say?" Jolene asked urgently.

Reluctantly, Mary Jane told them, "He said that she's awful sick and that . . . that she might. . . ." She was unable to continue.

"Might die?" Daniel queried, his voice breaking. She nodded.

Daniel's chin quivered and his eyes grew misty. "Mama . . . *Mama!*" he moaned.

Mary Jane wished she could bear his sorrow for him. She leaned her head against his shoulder and released a fresh flow of tears.

"You mustn't let Mama know that Delmar plans to hang Jolene and me. It would kill her."

"But Daniel, maybe Lucy can save you two! Masta John, he thinks a lot of Lucy. If Lucy asks 'im, he might let you and Jolene live!"

"There's nothing Mama can do to save us. She'd only kill herself trying. Mary Jane, I want your promise that you won't tell her what's happening."

At that moment one of the guards came inside and said to Mary Jane, "Come on, gal. You gots to leave 'fore the masta finds out that you's here."

"Do as he says," Daniel encouraged. "If Delmar learns you're with me, he'll punish you."

"I cain't leave you!" she sobbed, falling against his chest and hugging him with all her strength.

The guard, impatient, went to Mary Jane and forcefully pulled her away. Grasping her arms tenaciously, he began dragging her to the entrance.

"I love you, Daniel!" she cried.

"I love you, too," he called back as the man drew her outside and closed the door.

A heavy silence fell over the threesome. Then, speaking with remorse, Samson confided, "I got you two in this mess. I'd get you out of it if I could."

"There's nothing anyone can do," Daniel answered.

"I wish Kurt was here!" Jolene cried suddenly, her tone desperate.

Daniel, believing Kurt was on his way to New Orleans, told her gently, "Hon, you may as well wish for the moon."

Chapter Thirty-One

When Mary Jane slipped quietly into Lucy's room, she was startled to find John sitting beside the bed. She had hoped to avoid her master's presence. She despised him so intensely she was afraid he'd see her hate.

But Mary Jane had nothing to fear. Delmar was too worried about Lucy to notice his daughter's maid.

Going to a corner of the room, Mary Jane stood by as inconspiculously as she could and waited anxiously for the man to leave.

A soft moan came from Lucy's throat. Tensing, John leaned closer to the bed.

Lucy's dream had taken her back into the past. Now she was once again sixteen years old and deeply in love with Lazarus. Hand-in-hand, they'd strolled to the meadow, and when they came upon the babbling brook, Lazarus drew her into his arms, kissed her, then promised he'd always love her. Adoring the handsome young butler, Lucy swore that she, too, would love him forever.

Lucy's dream was blissfully peaceful, and when it began to fade, her subconscious fought to hold the beautiful vision close. But the image of her darling Lazarus became enshrouded in a misty fog. As the mist thickened, obscuring the man she loved, she called his name and tried to will him to come back.

"Lazarus . . . Lazarus, come back," Lucy groaned, her fever-racked body tossing fitfully.

Enraged, John leapt to his feet. After all he'd done for her, she still mourned for Lazarus! Why hadn't thirty years erased him from her mind?

Speaking his anger aloud, he grumbled, "I've taken care of this woman for over thirty years, yet she calls for Lazarus! After all this time, how can she still love him?"

John wasn't aware of Mary Jane's presence, and her voice startled him. "Masta, don't you know that love is ageless?"

He whirled about and faced her. "What do you know about love?" he asked irritably.

"Not much, thanks to my mastas. But what me and other slaves know 'bout love is special, 'cause it's an emotion our mastas always try to keep us from feelin'."

"That's ridiculous!" he denied heatedly; then he added, "Don't be impudent, girl! Considering my mood, I'd just as soon have you whipped as look at you!" With that he walked out of the room.

Dr. Evans and the patrollers were gathered in the drawing room drinking port. Preferring to avoid them, John went to his office.

He slumped into the chair at his desk. His

thoughts turned to Alan and tears filled his eyes: God, he could hardly believe his son was dead! He had been so young and had had his whole life ahead of him. God *damn* Samson for the murdering savage that he was! He'd relish watching the man die under the whip.

His thoughts went to Jolene and Daniel. John had convinced himself that they'd led the violent uprising. He was certain the pair had instigated the rebellion, for he couldn't imagine Samson and the others doing it on their own . . . there *had* to be an outside influence. A freed, educated slave and an educated quadroon were a dangerous combination, and his son had suffered the deadly consequences!

A soft knock on the door brought John out of his thoughts. "Come in," he called.

He was surprised to see Katherine. As she sat down in the chair across from him, he asked, "Is anything wrong? Sabrina's all right, isn't she?"

"Yes, considering what has happened," Katherine answered. A tendril of hair had fallen from her upswept coiffure, and she absently tucked it back into place. Her hand trembled slightly, and her face was visibly pale. The uprising had been traumatic, and Katherine was still somewhat shaken.

John let out a heavy sigh. "Katherine, I'm sorry about what happened. When I brought you to my home as a guest, I never dreamt your life would be in danger."

"You don't owe me an apology," she hastened to reply. "But I do want to express how sorry I am about Alan."

Her reference to his son caused fresh tears to

smart in his eyes. "I can only thank God that you and Sabrina weren't harmed!"

Katherine fidgeted uneasily. "That's why I came here to talk to you. Sabrina would be furious if she knew about this, but I couldn't live with myself if I didn't tell you what really happened."

John was baffled. "What are you talking about?"

"First, let me assure you that I consider Jolene insolent. I can barely tolerate the wench. She has Kurt utterly bewitched. If he weren't so blinded by her charms, he'd realize Sabrina would make him the perfect wife. Sabrina feels as I do. There's nothing we'd like better than to have Jolene out of Kurt's life for good. Now, however, that's all beside the point . . . you see, if it weren't for Jolene, Sabrina and I would be dead!"

Delmar was amazed. "What?"

"Jolene pleaded with Samson to spare us, and he told her that if she'd run away with him, he'd let us live. She didn't leave with Samson and the others because she was running. She left to save Sabrina's life—and mine."

"But Katherine, if you despise Jolene so much, why are you coming to her aid?"

"The wench saved my life, and although it galls me to say it, I'm grateful to her. If it weren't for Jolene, Sabrina and I would be dead."

"Katherine, it's admirable of you to defend Jolene. I've ordered that she be hanged alongside Daniel, but because of what you've told me, I'll consider lessening her punishment."

"I don't understand . . . *why* are you determined to punish her? What did she do?"

"She wrote a pass for Samson and the others and forged Sabrina's name."

"Then she was involved in the uprising?"

"Definitely," he replied. "The pass is written proof of it."

Katherine got to her feet. "Well, at least my conscience is clean," she said, but there was little emotion in her voice.

She started to leave but John detained her. "Why didn't Sabrina tell me the truth about Jolene?"

"She wants to marry Kurt and thinks he'll never notice her so long as Jolene is a part of his life."

Delmar frowned. "That's no excuse for dishonesty."

"Don't be too hard on her, John. She's so smitten with Kurt she's become desperate." Katherine paused, then asked, "Do you realize how furious Kurt will be when he finds out you ordered Daniel's hanging?"

"Yes—but there'll be nothing he can do about it. By then Daniel will be dead. I'm certain that Daniel was the brains behind the uprising. Furthermore, I warned him not to return to Willow Hill."

Katherine told him goodnight and left. Alone, John went to his liquor cabinet and poured himself a drink. He began to think of Alan, but finding his grief unbearable, he quickly thrust any thought of his son aside. Against his will his musings wandered to Lucy. My God, thirty years, and she still called for Lazarus! It was unbelievable!

He quaffed his drink, then went to join his guests in the drawing room. The group planned to stay for the remainder of the night, then at dawn assist

451

Delmar with the executions.

The eastern horizon was turning a pale pink, but dawn hadn't yet conquered the night, and the only light inside the barn was afforded by the burning lantern.

The three prisoners, plagued by thoughts of their impending executions, were too troubled to find solace in sleep.

Jolene was so tired that her body ached with fatigue, and she leaned her head against Daniel's shoulder.

He wished his arms weren't chained so he could hold her close and perhaps give her some comfort. Jolene's hanging had Daniel more upset than his own. If only there were some way he could save her! He felt as though he were letting Kurt down. He had rescued Jolene from the runaways only to let her be caught by the patrollers. He had failed not only Jolene, but Kurt as well.

Daniel was deeply impressed with Jolene's intrepid bearing. A woman with Jolene's bravery would make an ideal pioneer, for she'd stand firmly beside her man. Northern Texas was still somewhat untamed, a frontier that most women shied away from. He sighed remorsefully. Jolene would make Kurt the ideal wife, for she had the grit to help her husband tame the wild west.

Jolene was the first to notice a ray of daylight creeping in under the barn door. With a sharp intake of breath, she sat upright. "It's getting light outside," she murmured.

"Lord . . . Lord!" Samson moaned. "I's gonna die! Lordy, I's wishin' I hadn't tried to run! Wouldn't a done it if it hadn't been for that northern abolitionist a-tellin' me to!"

Jolene felt a pang of pity for the slave. Murder was wrong, and she couldn't pardon what he had done, but she believed the South's wicked system had turned Samson into a killer.

Samson, his huge body trembling, started to say more, but at that moment the barn door swung open. The sight of his master flanked by two guards caused Samson to groan. He longed to plead for his life, but even in his fear, he knew his pleas would fall on deaf ears.

Jolene's heart pounded as she watched Delmar's two slaves unchain Samson. Then, their master following, they dragged the condemned man outside.

Suddenly Jolene burst into tears. Her effusive grief was not just for herself, but for Daniel and Samson, too.

Frustrated, Daniel struggled against his chains. Damn the South, and damn this barbaric system that condoned slavery!

When the first sound of the lash, followed by Samson's scream, carried into the barn, Jolene turned to Daniel and buried her face in his shoulder. She wept as the ominous, death-dealing blows continued.

Every slave at Willow Hill had been summoned to witness Samson's execution so they could see firsthand what happened to a slave who took part in an uprising. They were also expected to watch the hangings that were scheduled to take place after the whipping.

The lashing was being administered close to the house, and the sounds carried into Lucy's room. Mary Jane, sitting beside the bed, held her hands over her ears, muffling Samson's agonizing screams.

The slave's bellowing cries penetrated Lucy's unconsciousness, waking her. She didn't have to be told what was happening. "Who's bein' whipped?" she asked feebly.

Mary Jane didn't hear her, and she had to reach over and touch her leg to get her attention. "Who's bein' whipped?" she repeated.

"Samson," Mary Jane replied.

"Why?" Lucy asked.

Breaking down, Mary Jane sobbed heavily. "Oh God, Lucy! There was an uprising, and it was led by Samson! He killed Masta Alan! All the runaways except Samson was shot! Now Masta John's havin' Samson whipped to death!"

By now the slave's cries were so weak that they no longer carried into the room.

"Poor Samson," Lucy whispered. Aware of the silence, she continued somberly, "I reckon he's just about dead. If I hadn't been so sick, maybe I could've stopped 'im from doin' it."

"I don't think anyone could've stopped 'im. He was determined to run away and to kill Masta Alan. He'd have killed Masta John, too, if the masta hadn't been in town."

"Where's Jolene?" Lucy asked, hoping she hadn't

somehow gotten hurt during the uprising.

Mary Jane was drawn between telling Lucy the truth or honoring Daniel's request for his mother not to be told. She knew, however, that Lucy was Jolene's and Daniel's only hope. She prayed Daniel would forgive her. As hard sobs racked her body, she let Lucy know Delmar had ordered her son's and Jolene's execution.

"When does the masta plan to hang 'em?" Lucy demanded urgently.

"As soon as Samson's dead," she cried.

"Help me out of this bed," Lucy said, sitting up and swinging her legs over the side. "I's got to save Jolene and my boy!"

Mary Jane assisted the woman to her feet. The room swam before Lucy's eyes, and she came close to passing out. She called upon the last of her strength, and as Mary Jane helped her slip on her robe, she prayed aloud, "Lord, you gots to help me, 'cause I cain't make it on my own!"

As the master of Willow Hill and his two male slaves came into the barn for the last two prisoners, Daniel made a frantic effort to change John's mind. "Mr. Delmar, for God's sake, you can't hang a woman! What kind of man are you?"

Ignoring Daniel's remarks, Delmar gestured for his men to unchain the captives. Before Daniel's chains could be removed, John drew his pistol. "Try anything, boy, and I'll kill you now!"

Daniel contemptuously eyed the gun and the man holding it. Then, turning to Jolene, he draped an

455

arm about her shoulder and escorted her outside.

The bright sunlight at first blinded Jolene, and she had to blink several times before she was able to keep her eyes open. She'd thought the hangings would take place farther from the house and was surprised to see that ropes had been slung over two nearby oaks. The nooses dangled over two bridled horses. Jolene had often admired the tall, full-branched oaks, never imagining someday they'd serve as gallows for her and Daniel. The area was surrounded by a multitude of slaves, including young children and babes in their mothers' arms. The stark silence was eerie, for even the youngsters seemed to know this was a grievous occasion, sensing, perhaps, a glimpse into their own hapless destinies. Dr. Evans and the patrollers, grouped beneath the oaks, stood watching stoically.

Daniel appraised the oak trees, and paying close attention to their branches, he knew they were too low to ensure quick death. The possibility of Jolene suffering a slow, painful demise caused his stomach to tighten.

Jolene, her voice weak, whispered, "Daniel, I hope I can die with dignity. God, I pray that I don't turn into a coward."

"You have more courage than most men," he replied sincerely, his heart aching for her.

She gazed helplessly into his eyes. "Last night I wished Kurt was here, but now I'm glad he isn't. At least he'll be spared watching us die."

"He wouldn't watch," Daniel answered. "He'd die trying to stop it. Don't you realize how much he loves you?"

456

She was about to tell him that Kurt didn't really love her, but before she could, Delmar walked up to them.

As he studied Jolene his thoughts ran wild. Reaching a final decision, he shoved her away from Daniel's side. "Mrs. Spencer told me you saved her life and my daughter's," he said to Jolene. "In return, I've decided to spare yours. I'll keep you imprisoned until Kurt returns, but if he doesn't punish you severely, I'll go into town and file a complaint with the constable. Forging a pass is a serious offense, and if necessary, I'll personally see to it that you pay for your crime."

Jolene, shocked, gaped at him as if she hadn't understood a word he'd said. Unconsciously she rubbed her throat, as though a noose that had been there had miraculously disappeared.

Delmar's next words brought Jolene out of her trance. "Put this damned buck on his horse!" he bellowed to his two slaves.

Reluctantly they went to Daniel, grabbed his arms, and led him to the horse. Coffer, holding a rope, stepped forward and tied Daniel's hands behind him. Then, with the slaves' assistance, they heaved him into the saddle.

Watching through a teary haze, Jolene prayed desperately for a miracle.

As Coffer slipped the noose about Daniel's neck, Lucy's frantic cry penetrated the quietness.

"Màsta John! Masta John, you gots to stop!"

Astounded, Delmar turned and watched as Lucy, leaning against Mary Jane, made her way through the throng of slaves.

457

"Lucy!" he bellowed. "You should be in bed!" He cast Mary Jane a look of rage. "Girl, I'll have you lashed for not taking care of her!"

Falling to her knees, Lucy clutched John's hands. "Masta, I's beggin' you not to kill my boy and Jolene!"

"Jolene isn't going to hang," he replied calmly.

Raising her gaze, she stared hopefully into his eyes. "And Daniel?"

"He must die."

"No!" she screamed piteously. "Masta, please . . . *please!*"

Spotting the slave Abe, Delmar called to him, "Take Lucy back to the house."

As the man stepped up behind Lucy, she shoved him aside, stood upright, and met her master's gaze. Pride and self-esteem suddenly overwhelmed her. She was through humbling herself before this man. She had shared his bed for over thirty years, and she'd be damned if she'd grovel at his feet!

Folding her arms beneath her breasts and lifting her chin proudly, Lucy said with dignity, "You've convinced yourself that Daniel planned the uprising 'cause you won't admit to yourself why you really want 'im dead. You want 'im dead 'cause he's your son, and you cain't stand the thought of Daniel bein' a Delmar." She eyed him emphatically. "Masta, if you kill our son, I'll hate you till the day I die. And every time you touch me, you're gonna know how much I hate you."

Daniel had been listening, and learning that John Delmar was his father made him sick inside. He'd rather the devil himself had fathered him.

458

Coffer had also heard what Lucy said, and afraid that Delmar was about to weaken, he stepped closer to Daniel's horse. The uppity buck had dared to hit one of his men, and Coffer wasn't about to be cheated out of the pleasure of watching the man hang. He held a quirt, and lifting it stealthily, he brought it down against the horse's flanks. The sudden blow caused the steed to take off with a bolt, leaving its rider dangling from the end of the rope.

Jolene, watching, felt as though life now passed in a kind of slow-motion. Everything happened within a matter of seconds, but to Jolene it always seemed an eternity. Inexplicably, Lucy's and Mary Jane's screams sounded far away, and as she tried to take a step forward, she found she couldn't move, for her legs were as heavy as lead. In Jolene's trancelike state, Lucy's collapse appeared to take forever. The woman fainted into John's arms, and kneeling, he eased her carefully to the ground.

Looking away from Lucy, Jolene's eyes flew wildly to Daniel. His body, hanging limply, was swinging ominously back and forth.

Jolene, coming out of her lethargic trance, fell to her knees and screamed; and the blood-curdling sound seemed to carry forever.

Chapter Thirty-Two

As Coffer was tending to Daniel's horse, Kurt was heading into the lane that led to the Delmar home. The night before when Kurt had returned to Heritage Manor, he'd been alarmed to learn Daniel had gone to Willow Hill. Kurt didn't doubt John would carry out his threat to kill Daniel. Worried, Kurt had stayed at his father's home only long enough to grab a bite to eat. He hoped to reach Willow Hill in time to keep Daniel out of trouble. Kurt was ready for whatever he might find, for he had his Winchester in its scabbard and his pistol strapped to his hip.

Now Kurt and his horse were tiring, for they had traveled through the night. Learning that Jolene had also gone to Willow Hill didn't concern Kurt, for he didn't think she was in any danger. But he'd been sorely disappointed to find she wasn't at Heritage Manor. He was anxious to apologize and to explain how he'd learned she was the true mistress of Cedarbrook. He also intended to assure Jolene that he would accompany her to her home and help her secure her rightful place.

Kurt's thoughts had drifted from Daniel to Jolene when suddenly, Lucy's and Mary Jane's screams rang out shrilly. For a moment, several horrible possibilities raced through Kurt's mind. As he urged his horse into a fast canter, Jolene's blood-curdling scream suddenly cut sharply into the still air.

Spurring his mount to a breakneck speed, Kurt raced swiftly down the winding lane. Nearing the house, he saw the large group of slaves congregated in a half-circle, and as he drew closer, he suddenly became aware of what was happening. The sight of Daniel hanging from the oak caused Kurt's heart to lurch.

The horse's thundering hoofs resonated over the eerie quietness, and the slaves scattered in various directions to avoid the charging beast.

The patrollers were too shocked to make a move and merely watched, dumbfounded, as Kurt rode up to Daniel's hanging body, lifted it onto his saddle, and released the noose.

Abe, running up to Kurt's horse, shouted excitedly, "Hand 'im to me, masta!"

Carefully Kurt eased his friend into Abe's arms, and the slave laid the man on the ground. Kurt dismounted quickly, knelt, and placed a hand on Daniel's throat, praying for a pulse.

As Mary Jane and Jolene ran up to them, Abe made room for Mary Jane to kneel beside Daniel. Tears streaming down her face, she cried, "Is he . . . Is he . . . ?" She couldn't bring herself to ask Kurt if he was dead.

A weak, rasping cough sounded from deep within Daniel's throat, and as his eyes slowly opened, Kurt's face was the first thing he saw. He tried to speak, but the effort was too painful.

Smiling shakily, Kurt murmured, "Don't try to talk. You're going to be all right, but you need to stay silent and give your throat time to heal."

Feebly, Daniel reached out and grasped Kurt's shirt sleeve. Hoarsely, he whispered, "Mama . . . Mama . . . How is Mama?"

Jolene had been so overwhelmed by Daniel's miraculous recovery that she'd completely forgotten about Lucy. Now, checking on the women, she saw that John was lifting her into his arms.

She started to go to Lucy, but was detained by Coffer's gruff remark to Delmar, "Ain't we gonna hang this nigger? The bastard's still alive!"

"There'll be no hanging," John answered tersely. He looked at Doctor Evans. "Come with me. Lucy's unconscious and her fever is raging."

Daniel had heard Delmar's report, and while tugging at Kurt's shirt, he pleaded raspingly, "Help me up. I've got to be with Mama."

"You're too weak. I'll see about Lucy and let you know how she is." Kurt spoke to Abe. "Get someone to help you and take Daniel to your cabin."

Abe motioned to a male slave, who came quickly. Together the two men lifted Daniel, and with Mary Jane following, they started toward the cabin.

Jolene waited with bated breath for Kurt to acknowledge her. The mere sight of him made her heart beat wildly.

But Kurt had another matter to take care of. He

turned to face the patrollers. Speaking to Coffer, he said in a cold, level tone, "Take your men and get the hell away from here."

Coffer took an immediate dislike to Kurt. "I don't take orders from no nigger-lover!"

"If you want to live to see tomorrow, you'll get on your horse and leave this plantation." Kurt, his gaze steely, was watching the man's every move.

Furious, Coffer reached for his revolver, but before his hand had even touched the handle, Kurt's pistol was drawn and aimed at his heart. The stranger's speed astounded Coffer and his men.

Reading their thoughts, Kurt said with a surly grin, "Where I come from, if a man isn't fast with a gun, he's dead." His eyes rested on Coffer as he continued threateningly, "This gun's got a hair trigger, and in about three seconds my finger's gonna get awfully tired."

Coffer was afraid. "Put your gun away, mister. We'll leave, but we gotta go to the stable and saddle our horses."

"Then move! You're wasting my time." Kurt holstered his pistol. He waited for the patrollers to leave before going to Jolene.

She longed to bury herself in his arms, but fearing rejection, she simply smiled timidly and said, "Kurt, thank God you got here in time to save Daniel. But why aren't you on your way to New Orleans?"

Holding back the urge to draw her into his embrace, he replied, "We'll talk later. Would you mind going to the kitchen and putting on a pot of coffee while I take my horse to the stable? He needs to be unsaddled and fed. Also I want to make damned sure that those men leave Willow Hill."

She turned away and hurried to the house.

After the coffee had brewed Kurt entered the kitchen and Jolene motioned for him to sit at the table. Joining him, she asked, "Are the patrollers gone?"

"Yes. Have you heard anything about Lucy?"

She shook her head. "The doctor and Mr. Delmar are still with her."

Kurt took a sip of coffee, then said, "I want you to tell me what's going on. You can start by explaining why part of the house has been damaged by fire."

Jolene took a deep breath. In detail, she told Kurt about the uprising, admitting that she had forged a pass for Samson. She assured him, though, that she had believed Samson was escaping peacefully with his brother, two women, and three children. She explained the reason why she'd been riding with the runaways, and how Daniel had rescued her during the ambush.

Tears filled her eyes as she told Kurt about Delmar's fury, giving a full account of the man's hostile behavior.

Kurt, listening intently, didn't interrupt as her story unfolded. He could well imagine how horrifying her ordeal had been, and as he pictured her chained in the barn, awaiting her execution, the vision cut painfully into his heart. Learning of Katherine's and Sabrina's maliciousness sent his anger surging, but it was mild compared to his rage for John Delmar.

Kurt watched Jolene as she went back to the stove

to refill their cups. He could no longer fight the urge to hold her close. Jolene's back was toward him, and getting to his feet, he stepped to her, grasped her shoulders, turned her about, and drew her against him.

Hanging onto him for dear life, she cried brokenly, "Oh, Kurt, I'm so glad you're here! Hold me! Please hold me close!"

"Sweetheart!" he groaned, pulling her as close as possible. "You've been through so much, and it's all my fault. God, how can you ever forgive me?"

Although she was reluctant to leave his comforting embrace, she pushed gently out of his arms. Gazing up at him with confusion, she asked, "Why do you think it's your fault?"

He led her back to the table, and when they were seated, he said contritely, "I've put you through hell."

"Kurt, what do you mean?"

Reaching across the table, he took her small hand into his, then proceeded to tell her about his talk with Cal Atkins. Kurt finished by saying, "I know now that you're the true mistress of Cedarbrook. I can imagine how much you must hate me, but if it's any consolation, you couldn't possibly hate me as much as I hate myself."

"I don't hate you, Kurt" she whispered.

A trace of tears glistened in his eyes. "Jolene, I'm sorry that I refused to believe you."

She sighed wistfully. "Kurt, I had lied to you so often that I can understand why you didn't believe me . . . I've always understood."

Standing, he drew her into his arms. "Darling, we made so many foolish mistakes."

She snuggled intimately against him, relishing his closeness.

Then, remembering she was in love with another man, Kurt released her abruptly. It wasn't his arms that she desired, but another's!

"What's wrong?" she asked.

"For a moment I forgot that you're in love with someone else." He sounded devastated.

Jolene smiled. "Kurt, I lied about loving another man. I was tired of you treating me as a bed wench. That's why I told you there was someone else."

At first Kurt grinned radiantly. Then a frown suddenly shadowed his face. "What do you mean, I treated you like a bed wench? I never did any such thing."

"Well, that wasn't the impression I got," she answered testily.

Taking Jolene by surprise, Kurt laughed heartily. "You delightful little minx. Don't you realize that I've always been in love with you? I loved you when I believed you were Cal's sister, and I loved you when I thought you were a slave . . . and I also love you as the mistress of Cedarbrook!" Throwing up his hands, he blustered powerfully, "Damn it! I love you! I love you! I love you!"

Overjoyed, Jolene flew into his waiting arms. Clinging tightly, she cried, "I love you too, Kurt!" Tears of happiness streamed down her cheeks.

Much had been left unsaid between them and there was still much to explain, but ironing out their past misunderstandings could wait. For now, only this moment was important.

Gently Kurt wiped away her tears. Then, bending his head, he pressed his lips passionately to hers.

Jolene responded with all her heart, for she knew this kiss would seal their future.

John, sitting beside Lucy's bed, asked the doctor, "Is she going to die?"

"I don't know," came the truthful answer. The physician placed a hand on Delmar's shoulder in a sympathetic gesture. He'd never seen a master so distraught over his slave. But Lucy was exceptionally beautiful, and he supposed that that might have a lot to do with it. The doctor gazed down at the sleeping woman. Despite her illness she was lovely.

Telling John that he was returning to town, Evans left the room, closing the door behind him.

Alone with his thoughts, Delmar tried to imagine his life without Lucy and Alan. Guilt overwhelmed him as he realized he'd miss Lucy more than he'd miss his own son.

John Delmar had been raised in a certain way, and in all his life, he never strayed from his father's teachings. He was taught that Negroes were an inferior race. A man could feel a fondness for his bed wench, but he certainly didn't fall in love with her. White women, however, were above reproach and were always treated with great respect. To this day, John had the fair sex of his own race on pedestals.

Because Delmar held to his convictions, he didn't admit to himself that he was in love with this beautiful, gentle slave who had not only borne him a child, but also shared thirty years of his life.

The bedroom door opened, and entering quietly, Jolene said in a low voice, "Kurt's waiting for you in your office. He needs to talk to you."

Rising, John slowly stepped across the room. He was haggard, and it was an effort to put one foot in front of the other. "Stay with Lucy until I get back," he said, his tone reflecting his fatigue.

Jolene didn't bother to reply, but she had no intentions of leaving Lucy.

Moving sluggishly, John went to his office. Kurt was waiting, and brushing past the younger man, Delmar slumped into the chair behind his desk.

John's apparent distress didn't lighten Kurt's anger. Leaning his arms on the desk top, Spencer leered darkly into Delmar's eyes. "You unfeeling son of a bitch!" he raged.

Kurt's wrath awakened John's senses. "How can you call me unfeeling when that nigger friend of yours caused Alan's death?"

"Daniel had nothing to do with the uprising, and if you call him a nigger again, I'm going to knock your teeth down your throat!"

"I can't understand how you can be so loyal to a man who used to be your slave!"

"Maybe it's because he saved my life more than once. From Indians as well as outlaws." It was a two-way street, though, for Kurt had come to Daniel's rescue several times. The west was untamed, and the two friends had fought side-by-side on numerous occasions.

John leaned back in his chair and folded his arms across his chest. "Can you prove Daniel wasn't involved in the uprising?"

"Yes, I can."

Delmar's surprise was evident.

Kurt continued, "On my way to Willow Hill, I rode through Mobile. I happened to see the sheriff, and we talked for a few minutes. He was on his way home to get some sleep—he'd been up all night hunting down a northern abolitionist. It seems the man tried to get the wrong slave to escape, and that slave went to his master and told him everything. The sheriff caught the abolitionist and he's now in jail. When the sheriff learned that I was on my way here, he said to tell you to be on your guard. He heard that the abolitionist had contacted a couple of your slaves. If you want to see who's responsible for inciting Samson and the others, then I suggest you visit the jail. Daniel wasn't responsible. Neither was Jolene."

"What you say may be true, but it doesn't change anything. Daniel called Alan a thief, and I warned him to stay away from Willow Hill."

"He called your son a thief because that's exactly what he was!"

"Alan had a lot of faults, but stealing wasn't one of them."

"In that case you shouldn't object to our going to his room and searching it thoroughly."

"What do you expect to find?"

"Daniel's five thousand dollars."

John, believing in his son's innocence, accepted the challenge.

Much later, when the two men returned from their search, Delmar's shoulders were drooping, and he moved lethargically. He held Daniel's money in his hand, and giving it to Kurt, he murmured, "I honestly believed Daniel lied about Alan stealing his money."

Kurt handed three thousand back to him.

"What's this for?" John asked.

"It's the amount Daniel owes you for Mary Jane."

He took the bills and placed them in a drawer. "I'll write out a bill of sale as soon as I get back from town."

Kurt was surprised. He didn't think John would leave with Lucy still so ill.

Delmar could tell that he was somewhat amazed. "I'll only be in town long enough to file a legal complaint."

"Against whom?"

"You and your quadroon wench. Daniel might be innocent, but I have written proof that Jolene was involved in the uprising."

"The pass?" Kurt asked.

"So you know about it."

"John, if you knew Jolene's true heritage, you'd tear up that pass, get down on your knees, and beg her forgiveness for the way you've treated her!"

Delmar was dumbfounded. "Hell will freeze over before I get down on my knees before a slave!" he bellowed.

A sudden loud rap sounded on the door. "Come in!" John called, irritable.

Delmar's butler took a hesitant step into the room and announced, "Excuse me, masta, but there's a Mista Warrington askin' for you."

"Sam Warrington?" he questioned, astounded. "I thought the man was dead!"

"He said his name was Thomas Warrington, masta, suh."

"Show him in."

Thomas had followed the butler, and he entered the room immediately. Lazarus, trailing, took a stance beside the door. The sight of his former

470

master hit him with a piercing force.

However, failing to recognize Lazarus, John merely gave him a cursory glance. As Thomas crossed the room, he moved out from behind his desk and offered him his hand.

Accepting the man's handshake, Thomas said cordially, "Allow me to introduce myself, sir. I'm Sam Warrington's brother."

Following the perfunctory courtesies, John introduced Thomas to Kurt, then went to his liquor cabinet to pour brandy for himself and his guest.

Kurt had declined a drink, and moving to the desk, he leaned against it and watched Thomas with keen curiosity. He was eager to question the man but had decided to wait and hear what he had to say.

His back turned to the others, John asked, "What brings you to Willow Hill, Mr. Warrington?"

"I'm looking for my niece. Her name's Jolene."

Delmar filled two glasses with brandy. "Niece?" he uttered disapprovingly. "Are you referring to that insolent little git your brother sired?"

Thomas despised the term "git" and everything it implied. "No, Mr. Delmar, I'm not."

Holding the filled glasses, John turned away from the liquor cabinet and waited for the man to explain himself.

"I'm referring to Sam and Charlotte Warrington's daughter. Jolene is white, and the mistress of Cedarbrook."

John paled, and the glasses fell from his hands. Hitting the floor, they shattered into tiny, jagged pieces, and the spilled brandy spread slowly into an amber puddle about his feet.

471

Chapter Thirty-Three

Kurt knocked softly on Lucy's door before entering, and going to the bed, he asked Jolene, "How is she?"

Rising from her chair, Jolene answered somberly, "I think she's worse. Oh Kurt, I'm so worried!"

Drawing Jolene into his arms, he held her close. Kurt had loved Lucy since childhood, and he shared Jolene's concern.

He relinquished her gently. "Sweetheart, there's someone here to see you."

"To see me?" she questioned, wondering who it could possibly be.

Kurt smiled. "I think you'll be very happy to see him."

"Who is it?"

Avoiding her question, he took her hand. "He's waiting for you in John's office."

Kurt started to lead her to the door, but she held back. "I don't want to leave Lucy alone."

"John's waiting in the hall. He'll stay with Lucy."

Conceding, Jolene allowed Kurt to usher her to the door. "Who wants to see me?"

"If I tell you who he is, it'll ruin the surprise."

Jolene was at a total loss, and she said no more as Kurt led her into the hall. She preferred to avoid Delmar and would have done so if he hadn't blocked her path.

"Jolene," he murmured hesitantly. He was perspiring profusely and fidgeting in his discomfort.

Kurt interjected, "John, anything you have to say to Jolene can wait." Taking Jolene's arm, he steered her away from Delmar.

Standing riveted to the spot, John watched the couple move away. He owed Jolene an apology, but how in God's name was he to find the right words? He had treated a genteel white lady like a slave! His conscience was killing him, and he hoped to make amends, but he doubted if it was possible. In John's opinion, treating a white woman as a quadroon slave was unforgivable! John was overcome with guilt, and his shoulders sagged under their heavy burden.

Slowly he opened the bedroom door and moved sluggishly to the side of the bed. He slumped into the chair and gazed sadly at Lucy. She was sleeping fitfully, her breathing ragged.

John groaned aloud. His only son was dead, he'd done a white woman a terrible injustice, and Lucy was seriously ill. His world was crumbling at his feet!

He reached out and took Lucy's hand in his. Gently he brought it to his face and placed it against his cheek. Giving in to his sorrow, he finally broke down and cried.

Jolene and Kurt went into Delmar's office, and

Jolene first become aware of Thomas. His resemblance to her father was uncanny, and for a moment she was taken aback. Then, becoming aware of another's presence, she turned her gaze to Lazarus.

She smiled radiantly, crossed the floor, and flung herself into his arms. He hadn't held Jolene since she'd been a child, and he was astounded by her warm reception. He returned her hug a bit hesitantly.

Then, leaving Lazarus' embrace, she looked at her uncle and exclaimed happily, "You must be Uncle Thomas!"

"How did you know?" he asked.

"You look so much like Papa."

He took time to study his niece. Despite her plain, colorless dress, she was striking. Her face was glowing, and her blue eyes sparkled. Evidently her ordeal as a slave hadn't been so bad as he had feared. Holding out his arms, he said cheerfully, "Don't you have a hug for me?"

She responded immediately, and Thomas' heart filled with love for his beautiful niece as he embraced her tightly.

Kurt poured a glass of sherry for Jolene and brandy for himself and Thomas. He asked Lazarus if he'd care for a drink, but the man declined.

Taking Jolene to the sofa, Thomas urged her to sit with him, and he then told her about the document Sam had sent.

After Kurt had brought them their drinks, Thomas explained his visit to Cedarbrook. He spoke in detail, even telling Jolene about Walker's death.

"Marshall's dead?" she cried. The news saddened her for she had always liked Marshall.

Lazarus knew a slave was forbidden to interrupt a conversation between whites, but he felt that where his mistress and Thomas Warrington were concerned, this rule didn't apply.

"Miz Jolene," he began, gaining her attention. "I ain't got no proof, but I think it's Miz Johanna's fault that Masta Marshall was killed."

"Why do you believe that?" she asked.

He told her about Johanna's infatuation with Marshall, and that he had overheard her telling the overseer that she planned to marry him.

"Speaking of Mr. Sullivan," Jolene remarked, "how has he been treating the field slaves?"

Lazarus didn't answer, but the pained look on his face confirmed her worst fears.

"I must return as quickly as possible to Cedarbrook and dismiss that horrible man! But Lucy's sick, and I can't leave until she gets better!"

"Lucy!" Lazarus exclaimed. He'd wanted to ask about Lucy from the moment Jolene had walked into the room. He'd postponed doing so because he was still torn between wanting to see Lucy, and keeping their love locked away in the past, where it had remained untouched by time.

Handing Thomas her glass of sherry, Jolene left the sofa and went to Lazarus, took his hands into hers, and said, "Oh Lazarus, I've been so involved with your arrival that I completely forgot about you and Lucy! Please forgive me!"

"You know 'bout me and Lucy?" He was surprised.

"Yes, I do. When Lucy learned that I'd lived at Cedarbrook, she asked me about you. She told me that you two had been deeply in love."

Lazarus was touched. "She never forgot me?"

"No, she didn't. And I don't think she ever stopped loving you . . . not really."

He understood. "Lucy's the only woman I ever loved. After I lost her, I swore I'd never be hurt like that again. I reckon she felt the same way I did."

"I think she did, too."

"I'd sure like to see her again, but I got a feelin' that Masta John won't let me."

Jolene spoke determinedly. "Of course you can see her. I'll take you to her room myself."

"How sick is she?"

"She's very ill, I'm afraid. The doctor said she has pneumonia."

"Can I see her now?"

Jolene was quick to give her permission, and telling her uncle and Kurt she'd return soon, she escorted Lazarus from the office. They went swiftly to the kitchen, and pausing at Lucy's door, Jolene knocked softly.

It was a minute or so before John responded. He was surprised to see that Warrington's valet was with Jolene. He looked closely at the servant, his close perusal bringing on recognition. "Lazarus!" he declared, stepping across the threshold and closing the door behind him.

"I wants to see Lucy, Masta John," he replied, meeting his former master's hard gaze.

"No!" John answered, adamantly. "She's too ill to have visitors." His jealousy raged.

476

Delmar made a half turn to go back into the bedroom, but he was deterred by Jolene. Her hand clutched his arm.

"I insist you allow Lazarus to see Lucy!" she cried.

As he faced Jolene, John's eyes clouded over with remorse. If it had been anyone but Jolene, he'd have flatly refused. But, God, he owed this woman so much! He'd do anything to make amends!

"Very well, Miss Warrington. Lazarus may see Lucy."

Jolene quipped bitterly, "So now I'm 'Miss Warrington,' am I? This morning I was 'gal,' or 'girl,' or 'wench!' I haven't changed. I'm the same person you bought from a slave jail."

"Please," John groaned. "There's nothing you can say that will make me feel worse than I already do." Unable to carry on, Delmar mumbled a hasty excuse and left.

Jolene turned to Lazarus. "I suppose I shouldn't be so hard on him. My behavior is hypocritical. I've lived in the south all my life and never once realized how wrong slavery was until I became a slave."

"You's always been a good mistress, Miz Jolene."

She smiled. "Lazarus, you have a heart of gold." She squeezed his hand fondly, then opened the door and stood back for him to enter.

"Ain't you comin' in with me?"

"You and Lucy have waited thirty years for this, and if she regains consciousness, the two of you should be alone. But Lazarus, if Lucy does wake up, be sure and let her know her son is alive. She thinks Mr. Delmar hanged him, but Kurt got here in time to save him." Seeing his confusion, she assured him that she'd explain everything later. Then, favoring him with an encouraging smile, she closed the door.

Lazarus' gaze went to the woman lying on the bed. He couldn't see her very well, but her closeness had sent his heart racing. On shaky legs he moved unsteadily across the room, reached the beside, and paused.

He looked down at Lucy and was amazed to find that she was still exceptionally beautiful. Tears welled and a strong gasp tore from deep within him. It was no wonder he'd never loved again! How could any woman have replaced his darling Lucy?

Without taking his eyes from the woman he loved, Lazarus drew the hard-backed chair closer to the bed and sat down. His hand trembled as he placed it within Lucy's, and the tears that were now streaming down his cheeks, fell onto their clasped hands.

"Lucy," he whispered, his voice a quiver, "I never stopped lovin' you."

Lazarus bowed his head and didn't see that Lucy's eyes had fluttered open. It was a short time before she was lucid. Then, realizing someone was holding her hand, she looked up at him.

At that precise moment Lazarus raised his head and his teary gaze met Lucy's. They didn't speak. Their eyes told it all.

Finally, finding her voice, Lucy cried weakly, "Oh, Lord, I must be dreamin'."

"It ain't no dream," he replied gently.

"Lazarus, is it really you?"

Getting to his feet, he leaned over and kissed her fevered brow. "It's me, Lucy."

Her eyes roamed lovingly over his face. "You's

still a handsome man." Then large teardrops dampened her cheeks as she sobbed. "I asked God to let me see you 'fore He took me away. I knew I was prayin' for a miracle. But praise the Lord, he done answered my prayers!"

"Lucy, don't talk 'bout God takin' you away. You's gonna get better."

Lucy moved over and patted the bed. "Lie beside me, Lazarus, and hold me in your arms. For over thirty years, I dreamed of bein' in your arms again."

He lay at her side and drew her snugly against him. Her flesh was hot, and he knew her fever was raging.

Resting her head on his shoulder, Lucy murmured brokenly, "Lazarus, I done lost my son. Masta John hanged 'im."

"Your boy is alive," he told her quickly. "Miz Jolene said that Masta Kurt got here in time to save 'im."

"Thank God!" she cried, fresh tears flowing. Although her heartbeat was weak, it was filled with joy.

"You got to get well, Lucy. I wants you to come to Cedarbrook with me."

"Don't talk 'bout goin' to Cedarbrook," she pleaded, her voice growing faint. "Just hold me close, 'cause there ain't nothin' I want more than to be in your arms."

She wondered how he'd come to be at Willow Hill, but she felt she didn't have the strength to ask, nor the time to listen. "Lazarus," she managed to whisper, "promise you'll stay with me until I . . . go to sleep."

He swallowed the sob that had risen in his throat. "Gonna stay right here, Lucy. I promise you I will."

The office door was open, and as Jolene swept into the room, she saw that Delmar was seated at his desk with Thomas sitting across from him. Kurt stood poised beside the window.

At her entrance, the two men got to their feet and Kurt asked, "Has Lucy regained consciousness?"

"She was asleep when Lazarus went into the room. I didn't stay . . . I thought they should have this time alone."

"I need to let Daniel know how she's doing."

"I'll go with you, but first I want to talk to Mr. Delmar."

Kurt accompanied her to the desk, and Thomas gave her his chair. John waited for her to sit down before saying uneasily, "Miss Warrington, is there anything I can do to make amends?"

It was Kurt who responded to his request. "You can tear up that pass."

"Of course," Delmar agreed without hesitation. "I'll also refund the four thousand you paid me for Miss Warrington." Unlocking a desk drawer, he removed the pass and handed it to Kurt. "Here—feel free to rip it to shreds."

Kurt tore it into tiny pieces and pitched them into a wastepaper basket.

Sitting, John's eyes went over the threesome. He folded his hands on the desk and asked, "Is there anything else I can do?"

"Yes!" Jolene remarked strongly.

The man raised an eyebrow. "Just name it, Miss Warrington."

"You can set Lucy free."

Delmar inhaled sharply. "Miss Warrington, I'd do anything, within reason, to prove that I'm sincerely sorry. But I'll not release Lucy!"

Jolene sprang to her feet. "You unfeeling, cold-hearted monster! For God's sake, set her free!"

John rose to his feet and his level gaze locked with Jolene's. "I've lost my son, and someday soon Sabrina will marry and go away. Lucy's all I have left. I'll say this once, young lady, and only once . . . Lucy's staying at Willow Hill!"

"Damn you!" Jolene declared heatedly, her blue eyes shooting daggers at him. "Give Lucy her freedom so she can choose where she wants to live!"

John and the others were too involved to notice that Lazarus had entered the room. The butler paused in the doorway and listened.

Delmar, his face red with rage, bellowed, "I'll never set Lucy free!"

"There ain't no reason for y'all to argue 'bout Lucy," Lazarus suddenly remarked, his voice startling the group. All eyes turned to look at him, their gazes questioning.

Lazarus, his chin held high, his posture ramrod-straight, took a step into the room. He addressed his mistress, "Miz Jolene, you don't have to worry 'bout Lucy's freedom. The good Lord done set Lucy free."

Kurt's heart was heavy as he walked into Abe's cabin. He was alone, for Jolene had been too

481

overcome with grief to accompany him.

Daniel was lying down, and Mary Jane was sitting beside his bed. Glancing about the sparsely furnished cabin, Kurt saw that the couple were by themselves.

"How's the patient?" Kurt asked Mary Jane.

"He's fine, only it hurts 'im to talk."

Kurt moved to the bed with hesitant steps.

Daniel, seeing Kurt's hesitation, knew at once that something was wrong. A cold foreboding coursed throughout his veins.

Kurt paused beside the bed and looked down at his friend. Daniel's throat was bandaged and he asked Mary Jane, "How bad is the rope burn?"

"It's gonna heal," she was pleased to reply.

Despite the pain it cost him to talk, Daniel whispered raspingly, "How's Mama?" Deep in his heart, he already knew the answer.

Kurt swallowed heavily, placed a hand on Daniel's shoulder, and replied as gently as possible, "I'm sorry, but Lucy died a few minutes ago."

Mary Jane fled from the cabin, her hasty departure taking Kurt by surprise. He had thought she'd want to be with the man she loved. Kurt returned his attention to Daniel, and sharing his friend's grief, sat on the edge of the bed. His grip on Daniel's shoulder tightened as heartrending sobs shook the man's body.

Kurt had stayed with Daniel a long time before leaving Abe's cabin to search for Mary Jane. He wondered why she'd run away. Looking about, he spotted her in the distance, sitting beneath a tree, leaning back against its trunk.

Reaching into his pocket, Kurt removed a cheroot and lit it before going to Mary Jane. As he drew closer, the young woman got to her feet.

Her eyes were red and puffed, and Kurt knew she'd been crying. "Why did you leave?" he asked softly.

"It's my fault Lucy died! Daniel will never forgive me!"

Kurt was perplexed. "Why do you think that?"

Her explanation verged on incoherence. "Daniel asked me not to tell Lucy that Masta John was gonna hang 'im! He said Lucy would kill herself tryin' to stop the hangin'! If I hadn't told her, she wouldn't have gotten out of bed!"

Kurt spoke kindly. "Mary Jane, I doubt that Lucy's getting out of bed brought on her death. God had already decided to take her."

Mary Jane's eyes pleaded with his. "Do you really believe that, Masta Kurt?"

"Yes, I do," he answered with sincerity.

"But Daniel ain't gonna feel that way," she sighed.

"I think you're jumping to false conclusions. Daniel's been asking for you." He took her hand and squeezed it encouragingly. "He loves you."

Mary Jane's face brightened. "I love 'im too, Masta Kurt. I swear I do!"

"Then go to him. . . . he needs you."

She wheeled about to hasten to Abe's cabin, but

then, hesitating, looked back at Kurt. "My heart's breakin' for Daniel. First the hangin', then learnin' 'bout Masta John, and now Lucy's death! How much more can he take?"

Confused, Kurt asked, "What did he learn about John Delmar?"

"Didn't Jolene tell you?"

"We haven't had time to do a lot of talking."

"I reckon she's plannin' to tell you later."

"Tell me what?" He was growing impatient.

"Masta John is Daniel's pappy. When Lucy was tryin' to stop the hangin', she told the masta that he was hangin' Daniel 'cause he couldn't stand 'im bein' his son."

"And Daniel heard what she said?"

"Yes, suh."

He dismissed Mary Jane with a wave of his hand. "Go on; Daniel needs you."

She hurried away.

Taking a long drag from his cheroot, Kurt blew out the smoke slowly. He knew Delmar couldn't resent Daniel being his son any more than Daniel resented having him for a father.

Meanwhile, Mary Jane had reached the cabin. Drawing a deep breath, she hurried inside.

"Why did you run away?" Daniel asked hoarsely.

She sat on the bed beside him. "Oh, Daniel, I was afraid you'd blame me for Lucy's death. You asked me not to tell her 'bout the hangin'!"

Talking was very painful for him, and he replied with a grimace, "I don't blame you. In your place, I'd probably have done the same thing. It's no one's fault that Mama died."

484

She went into his arms. "Daniel, I's so sorry that she's gone. I loved her, too."

"I know you did," he whispered. "Mama was special, wasn't she?"

"I ain't never known nobody as nice as Lucy."

Once again, Daniel's grief emerged, and while holding him close, Mary Jane's tears mingled with his.

Chapter Thirty-Four

Daniel had been convalescing for seven days when he informed Kurt that he was well enough to make the long journey to Cedarbrook. Spencer decided that they would leave the following morning, for he was anxious to see Johanna's cruel reign come to an end.

A heavy, somber cloud hung over Willow Hill, and Kurt was also eager to get Jolene and Daniel away from this plantation, which held so many painful memories.

Although he was anticipating leaving Willow Hill and beginning their journey to Cedarbrook, Kurt was deeply troubled. Once Jolene was reinstated in her rightful position, would she be willing to turn her back on such luxury to accompany him to his ranch? His home in Texas seemed sorely lacking, compared to the life of comfort in a flourishing southern plantation. Kurt wanted to ask Jolene to marry him, but he was uncertain whether she'd leave Cedarbrook to live in the rugged country out west.

Would she want him to give up his ranch and live with her on her plantation? If so, could he sell his ranch and turn his back on the life he loved? He had no desire to be a planter; his beliefs conflicted with the South's. But Kurt adored Jolene, and deep in his heart he knew he'd make any sacrifice to marry her. He loved his ranch and he loved the West, but he loved Jolene more. He could live without his ranch, but he felt as though he couldn't live without Jolene. She was his heart and soul, and she meant the world to him.

The night before they were to leave Willow Hill, Kurt left his bedroom and went down the hall to Jolene's. He intended to ask her to be his wife, but he wouldn't put her on the spot by suggesting she abandon Cedarbrook. He loved her too much even to hint that she might make such a sacrifice. The untamed West was no place for a lady who had been raised as the daughter of a rich aristocrat. On his ranch there would be no servants to wait on her and no cook to prepare any of the meals.

Now, as Kurt knocked softly on Jolene's door, his mood was somewhat gloomy. Selling his ranch was disheartening, and he dreaded living at Cedarbrook. But Jolene's happiness came before his own.

Jolene was pleasantly surprised to see him. Every night for the past week, she'd been hoping he'd come to her room. His failure to do so had begun to worry her . . . didn't he love her as much as she loved him? And why hadn't he asked her to be his wife?

As Kurt entered and closed the door, his eyes traveled over her with appreciation. She was wearing a plain white nightgown, and the simple garment made her even more desirable, for it did nothing to distract him from her own natural beauty. Her shiny black hair, cascading gracefully past her shoulders, contrasted beautifully with her dark blue eyes. Her bangs were now too long to fall impishly over her brow and were brushed back from her face and held in place with a white ribbon. He looked closely at her forehead. The scar was completely gone.

Jolene was puzzled by his somber mood and asked nervously, "Kurt, is anything wrong?"

His smile was loving. "I was just admiring you. Jolene, you're so beautiful."

"Thank you," she replied, returning his smile. "You're very handsome yourself."

Delmar had given Jolene one of his finest and largest guest rooms, and as Kurt began to pace the length of it, she watched him with pangs of worry. Regardless of what he'd said, she knew something was amiss.

Going to Kurt and touching his arm, she halted his pacing. "Please tell me what's on your mind," she pleaded.

His strong hands went to her shoulders, and as he gazed down into her azure eyes, he felt as though he were drowning in their fathomless blue pools. "Sweetheart, will you marry me?" he asked.

She answered joyfully, "Yes, Kurt, I'll marry you!"

Bringing her into his embrace, he kissed her endearingly, and entwining her arms about his neck, she responded with feverish enthusiasm.

Releasing her gently, Kurt queried, "If it's all right

with you, on our way to Cedarbrook we'll stay over a couple of days in New Orleans and get married."

"Oh, Kurt! I can hardly wait to be your wife!" Her eyes sparkled brightly. "I love you so much!"

"And I love you," he assured her. He moved away from Jolene, stepped to the bed, sat down, and forcing eagerness into his voice, remarked, "I'll have to get used to my new title."

"New title?" she repeated, confused.

"Yes. As the master of Cedarbrook."

For a moment, Jolene was dumbfounded. She had been so certain that Kurt would want them to live on his ranch. She was also disappointed. She didn't want to make their home at Cedarbrook—she wanted to move to Texas!

Sitting beside him, she asked somberly, "Are you planning to sell your ranch?"

He nodded. "I'm sure my foreman will be anxious to buy it."

"Has he been taking care of the ranch during your absence?"

"Yes. He's also overseeing Daniel's. He's a good man, and I trust him implicitly."

Jolene expelled a long sigh. "Uncle Thomas will be very disappointed."

Kurt was baffled. "Why is that?"

"I was certain you'd want to live on your ranch. So the other day, I told Uncle Thomas that if you asked me to marry you, I'd give Cedarbrook to him. I never imagined you'd choose Cedarbrook over your ranch. I *know* how much you love the West. Furthermore, I never dreamed you'd want to become a planter. Your beliefs are so different from

489

most southerners'."

A trace of tears came to her eyes, and she brushed them away. "And to be perfectly honest, I was looking forward to living on a ranch. Neither of us condones slavery, so I'm afraid it's going to be difficult for us to be happy on a plantation. Also, I have enough adventure in me to want to tame the West. I was looking forward to sharing your life with you and raising our children away from the South and all its bigotry."

She reached over and placed her hand on his. "But I love you so much that I'm willing to live wherever you choose."

Kurt's grip on her hand was so tight that it was almost painful. "Jolene," he began excitedly, "are you telling me that you prefer my ranch over Cedarbrook?"

"Yes—why?" she answered.

"Don't you realize there'll be no servants, and that my home is small in comparison to a plantation mansion?"

"What does it matter?" she questioned.

"Are you *really* willing to give up such luxuries?"

"The only luxuries I want are to be able to sleep in your arms every night, bear your children, and share your life with you."

Taking her unawares, he drew her into his arms, hugging her enthusiastically. "Jolene, you've made me the happiest man on earth!"

She looked at him dubiously, "Kurt, I don't understand . . . why are you now so happy?"

"I *never* wanted to live at Cedarbrook! But I thought that you *did!* I just couldn't bring myself to ask you to give up your plantation for the hardships of life on a ranch."

"You love me that much?" she asked. "You'd have given up your ranch for me?"

"Darling, you mean more to me than anything or anybody. Your happiness will always come before my own."

It was now her turn to hug him with enthusiasm. "Oh, Kurt, I *do* love you! And I'm excited about becoming a rancher's wife!" She laughed merrily. "I bet if you'd fallen in love with Sabrina, she'd never have agreed to live in Texas."

"What makes you think there was ever any chance I could fall in love with Sabrina?"

"Well, I saw you kissing her twice—in the garden, and then in the hallway."

Kurt smiled. "Neither time was I kissing her—she was kissing me. There *is* a difference, you know. Besides, Sabrina isn't my type."

"And what *is* your type?" she asked pertly.

"I like rebellious little wenches," he answered, grabbing her hand and planting a fervent kiss upon it.

"I's glad, masta, suh." She giggled.

"What kind of man appeals to you?"

"Texas cowboys," she replied at once. She smiled suggestively. "There's one cowboy in particular I fancy. When I'm with him, I become a wanton little wench."

Subtly her hand moved to his leg, where she daringly let it roam even higher until she was able to fully grasp him. His trousers didn't prevent her from feeling his immediate erection. Becoming even

491

bolder, she nimbly undid his pants, wrapped her fingers about his bare flesh, and stimulated him with an up-and-down motion.

Leaning closer and nibbling at his earlobe, she teased, "I especially love my handsome cowboy when he's armed and ready for action."

"You teasing little minx," he uttered thickly, his hand slipping beneath her gown and moving upward to caress the womanly softness between her thighs.

His touch caused her to gasp softly, and as he urged her to lie back on the bed, her legs parted so that he could fondle her completely.

His lips met hers in a demanding kiss, his tongue entering and relishing the inside of her mouth as, simultaneously, his finger probed intimately.

Their passions were soon fully aroused, and Kurt left her side long enough to undress. Then, as he returned to her embrace, he entered her powerfully.

"Kurt," she purred tremulously, "I adore you."

"I know you do, my beauty," he murmured. "I adore you, too."

She clung to him tenaciously, for she needed him desperately. He was the very center of her life, and everything else merely revolved around him. Through Kurt she had learned the rapturous power of love, and she surrendered breathlessly to the sensuous pleasure of his throbbing manhood deep inside her.

Kurt, his emotions every bit as intense as Jolene's, thrust against her strongly. Her moist warmth titillated his senses, driving him wild with desire.

Clinging to each other, they drifted blissfully into the fiery culmination of a lovemaking that sealed their promise to wed.

Alone in his office, John was slumped in his chair, and a half-filled bottle of bourbon dangled from his hand. His thoughts were on Lucy, he dreaded living out the rest of his years without her. Her death had left a void in his life that was deeper than Alan's.

Suddenly the door swung open and Daniel barged into the room.

Sitting up straight, Delmar thundered, "How dare you come into my office without asking permission!"

Unintimidated, Daniel crossed the room and sat in the extra chair. Eying the man, he insinuated caustically, "Is that any way for a father to talk to his son?" His throat was completely healed and there was no trace of hoarseness.

John's face reddened. "I'll not tolerate your insolence!" He waited for a reply, but when Daniel remained unresponsive, he demanded, "What do you want?"

"I want Mary Jane's bill of sale."

Reaching into a desk drawer, John drew out the paper and handed it to him. As Daniel was looking it over, Delmar lifted the bottle of bourbon to his lips and helped himself to a liberal swallow.

Folding the document, Daniel shoved it into his shirt pocket. He studied the master of Willow Hill. The man's clothes were wrinkled, his eyes were bloodshot, his beard was ungroomed.

Lifting up the bottle, John took another large swig. He wiped his mouth with the back of his hand, then met Daniel's intense gaze. Although he was intoxicated, his words were steady. "You look a lot like your mother. But I can also see a resemblance between us. It's in the way you move, your smile, the shape of your chin. You've got Delmar blood, there's no denying it." He sounded sick with disappointment.

Daniel smirked. "I don't like having you for a father any more than you like having me for a son."

"Well, at least we agree on something," he said sarcastically.

Daniel's brow furrowed. "Why did Mama lie about the overseer being my father?"

"If I'd known you were mine, I'd have sold you even before you were weaned. Later, after you moved to Heritage Manor, I'm not sure why Lucy didn't tell you the truth."

"Maybe she figured what I didn't know wouldn't hurt me. How long have you known?"

"Just a few weeks."

The younger man waited for a moment, then with a malicious grin, commented, "One useful thing came out of all this."

"Oh?" John asked, curious.

"I now know my last name."

Delmar was instantly outraged. "Surely you don't intend to take my name!"

"Of course I do. What's more, I do so vindictively. I can imagine how much it galls you to know that future black generations will carry the Delmar name. I'll be sure to tell my sons about you so your grandchildren, and their children, and all the generations that follow will know their true roots.

494

And the family tree will begin with you."

John laughed harshly. "Well, if you're planning to marry Mary Jane, you'll never have any children! The woman's barren!"

Daniel smiled imperceptibly. "How do you know such a thing?"

"She hasn't been a virgin for years, yet she's *never* conceived."

"You're wrong. When she was fifteen, she became pregnant and miscarried. The woman slave who tended her showed her how to prevent unwanted pregnancies. If she conceived at fifteen, there's no reason to think that she couldn't conceive now."

"You bastard!" John seethed with fury.

"You hit the nail on the head," was Daniel's bitter riposte. He got to his feet. "Just remember that I'm your bastard, you cold-hearted son of a bitch!"

John leapt from his chair. "No nigger has ever talked to me like that and lived!"

"Well, now one has!" Daniel spat. He grinned abjectly as he said, "Good-bye, *Dad."* Whirling about, he headed for the door.

"After you leave Willow Hill, I hope I never set eyes on you again—not for as long as I live!" Delmar raged.

"You won't—you can count on it!" Daniel stalked out the door.

Daniel went to the kitchen. The new cook, a slave woman, had gone to bed, and Lazarus was now sitting at the table by himself, drinking a cup of coffee. As Daniel came into the kitchen, Lazarus asked the young man if he'd like to join him.

Accepting, Daniel poured some for himself, went

to the table, and sat down. He'd been hoping for a chance to talk with Lazarus in private. As he sipped his coffee, he studied the older man. Jolene had told him that Lazarus and Lucy had been in love.

Lazarus smiled wistfully. "I guess you're thinkin' 'bout me and your mama."

It was a moment before Daniel replied. "You two never stopped loving each other, did you?"

The older man sighed. "I don't reckon anyone ever completely forgets his first true love."

"When I was a boy, I used to ask Mama about her life before Willow Hill, and if she'd ever been in love. She always avoided my questions. I suppose she found talking about the past too painful to bear."

"You want me to tell you 'bout your mama?"

"Would you?"

As they drank their coffee, Lazarus told Daniel about Lucy's life before she was sold to John Delmar, and then he reflected ruefully on his and Lucy's love. He explained why he and Lucy had tried to flee, and that he was given thirty lashes for running. He ended his story by saying, "I never loved any woman but Lucy. Not that I wasn't capable of lovin' again . . . I just didn't want to get hurt."

A look of pain crossed Daniel's face. "If Mama had lived, she could've decided between going to Cedarbrook or to my ranch. She'd have been free!"

Lazarus said kindly, "Son, don't make the mistake of thinkin' Lucy could've been free. Masta John, he'd never have set her free. If Lucy was still alive, we'd be leavin' without her."

"I suppose you're right," Daniel admitted somberly.

496

"Masta John was in love with your mama, and that's why he wouldn't set her free. Regardless of what you or Miz Jolene could've said or done, he'd have kept your mama right here at Willow Hill. When I saw Lucy, I kinda hoped Masta John would let her move to Cedarbrook so we could share our remainin' years. But when I came into the masta's office and heard how determined he was to keep Lucy, I knew that even if she hadn't died, he'd never have set her free . . . no matter what. A man don't want to lose the woman he loves."

Daniel spoke more to himself than to Lazarus. "I wonder if Delmar knows he was in love with Mama?"

Lazarus chuckled dryly. "Masta John ain't gonna ever admit to himself that he loved a colored wench."

Daniel pushed back his chair and got to his feet. "Kurt wants to get an early start in the morning, so I guess we'd better get some sleep."

"Goodnight, son," he murmured.

Daniel left quickly, and Lazarus took their empty cups and placed them in the large dishpan, then went out the back door. Before retiring, he'd visit Lucy's grave and tell her good-bye

Edward had arrived at Willow Hill a couple of days after the uprising, and he was on the front porch with Katherine and John to bid Kurt and the others farewell.

The travelers were eager to get on the road and were packed and ready to leave before the morning

497

dew had evaporated.

Thomas and Lazarus were mounted and waiting fo Kurt to tell his parents and John good-bye. Delmar had given Kurt a buckboard and a pair of horses. Daniel and Mary Jane were seated in the back, and Jolene was on the front seat. Kurt's and Daniel's saddle ponies were tied to the back of it.

Now, as Kurt talked to his father, Jolene turned and said to Mary Jane and Daniel, "When we reach New Orleans, Kurt and I are planning to get married."

Mary Jane's face brightened, "So are we!"

"That's wonderful!" Jolene exclaimed. She glanced at her fiancée. "I wish Kurt would hurry. I'm dying to leave this place."

Kurt, his thoughts coinciding with Jolene's, embraced his father and promised to write as soon as he could. He turned to Katherine and said in a cold tone, "Good-bye, Mother."

"Good-bye," she whispered sadly. She had a feeling that her stepson would never forgive her for the way she'd treated Jolene. When Katherine had learned that Jolene was white, she'd made a couple of attempts to befriend her, to no avail. Too much had happened for them ever to be true friends.

Hesitantly John offered young Spencer his hand. Kurt was about to refuse, but then, deciding it wasn't his place to judge Delmar, he accepted the man's limp handshake.

Edward accompanied his son down the steps and to the buckboard. As Kurt was climbing onto the seat, the elder Spencer looked up at Jolene and said with a warm smile, "This son of mine is a poor correspondent, so I hope you'll find time to write."

"I will," she replied, "I *promise.*" Jolene had always liked Kurt's father.

"I wish you both every happiness," he said sincerely. He extended his good wishes to Mary Jane and Daniel.

As Kurt picked up the reins, Jolene had the weird sensation that she was being watched. Her gaze went to the second floor, where she saw Sabrina peeking out the window. For a moment their eyes met, and Jolene recognized the other woman's intense jealousy. Then Sabrina closed the curtains with a flourish.

Kurt had seen the exchange, and favoring Jolene with a loving smile, he asked, "Are you ready to leave?"

"Yes!" she remarked strongly. "And I never want to set eyes on this place again!"

Mary Jane spoke up, "That makes two of us!"

"Three!" Daniel declared.

"I make it unanimous," Kurt chipped in. He slapped the reins against the team of horses and the wagon rolled into motion. Thomas waved to Edward and John, then he and Lazarus urged their horses into a trot.

The group traveled quickly down the meandering lane, and soon Willow Hill was far behind them.

Chapter Thirty-Five

Johanna was complacent, and she had a large smile on her face as she poured a sherry for herself and a brandy for Robert.

She and the lawyer had been at James Mitchell's trial, and upon their return to Cedarbrook, Johanna had suggested they celebrate with a couple of drinks. The trial had lasted only two days, and today had brought it to an end. In Johanna's opinion, it had finished satisfactorily. Because of her testimony, young Mitchell had been found guilty of murder and sentenced to hang.

Now, as she crossed the parlor and handed Robert his brandy, she was still smiling.

Hawkins' eyes bore into hers as he accepted the drink. Then, putting the glass to his lips, he downed the brandy.

Johanna watched him guardedly. "Robert, what is bothering you?"

He stepped to the liquor cabinet, poured himself another drink, finished it, then wheeled about to face her. "You lied, didn't you? Everything Amanda and James said was true."

"What makes you think such a thing?"

Robert didn't answer. Instead, he reflected back on the day, recalling how Amanda had followed them from the courthouse and had begged Johanna to admit what had really happened. There was something in the way the young woman had pleaded that had convinced Robert that Johanna was lying. . . .

Hawkins stepped quickly to Johanna, grabbed the sherry from her hand, and threw the glass to the floor. Clutching her shoulders, he shook her roughly. "Damn it, Johanna! If James is innocent, you've got to admit that you lied! In God's name, how can you let an innocent man go to the gallows?"

Forcefully, she wrested free of him. "How *dare* you manhandle me! Have you gone mad?"

He was about to continue pressuring her, but at the sound of the front door opening, he grew silent. Thomas' voice carried into the parlor.

"Uncle Thomas has returned," Johanna remarked, thankful for the man's interruption. She needed time to figure out the best way to deal with Robert. The lawyer was becoming a nuisance, and she must find a way to extricate him from her life.

Composing herself, Johanna moved to the center of the room, and she awaited her uncle's entry with a forced smile.

Thomas stepped into the room, and he was followed by the constable, Jolene, and Kurt. Johanna's smile froze and her face paled noticeably. For a moment she tottered precariously. Then, regaining her balance, she gasped hoarsely, "Jolene! I thought you were . . . !"

"Dead?" Jolene completed. "You should've known you couldn't trust a man like Cal Atkins."

Robert inhaled sharply. *Dead?* My God, had Johanna bribed Atkins to kill Jolene? She had sworn to him that Jolene had gone up north!

Johanna was shocked not only by her sister's presence, but also by her costly attire. In New Orleans Kurt had taken Jolene shopping, and she was wearing a stylish royal-blue traveling gown. She wore a white straw bonnet trimmed with dark blue velvet on her raven tresses, which were caught up into a cluster of curls at the nape of her neck.

Johanna, her old jealousies emerging, eyed Jolene resentfully. "Well, for a quadroon wench you've done rather well."

"I'm not a quadroon," Jolene replied calmly.

Johanna looked at her skeptically. *"Oh? Papa's will says you are."* She turned to Kurt and was immediately taken aback by his good looks. She noticed how his beige shirt fit tightly across his wide chest and how snugly his tan trousers fit. Good Lord, she'd never seen such a virile man! She wondered who he was and why he was accompanying Jolene.

The constable stepped forward and spoke to Robert. "Mr. Hawkins, Thomas Warrington and his niece stopped by my office and asked me to ride out here with them. They've accused you of a very serious crime, and it's my job to investigate their allegations thoroughly. I need to see Sam Warrington's will. Is it here, or at your office?"

"My office," he answered.

Johanna intervened, her voice shaky. *"Why do you want to see Papa's will?"*

"I think a close perusal will verify that the will was tampered with," the lawman explained.

"Well, I refuse to let you examine it!" Johanna spat.

"Your charade's over," Thomas told Johanna. "I have a legal document—Sam sent it to me—which states *you're* the quadroon." He looked sternly at Robert. "I demand to see my brother's last will and testament."

Hawkins groaned audibly. He knew it was useless to claim his and Johanna's innocence. Thomas' document and the changed will proved their guilt. He'd always known that the will wouldn't hold up under close examination. "You can see the will, but first I'd like to make a complete confession."

"No!" Johanna cried desperately. *"Robert, no!"*

"It's no use, Johanna. We're caught, and the only chance we have is to throw ourselves on Jolene's mercy." He turned to Jolene. "Please believe me. I didn't know Johanna had hired Atkins to kill you. She told me you'd gone up north. I would never have condoned murder."

The constable asked, "Mr. Hawkins, are you admitting that you changed Sam Warrington's will?"

"Yes, I am," he replied.

Johanna stepped shakily to the sofa and sat down. It was all over! A cold chill ran up her spine. Would Jolene get even by selling her to Cal Atkins? Would she end up on a vendue block?

503

The constable continued, "Mr. Hawkins, you are under arrest. Since Johanna is legally a slave, her punishment is in the hands of her mistress."

The law officer took a step toward Robert, but was deterred by Jolene. "No. I don't want him arrested."

"What!" the constable exclaimed.

Jolene spoke to Robert. "If you'll go to town, pack your clothes, return, and take my sister north, I won't press charges."

The attorney was astounded. "Jolene, I don't know what to say! Your generosity is admirable, to say the very least."

Johanna, as shocked as Robert, gaped speechlessly.

Slipping her arm in Kurt's, Jolene replied, "My husband and I talked this over at length, and we decided to let you and Johanna go free." She smiled coldly. "You two deserve each other."

Johanna's shock was now coupled with jealousy, for she envied Jolene her handsome husband.

"I'll leave immediately, pack my belongings, and return for Johanna," Robert said quickly.

"If you aren't back wihtin a reasonable amount of time," Kurt began, "you'll be hunted down, arrested, and sent to prison."

"What makes you think I'd try to leave without Johanna?"

Kurt eyed him levelly. "It's just a warning, Mr. Hawkins, in case the idea might cross your mind."

"I'll ride to town with you," the constable told Robert. "I need to set James Mitchell's release into motion."

"Release!" Johanna exclaimed. "You have no grounds to set that murderer free!"

"Grounds?" the law officer repeated bitterly. "The whole trial was a farce. It was *your* testimony that convicted James, and a slave cannot testify against a white person. Furthermore, considering who you really are and what you've done, it's apparent to me that you lied on the witness stand. Fortunately for young James, everyone will believe what I do: Marshall Walker's death was an accident."

As the constable and Robert left, Johanna withdrew into a sulk.

Watching her, Jolene said firmly, "Don't you think you should go to your room and pack? Robert will be back soon, and when he arrives, I want you ready to leave."

'Don't worry," Johanna replied irritably. "I'll have Patsy pack my belongings."

"No, you won't. Patsy is no longer your maid. You'll pack your own clothes."

Johanna sprang to her feet, cast Jolene a hateful glare, then left the room in a flurry.

Smiling, Kurt turned from his wife to Thomas. "Would anybody care for a drink?"

When the beverages were poured, Jolene held up her glass, looked at her uncle, and toasted, "Here's to you, Uncle Thomas. The new master of Cedarbrook!"

Johanna was packing when Jolene opened the door and entered without being asked to.

"How *dare* you barge into my bedroom!" Johanna cried petulantly.

"*Your* bedroom?" she questioned. "It happens to be *mine*. You *stole* it from me."

Johanna stepped away from the bed, went to the large wardrobe, removed a gown, and returned to her packing. "I don't have enough luggage for all my clothes," she complained in a whine.

"You don't have to try and take everything. When you settle someplace, write and let Uncle Thomas know your address, and he can send the rest of your things. He'll also mail you your manumission papers. You might need them if you ever return to the South."

Jolene held an envelope, and she stepped to Johanna and handed it to her.

"What's this?"

"Money. It's more than Papa left you in his will. It may not be a fortune, but it's enough to help you and Robert get started."

Taking the envelope and putting it inside her suitcase, Johanna replied with agitation, "Don't talk as though Robert and I will always be together, because we won't. I don't love him, and now that he knows I hired Atkins to kill you, I doubt he still loves me. Our separation is inevitable."

Johanna sat on the edge of the bed and continued in a smooth confident tone, "I've decided to move to Boston. The city is full of rich shipping tycoons, and I plan to snare one of them . . . preferably an old one who'll soon die and leave me a rich widow."

Jolene smiled without mirth. "I don't doubt that you'll get exactly what you want."

"Of course I will. I'm a survivor." Johanna studied

her sister thoughtfully. "But then, so are you, aren't you? I used to think that you had no gumption whatsoever. But I was wrong."

"My days as a slave made me a much stronger person."

"Yes. It also matured you." Johanna suddenly shrugged as though the change in Jolene wasn't important. "I suppose you now hate me as much as I hate you."

"Quite the contrary," Jolene refuted, her eyes gleaming. "I'm very grateful to you. If you hadn't sent me away with Atkins, I'd never have met Kurt. Ironically, you did me a great favor."

Johanna spitefully replied, "Your husband probably married you to get his hands on Cedarbrook!"

"I hardly think so. He owns a ranch in Texas, and that's where we plan to live. I intend to give Cedarbrook to Uncle Thomas."

The other woman was amazed. "You mean you're going to give up Cedarbrook to live on a ranch? You must be mad!"

"I am. I'm mad about my husband." Pleased, Jolene smiled, turned about, and walked to the door. She opened it, then looked back at her sister. "Uncle Thomas will let you know when Robert arrives. Kurt and I are going to the overseer's house and dismiss Mr. Sullivan. So I probably won't see you again." Jolene wanted to remain aloof, but against her own volition, feelings for her sister surfaced. "Johanna," she began sincerely, "despite everything that has happened, you are still my own flesh and blood. If you should ever. . . ."

Leaping from the bed, Johanna leveled her gaze at

her sister. "I know what you're about to say, and you may as well save your breath. I'll never change . . . I'll always despise you! And if you think taking Cedarbrook away from me will destroy me, you're badly mistaken! I'll overcome this setback!"

"Yes, I'm sure you will. Like a cat, you'll always land on your feet." With that, Jolene stepped across the threshold and closed the door. She had a feeling she'd never see or hear from her sister again.

Patsy's mood was chipper as she stood behind her mistress' chair and brushed the woman's hair. Johanna and Sullivan were gone! It was so wonderful that she could hardly believe it.

Jolene had decided to use her mother's bed-chamber. She had no wish to use her own bedroom, for it was still filled with Johanna's belongings.

Now, as she looked in the mirror at Patsy's reflection, Jolene could see the happiness in the servant's eyes. Kindly, she asked, "Was it terrible, being Johanna's maid?"

"That woman is a monster!" she answered, frowning.

Her thoughts on Sabrina, Jolene replied intro-spectively, "I know what you mean." She paused, then went on, "Patsy, you know that I'm moving to Texas. There'll be no mistress at Cedarbrook for you to attend. So what would you like to do? Is there a special position in the household that you'd espe-cially like to have?"

The young woman smiled timidly. "Miz Jolene, the carpenter's son, Josh. . . ."

Her voice faded, and Jolene encouraged, "Go on."

"Well, Masta Thomas told me he's gonna let us slaves get married if we wants to. Josh, he wants me to marry 'im."

"Is that what you want?"

"Oh, yes'm. I loves 'em a powerful lot!"

"Then I think you should marry him at once."

"You know, Miz Jolene, I was awful suprised to learn that you is married. Did you have a big weddin'?"

"No . . . Kurt and I were married a few days ago in New Orleans. We got married at the Reverend's house."

Jolene grew warm inside at the thought. Although her wedding had been small and simple, it had been wonderfully romantic; and her wedding night had been pure heaven. Mary Jane and Daniel had been married in the colored section of town, the ceremony performed by a Negro preacher. Mary Jane, too, had found her small wedding romantic.

Putting down the brush, Patsy asked, "Mistress, ma'am, is you through with me for the night? I's kinda anxious to see Josh."

"Yes, you may leave."

Patsy was heading for the door when it suddenly swung open; and as Kurt entered, he almost collided with the young maid.

"Excuse me, masta, suh," she mumbled, brushing past him and rushing from the room.

"Where is she going in such a hurry?" Kurt asked.

"To her true love." Rising from her dressing stool, Jolene let her eyes sweep adoringly over her husband. He looked quite distinguished in his burgandy smoking jacket.

Returning her perusal, Kurt took in his wife's supple curves, which were temptingly outlined beneath her pink negligee.

Stepping to her side, he drew her into his arms and kissed her possessively. "I love you, Mrs. Spencer."

"And I love *you,* Mr. Spencer." Her eyes shone with adoration.

A small balcony led off the bedroom, and taking Jolene's arm, Kurt led her through the open doors and onto the terrace. The full moon, splendid in the dark sky, shone down brilliantly on Cedarbrook.

"Now that Johanna and Mr. Sullivan have gone," Jolene murmured, "Cedarbrook seems so tranquil. There's an aura of happiness about it."

"Yes, but I'm afraid it's only temporary."

"Why do you think that?"

"A war between the South and the North is inevitable. Battles will take place on southern soil, and many plantations will fall to ruin."

"If the North wins, will Uncle Thomas lose Cedarbrook?"

"I don't think so. Thomas told me that the bulk of his money is in a bank in London, and he intends to keep it there. He'll run Cedarbrook with your father's money, but if there's a war and the South loses, he can use his own money to rebuild Cedarbrook."

"Kurt," she began anxiously, "if they declare war, will you fight?"

He smiled tenderly, wrapped an arm about her waist, and drew her close. "I used to wonder about that myself . . . but that was before I became a married man. If the North and South go to war, both sides will have to get along without my services. It'll probably drag on for years, and there's no way I'm going to leave you alone on a secluded ranch for an extended period of time. There are still too many Comanches in the area, not to mention other unsavory characters. You must understand that the West is partially untamed."

"Yes, I know." Her eyes glittered with excitement. "But Darling, I'm looking forward to our life."

"I talked to Daniel a short time ago, and he and Mary Jane are ready to leave whenever we are."

She smiled with love. "You're anxious to return to your ranch, aren't you?"

"I've already been away much longer than I'd planned."

Draping her arms about his neck, she stood on tiptoe and kissed him softly. "Darling, I know the life we've chosen will not always be an easy one, and I also know that it entails a certain amount of danger. But I think we both thrive on adventure. Furthermore, our marriage will never become a boring one. It'll be filled with excitement, passion, and love!"

Swooping her into his arms, he carried her inside to the bed. Laying her down with care, he stretched out at her side and drew her small frame snugly against his.

"I can hardly wait to take you to my ranch," Kurt began. "I plan to carry you across the threshold and put you permanently in my bed."

Jolene laughed softly. "And am I never to leave it?"

511

"Only to clean house, cook my meals, and wash my clothes. When you aren't taking care of chores, I'll expect you to be in my bed like a good little bed wench." He grinned teasingly.

"Masta, suh, ain't you forgettin' somethin'?"

"What's that?"

"Your little bed wench is rebellious."

"But passionate," he added, hugging her so tightly that they seemed inseparable.

Then, as Kurt's lips descended to meet hers, Jolene, her heart overflowing with love, returned her husband's kiss ardently.

Jolene was as eager as Kurt to leave the South and embark on their new life, and as his lips left hers, she murmured, "In the morning, I'm signing Cedarbrook over to Uncle Thomas, so I don't see any reason why we can't leave the day after tomorrow."

"Good," he replied.

She smiled happily. "Darling, let's go home."